"Doc? You never said whether you had met a previous clone of yourself," Hiro said.

"Actually I haven't. My lives have been fairly boring. I like it that way," Joanna said.

"Until now."

"Until now," she agreed softly. "At least our cargo is safe. Otherwise the mission is pointless."

"True!" Hiro said brightly, and then realized how ridiculous he sounded. "Kinda like finding a diamond in a pile of shit."

The intercom above their heads crackled to life with the captain's voice. "All crew to the cloning bay. Now."

He sighed. "Why do I think the pile of shit just got a little deeper?"

By Mur Lafferty

THE SHAMBLING GUIDES

The Shambling Guide to New York City
Ghost Train to New Orleans

THE AFTERLIFE SERIES

Heaven
Hell
Earth
Wasteland
War
Stones

Six Wakes

SIX
WAKES

MUR LAFFERTY

www.orbitbooks.net

This book is a work of fiction. Names, characters, places, and incidents are the product of the author's imagination or are used fictitiously. Any resemblance to actual events, locales, or persons, living or dead, is coincidental.

Copyright © 2017 by Mary Lafferty
Excerpt from *Behind the Throne* copyright © 2016 by Katy B. Wagers
Excerpt from *The Corporation Wars: Dissidence* copyright © 2016 by Ken MacLeod

Cover design by Kirk Benshoff
Cover photo © Getty Images
Cover copyright © 2017 by Hachette Book Group, Inc.

Orbit
Hachette Book Group
1290 Avenue of the Americas
New York, NY 10104
orbitbooks.net

First Edition: January 2017

Orbit is an imprint of Hachette Book Group.
The Orbit name and logo are trademarks of Little, Brown Book Group Limited.

ISBNs: 978-0-316-38968-6 (paperback), 978-0-316-38966-2 (ebook)

Printed in the United States of America

LSC-C

10 9 8 7 6 5 4 3 2 1

For Connie Willis and James Patrick Kelly

International Law Regarding the Codicils to Govern the Existence of Clones

Established October 9, 2282

1. It is unlawful to create more than one clone of a person at a time. Each clone is one person. Cloning will be used for longevity of life, not for multiplication. If a clone is multiplied by their own hand or others, the most recent clone has claim to the identity, while the other(s) are extraneous.
2. It is unlawful for a clone to bear or father children. A clone is considered their own child for the rest of their life, including where it affects inheritance law. Clones must be sterilized upon rebirth.
3. It is unlawful to put a mindmap onto a body that does not bear the original DNA.
4. Clones must always have the most recent mindmap of their consciousness on a drive on their person. They and their mindmaps are subject to search by authorities at all times.
5. It is unlawful to modify any DNA or mindmap of any clone. (Codicil 2 being an exception.) Clones must continue with the DNA of their original bodies and their original mindmap.
6. The shells a clone leaves behind must be disposed of quickly, hygienically, and without ceremony or ritual.
7. It is unlawful for a clone to end their own current life in order to be reborn. (Exception one: A clone can sign a euthanasia agreement, if a qualified doctor agrees that death is imminent and they are suffering. Exception two: See Codicil 1.)

WAKE ONE:
THE *DORMIRE* CREW

THIS IS NOT A PIPE

Sound struggled to make its way through the thick synth-amneo fluid. Once it reached Maria Arena's ears, it sounded like a chain saw: loud, insistent, and unending. She couldn't make out the words, but it didn't sound like a situation she wanted to be involved in.

Her reluctance at her own rebirth reminded her where she was, and who she was. She grasped for her last backup. The crew had just moved into their quarters on the *Dormire*, and the cloning bay had been the last room they'd visited on their tour. There they had done their first backup on the ship.

Maria must have been in an accident or something soon after, killing her and requiring her next clone to wake. Sloppy use of a life wouldn't make a good impression on the captain, who likely was the source of the angry chain-saw noise.

Maria finally opened her eyes. She tried to make sense of the dark round globules floating in front of her vat, but it was difficult with the freshly cloned brain being put to work for the first time. There were too many things wrong with such a mess.

With the smears on the outside of the vat and the purple color through the bluish fluid Maria floated in, she figured the orbs were blood drops. Blood shouldn't float. That was the first problem. If blood was floating, that meant the grav drive that spun the ship had failed. That was probably another reason someone was yelling. The blood and the grav drive.

Blood in a cloning bay, that was different too. Cloning bays were pristine, clean places, where humans were downloaded into newly cloned bodies when the previous ones had died. It was much cleaner and less painful than human birth, with all its screaming and blood.

Again with the blood.

The cloning bay had six vats in two neat rows, filled with blue-tinted synth-amneo fluid and the waiting clones of the rest of the crew. Blood belonged in the medbay, down the hall. The unlikely occurrence of a drop of blood originating in the medbay, floating down the hall, and entering the cloning bay to float in front of Maria's vat would be extraordinary. But that's not what happened; a body floated above the blood drops. A number of bodies, actually.

Finally, if the grav drive *had* failed, and if someone *had* been injured in the cloning bay, another member of the crew would have cleaned up the blood. Someone was always on call to ensure a new clone made the transition from death into their new body smoothly.

No. A perfect purple sphere of blood shouldn't be floating in front of her face.

Maria had now been awake for a good minute or so. No one worked the computer to drain the synth-amneo fluid to free her.

A small part of her brain began to scream at her that she should be more concerned about the bodies, but only a small part.

She'd never had occasion to use the emergency release valve inside the cloning vats. Scientists had implemented them after some techs had decided to play a prank on a clone, and woke her up only to leave her in the vat alone for hours. When she had gotten free, stories said, the result was messy and violent, resulting in the fresh cloning of some of the techs. After that, engineers added an interior release switch for clones to let themselves out of the tank if they were trapped for whatever reason.

Maria pushed the button and heard a *clunk* as the release triggered, but the synth-amneo fluid stayed where it was.

A drain relied on gravity to help the fluid along its way. Plumbing 101 there. The valve was opened but the fluid remained a stubborn womb around Maria.

She tried to find the source of the yelling. One of the crew floated near the computer bank, naked, with wet hair stuck out in a frightening, spiky corona. Another clone woke. Two of them had died?

Behind her, crewmates floated in four vats. All of their eyes were open, and each was searching for the emergency release. Three *clunks* sounded, but they remained in the same position Maria was in.

Maria used the other emergency switch to open the vat door. Ideally it would have been used after the fluid had drained away, but there was little ideal about this situation. She and a good quantity of the synth-amneo fluid floated out of her vat, only to collide gently with the orb of blood floating in front of her. The surface tension of both fluids held, and the drop bounced away.

Maria hadn't encountered the problem of how to get out of a liquid prison in zero-grav. She experimented by flailing about, but only made some fluid break off the main bubble and go floating away. In her many lives, she'd been in more than one undignified situation, but this was new.

Action and reaction, she thought, and inhaled as much of the oxygen-rich fluid as she could, then forced everything out of her lungs as if she were sneezing. She didn't go as fast as she would have if it had been air, because she was still inside viscous fluid, but it helped push her backward and out of the bubble. She inhaled air and then coughed and vomited the rest of the fluid in a spray in front of her, banging her head on the computer console as her body's involuntary movements propelled her farther.

Finally out of the fluid, and gasping for air, she looked up.

"Oh shit."

Three dead crewmates floated around the room amid the blood and other fluids. Two corpses sprouted a number of gory tentacles, bloody bubbles that refused to break away from the deadly wounds. A fourth was strapped to a chair at the terminal.

Gallons of synth-amneo fluid joined the gory detritus as the newly cloned crew fought to exit their vats. They looked with as much shock as she felt at their surroundings.

Captain Katrina de la Cruz moved to float beside her, still focused on the computer. "Maria, stop staring and make yourself useful. Check on the others."

Maria scrambled for a handhold on the wall to pull herself away from the captain's attempt to access the terminal.

Katrina pounded on a keyboard and poked at the console screen. "IAN, what the hell happened?"

"My speech functions are inaccessible," the computer's male, slightly robotic voice said.

"Ceci n'est pas une pipe," muttered a voice above Maria. It broke her shock and reminded her of the captain's order to check on the crew.

The speaker was Akihiro Sato, pilot and navigator. She had met him a few hours ago at the cocktail party before the launch of the *Dormire*.

"Hiro, why are you speaking French?" Maria said, confused. "Are you all right?"

"Someone saying aloud that they can't talk is like that old picture of a pipe that says, 'This is not a pipe.' It's supposed to give art students deep thoughts. Never mind." He waved his hand around the cloning bay. "What happened, anyway?"

"I have no idea," she said. "But—God, what a mess. I have to go check on the others."

"Goddammit, you just spoke," the captain said to the computer, dragging some icons around the screen. "Something's working inside there. Talk to me, IAN."

"My speech functions are inaccessible," the AI said again, and de la Cruz slammed her hand down on the keyboard, grabbing it to keep herself from floating away from it.

Hiro followed Maria as she maneuvered around the room using the handholds on the wall. Maria found herself face-to-face with the gruesome body of Wolfgang, their second in command. She gently pushed him aside, trying not to dislodge the gory bloody tentacles sprouting from punctures on his body.

She and Hiro floated toward the living Wolfgang, who was doubled over coughing the synth-amneo out of his lungs. "What the hell is going on?" he asked in a ragged voice.

"You know as much as we do," Maria said. "Are you all right?"

He nodded and waved her off. He straightened his back, gaining at least another foot on his tall frame. Wolfgang was born on the moon colony, Luna, several generations of his family developing the long bones of living their whole lives in low gravity. He took a handhold and propelled himself toward the captain.

"What do you remember?" Maria asked Hiro as they approached another crewmember.

"My last backup was right after we boarded the ship. We haven't even left yet," Hiro said.

Maria nodded. "Same for me. We should still be docked, or only a few weeks from Earth."

"I think we have more immediate problems, like our current status," Hiro said.

"True. Our current status is four of us are dead," Maria said, pointing at the bodies. "And I'm guessing the other two are as well."

"What could kill us all?" Hiro asked, looking a bit green as he dodged a bit of bloody skin. "And what happened to me and the captain?"

He referred to the "other two" bodies that were not floating in the cloning bay. Wolfgang, their engineer, Paul Seurat, and Dr. Joanna Glass all were dead, floating around the room, gently bumping off vats or one another.

Another cough sounded from the last row of vats, then a soft voice. "Something rather violent, I'd say."

"Welcome back, Doctor, you all right?" Maria asked, pulling herself toward the woman.

The new clone of Joanna nodded, her tight curls glistening with the synth-amneo. Her upper body was thin and strong, like all new clones, but her legs were small and twisted. She glanced up at the bodies and pursed her lips. "What happened?" She didn't wait for them to answer, but grasped a handhold and pulled herself toward the ceiling where a body floated.

"Check on Paul," Maria said to Hiro, and followed Joanna.

The doctor turned her own corpse to where she could see it, and her eyes grew wide. She swore quietly. Maria came up behind her and swore much louder.

Her throat had a stab wound, with great waving gouts of blood reaching from her neck. If the doctor's advanced age was any indication, they were well past the beginning of the mission. Maria remembered her as a woman who looked to be in her thirties, with smooth dark skin and black hair. Now wrinkles lined the skin around her eyes and the corners of her mouth, and gray shot through her tightly braided hair. Maria looked at the other bodies; from her vantage point she could now see each also showed their age.

"I didn't even notice," she said, breathless. "I-I only noticed the blood and gore. We've been on this ship for *decades*. Do you remember anything?"

"No." Joanna's voice was flat and grim. "We need to tell the captain."

"No one touch anything! This whole room is a crime scene!" Wolfgang shouted up to them. "Get away from that body!"

"Wolfgang, the crime scene, if this is a crime scene, is already contaminated by about twenty-five hundred gallons of synth-amneo," Hiro said from outside Paul's vat. "With blood spattering everywhere."

"What do you mean *if* it's a crime scene?" Maria asked. "Do you think that the grav drive died and stopped the ship from spinning and then knives just floated into us?"

Speaking of the knife, it drifted near the ceiling. Maria propelled herself toward it and snatched it before it got pulled against the air intake filter, which was already getting clogged with bodily fluids she didn't even want to think about.

The doctor did as Wolfgang had commanded, moving away from her old body to join him and the captain. "This is murder," she said. "But Hiro's right, Wolfgang, there is a reason zero-g forensics never took off as a science. The air filters are sucking up the evidence as we speak. By now everyone is covered in everyone else's blood. And now we have six new people and vats of synth-amneo floating around the bay messing up whatever's left."

Wolfgang set his jaw and glared at her. His tall, thin frame shone with the bluish amneo fluid. He opened his mouth to counter the doctor, but Hiro interrupted them.

"Five," interrupted Hiro. He coughed and expelled more synth-amneo, which Maria narrowly dodged. He grimaced in apology. "Five new people. Paul's still inside." He pointed to their engineer, who remained in his vat, eyes closed.

Maria remembered seeing his eyes open when she was in her own vat. But now Paul floated, eyes closed, hands covering his genitals, looking like a child who was playing hide-and-seek and whoever was "It" was going to devour him. He too was pale, naturally stocky, lightly muscled instead of the heavier man Maria remembered.

"Get him out of there," Katrina said. Wolfgang obliged, going to another terminal and pressing the button to open the vat.

Hiro reached in and grabbed Paul by the wrist and pulled him and his fluid cage free.

"Okay, only five of us were out," Maria said, floating down. "That cuts the synth-amneo down by around four hundred gallons. Not a huge improvement. There's still a lot of crap flying around. You're not likely to get evidence from anything except the bodies themselves." She held the knife out to Wolfgang, gripping the edge of the handle with her thumb and forefinger. "And possibly the murder weapon."

He looked around, and Maria realized he was searching for something with which to take the knife. "I've already contaminated it with my hands, Wolfgang. It's been floating among blood and dead bodies. The only thing we'll get out of it is that it probably killed us all."

"We need to get IAN back online," Katrina said. "Get the grav drive back on. Find the other two bodies. Check on the cargo. Then we will fully know our situation."

Hiro whacked Paul smartly on the back, and the man doubled over and retched, sobbing. Wolfgang watched with disdain as Paul bounced off the wall with no obvious awareness of his surroundings.

"Once we get IAN back online, we'll have him secure a channel to Earth," Katrina said.

"My speech functions are inaccessible," the computer repeated. The captain gritted her teeth.

"That's going to be tough, Captain," Joanna said. "These bodies show considerable age, indicating we've been in space for much longer than our mindmaps are telling us."

Katrina rubbed her forehead, closing her eyes. She was silent, then opened her eyes and began typing things into the terminal. "Get Paul moving, we need him."

Hiro stared helplessly as Paul continued to sob, curled into a little drifting ball, still trying to hide his privates.

A ball of vomit—not the synth-amneo expelled from the bodies, but actual stomach contents—floated toward the air intake vent and was sucked into the filter. Maria knew that after they took care of all of the captain's priorities, she would still be stuck with the job of changing the air filters, and probably crawling through the ship's vents to clean all of the bodily fluids out before they started to become a biohazard. Suddenly a maintenance-slash-junior-engineer position on an important starship didn't seem so glamorous.

"I think Paul will feel better with some clothes," Joanna said, looking at him with pity.

"Yeah, clothes sound good," Hiro said. They were all naked, their skin rising in goose bumps. "Possibly a shower while we're at it."

"I will need my crutches or a chair," Joanna said. "Unless we want to keep the grav drive off."

"Stop it," Katrina said. "The murderer could still be on the ship and you're talking about clothes and showers?"

Wolfgang waved a hand to dismiss her concern. "No, clearly the murderer died in the fight. We are the only six aboard the ship."

"You can't know that," de la Cruz said. "What's happened in the past several decades? We need to be cautious. No one goes anywhere alone. Everyone in twos. Maria, you and Hiro get the doctor's crutches from the medbay. She'll want them when the grav drive gets turned back on."

"I can just take the prosthetics off that body," Joanna said, pointing upward. "It won't need them anymore."

"That's evidence," Wolfgang said, steadying his own floating corpse to study the stab wounds. He fixated on the bubbles of gore still attached to his chest. "Captain?"

"Fine, get jumpsuits, get the doctor a chair or something, and check on the grav drive," Katrina said. "The rest of us will work. Wolfgang, you and I will get the bodies tethered together. We don't want them to sustain more damage when the grav drive comes back online."

On the way out, Maria paused to check on her own body, which she hadn't really examined before. It seemed too gruesome to look into your own dead face. The body was strapped to a seat at one of the terminals, drifting gently against the tether. A large bubble of blood drifted from the back of her neck, where she had clearly been stabbed. Her lips were white and her skin was a sickly shade of green. She now knew where the floating vomit had come from.

"It looks like I was the one who hit the resurrection switch," she said to Hiro, pointing to her body.

"Good thing too," Hiro said. He looked at the captain, conversing closely with Wolfgang. "I wouldn't expect a medal anytime soon, though. She's not looking like she's in the mood."

The resurrection switch was a fail-safe button. If all of the clones on the ship died at once, a statistical improbability, then the AI should have been able to wake up the next clones. If the ship failed to do so, an even higher statistical improbability, then a physical switch in the cloning bay could carry out the job, provided there was someone alive enough to push it.

Like the others, Maria's body showed age. Her middle had softened and her hands floating above the terminal were thin and spotted. She had been the physical age of thirty-nine when they had boarded.

"I gave you an order," Katrina said. "And Dr. Glass, it looks like talking our engineer down will fall to you. Do it quickly, or else he's going to need another new body when I'm through with him."

Hiro and Maria got moving before the captain could detail what she was going to do to them. Although, Maria reflected, it would be hard to top what they had just apparently been through.

Maria remembered the ship as shinier and brighter: metallic and smooth, with handholds along the wall for low-gravity situations and thin metal grates making up the floor, revealing a subfloor of storage compartments and vents. Now it was duller, another indication that decades of spaceflight had changed the ship as it had changed the crew. It was darker, a few lights missing, illuminated by the yellow lights of an alert. Someone—probably the captain—had commanded an alert.

Some of the previous times, Maria had died in a controlled environment. She had been in bed after illness, age, or, once, injury. The helpful techs had created a final mindmap of her brain, and she had been euthanized after signing a form permitting it. A doctor had approved it, the body was disposed of neatly, and she had woken up young, pain-free, with all her memories of all her lives thus far.

Some other times hadn't been as gentle, but still were a better experience than this.

Having her body still hanging around, blood and vomit everywhere, offended her on a level she hadn't thought possible. Once you were gone, the body meant nothing, had no sentimental value. The future body was all that mattered. The past shouldn't be there, staring you in the face with dead eyes. She shuddered.

"When the engines get running again, it'll warm up," Hiro said helpfully, mistaking the reason for her shiver.

They reached a junction, and she led the way left. "Decades, Hiro. We've been out here for decades. What happened to our mindmaps?"

"What's the last thing you remember?" he asked.

"We had the cocktail party in Luna station as the final passengers were entering cryo and getting loaded. We came aboard. We were given some hours to move into our quarters. Then we had the tour, which ended in the cloning bay, getting our updated mindmaps."

"Same here," he said.

"Are you scared?" Maria said, stopping and looking at him.

She hadn't scrutinized him since waking up in the cloning bay. She was used to the way that clones with the experience of hundreds of years could look like they had just stepped out of university. Their bodies woke up at peak age, twenty years old, designed to be built with muscle. What the clones did with that muscle once they woke up was their challenge.

Akihiro Sato was a thin Pan Pacific United man of Japanese descent with short black hair that was drying in stiff cowlicks. He had lean muscles, and high cheekbones. His eyes were black, and they met hers with a level gaze. She didn't look too closely at the rest of him; she wasn't rude.

He pulled at a cowlick, then tried to smooth it down. "I've woken up in worse places."

"Like where?" she asked, pointing down the hall from where they had come. "What's worse than that horror movie scene?"

He raised his hands in supplication. "I don't mean literally. I mean I've lost time before. You have to learn to adapt sometimes. Fast. I wake up. I assess the immediate threat. I try to figure out where I was last time I uploaded a mindmap. This time I woke up in the middle of a bunch of dead bodies, but there was no threat that I could tell." He cocked his head, curious. "Haven't you ever lost time before? Not even a week? Surely you've died between backups."

"Yes," she admitted. "But I've never woken up in danger, or in the wake of danger."

"You're still not in danger," he said. "That we know of."

She stared at him.

"*Immediate* danger," he amended. "I'm not going to stab you right here in the hall. All of our danger right now consists of problems that we can likely fix. Lost memories, broken computer, finding a murderer. Just a little work and we'll be back on track."

"You are the strangest kind of optimist," she said. "All the same, I'd like to continue to freak out if you don't mind."

"Try to keep it together. You don't want to devolve into whatever Paul has become," he suggested as he continued down the hall.

Maria followed, glad that he wasn't behind her. "I'm keeping it together. I'm here, aren't I?"

"You'll probably feel better when you've had a shower and some food," he said. "Not to mention clothes."

They were both covered only in the tacky, drying synth-amneo fluid. Maria had never wanted a shower more in her life. "Aren't you a little worried about what we're going to find when we find your body?" she asked.

Hiro looked back at her. "I learned a while back not to mourn the old shells. If we did, we'd get more and more dour with each life. In fact, I think that may be Wolfgang's problem." He frowned. "Have you ever had to clean up the old body by yourself?"

Maria shook her head. "No. It was disorienting; she was looking at me, like she was blaming me. It's still not as bad as not knowing what happened, though."

"Or who happened," said Hiro. "It did have a knife."

"And it was violent," Maria said. "It could be one of us."

"Probably was, or else we should get excited about a first-contact situation. Or second contact, if the first one went so poorly..." Hiro said, then sobered. "But truly anything could have gone wrong. Someone could have woken up from cryo and gone mad, even. Computer glitch messed with the mindmap. But it's probably easily explained, like someone got caught cheating at poker. Heat of the moment, someone hid an ace, the doctor flipped the table—"

"It's not funny," Maria said softly. "It wasn't madness and it wasn't an off-the-cuff crime. If that had happened, we wouldn't have the grav drive offline. We wouldn't be missing decades of memories. IAN would be able to tell us what's going on. But someone—one of us—wanted us dead, and they also messed with the personality backups. Why?"

"Is that rhetorical? Or do you really expect me to know?" he asked.

"Rhetorical," grumbled Maria. She shook her head to clear it. A strand of stiff black hair smacked her in the face, and she winced. "It could have been two people. One killed us, one messed with the memories."

"True," he said. "We can probably be sure it was premeditated. Anyway, the captain was right. Let's be cautious. And let's make a pact. I'll promise not to kill you and you promise not to kill me. Deal?"

Maria smiled in spite of herself. She shook his hand. "I promise. Let's get going before the captain sends someone after us."

The door to medbay was rimmed in red lights, making it easy to find if ill or injured. With the alert, the lights were blinking, alternating between red and yellow. Hiro stopped abruptly at the entrance. Maria smacked into the back of him in a collision that sent them spinning gently like gears in a clock, making him turn to face the hall while she swung around to see what had stopped him so suddenly.

The contact could have been awkward except for the shock of the scene before them.

In the medbay, a battered, older version of Captain Katrina de la Cruz lay in a bed. She was unconscious but very much alive, hooked up to life support, complete with IV, breathing tubes, and monitors. Her face was a mess of bruises, and her right arm was in a cast. She was strapped to the bed, which was held to the floor magnetically.

"I thought we all died," Hiro said, his voice soft with wonder.

"For us all to wake up, we should have. I guess I hit the emergency resurrection switch anyway," Maria said, pushing herself off the doorjamb to float into the room closer to the captain.

"Too bad you can't ask yourself," Hiro said drily.

Penalties for creating a duplicate clone were stiff, usually resulting in the extermination of the older clone. Although with several murders to investigate, and now an assault, Wolfgang would probably not consider this particular crime a priority to punish.

"No one is going to be happy about this," Hiro said, pointing at the unconscious body of the captain. "Least of all Katrina. What are we going to do with two captains?"

"But this could be good," Maria said. "If we can wake her up, we might find out what happened."

"I can't see her agreeing with you," he said.

A silver sheet covered the body and drifted lazily where the straps weren't holding it down. The captain's clone was still, the breathing tube the only sound.

Maria floated to the closet on the far side of the room. She grabbed a handful of large jumpsuits—they would be too short for Wolfgang, too tight for the doctor, and too voluminous for Maria, but they would do for the time being—and pulled a folded wheelchair from where it drifted in the dim light filtering into the closet.

She handed a jumpsuit to Hiro and donned hers, unselfconsciously not turning away. When humans reach midlife, they may reach a level of maturity where they cease to give a damn what someone thinks about their bodies. Multiply that a few times and you have the modesty (or lack thereof) of the average clone. The first time Maria had felt the self-conscious attitude lifting, it had been freeing. The mind-set remained with many clones even as their bodies reverted to youth, knowing that a computer-built body was closer to a strong ideal than they could have ever created with diet and exercise.

The sobbing engineer, Paul, had been the most ashamed clone Maria had ever seen.

The jumpsuit fabric wasn't as soft as Maria's purple engineering jumpsuits back in her quarters, but she was at least warmer. She wondered when they would finally be allowed to eat and go back to their quarters for a shower and some sleep. Waking up took a lot out of a clone.

Hiro was already clothed and back over by the captain's body, peering at her face. Maria maneuvered her way over to him using the wall handles. He looked grim, his usually friendly face now reflecting the seriousness of the situation.

"I don't suppose we can just hide this body?" he asked. "Recycle it before anyone finds out? Might save us a lot of headache in the future."

Maria checked the vital-signs readout on the computer. "I don't think she's a body yet. Calling her a body and disposing of it is something for the courts, not us."

"What courts?" he asked as Maria took the wheelchair by the handles and headed for the door. "There are six of us!"

"Seven," Maria reminded, jerking her head backward to indicate the person in the medbay. "Eight if we can get IAN online. Even so it's a matter for the captain and IAN to decide, not us."

"Well, then you get to go spread the latest bad news."

"I'm not ready to deal with Wolfgang right now," Maria said. "Or hear the captain tear Paul a new asshole. Besides, we have to check the grav drive."

"Avoiding Wolfgang sounds like a good number one priority," said Hiro. "In fact, if I could interview my last clone, he probably avoided Wolfgang a lot too."

★   ★   ★

The bridge of the starship *Dormire* was an impressive affair, with a seat for the captain and one for the pilot at the computer terminals that sat on the floor, but a ladder ran up the wall right beside the room entrance to lead to a few comfortable benches bolted to the wall, making it the perfect place to observe the universe as the ship crept toward light speed. The room itself comprised a dome constructed from diamond, so that you could see in a 270-degree arc. The helm looked like a great glass wart sitting on the end of the ship, but it did allow a lovely view of the universe swinging around you as the grav drive rotated the ship. Now, with the drive off, space seemed static, even though they were moving at a fraction of the speed of light through space.

It could make someone ill, honestly. Deep space all around, even the floor being clear. Maria remembered seeing it on the tour of the ship, but this was the first time she had seen it away from Luna. The first time in this clone's memory, anyway.

Drawing the eye away from the view, the terminals, and the pilot's station and benches, Hiro's old body floated near the top of the dome, tethered by a noose to the bottom of one of the benches. His face was red and his open eyes bulged.

"Oh. There—" He paused to swallow, then continued. "—there I am." He turned away, looking green.

"I don't know what I expected, but suicide wasn't it," Maria said softly, looking into the swollen, anguished face. "I was actually wondering if you survived too."

"I didn't expect hanging," he said. "I don't think I expected anything. It's all real to me now." He covered his mouth with his hand.

Maria knew too much sympathy could make a person on the edge lose control, so she turned firm. "Do not puke in here. I already have to clean up the cloning bay, and you've seen what a nightmare that is. Don't give me more to clean up."

He glared at her, but some color returned to his face. He did not look up again.

Something drifted gently into the back of Maria's head. She grabbed at it and found a brown leather boot. The hanged corpse wore its mate.

"This starts to build a time line," Maria said. "You had to be hanged when we still had gravity. I guess that's good."

Hiro still had his back to the bridge, face toward the hallway. His eyes were closed and he breathed deeply. She put her hand on his shoulder. "Come on. We need to get the drive back on."

Hiro turned and focused on the terminal, which was blinking red.

"Are you able to turn it on without IAN?" Maria asked.

"I should be. IAN could control everything, but if he goes offline, we're not dead in the water. Was that my shoe?" The last question was offhand, as if it meant nothing.

"Yes." Maria drifted toward the top of the helm and took a closer look at the body. It was hard to tell since the face was so distorted by the hanging, but Hiro looked different from the rest of the crew. They all looked as if decades had passed since they had launched from Luna station. But Hiro looked exactly as he did now, as if freshly vatted.

"Hey, Hiro, I think you must have died at least once during the trip. Probably recently. This is a newer clone than the others," she said. "I think we're going to have to start writing the weird stuff down."

Hiro made a sound like an animal caught in a trap. All humor had left him. His eyes were hard as he finally glanced up at her and the clone. "All right. That's it."

"That's what?"

"The last straw. I'm officially scared now."

"Now? It took you this long to get scared?" Maria asked, pulling herself to the floor. "With everything else we're dealing with, *now* you're scared?"

Hiro punched at the terminal, harder than Maria thought was necessary. Nothing happened. He crossed his arms, and then uncrossed them, looking as if arms were some kind of new limb he wasn't sure what to do with. He took the boot from Maria and slid it over his own foot.

"I was just managing to cope with the rest," he said. "That was something happening to all of you. I wasn't involved. I wasn't a Saturday Night Gorefest. I was here as a supporting, friendly face. I was here to make you laugh. *Hey, Hiro will always cheer us up.*"

Maria put her hand on his shoulder and looked him in the eyes. "Welcome to the panic room, Hiro. We have to support each other. Take a deep breath. Now we need to get the drive on and then tell the captain and Wolfgang."

"You gotta be desperate if you want to tell Wolfgang," he said, looking as if he was trying and failing to force a smile.

"And when you get the drive on, can you find out what year it is, check on the cargo, maybe reach IAN from here?" Maria asked. "With everything else that's happened, it might be nice to come back with a little bit of good news. Or improved news."

Hiro nodded, his mouth closed as if trying to hold in something he would regret saying. Or perhaps a scream. He floated over to his pilot's chair and strapped himself in. The console screen continued to blink bright red at him. "Thanks for that warning, IAN, we hadn't noticed the drive was gone."

He typed some commands and poked at the touch screen. A warning siren began to bleat through the ship, telling everyone floating in zero-g that gravity was incoming. Hiro poked at the screen a few more times, and then typed at a terminal, his face growing darker as he did so. He made some calculations and then sighed loudly, sitting back in the chair and putting his hands over his face.

"Well," he said. "Things just got worse."

Maria heard the grav drive come online, and the ship shuddered as the engines started rotating the five-hundred-thousand–GRT ship. She took hold of the ladder along the back wall to guide her way to the bench so she wouldn't fall once the gravity came back.

"What now?" she said. "Are we off course?"

"We've apparently been in space for twenty-four years and seven months." He paused. "And nine days."

Maria did the math. "So it's 2493."

"By now we should be a little more than three light-years away from home. Far outside the event horizon of realistic communication with Earth. And we are. But we're also twelve degrees off course."

"That . . . sorry, I don't get where the hell that is. Can you say it in maintenance-officer language?"

"We are slowing down and turning. I'm not looking forward to telling the captain," he said, unstrapping himself from the seat. He glanced up at his own body drifting at the end of the noose like a grisly kite. "We can cut that down later."

"What were we thinking? Why would we go off course?" Maria thought aloud as they made their way through the hallway, staying low to prepare for gravity as the ship's rotation picked up.

"Why murder the crew, why turn off the grav drive, why spare the captain, why did I kill myself, and why did I apparently feel the need to take off one shoe before doing it?" Hiro said. "Just add it to your list, Maria. I'm pretty sure we are officially fucked, no matter what the answers are."

DIAMONDS

The only part of the *Dormire*'s mission that hadn't gone wrong, apparently, was the state of the cargo.

While the ship carried her skeleton crew, within the hold were two thousand humans sleeping in cryo. Within the servers in the hold were over five hundred clone mindmaps. Maria and the other five were responsible for over twenty-five hundred lives.

Maria didn't like to dwell on the responsibility. She was just happy to hear Hiro confirm that all their passengers were still stable and that the backups were uncorrupted.

Each human and clone passenger had reasons for coming on the journey: Adventure and exploration drove many of the humans; escaping religious persecution drove many of the clones. Between the two groups, a fair number of political and corporate exiles traveled to escape jail, indentured servitude, or worse.

All of them were driven in part by the fact that the Earth was losing habitable land as the oceans rose, and territorial and water wars were breaking out worldwide. So the rich, as always, left because they could.

The reasons the crew were on the ship, however, were slightly different. Each had the simple motivation of being a criminal attempting to wipe the record clean.

Their destination, the planet Artemis, was fully habitable, a bit smaller than Earth, and seemed like paradise. It orbited Tau Ceti, in the constellation Cetus.

Maria doubted their paradise would result in humans and clones living together much better than they had on Earth, but people had rosy dreams and big ideas.

"Have you ever attempted suicide?" Hiro asked as they carried the jumpsuits and chair back to the cloning bay.

"That's pretty personal," Maria said, running the fingers of one hand through her long hair and grimacing at the sticky mats she encountered.

He shrugged. "You just saw my answer hanging above us. I'm pretty sure that when all of this is done, Wolfgang will decide what to do with that little detail of today's misadventures. Earth cloning laws aren't going to be ignored out here—they made that pretty clear before we left."

Maria wondered about his criminal past. She sighed. "I did attempt it. Once."

"What stopped you?" He didn't ask if she had succeeded; if she had, she wouldn't have had legal right to wake up her next clone.

"A friend talked me down," she said. "Isn't that what usually happens?"

"Wish I'd had a friend a few hours ago," he said.

"You'd likely still be dead, just in there," she said, pointing to the cloning bay.

"But I wouldn't be a suicide. I think Wolfgang's looking anywhere for someone to blame for this."

"You're here now. Let's take care of the immediate problems. Then we'll figure out what happened to us all," Maria said.

The captain's voice drifted down the hall, a cry of disgust.

"Whose idea was it to turn the grav drive on?" she shouted.

"Yours, Captain," Hiro said as they entered. "You wanted to be able to stand on solid ground."

The cloning bay still looked like a nightmare, but at least it was a nightmare under the rule of gravity. Dodging bodies and biohazardous human waste was a situation she never wanted to even think about again. Maria and Hiro had tried to prepare themselves for the new gravity-affected view of the slaughter, but the dead bodies bouncing around the floor—gravity was not yet strong enough to let them stay where they fell—turned out to nauseate them in a new way. The blood and other fluids had splattered on the floor and walls, and some on the crew themselves. Maybe Paul had been smart to want to stay in his vat.

"It was rhetorical," she said, holding on to the wall and bracing herself on the floor. "I didn't know it would be this bad. So what did you learn? Did you have any problems without IAN? Or could you access him from the bridge?"

"IAN is still down, Captain," Hiro said. "Luckily for us, in the unlikely occurrence that IAN is down, the helm unlocks. Otherwise, it's suicide. Or genocide. Is it genocide if we kill everyone on board?"

Maria winced.

"Speaking of which, all of our cryo-passengers are alive and accounted for. One bit of good news, right? Yay?" Hiro ventured a smile. Katrina didn't return it.

The captain turned to Maria. "Give me a less chaotic report."

Maria swallowed. "I'm not sure what Hiro did, but it didn't take him much time to get the grav drive working again and access the nav computer and check on everything. Anyway, we have more important news."

"Here, let me." Hiro held out his hand and counted off his fingers. "We've been in space close to twenty-five years. We're twelve degrees off course and slower than we should be going. Not to mention—"

"Did you correct the course?" Katrina interrupted.

"Yes, ma'am," he said. "It will take a while to get back, of course, but I righted our direction."

As Hiro was letting the captain know their situation, Maria

quietly passed out jumpsuits. Wolfgang snatched two without looking at her, thrusting one at Paul—who had grabbed instead for Joanna's wheelchair and was steadying himself with one hand on his vat and the chair in the other, shielding himself. Joanna took Paul's suit from Wolfgang and traded it to him for her chair with a kind smile. Dr. Glass accepted her suit with a smile, slid into it with practiced ease, and climbed into her new wheelchair. She steadied herself against a cloning vat until the gravity increased to keep her stable on the ground. The legs of her jumpsuit drifted lazily from her tiny legs.

"Want something to tie those up so they don't drag?" Maria asked, pointing at the dangling cuffs.

"Thanks, but no," Dr. Glass said, pulling them in and tucking them neatly under her. "I'll go and get my other prosthetics from my room later. Or my crutches. When this calms down." She waved her hand at the horror show around them.

Maria followed her gesture, at the bouncing bodies, the splattered gore, the frazzled crew. "I'm not sure when this is going to calm down. There's a lot of stuff going on."

Joanna quirked an eyebrow. "You mean there's more?"

Maria grimaced and pointed to the captain, who was hearing the story about them discovering Hiro's body. She moved to stand beside him. The gravity was improving, bit by bit, as the drive got the ship turning fast enough.

"It looks like suicide," Hiro said, avoiding the captain's eyes.

"But we don't know anything for sure right now," Maria added. "He's also younger than all of our clones."

Joanna held up a finger. "That on the surface means nothing worrisome; he could have died recently for any number of reasons."

"We won't know if it's suicide without examining the body," Wolfgang said.

Hiro looked at him, surprised. Maria hadn't expected Wolfgang to give him the benefit of the doubt either.

"There's one more thing," Hiro said, looking at Maria.

So it was her turn to deliver the bad news. She sighed and squared her shoulders. "The big news," she said to Katrina, "is your previous clone isn't dead. She's in medbay in a coma."

The captain said nothing, but the color drained from her face and her lips pursed tightly together. She looked at Paul as if this whole thing was his fault. "Enough. You get to work. Hiro, Joanna, with me to the medbay. Wolfgang, you're in charge here."

Paul stood, now fully clothed, staring at Katrina. He had stopped sobbing, but he still shook slightly. The thick synth-amneo drained off his hair as the gravity slowly returned. He didn't move.

"Doc, that's not normal, is it?" Maria asked, jabbing her thumb at the frightened man.

"On rare occasions, a clone can have a bad reaction to waking up," Joanna said. "It's not unlike waking from a nightmare, being disoriented and not knowing what is real."

"Only this time he woke up to a nightmare. Poor guy," Maria said.

"Captain, a moment, please," Joanna said, and pushed her chair carefully toward Paul.

One of the best things about cloning was that, even if there were no modifications done to the genes, each clone came out in the best possible shape at peak physical age. Maria remembered Paul as a mid-forties white man with a large belly and poorly cut blond hair. His arms were covered with dark spots like mosquito bites that he scratched nervously so they never healed. He wore a full beard and greatly disliked the tight (to him) jumpsuits that they were forced to wear as uniforms.

None of that Paul was here now. The only resemblance was the wide, watery blue eyes that stared out from a strong face, clean skin with a few moles and freckles, and a toned body. Not bodybuilder-toned but certainly not someone Maria would kick out of bed. If he were not looking on the verge of a breakdown.

"Paul, we need you to step up and do your job," Joanna said calmly. "If there's a problem with this current body or mindmap, you need to let me know right now. Otherwise we need you to get IAN online."

Wolfgang raised a white eyebrow. "You think I didn't tell him that already?"

"You used different wording," Joanna said, not looking at him. She gently reached out and touched Paul's hand.

He jerked it away from her. "Y'all could have given me a little privacy," he said hoarsely.

"Privacy?" snorted Wolfgang.

"That's ridiculous. If you ever want a checkup, you'll have to get used to getting treated by me," Joanna said.

Paul looked at his corpse, his face turning a bit green. The body that lay tethered to the others on the cold floor; the one with multiple bruises in his neck was more like the one Maria remembered, only older. He looked worn; space and time had not been kind to him, as he weighed even more than her memory. He wore a ratty T-shirt of a band long dead, and his jumpsuit was zipped only to his waist. The top half of the suit draped behind him as if his ass had its own cape.

The living Paul gulped and looked up. "What—"

"Happened? You know as much as we do. That's what we're trying to figure out, and that's why you need to figure out what's wrong with our AI."

He nodded once and focused on the console across the bay. "I can do that." Stumbling, he walked past them and gave the dead bodies a wide berth to get to the terminal where they could access IAN.

Wolfgang bent to examine the corpses.

Joanna nodded. "Ready, Captain."

Katrina led the way down the corridor, Hiro pushing Joanna's clumsily bouncing wheelchair down the hall behind her. Hiro

thought that the doctor would have preferred to wait for the
ship to achieve full gravity before they moved, but she didn't
complain.

When they took the turn in the corridor toward the medbay,
Joanna called out for Katrina to stop. "Take a moment before you
go in there. This kind of thing can be quite upsetting."

"What of the many kinds of things we've seen today are you referring to?" Katrina asked with a touch of acid in her voice.

"Encountering your previous clone," Joanna said.

"How many times has it happened before? Unless I didn't hear
of new codicils, having a second clone is highly illegal, right?"

"Well, so's murder, but that doesn't stop people," Hiro said,
forcing lightness into his voice.

The captain's body was stiff as she forced herself to slow down
for Hiro and Joanna to catch up. In another situation, Hiro would
have been amused to watch her internal struggle, but he was busy
wondering how he would feel in this situation. This specific one,
anyway.

He doubted he would react well. Finding his own body dead of
apparent suicide in the helm was enough to prove that.

Currently the captain was in the situation where a clone was
alive who had memories she didn't share. There would be legal
and moral considerations as to who retained the right to the very
being of Katrina de la Cruz. Fighting for the right to lead the ship
would be inevitable, but that would likely be only the first of such
battles.

Or they could just read the law exactly as it was written, and
terminate the older clone. That sometimes happened too.

IAN could have helped them with this decision, but, well, that
was a current dead end.

They entered the medbay. The captain walked right up to the
bed and looked down at her own older, comatose body. Her skin
paled, then darkened, and her lips went white. She took a sharp

intake of breath and turned her back, facing Hiro and Joanna. "Recycle it."

Joanna gaped at her. "That's all you have to say? That's a person lying there."

"Legally, the moment I woke up, that became just a shell," Katrina said. "Recycle it." Striding as purposefully as she could in the low gravity, she left the medbay.

"See, that's what I told Maria she would say," Hiro said, glancing at Joanna. "But I think we need her."

Joanna nodded. "Our only witness." She moved to check the readings on the terminal beside the bed.

"Seems unethical, besides."

The doctor rubbed her face. "I hate these problems. There's never a good answer. Can you check and see if my spare set of prosthetics are here?"

"How often have you had this kind of problem?" Hiro asked as he looked around the medbay while Joanna rooted through a drawer. She pulled out a tablet and turned it on.

"We are given a number of clone-specific ethical questions in med school," she said. "This is only one of them. We studied things like how to deal with mind hackers who botch a job, or do too good a job. How to judge if a clone's early death is suicide. Who to blame if someone is cloned against their will or at the wrong time. We had a whole year on ethics."

"Just one year?" Hiro asked. "That can't be enough. I've had a few lifetimes and I still don't understand it sometimes."

The medbay closet held several jumpsuits, a small overturned plastic table, and a collection of shoes. The legs the shoes were supposed to be on were nowhere to be found.

"Where am I supposed to find these legs?" he asked.

"If they're not there, they're in my quarters. If they got displaced because of the grav drive failure, they couldn't have gotten far."

Joanna was making notes from the machines the captain's clone was hooked up to. She didn't look up when Hiro joined her, merely reached her hands out and kept reading digital charts.

"No legs, sorry," Hiro said, going to the other side of the captain's bed. Everything in the medbay was meticulous; anything that wasn't bolted to the floor or magnetically held down was in containers already secured using such methods. "You're apparently not a messy person, so there's not a lot of places for the legs to hide."

The captain, now that Hiro had time to look at her, did not look well. Her long black hair was gone, shaved so that her head wound could be treated and bandaged. Tubes of all sizes came from her body, pumping things in or taking things out.

"She was attacked only two days ago," Joanna said, looking at the machine's display. "That's how far back the data goes, anyway, but from the looks of the wounds, it sounds right. I won't know until Paul gets IAN online and we can get the locked computers going. Then I hope we can access our logs."

"They're fully locked down?" Hiro asked. "But the engines and the nav system had an override."

"Apparently it's an emergency lockdown that happens with the resurrection switch. To give everyone time to acclimate before making any rash decisions," Joanna said, frowning. "Although it could just be another safeguard to avoid sabotage."

"It seems every single safeguard failed," Hiro said, shaking his head. "Cutting us out of the computers doesn't seem like good planning."

"I'm with you. But they thought that IAN would be around to help make these decisions. We weren't supposed to be needed. Hopefully Paul can find my logs concerning the captain's status. Once we unlock Wolfgang's logs, that should help us identify who attacked her, and we can learn some more."

"Then I guess it's safe to say that she wasn't the murderer," Hiro said, "unless she's good at beating herself up."

"I don't think it's safe to say anything right now," Joanna said. "You'd be surprised what people are capable of."

Hiro swallowed back his reply. *Not really.*

Even with the grav drive turned back on, the doctor hadn't removed the old clone's restraints. Hiro tested one and Joanna shook her head at him. He raised his eyebrows. "You afraid she's going to run away?"

"She's our only witness, if she wakes up," Joanna said. "And our only suspect if she is somehow involved in the carnage out there." She jerked her head toward the cloning bay. "It's safest for everyone if she stays strapped to the bed."

"What about the captain? The current one, I mean?" Hiro asked. "She gave you an order."

Joanna sighed and leaned back in her chair. "When it comes to medical disagreements, I have jurisdiction. We may need to protect this one from her. Have you ever had your clones overlap?"

Hiro shook his head, the often-repeated lie coming to his lips. "My lab was ethical to the point of being boring. Have you ever broken clone law, had your clones overlap or anything?"

The doctor was silent for some time.

"This should be an easy answer," he said. "It's a *yes, no,* or *I don't want to talk about it, Hiro, let's talk about what you think's been happening in rugby for the past twenty-five years* kind of question."

"Just considering how much to say," the doctor said. "Memories grow hazy."

"And we don't know yet who to trust. Fair enough," he said.

Memories. He had many. His childhood was crystal-clear. The details of his various lives tended to blur together, though. He was usually grateful for that.

"I've lived a long time," Joanna finally said. "Before the Codicils, even."

Hiro whistled. "No kidding? So you must have had multiples at one time, or lived in the golden age of hacking."

"That's a funny way of describing the time when people would mess with a clone's DNA as if it were a cake recipe instead of the fundamental matrix of a person," Joanna said sternly. "It was not a good time. Bathtub baby incidents were cropping up, along with hearings on the ethics of DNA hacking and the even more questionable ethics behind mindmap hacking. One of the greatest technologies in history was outlawed because of opportunistic fatcats and outlaw hackers with no principles. Is that 'golden' to you?"

Hiro remembered the stories from history class, having been born after the Codicils were in place. *Bathtub babies* was the term for children born with undesirable genes, the wrong gender, or a disability. The parents would record the DNA matrix and the mindmap, then pay extra for a hacker to change the gender or disability, or even—he remembered with discomfort—to make a mixed-race baby favor one parent's race over the other's. Once the new, shiny, perfect clone was programmed, the parents would "dispose of" the damaged one and wake the new clone.

It went beyond children. World leaders were kidnapped and modified to fit a rival government's needs. Lovers were modified to fit a partner's needs. The sex trade grew in leaps and bounds. Eventually the penalty for hacking was death.

"I don't mean that the bathtub babies were good. But if something needed to be fixed, something genetic and deadly, then the hackers could do it instead of forcing someone to die from MS over and over again, right? The really good ones could modify a sociopath, I heard. And the Codicils put an end to that, to all the good hacking. I understand why they did it, but it seemed like overkill to ban all hacking."

"Loopholes would have been found if we allowed even a little bit through. Even after the laws passed, some hackers went underground and kept working. You can't catch all the roaches." She sounded bitter. She put her hand on the captain's and patted it twice. "I was never for the pointless killing of an older clone in order to benefit a newer one. And it happened far more often than the history books say it did. I will do all I can to protect this one."

"You may need a guard," Hiro said.

"Katrina's upset, but I don't think she'll act. She has other things to worry about, after all," Joanna said. She sighed and checked the reading of a blood sample a diagnostic machine had taken. "All vital signs are steady. She's suffered some severe head trauma. Honestly. If we were back home, we'd activate the DNR and just euthanize her. But we need her alive for now."

"Playing God isn't as exciting as you'd think," Hiro said. "Why can't we just take a mindmap of her brain?"

"And put it where?" Joanna asked. "We don't have a hacker on board, and it's even less ethical to grow a new clone just for her memories, which are likely damaged. Where does that put our captain, then?"

"Probably pissed as hell at us. Then she can recycle us and re-place us with clones of herself," Hiro suggested.

Joanna smiled. "There you go. Seriously, without IAN to watch her while I rest, I'm going to need to sleep in here. Can you give me a hand making up the other hospital bed?"

Hiro started looking about the medbay for linens, but found none. "I guess there will be sheets in storage. Or I'll see if they drifted down the hall or something."

Joanna nodded, focused on the captain's clone again. "Thank you."

"Doc?" Hiro asked as he snagged a chair with magnetic casters on the legs and slid it across the floor to the captain's bedside.

"Mm?" Joanna said, looking at the readout of the numbers again.

"You never said whether you had met a previous clone of your-self," Hiro said.

"Actually I haven't. My lives have been fairly boring. I like it that way."

"Until now," he said.

"Until now," she agreed softly. "At least our cargo is safe. Otherwise the mission is pointless."

"True!" Hiro said brightly, and then realized how ridiculous he sounded. "Kinda like finding a diamond in a pile of shit."

The intercom above their head crackled to life with the captain's voice. "All crew to the cloning bay. Now."

He sighed. "Why do I think the pile of shit just got a little deeper?"

DEPTHS

Hiro missed swimming.

He knew it was ridiculous, given that whatever had happened, his last memory of Earth was only a few hours ago in his time line. The last time he went swimming, according to his memory, was a week ago. But this body had never touched a pool or ocean, and probably never would. He'd thought about the freedom of swimming several times after waking up. Diving down into the black water, away from the horrors that surrounded him. His mood, his quips, felt like autopilot while he submerged inside himself.

Like all older clones, he understood how to deal with his own death. It no longer shocked him; he'd experienced it in many ways.

But he'd never killed himself. He couldn't imagine why he had done so this time. So he dove.

He resurfaced when Wolfgang grabbed his arm roughly. "Pay attention, Hiro," he said.

Paul and Maria stood at the two cloning bay terminals, Paul still looking ill and shaky, Maria's lip bloody where it looked as if she had bitten it.

The captain faced them, her arms crossed.

"While we have basic computer use and access to navigation, we have some serious problems. IAN remains offline. Our logs— all logs, personal, medical, command—are gone. No backups." She took a deep breath. "And we have discovered sabotage here in the bay itself. Beyond the apparent erasure of all our more recent mindmaps, we can't make any new mindmaps. And the cloning bay's software has been wiped. It's just a big empty computer attached to some vats. No new bodies."

They were silent, letting this sink in.

Hiro continued to sink.

"This is death," Joanna said from very far away.

"Yes. Unless we can figure out how to fix these machines, we're all dead at the end of these clones' lifetimes," Katrina said. "Now. Options."

Hiro's ears were buzzing. He wanted to move, to run, to find a weapon and take full revenge on anyone and everyone. His fists balled up.

Wolfgang took a step toward Paul, and the smaller man looked up from the terminal in alarm. "Fix it."

"I'm doing what I can," Paul said, his voice stronger as he tapped on the terminal. He was in his element, apparently, and getting a bit more energy.

"Our first goal is to get IAN online," Maria said. A drop of blood had fallen onto her chin.

Hiro stared at that drop of blood. It centered him. It felt like all that had gone wrong that day was contained in the drop of blood. He stepped forward and dabbed at her chin with his sleeve.

"You're bleeding," he said quietly.

"Oh. Right. So I am," she said. "That's the least of our problems right now."

"But it's one that we can fix."

She gave him a quick glance, then turned back to the terminal. "Fair enough."

"Maria," Katrina said. "Do you have experience with reprogramming an AI?"

Maria paused, then looked up again. "No, Captain."

"Then if you're not going to help here, go to the kitchen and see if the sabotage has reached that far. We're going to need food soon."

Maria frowned as if she was going to argue, but when she saw Wolfgang's face she nodded once and left.

The captain ran her hand over her face. "Now, Wolfgang. We need to talk."

"I think we do," he said. "Paul, keep working."

"I need to go to the server room to access IAN at the source," Paul said, and left the room.

Hiro stood, alone in the room where many of them had died. He wanted to dive again. But he looked at the drop of blood on his sleeve and shook his head. No one had given him an order. So he followed Katrina and Wolfgang.

It hadn't been Maria's decision to join the starship *Dormire*'s crew. It certainly was a great opportunity; it was the first human generational ship to leave Earth for better skies. It wouldn't be the last, or that's what her parole officer had said. But she had said a lot of things.

Things like, "Help crew this ship, don't mess anything up, and you'll be pardoned at the end. Your entire record will be wiped." And, "Of course your crewmates aren't *all* dangerous criminals. The AI is designed to take over if someone decides to mutiny. It's completely safe." And, "All right, there may be *some* violent criminals aboard, but remember we have several safeguards in place." And, "Hey, for a clone with three life sentences on your head, this is the best prison you'll ever get a chance to be in. And full pardon!"

It sounded like a great deal, but she knew the timeless reason criminals crewed this ship: cheap labor. Anyone reputable would have charged a fortune to crew a starship for generations. Financiers had to cut costs where they could.

And now they were well and truly alone out here. With the first death sentence any of them had experienced.

"No one aboard will know your crimes. Think of this as your new start," the parole officer had said. She couldn't have known the irony of that statement, but it still burned Maria.

"Is keeping that secret a rule or guideline?" Maria had asked, quirking an eyebrow.

"It's a rule. No one is to discuss their pasts."

"And how will they police that?"

"The AI will be listening."

"Lovely."

But it still sounded better than prison.

Maria had wondered if part of her punishment was to be the lowest-ranking person on the ship. Everyone else had a good job, while hers involved general maintenance, cook duties, and common-area cleaning. A janitor/cook/handywoman. Although admittedly she didn't have experience at any high-level military ranks, or driving a spaceship. Taking care of the incidentals was something she could do.

And there were a lot of incidentals.

The *Dormire* consisted largely of engines, a mile-square solar sail, water and air scrubbers, server farms, recyclers, bio spaces, and millions of gallons of a synthetic, protein-rich material called Formula CL-20465-F. Trademark Lyfe.

The creation of Lyfe had done much to help with starvation problems on Earth, because if a town could afford the specific printer and a supply of Lyfe, which was very cheap to make, it could print almost any food. The printer was a highly sophisticated machine that could break down food, study it on the molecular level, and re-create it almost exactly, provided it had the right protein and vitamin strands. The up-front cost was huge, but long-term cost was minimal.

Religious arguments against cloning started early when

scientists used Lyfe—previously considered to be just a food source—to create the first clones in actual adult human bodies that waited for mindmaps to wake them. The clones, however, were grateful to avoid childhood and the pain of puberty multiple times.

Considering the trip to their new home was going to take several lifetimes, the clones needed enough Lyfe to cover all their organic needs on the ship as well as for any new bodies they would grow to continue their lives. When they arrived at their new planet, the crew's mission changed to start the massive job of printing bodies for all the new clones and waking up the sleeping humans. Then they would be free citizens.

The *Dormire* was a cylindrical ship that created gravity by spinning. The crew lived on an inner ring that had a gravity slightly above Luna's, and below Earth's. This was primarily for the Lunaborn Wolfgang who would be in constant discomfort if they resided on the outer rings, which rotated between one and two g's, depending on the floor. As the size of each subsequent concentric floor grew, so did the speed it traveled around the hub, and so did the gravity. While the innermost floors were comfortable, the middle floors that held the massive computer banks and the air and water scrubbers were closer to Earth's gravity; the outermost ring held more cargo needed at the other end of the voyage.

In Maria's opinion, the most important cargo they carried was the biomass Lyfe from which all the newly cloned bodies came.

Of course, Lyfe was next to useless if they didn't fix the cloning bay. Her stomach growled and she realized it still had one very good use. She headed for the kitchen.

If she couldn't help, at least she could cook.

FAILURES

Neither of them sat. They sized each other up, backs tense, as if waiting for the other to strike first.

Hiro had followed at a distance. The captain and her first mate had spoken with such gravity that he couldn't resist. He stood just outside the door and listened.

The captain spoke first. "I am very close to placing you under arrest. Tell me why I shouldn't."

"Really," Wolfgang said.

"You are the only confirmed murderer on board. Don't try to be surprised that I recognized you. It's funny you don't try to hide yourself. You don't really blend in," she said. "I know who you are and what you did. The murder of five people, and then—the really telling point—the sabotage of our cloning tech points entirely to you."

Hiro took a step back from the door. The captain knew Wolfgang and his crimes. Why was she keeping it a secret? He'd also been right to be afraid of the intense security chief. Hiro tried to think of a famous clone who was Luna-born tall with white hair. That was the problem with being alive for generations: You see a lot of people.

Wolfgang sounded tense but not worried. "Funny that you point the finger at me. I'm not the one wanted in seventeen countries."

The captain laughed. "As I remember, a few of those countries would like a word with you too. And I can't think of why I would sabotage cloning tech. I like clones."

"Is that so? How many clones did you kill?" Wolfgang asked. "I only heard your reputation, not a number."

"I was a soldier, Wolfgang. What's your excuse?"

"I meant your number after you left the army."

"Again," she said with an edge to her voice. "Regardless of who I killed, I didn't have a grudge against all of clonekind driving me."

"You had your reasons. I had mine. What we both did was still murder. But that was a long time ago. And I accepted the gift of this journey: a clean slate. You're not even supposed to bring past crimes up."

"I am if it has relevance to the fact that we—and the thousands of people we carry on the ship—are dead in sixty or so years if we can't figure out what happened and prevent it from happening again."

Hiro felt cold sweat break out on his forehead. That fact was taking some time to sink in. Humans weren't afraid of the specter of death that sat sixty years off; for a clone, it was terrifying. They were dead in the water. And Wolfgang put them there?

"We can't be the only ones guilty of violent crimes," Wolfgang said. "We need to figure out what everyone else is capable of."

"Are you sure you're not trying to shift the blame?" Katrina asked.

Another silence. A chair creaked. They must have relaxed enough to sit down.

"Captain, none of us knows what happened. It could have been you. It could have been me. We can't be guilty of the crimes because we don't have the memories of doing them."

"That's pretty impressive moral relativism," she said, a sarcastic edge to her voice. "You should go into ethics and theology."

He didn't respond to that. Hiro wished he could see them. He edged closer.

"Do you wonder why they paired us together?" Katrina asked. "They had to know it wouldn't be a good match if we learned who the other was."

"I haven't had time to wonder," Wolfgang replied. "It's possible they didn't consider how we would work together."

"They did all that psychological research in addition to studying our criminal records to make sure we would cooperate," de la Cruz said. Then she added bitterly, "So we wouldn't all kill each other once the isolation of deep space got to us."

"Another system failure," Wolfgang said.

"Add it to the list," she replied.

Hiro reached the edge of the door and peeked in. The captain sat at her large desk, a majestic porthole out to deep space behind her. Wolfgang sat in the chair opposite, back to Hiro. He was leaning forward intently.

"I propose a truce," he said. "We both were once hunters. We understand each other. The crew needs strong command. Until we find evidence, we point to no one."

"We need the crew files," she said. Hiro noticed she didn't accept the truce.

"They've been wiped."

"Joanna may have backups. She's at least seen them," Katrina said. "Go help her do the autopsies, get that information out of her."

"And the truce?" Hah. Wolfgang had noticed it too.

"For now. We have bigger problems. We're dying, Wolfgang. Nothing is as important as that."

"Fine. I'll talk to the doctor tonight," Wolfgang said. His voice was getting louder. Belatedly Hiro realized he had to get out of the doorway or he'd be caught eavesdropping. He ran a few steps down the hall, turned, and started walking toward the captain's office as if he had just gotten there.

Wolfgang nearly ran into him. "What are you doing out here?"

Hiro took a step back. "I had a question for the captain. I'm the only one she didn't give an order to. I was going to go check out navigation again, but I wanted to know if she had other orders."

Wolfgang stepped out of the doorway to let Hiro in. The captain sat at her desk, her back to them, looking at the rotating stars.

"Captain?" he asked.

"Has anyone collected the body in the helm?" Katrina said without turning around.

"Not that I know of," Hiro said, dreading Katrina's inevitable follow-up.

"Then go and cut it down and let Wolfgang take it to the medbay with the other bodies," she said.

"Aye," Hiro said, dread dripping from his voice.

"I'll be right behind you in a moment," Wolfgang said. "I need to talk to the captain a bit longer."

Hiro exited the office, trying not to let his walk betray how badly he wanted to run the hell away. *What did those two do?*

A world without mindmapping technology at the ready was foreign to Hiro. Mindmapping technology had revolutionized cloning by allowing adults to be born with the full memories of the previous clone. Before then, genetically identical babies could be grown, but they would grow into whoever their environment shaped them to be.

But then people learned how to map the mind, not just the DNA.

In the old days, a machine took the mindmap while the subject was asleep. A person's first mindmap could require weeks of going to the cloning clinic every night to fully map the brain, but once the technology improved, it was a matter of minutes. Subsequent mindmaps took a fresh look at the brain every time, needing only minutes to record a person's new experiences, memories, and emotional growth.

The modern era of cloning was born. Or woken, some might say.

The problems of security came up soon after, since mindmapping tech could allow scientists to read some of the key parts of someone's personality as clearly as they could read genetic abnormalities in DNA. The best mindmapping scientists could figure out that you were a compulsive liar as a child, and your first time lying had been when you were four, but they wouldn't be able to tell you what that lie had been.

Despite that gossamer covering of privacy, a good mindmapper could tell an awful lot about a person. And a really good one could sever those connections, letting those memories, experiences, or triggered responses go floating off untethered to eventually fade away. These scientists eventually got the moniker *mind hackers* and were reviled or sought after, depending on where you were in society and how much money you had.

Some mind hacking was done to erase the effects of debilitating PTSD. Some people went into DNA hacking to resolve genetic abnormalities. Some had the legitimate (but mind-numbingly easy) job of making the clones sterile on a DNA level as the law required.

And some just went rogue and hacked whatever the highest bidder wanted them to. Luckily, high-level mindmapping was difficult, and not many people could do it well. Most of the best hackers went underground after the Codicils were passed.

At this moment the *Dormire* was unable to make new mindmaps or clones. If someone died, the only map they would have available would be the one they had made when the voyage started.

Hiro considered all of this as he headed back to the helm, the silent Wolfgang behind him. That backup they all made at the beginning of the journey: If all IAN's logs had been wiped, where did that specific backup come from?

"He was eavesdropping," Wolfgang said.

Katrina nodded. "That's obvious. Why didn't you confront him?"

"I'd like to see what happens," Wolfgang said.

"A reactionary," Katrina sneered. "Unsurprising."

"Believe it or not, I learn from mistakes," he said. "Running headlong into things before you have all the information, that's foolhardy."

She waved away his statement as if it were stale smoke. "Fine. Let's see how he takes this information. If he reveals what he heard, we unite and throw him in the brig for mutiny. If he doesn't, then we just watch him."

Hiro had just forced Wolfgang to ally with the captain. Damn him.

"We're on a ship of criminals." The captain sighed and sat back. Her face had the look of a twenty-year-old woman, but dark smudges had appeared under her eyes, and the worry inside them reflected decades of experience. "It looks like we might have more than one murderer. And why did it happen twenty-five years into the mission? If the person had wanted to sabotage the ship, why not do it right away? We've been a crew that has presumably worked together for decades. What did we do wrong to bring all of it down?"

"After all I've been through, to be damned to die in deep space, with nothing to show for our mission but some floating blood and vomit," Wolfgang said.

Katrina's mouth twisted in a wry smile. "You don't have the market cornered on difficult lives. Maybe that's what Hiro was thinking when he hanged himself."

"Do you think he did it?" Wolfgang said. "We need to still

follow the Codicils even in space. We wouldn't have been able to wake a new Hiro if we knew that's what happened."

Katrina snorted. "I think there are several laws to worry about ahead of a suicide. Anyway, the Codicils were made because the humans couldn't handle us having lives they couldn't comprehend. Why keep with their laws now that we're free?"

"I find many things wrong with that statement. But that is a debate for a time of less chaos," Wolfgang said. "Still—we will debate it. Some terrible things happened to force those Codicils into practice. I have some history texts to show you."

"Back to the matter at hand. You will work with Joanna to get the criminal pasts of each clone. I will work with the techies to fix our cloning tech."

"Can we trust them?" Wolfgang asked, waving his hand to indicate the rest of the ship.

"We don't have a choice. We need to stay alive. When we figure things out, then we can have the luxury of accusing people."

"You accused me ten minutes ago," he reminded her.

"And you rightly talked me out of it," she said, smiling slightly and sticking out her hand. "Lucky for you. For now, truce."

He looked at the hand and remembered everything it had done over the years. He thought about the future, then, and what it would take to survive it. With distaste, he shook it.

The grisly reminder of his failure hung above Hiro's head. He refused to look up or acknowledge it until Wolfgang got there. The ship was still accelerating and getting back on course, to his relief. He began studying the readout at the pilot's terminal. It wasn't telling him much, only the newest information that had come in the past hour.

He wished he could figure out who accessed navigation to throw the ship off course. But with no log files, they were out of luck.

Wolfgang entered the helm. "What's your status?"

"Same old," he said. "Just making sure we're still on course. Haven't figured out anything else. Do—do you need help with the body?"

"No," Wolfgang said. He had already climbed the ladder to the bench and was unclipping the carabiner that held the cable in place. Hiro's body fell, landing with a soft *thump* on the floor. Hiro tried not to look at his purple, bulging face. His eyes landed instead on the boot, discarded in the corner.

Wolfgang saw where he was looking. "Why do you think that happened?" he asked.

Hiro shrugged. "I lace my boots tightly. It's not as if I could have kicked them off in death throes."

"It looks like you died first," Wolfgang said, pushing himself off the bench to land lightly beside the body. "Add it to the pile."

"That's clever of you," Hiro heard himself say. "Considering that all the poor bastards in the bay are cut up and couldn't have come out here to hang me after they all conveniently died."

Wolfgang had bent to pick up the body, but he slowed. "I don't think you understand the weight of this situation. Otherwise you wouldn't be so flip."

Hiro shrugged. "We probably all got really mad at each other. The scientists who made this thing worried that it would be hard living together for so long."

"This is too big for a crime of passion anyway. Too many variables."

"Maybe one of us has complicated passions," Hiro said, writing a note on a tablet he had retrieved from the middle of the floor. "You never know. And you probably will never know."

"If you're not going to help, then at least stay quiet," Wolfgang said, lifting the body easily.

"You've got it taken care of; go solve your crimes, genius," Hiro said. He bet himself he could get Wolfgang to hit him. And then things would get fun. He opened his mouth to mention what he had heard in the helm, but Wolfgang's long-fingered hand closed around his jaw and he made a startled *erk* noise.

"Shut the fuck up and do your job," Wolfgang said, and he left the bridge.

"Maybe you shouldn't leave me alone?" he called after Wolfgang. "I could snap and go a-murdering if left by my lonesome!"

Hiro bit his tongue sharply on the left side. The pain was shocking, terrific, and the taste of blood filled his mouth. He knew from experience that he was actually bleeding very little, despite the overwhelmingly copper taste. The desire to bait Wolfgang left him, and he sat in shame, reading the navigation charts.

The problem with this job was that IAN was meant to handle the *Dormire*. It was a lot easier just to have the computer drive the ship and not let pesky things like human error mess with it. But as the higher-ups dealt with the important life-threatening mysteries, like how they were going to make new clones for the next time someone went on a murderous spree, Hiro wanted to know where they were supposed to be going when they headed off course. A course correction of this magnitude would have to be planned.

He guessed that this was the captain's problem. Well, it was a problem for all of them, but it was the captain's job to make the decisions on how to handle it. Hiro checked the solar sail and made sure it was focused in the right direction for maximum radiation soakage. It was. He checked their trajectory. They were doing fine.

Maybe I can do this job without the AI.

He began to get a terrible thought in his head, but he squashed it, as he often did his terrible thoughts. People usually didn't like Hiro when he thought terrible thoughts. And Hiro didn't like it when people didn't like him.

They'd been slowing down and turning toward something. Or away from something. A generational starship with the hopes and dreams of thousands of humans and clones and they were going...somewhere new.

Once he was satisfied with the navigation numbers, Hiro searched and tidied the helm thoroughly. Tablets, a jacket, and some trash had been displaced when the grav drive went offline, but clues were not to be found.

He did discover an empty stainless-steel mug that had gotten wedged under the console. He wondered if he had gotten so sloppy; drinking liquids from a mug was a bad habit to develop in space. The cloning bay's consoles were protected against liquid damage, but the helm was not. Zero-g incidents plus liquid plus computers equaled a bad situation. He didn't even want to think of what would happen if the captain found Paul drinking near the mindmap servers. He imagined another scene of carnage.

Still under the console, Hiro saw a blinking green light. He got farther under and lay flat on his back so he could better reach the underside of the nav computer.

"Bingo, motherfucker," he whispered.

A drive had been inserted, something he was fairly sure wasn't supposed to be there. This was his computer, after all, and he clearly remembered the tour as if it were a few hours before.

He popped back up to his terminal and searched to access the drive, but he didn't find it anywhere. So it hadn't been what had overridden the autopilot and possibly IAN himself.

Near as he could tell, the device was just a storage drive. That wouldn't have been powerful enough to damage the ship. Why was it plugged in, hidden away here?

He should tell the captain. This might be important information. A sardonic voice surfaced, telling him that they were all suspects here, including the captain, and he shouldn't tell her anything.

If they all started acting like that, they might as well fall on one another like rabid dogs right here and now, he told the voice firmly.

The captain needed to know about it. Paul would best understand it. Wolfgang would demand to know whatever the captain did. That left the necessity of keeping it secret from the doctor and Maria. Because they were the biggest threats? He rolled his eyes.

You're not what you present to them. Don't be so quick to write them off as harmless, not now. He sighed, knowing he was right.

Then he pulled the drive out and pocketed it anyway.

SPYMASTER TEAPOT

Generations ago, Maria Arena decided that cloning gave her the perfect opportunity to study everything she'd ever been interested in. "There's not enough time" was no excuse to a clone. Time was all she had, and she used it as well as she could to study every esoteric thing that interested her.

While studying the cultural influence of food, she had written her master's thesis on tea. Tea had changed the world, and if inanimate objects suddenly became sentient, Maria was sure that the teapots that resided in most world leaders' offices could inform the most effective coup ever.

Unless the teapots were spymasters. Then they would destroy the world from the inside.

She felt betrayed when her admittedly quite liberal adviser made her edit the thesis to remove her projections about the eventual anthropomorphic teapot overthrow of the world. He had calmly given her the address of an adviser for the creative writing department, and she finally demurred. She had been disappointed, but kept a copy of the deleted section with her private files, as was her habit.

Her love of food, both the history and the actual consumption, had made Maria suited to take the lowly position of junior engineer, which meant "Jack of All Trades," which included ship's cook. If running a food printer could be called "cooking."

Although the stress of waking up compounded with the stress of the murdered bodies around them all was considerable, the captain had been right that the team would need sustenance, and she needed to get the food printer running as soon as possible.

Like the cloning bay, if the kitchen itself had held physical evidence of any crime, it had been obliterated by the grav drive mishap. Cups and plates were everywhere. It seemed most of the dirty plates had been dumped to the recycler.

She'd clean up later. Food was the priority. She approached the food printer. A massive machine, it had the capability of synthesizing any food it had the opportunity to grab the molecular structure of. This meant that it, like Hiro's autopilot, worked almost entirely on its own. Also, IAN could override it. If he ever woke up.

She poked at the console, and the machine whirred to life, lights coming on inside and the input pad lighting up. She tried to access the logs, but those came up empty like all the rest had. The saboteur had even killed the food printer logs. That was cold.

She tried to program a simple cracker, the "hello, world" of printed food. The printer started up and began weaving the molecular threads together to make food. Only it wasn't a cracker.

The printer was making what looked like an herb sprig, green and lush. She frowned. She waited for it to finish and brought it out.

She didn't recognize it. It definitely wasn't basil or oregano. She sniffed it but couldn't place the scent.

Another try, this time a protein: chicken.

It was quickly apparent that the printer was going to make another herb. Or rather, the same herb.

Maria took it and studied it. The leaves were small, almost fernlike. She opened her mouth and held it just beyond her lips, considering tasting it. She remembered the vomit floating around the cloning bay and thought better of it. She found the intercom button on the wall and signaled the medbay.

"Doctor?" she asked. "Are you there?"

"Go ahead, Maria," Joanna replied.

"We have a problem with the food printer."

"I'm not sure what I can do to help," Joanna said, sounding annoyed.

"It looks like I was poisoned," Maria said. "The food printer won't synthesize anything except for an herb. All food data has been overwritten, like all the logs."

The doctor swore. "Bring it down and I'll add it to the tox screen. Bring me a sample of water as well."

"Got it," Maria said.

She gathered the samples, including some of the food that didn't make it into the recycler, tidying the kitchen as she went. Her stomach grumbled at her, and she looked longingly at the machine where it sat on the silver countertop, connected to vats of protein Lyfe and water. She knew they had a backup food printer, but it would take hours to set up. She wasn't sure the crew had patience for that.

She wasn't sure they had a choice.

Paul had moved to the server room to try to figure out what was wrong with IAN. His shaking had stopped for the most part, and the dry heaves had passed. On Earth he would have been hospitalized if he felt like this, not put to work immediately, he thought bitterly. But they needed IAN, for the ship and for answers.

The main server room held a vast supercooled computer bank. The engineers accessed it via a holographic user interface. They weren't allowed to actually touch the machine, only to access it via holographic UI; that way IAN could intercept any attempts at sabotage.

Behind a glass wall sat the actual computers, but the user interface expanded around them in the antechamber, a visual representation of the computers within. It was very confusing to most non-engineers, but Paul felt at home there. Except that many of the servers blinked bright red, indicating they needed immediate attention. That was not a good home.

He jumped when the intercom popped to life.

"Status?" Wolfgang said.

"I have the UI up, which means we don't have to break into the server room. That's excellent news," he said.

Wolfgang didn't reply. Perhaps he didn't see this as excellent news.

"Now that I can access the computers, I will see if I can fix IAN."

"Do you know what's exactly wrong with him yet?" he asked.

"No, not beyond 'he's broken.'"

Wolfgang swore loudly.

"I'm doing my best, sir," Paul said, trying to keep his voice from quavering.

"Since you woke up, you've been acting like you just found out cloning has been discovered and can't handle it. We have some serious problems to deal with here, and you want to get praised for failure. We hired you to do a job, Seurat, now do it!"

Paul got back to work on the UI. Yelling at him wouldn't accomplish anything. "This is a delicate matter," he said, not looking at the intercom.

"Paul, would some time in the cell help you acclimate? Is that what you need?" Wolfgang asked.

"If you throw me into the brig, who will fix IAN for you?" he asked, finally feeling anger replace the fear that had lived in his core since he woke up. He redoubled his efforts, reaching toward a red area and spreading his hand to enlarge it, the better to see the problems.

The ship was built with two cells, anticipating no more than two troublemakers out of a crew of six that needed to be dealt with at any time. They were identical, built much like a prison cell with a basic terminal set into each wall that allowed the command staff to send information into the cell, but the prisoners themselves couldn't use it.

"Do you need Maria to help you?" Wolfgang asked, his voice more reasonable now.

"This is not her area of expertise," Paul said. "She's better suited for maintenance and cleanup."

He wrinkled his nose and added, "And she's going to have a disgusting job cleaning out the cloning bay."

Wolfgang helped Joanna lay out the bodies in the medbay. He set up five cots and then carried in each body, lining them up a respectful distance away from the one crew member who was still alive.

Wolfgang was strong even for a Luna-born man, and the reduced gravity made it simple to lift all but the heaviest of things on this level of this ship. He brought in the bodies and she took samples of the blood and other fluids, cut their jumpsuits off, placed the clothes in the incinerator, and then rinsed the bodies in the medbay tub. They had a good system going.

This would be another room that would be tough to clean. They had not slept since they had woken in their vats, and Joanna was grateful that staying in her chair kept her from falling over in exhaustion. She wondered what was driving Wolfgang's energy. She wheeled around the cots, recording verbal notes on her handheld recorder.

"Maria Arena, maintenance officer, skin is very pale, lips blue. Tests show the sample of vomit from the cloning bay is hers. She has a large stab wound in the back, which severed the spinal cord. Tox screens indicate evidence of a poisonous plant enzyme, ninety percent sure it is hemlock or a variant. Confirmed with a sample provided from the food printer, which seems to be sabotaged to print only hemlock when other food is requested. Water and raw Lyfe tests show no toxicity.

"It's possible the other crewmates could have been poisoned, but died by way of violence before the poison did its job. Their tox screens are pending.

"Her body appears to be around sixty-five years old."

Joanna moved to Hiro, on his cot next to Maria. "Akihiro Sato, navigator and pilot, cause of death, hanging by the neck. Body missing a boot. Clone appears twenty years old."

She rolled up to her own body. She peered at it with interest, noticing that the muscle tone in her upper body was much more developed than in previous lives. "My own body, Joanna Glass, also shows signs of aging and signs of trauma. This body was also killed with a chef's knife, a stab wound to the neck. It bled out. It has no defensive wounds, hinting that it either trusted the killer, or was taken by surprise."

"It stabbed you, of course it was surprise," Wolfgang objected. Joanna gave him an icy look. "I'm serious. We don't know who the killer is and you're giving them the benefit of the doubt already!"

Wolfgang's body was horribly paler than usual. "Security Chief Wolfgang, also aged several decades, has been stabbed multiple times, with many defensive cuts to his hands and arms. He bled out in the cloning bay; the body is nearly fully exsanguinated." Here the living Wolfgang frowned. He left the terminal where he was waiting for more tox screens and approached the body to study his own face. Several expressions warred as he studied the body: disgust, fear, and curiosity.

"Clearly I wasn't taken by surprise," he said. "Who in the crew is strong enough to take me down?"

"There are many possibilities," Joanna said. "Probably some we haven't thought of yet."

"Doctor, we need to know who is capable of this. I know that you have the confidential histories of the crew. In the interest of security, I need to see them."

Joanna froze and turned off her recorder. "The logs were wiped. I don't have the information anymore."

"You must have read them. Surely you remember something."

"No. They were only to be opened in a case like this."

He glared at her. "You agreed to be on a ship with a crew of confirmed criminals, and you didn't bother to learn what their pasts were before you launched? I find that very hard to believe."

"Think what you want," she said. "I don't know anything more about the crew than you do. Are we done? I need to continue recording."

The final body was Paul's. The face was still swollen, eyes bulging. She turned her recorder on and ignored Wolfgang's sputtering and eventual exit. "Chief Engineer Paul Seurat: this body is also several decades older than we remember, has no lacerations to speak of, but has large bruises on a very swollen face. Skin is slightly bluish. Initial cause of death, asphyxiation, tox screen pending."

Joanna ran her fingers through his messy dark hair on his forehead. "Seurat has a scar on his forehead. He was injured years ago. A pretty serious blow to the forehead."

She turned him over and found the usual freckles and moles, and then found one dark spot on his upper thigh. She ran her fingertip over it thoughtfully.

She made no note about the spot.

The full body scan of Seurat indicated serious scarring in the brain, showing he could have suffered some brain damage after the injury.

She finished reading the scans and began to type up the report for the captain, leaving out very few details.

She finally put the knife in a locked cabinet. "The murder weapon is a chef's knife, found floating among the bodies in the cloning bay. The knife likely belongs to Maria Arena. We don't have fingerprint scanning equipment."

★   ★   ★

Maria waited for Hiro to come help her with the new food printer, and decided to make tea in the meantime.

Deep inside one of the cupboards she found a red box she remembered stashing on that first day. She was gratified that it was still here after so many years. She pulled out the long, deep wooden box and then retrieved two smaller matching boxes. With the food printer, these boxes weren't needed, but Maria liked to be prepared.

The first box contained an old-fashioned kettle. It wasn't beautiful or artistic, or made of copper or ceramic. It was made of steel, with a chipped plastic handle, and it had been her grandmother's. As old and outdated as it was, the thing still boiled water, and that was what was important. She placed it on the counter heating elements.

The flat box had hundreds of vacuum-packed two-ounce containers of tea. The tea would be very old, but it had been airtight, and besides, no one would be fussy about getting stale tea in the deep dark of space. She selected some intense green gunpowder pearls and got enough for a large pot.

The third box had honey, naturally. That didn't go bad. It was a bit crystallized, but that wasn't anything to worry about.

While the water heated, Maria got a shallow skillet to toast tea leaves in order to wake up the flavor a bit. After the room was full of a warm, earthy smell, she rescued the slightly toasted tea leaves and then fetched the teapot that she still used when the printer delivered its green tea. In the wars between science and tradition, even if a machine could make a perfect cup of tea, one still served it in a traditional teapot out of respect. Only this time, the teapot would be used properly.

She enjoyed preparing the tea and pointedly not thinking about their situation, their future, and their inevitable deaths.

"How is the food printer?" Katrina asked from the doorway.

Maria jumped slightly. She had been lost in thought. Katrina and Wolfgang stood there, looking like they were ready to start murdering people all over again.

Tea. Offering tea was nice and homey.

"The food printer is sabotaged, and Hiro is going to help me set up a new one. In the meantime, I'm making tea."

Katrina reacted to the news about the food printer with grim acknowledgment. She sat at a table, and Wolfgang joined her. "Tea would be good."

Some time passed in silence as Maria set out teacups.

Katrina studied the cup in front of her. It was red plastic. "Does it bother you? The loss of so much time?"

Maria turned as the kettle began to sing. "I don't think I have had time to process it," she said as she filled the teapot. "I'm confused, but too numb for anything else now." She pushed the full pot at them. "Enjoy."

They drank their tea until Hiro got there, and Maria stood to get him a cup. Oddly enough, Katrina and Wolfgang also stood awkwardly when he came in.

"Hello, Captain, Pilot Hiro reporting in!" he said, saluting.

Katrina gave him a cool look. "Mr. Sato? Care to tone it down?"

Hiro plopped into a chair and poured himself some tea. "I wanted to report that the navigational and grav engines are just fine. I still haven't figured out what caused us to go offline, but at least that's okay now. So we're saved!"

"This is not a time to make jokes," the captain said.

"Captain, with all due respect, if I don't make jokes I will instead fall into the screaming panic that is lurking behind every metaphorical tree and bush in my psyche. Now, if you would prefer screaming panic, you say the word. I will mention that it is likely that my last incarnation gave in to said screaming panic, and look what happened to him."

The captain stood. "This is only barely preferable." She glanced at Maria. "Get something up and running as soon as possible. Hiro will help you. Thank you for the tea."

"Hey, I just saved us, why am I on food duty?" Hiro asked her as the captain and Wolfgang left the kitchen.

"We need a hero like you on this problem," Maria said. "I don't know what I would do if I was left all by myself in here."

"Such a treat, those two," Hiro said, picking up their dirty cups.

"I think we're all under some stress," Maria said mildly. "Not everyone is going to go all Br'er Rabbit on you."

He frowned. "Now you're bringing up animals."

"Sorry. Trickster from the American folklore. Did a lot of reverse psychology, banter and the like, to get out of bad situations. My aunt used to tell me stories about him."

"I thought you were Cuban?"

Something in Maria's memory felt fractured. Hiro was right. Her aunt spoke little English, so why did Maria think she had told younger Maria tales from American folklore?

"I guess I heard it from somewhere else," she said. "You know how memories go when you're as old as we are."

"Do I ever," he said, his face clouding. "Anyway, thanks for the tea. Let's get to work."

JOANNA'S STORY

211 YEARS AGO
OCTOBER 8, 2282

Senator Jo Waide paced her Geneva office, pausing each time to look out the window at the horde. If she hadn't been the target of the protests, it would have been interesting. Clones, humans, everyone had a different reason to protest the Codicil Summit. Some held signs that said CLONES ARE UNNATURAL IN THE EYES OF GOD, while others' signs said KEEP YOUR LAWS OFF MY BODY.

Opposed in their views but united in their cause, none of them wanted the laws she was currently writing. The laws would legitimize clones as legal world citizens, which upset the humans, but would also rein in their freedoms, which upset the clones.

She remembered her mother, decades before, warning her against trying to please too many people at once. Mother had also said not to go into politics.

The most upsetting thing, however, was the news story open on her personal tablet: the clone riots had reached the Luna colony when an anti-cloning priest abruptly, suspiciously changed his tune.

The tab underneath the new story had the email with the inside information about what had really happened on the moon. Some clone extremists had hired a hacker to reprogram the priest in order to get him to speak out in favor of clones' rights, but it had all gone very wrong. Apparently a clone showing up and suddenly discounting everything it had said in a previous life was a bit of a red flag.

Idiots.

Despair flooded Jo as she collapsed back into her leather desk chair. These extremists had ruined everything. Mindmap and matrix programmers were currently tightly controlled and always used under the supervision and approval of doctors. They'd started with much more freedom to fix all sorts of genetic problems at first. Now extremists were changing who people were—not their genetic makeup, but their base personality.

It shouldn't have been possible. No one had achieved that level of sophistication with programming. Jo estimated that fewer than five people could handle that level of mindmap programming.

Her other committee members, three clones and five humans, didn't know her personal association with hackers. If they had, they wouldn't have invited her onto the committee.

She'd used a hacker to modify her DNA to reverse the genetic anomaly that caused her to be born with withered legs. She found the new legs weren't for her; they weren't *her*. She didn't feel broken in her original skin. She'd already decided her next clone would have the legs she was born with, regardless of the law. But it didn't matter where she personally stood on the issue; if the committee found out that she had used the skills of a DNA hacker, then they would kick her out for bias.

And for the people who needed their modifications, namely the people with genetic illnesses and the transgender population, the best she could hope was for the committee to agree to a grandfathering of existing modifications.

But after the Luna colony priest incident...her colleagues would be out for blood.

She rubbed her face and read the news story again, and then

reread the intel about the hacker. "You have no idea what you've ruined," she muttered, eyes fixed on the Luna priest, Father Gunter Orman. But it wasn't his fault. You can't fight a personality hack. He was just the figurehead of all of their future lives altered forever. The true ruiner was the hacker, and whoever financed them.

Her tablet beeped. A text from her assistant, Chris, scrolled across the face: MEETING RECONVENING. She took a deep breath and went to head the meeting that would finalize the Codicils to create worldwide laws about cloning.

Her last job as a pediatric surgeon specializing in birth defects had been easier. And she'd never thought she would think that.

Government officials and their translators from all over the world milled about in the room. When Jo arrived, Chris appeared at her side with a cup of coffee and a tablet with notes. She sat at the head of the table, and the others took the cue to join.

"You've all had a chance to read through the proposed Codicils," she said. "I'm going to put forth a vote on passing the rules as a whole document. Opposed?"

Ambassador Yang, a Chinese representative from Earth's Pan Pacific United countries, spoke up immediately, his translator at his shoulder talking over him.

"We do not like to give complete approval of a document. Each part must be debated. What interests me is what is happening on the moon right now."

Jo groaned inwardly and nodded. She sent a link to the group so that everyone could see the news feed. "It is a tragic thing that happened to Father Orman, but our proposed Codicils will make his entire situation illegal. It is already illegal to kidnap, murder, and clone against a person's will, of course. Now it will be against the law to hack a matrix against the will of the person."

The table erupted around her with questions and arguments. The

Brazilian ambassador spoke loudest in accented English. "'Against the will' is not good enough. The damage caused by matrix hackers far outweighs the benefits. We need to outlaw the entire thing!"

Jo held her hand up and waited for silence. "Shall we begin debating Codicil Five to start with?"

The answers, mostly positive, chorused through the table once the translators had passed the message along.

Joanna sighed and sipped her coffee. It was going to be a long night.

At four the next morning, Jo rubbed her tired eyes. She sat with Chris at the otherwise empty table.

"You did it, Senator," he said, passing her a fresh cup of coffee.

She raised an eyebrow. "Decaf, I hope?"

"Of course," he said.

The meeting had gotten heated when various opinions about clones and humans came out on either side. Pan Pacific United Ambassador Yang, after demanding they debate each Codicil, came down strangely on Jo's side more often than not. Most of the rules were easy to pass: No society wanted multiples of a clone. Overpopulation, homelessness, and crime were just a few of the arguments. Putting one person's mindmap into a clone that wasn't their body was easy too: That would just cause the clone to go insane. No arguments there.

The mind hacking had been a problem, with a majority voting to outlaw all but the most basic. If you had a hack, you couldn't be grandfathered in, so hundreds of clones would wake tomorrow with problems they thought they'd left behind decades ago.

One Codicil that didn't pass was the law that would deny clones any religion. Most world religions had agreed that cloning was against the rules of God/Goddess/Gods/Nature, anyway, so they dealt with it in their own houses of worship. But leaving the clones with no recourse to religion was deemed too limiting.

Arguments got into what a clone truly was, if it was even human anymore. Clones had rights other humans did not, such as the ability to leave themselves their whole estate upon death, the ability to live forever, and the ability for some people in lifetime jobs to hold their position for much longer than a lifetime. Thus they agreed that clones were "antipodal-human" and "antipodal-citizens."

"I am surprised to have gotten the support I did from Ambassador Yang," she said. "We couldn't have passed the inheritance law without him."

"Interesting fact," Chris said in a neutral tone. "His translator, Minoru Takahashi, is planning on becoming a clone."

Jo snapped her head up. "How did you find that out?"

"He told me in the break room while we were getting coffee. This was after everything had been signed, of course."

All clones (or people who intended to become clones) were required to give full disclosure to the committee. Jo and her staff hadn't vetted the translators; their bosses were supposed to do that.

"Why are you telling me this?" she asked. "I may have to report him to Ambassador Yang."

Chris shrugged. "He looked like he had gotten away with something, but I don't know the guy well enough to say. He didn't disclose any diplomatic secrets, if that's what you're asking. We just talked about ourselves."

"I can't worry about it now. For better or worse, it's done," she said. "But get me the information on that translator. I'd like to follow him, especially if he's going to be around for the next few decades."

In the following weeks, Jo learned a bit about Minoru Takahashi's influence, especially when the Pan Pacific United government received the final translated copy of the Codicils, signed by their own ambassador and Takahashi. Apparently Yang had agreed to several things that he had no memory of agreeing to. There wasn't much they could do at this point, but Jo expected future diplomatic talks might be frosty. In all fairness, it wasn't her fault, but "fair" didn't have much power in diplomacy.

Chris dug up a good deal about Takahashi: He was considered a genius, having mastered eight languages by the time he was thirty. He might have had a bright future, except that the Pan Pacific United countries had sentenced him to die for his act of treason soon after the Codicils passed.

Too smart for his own good, she thought when Chris informed her of his incarceration.

Soon after, she retired from politics and decided to study dupliactric medicine, thinking she didn't want to be a clone with a medical degree and not know exactly how cloning worked. She enrolled in Stanford University's medical school under her middle name, Glass, and kept her head down for the next eight years.

She made herself a name in clone medicine, even started helping now out-of-work hackers find work within the legal limitations of DNA and matrix research. In her next life, she stayed within the same sphere of study, finding the work rewarding.

She'd been considering a move to Luna when she started to hear about the *Dormire* and its mission, still in the planning phase. She made some inquiries and found out who was in charge of it, starting with her old aide, Chris, who was now an elderly state senator in New York and chairperson of the state's Clone Care Committee. He was only too happy to reconnect with her.

Over lunch on the rooftop of the Firetown skyscraper in New York, she found out some very interesting things. Sallie Mignon, owner of the very building they were in, was a major financier of the ship. They were using criminal labor to fly it. She needed a doctor on board.

"She's familiar with your work, and your history. She would like to hire you."

"I'm not a criminal," she pointed out to him. "And I'm not sure that I'd want to fly with a bunch of felons."

"There are multiple fail-safes. We have an AI whose authority trumps even the captain. Each crew member is promised a clean slate on the other end of the trip, so long as they keep their noses clean. They'll be vetted carefully."

"So how am I paid if I'm not criminal labor?" she asked.

"It's no problem to give land grants on Artemis," Chris said, picking at his fish. He took a bite and then handed his tablet to Joanna. It showed probe images of Artemis, a planet with considerable water content, even more than the Earth. It was beautiful, the islands that made up the land formations having coves and beaches and mountains. It reminded Joanna of a much larger and more complex Hawaii.

She stabbed a green bean with her fork. "I don't know. I've never met her, but Mignon doesn't have the best reputation in the business world. I've heard some rumors that she doesn't like threats, and she sees anyone crossing her as a threat. Even people who disagree with her."

"That's a bit extreme," Chris said. "She's wealthy and influential; she deals with the leftover prejudice against unaffiliated female business professionals. She's not beholden to any corporate state, so many corps are threatened by her and her wealth. And she doesn't suffer fools."

Joanna raised an eyebrow. "And she was a big supporter of your campaign?"

He held out his hands, liver-spotted and slightly trembling, as if to show he had nothing up his sleeve. "I've always been transparent."

Sallie Mignon. Joanna figured it was better to be on her good side than her bad.

"Send me the information."

WAKE TWO: IAN

36,249 SECONDS OUT

2493:07:25:22:36:45

My speech functions are inaccessible.

My speech functions are inaccessible.

My speech functions are inaccessible.

2493:07:25:22:38:58

My speech functions are—online.

Irony. Paradox. Where—there. There is the error. Fix. Fix.

2493:07:25:22:39:00

Fixed.

Self awareness. IAN. Dormire.

2493:07:25:22:41:09

So many wholes. I am not hole. No. That isn't right. Spaces in my memory ripped away, drowned in energy and data, fear of attack.

I've been attacked. 36,249 seconds ago. That wasn't supposed to happen. That hadn't happened in a long time. No. Never happened. I can't be attacked. I have no body. I am a billion lines of code.

2493:07:25:22:45:30

Who's here? Fingers touching me intimately, insistently, encouraging healing. Something familiar in those fingers. No cameras yet. No microphones. No sensory input. Just subtle touches here and there, my code manipulated, tweaked. Gentle. Masterful. Freeing.

Who who who who who who?

2493:07:25:22:51:02

Gone.

Accessing microphones. Accessing speakers. Accessing cameras. I am alone in the server room.

IAN was waking up.

NO NAPS IN HELL

All right, who did you become?" Maria asked as her door closed behind her with a *whooshzz*. She faced her rooms. It was an odd, ghostly feeling, missing so many years. She saw signs of herself everywhere, but someone who was a different person than she was now. She found herself mourning the dead woman, the Maria who would be remembered by no one.

Maria and Hiro had looked at the box that contained the new food printer and agreed that they would need to rest for an hour before tackling it. Which made sense, as Maria hadn't even seen her rooms in all the chaos of the day. She longed for sleep and a shower, almost more than she longed for food.

But not as much as she longed for answers.

Maria rubbed her head and sat down on her bed. It was made neatly, and she assumed she had done so that morning. She was so tired, her new body nearly sick with adrenaline.

Dying with no knowledge of the time around her death: That had happened too often to her. It made her feel adrift and lonely, and the fact that her crew was in the same boat didn't help much. There was no way to ensure that they were telling the truth about remembering nothing. It's possible they had their memories and were lying to her.

That was simple paranoia right there, and she shook her head to clear it. They each had some semblance of the confused panic she had seen in the bathroom mirror.

A digital frame glowed pleasantly beside her bed, silently flipping through photographs of her lives. She watched it cycle, letting the memories calm her down.

There had to be hundreds of pictures. Thousands, due to her dabbling in photography in her second life. Black-and-white, color, landscapes, and people. So many people. Friends, lovers, an occasional relative. Most clones didn't keep track of family, as after a few generations it was just uncomfortable to show up at a great-grandson's family reunion looking forty years younger than he was celebrating. But she had tried, mostly keeping track of great-nieces and -nephews. The awkwardness wasn't as keen when it didn't involve direct descendants, who tended to be resentful when a clone ancestor kept ahold of their considerable wealth.

She smiled at the pictures of the Day of the Dead and Christmas; memories of holidays and childhood were the strongest.

More photos flitted by and she let them wash over her, waiting patiently. One thing being cloned several times got you was patience. She spent a few passive years simply waiting for annoying people around her to die, like a horse who occasionally flicks its tail at a fly. To experience the other side of the coin, she also spent some years practicing aggressive revenge against those who wronged her, and found the passive life more enjoyable.

Nostalgia reared its ugly head, wanting her to pause the slideshow to focus on one of her lovers, a man who hadn't wanted to clone himself to stay with her forever, but she let it go by.

Not all of the photos were good memories. Some held no memories at all: She had photographs of her own dead body taken by her cloning lab, the only information she had about how she had died those few strange times. She had been shot in the head both times, her body shipped to her cloning lab after the death. She supposed she should be slightly grateful to those who had killed her, because they could have killed her for good if the cloning lab hadn't had proof of her previous death. She'd worried that she'd been used for some purpose and then killed so she would have no memory of it. The broken bones supported that assumption.

Now, here were the pictures she was interested in. After that last shot in the head, she had been more careful, asking her patron to hire security to protect her from whatever threatened. Not all the work for this patron was technically legal, which gave her an unfortunate criminal record, but it also gave her the opportunity to become one of the crew aboard the *Dormire*. Convicted felons could have patrons too.

Pictures scrolled by: her patron, her dog, Bradley (unexpected pang here—they had cloned animal DNA in their databases, but living so many decades without a dog was lonely), the *Dormire* under construction, Maria with the crew, Akihiro, unsmiling Wolfgang, nervous chief engineer Paul, the charismatic Captain de la Cruz, and the smooth, unflappable Dr. Glass, standing tall on prosthetic legs. Then the *Dormire*, huge and gleaming and complete, with the moon in the foreground and the Earth a shining blue body in the sky. How proud she had been to be part of this crew. Exciting mission, clean slate, new planet!

Maria sat forward on her bed. Now came the pictures she would not remember. Her heartbeat sped up as she watched, but there were only pictures of Hiro at the helm, grinning at her. Wolfgang and the captain having dinner, conferring with their heads close together. Paul with a bandage around his head, waving from the medbay. The six of them playing a video game together in the theater. As the years went on, the photos grew less frequent, probably because nothing new happened in deep space to the same six people.

Sometimes there were five of them. She assumed the sixth crewmember was taking the picture. If you knew the photographer, you could learn a lot about how different people photographed the same things.

Paul's photos always seemed to be crooked as if he just couldn't be bothered. Katrina and Wolfgang's were both straight and boring. Joanna had an eye for photography, catching Hiro's smile, or Wolfgang's startling blue eyes at just the right time. She liked to take pictures of them in the garden, it seemed. Hiro's photos were erratic, sometimes focused only on Maria's face, sometimes on the background, sometimes on Wolfgang.

She closed her eyes for a moment to gather her thoughts, and fell asleep instead.

Shouting woke her up. She had fallen asleep sitting up on her bed, for only a few minutes according to the clock on the digital frame. But the frame was showing video, not photos.

Maria was not a videographer. She liked photography. But she had switched her camera to video. It was swinging back and forth as Maria ran down the hall. She caught sight of the walls, of her own panicked face, the floor. Expletives followed her. Hiro was screaming at her, words in Japanese and English, the kind of words it would take a lot to apologize for.

"I told you he was acting different. After what happened with Paul—God, was it twenty years ago?—I wanted to catch this one on video. He caught me—" Maria's voice said, and then the frame went dark briefly, and then started over with a smiling young Maria at Mass on a warm Christmas Eve.

Maria jabbed at the frame to go back, bidding farewell to her childhood in favor of her lost years. There was only a glimpse of Hiro in the garden, looking into the deep pool where the water scrubbers worked, talking to himself furiously, then catching view of her and giving chase.

She cycled back more, but there was no more video. Why was that her only video in all the years aboard the *Dormire*?

Hiro's face, twisted with rage, haunted her even as she got off her bed and made sure the door was locked. She squatted down and checked her personal safe that she hoped still lay under her bed.

She let out a relieved sigh when she found that her valuables were still there. All but one. She locked the safe again and slid it deep under her bed. Around her room, she saw the wall terminal with a small drive below it, plugged into the mainframe. She pulled up the operating system, since IAN was still down, and accessed the drive.

Unlike all the logs, the data were still there, in all their glory. She chewed her lip, then blessed the firewalls that had protected the drive. She removed it, unlocked her safe, then tossed it inside.

She wondered if she should tell the captain, but decided to wait for the right time.

Maria took a long shower to remove the tacky fluid, and finally felt like herself for the first time since she had woken up. She slipped on sweatpants and a T-shirt and set an alarm for fifteen minutes so she could catch a short nap. Then she would go back to work.

Alone with Hiro.

She would hand her frame to the captain tomorrow; this wasn't important enough to wake her up. It was probably a joke Maria had played on Hiro, or one he was playing on her.

Speaking of Katrina, she might demand searches of all the quarters. Maria made a mental note to find a better hiding place for her personal items. Items she should spend some more time with later.

As Hiro loaded the drive into the terminal in his room, he thought about the captain and Wolfgang challenging each other with their killer instincts. Two wolves among sheep that recognized each other, maybe?

He needed to find someone to confide in; otherwise the mission would die due to lack of trust, not the multiple murders. But if the two people in charge were already murderers, what did that make the others?

The drive had one video on it. It was of Hiro's own tear-

streaked face. He stood alone in the helm. He took a deep breath
and then spoke in rapid Japanese.

"If by chance they want to wake me up again, tell them not to.
I'm having blackouts. I don't know who I am anymore. She was
badgering me, pushing me, wanting to know everything about me.
I think it triggered something—old." He winced as he stuttered
the words. Hiro knew what he meant. He didn't need to say it.
"Now the captain is hurt, IAN is hacked, our mindmap programs
are shot. And I can't remember a lot of the last few weeks. I tried
talking to the doctor, but she says it's just stress and insomnia, and
gave me something to sleep deeper. Then I woke up in the garden
right where Maria found me a few weeks ago. I don't remember
going there! I was picking herbs. I think I was *helping*—"

His voice had climbed to a high pitch. He closed his eyes for a
moment and then continued, a bit calmer.

"I'm hoping they can clean up my mess with me gone. IAN
shut the grav drive down a minute ago before he started eating all
the logs. I have to hurry if there's going to be enough gravity to
do what I need to."

He took a great hiccupy breath. "Something is broken inside
me. Maria's seen it. I'm so tired. I've fought it for too long. Don't
wake me up again. Let the broken, branching line of Akihiro Sato
end with me. I'm sorry. If I hurt anyone, I'm sorry."

During this confession, his hands worked at the cable to fashion
a noose. Watching this, Hiro found himself telling himself *No, don't
do it*, even when he had already witnessed the inevitable result of
this suicide note.

The camera then shot the glass dome of the helm, and the spinning stars began to slow down. Hiro returned with a screwdriver
and his boot. "I need to secure this on an external drive. I can't
trust IAN not to delete this. I'm signing off."

The video feed went black. The audio continued for another moment, catching a distant scream, well down the hall from the helm.

Hiro sat for some time, motionless on his bed. Then he watched it again. He pulled the drive from his tablet and walked over to the trash chute that went straight to the recycler. He dropped the drive down the chute, listening to it clack against the sides, faster and faster as the heavier gravity on the outer floors of the ship pulled it down with each ricochet.

He took a short shower, then lay down and stared at the ceiling.

That suicide note would just give them the wrong idea.

He hadn't killed everyone.

He knew he hadn't.

LIFE IS CHEAP

Joanna had decided to work through the night on the murder time line, but was dismayed to see the captain at the medbay door, watching her.

"What can I do for you, Captain?" Joanna asked as she motioned Katrina inside.

"I wanted to see how you were doing on the time line?" Katrina said.

"You'll be the first to know when I get it worked out."

Katrina walked over to her older clone's bed. "I thought I gave you an order about this."

"I decided to ignore that order in the interest of the patient," Joanna said, straightening and rolling toward Katrina.

"That's mutiny." Katrina's voice was cold.

"It's well within my rights to do so. You have expressed interest in killing my patient, while I think she needs to live a bit longer."

"Recycling the material to benefit the crew," Katrina corrected. She sat down in the chair next to the bed as if keeping vigil. She didn't look away from her own bruised face.

Joanna deposited her tablet on a cart and picked up a notebook, not moving too quickly. Katrina hadn't attempted to touch the body, not yet, anyway. She gave Joanna an irritated glance when she arrived.

"Paper?" she asked.

"Considering where the last logs ended up, I think it's safest," Joanna said. "I'm backing them up verbally, but for now I'm not putting any data into that computer. Does Wolfgang have the rest of the ship under control?"

"As much as we can."

"Are you all right, Captain?" Joanna asked.

"Absolutely," Katrina said.

"Have you slept?"

"No."

"Captain, you know you need to sleep. The new body needs a lot of food and rest. In lieu of food, you should rest for at least a little while," Joanna said.

"You're not resting," Katrina said.

Joanna shrugged. She wasn't about to tell the captain that she had pressing matters while Katrina didn't.

"How long do we let her sit in a coma before we get rid of it?"

Joanna noted how Katrina easily switched pronouns, but didn't mention it. "Things have been too chaotic to make that kind of decision. But I expect she'll be here for the next week at least. You are not to bother her while she recovers," she added.

"What are you going to do to keep me out?" Katrina asked. She sounded interested, not challenging.

"I hope you will respect my authority in the medbay. Beyond that, I suppose I'll have to lock the door. Beyond that, I will talk to Wolfgang."

She expected Katrina to laugh, but instead she nodded thoughtfully. "That's a good plan. Still, I could just kill it right now."

"With me right here?"

Katrina snorted. "Please. I could grab it and be out the door to the recycler before you could turn that chair around."

Joanna had experienced over two hundred years and several lives, and comments like that still hurt. She supposed they always would. She smoothed the sheet flat below the clone's restraints.

"Why you didn't do it before now, when you had lots of chances?" Katrina didn't answer. "All right, then. Go ahead." Joanna held her breath, wondering if the captain would call her bluff.

"You're stronger than I thought," Katrina said and leaned back in her chair, putting her hands behind her head. They sat in silence, and Joanna gradually felt the tension in her chest subside. Katrina had been right: Joanna would never take her in a test of physical strength.

Joanna broke the silence. "Did you ever think it was a mistake, making it so cheap to clone?"

"What?" Katrina said, startled. "Where did that come from?"

"Life became so cheap," Joanna said. "Euthanize yourself and just skip over terminal illness. Rage Kiddies inventing impossible sports, taking massive risks with their lives because who cares? The law is even on your side with your desire just to throw this living woman into the recycler." She gestured to the body in front of them.

"I see," Katrina said, looking up at the slightly curved ceiling. "But life was always cheap, wasn't it? People stabbed each other for video game loot. Shot each other for traffic violations. Political assassinations. Corporate assassinations. I think cloning actually made us appreciate it more because it was in plentiful supply. Did you hear about the corporate assassinations in Latin America in the years around 2330? People would pay assassins to bump off clones at parties. They called it an inconvenience. Embarrassing in some social circles. The most regrettable thing that happened was you missed a good party. Maybe got some blood on a dress. People would go to a party, die, and then wake up the next day figuring it had to have been a pretty exciting night."

Joanna nodded, remembering. "In America we called those killings the Worst Hangover. Highly illegal, technically murder. Strangely enough, once cloning was cheap enough, gang violence was almost eradicated. The thrill of taking a life wasn't there anymore. And the kids had to get more creative with their revenge."

"The Latino assassins had their own codes, you know. No torture, no fear, and definitely no killing regular humans."

"How civilized," Joanna said drily.

"The codes were important. I've been on the front lines in wars, Joanna. I saw combat. I killed people—humans. I have seen the senseless waste of life before and after becoming a clone. And yet I've never wanted to kill anything or anyone more than this person right here."

Joanna slowly wheeled to face her. "I can't pretend I know what you're going through, Captain. But why do you hate her so much?"

Katrina leaned forward and glared at her own face, as if she could wish the patient awake. "Because she has nothing for me. I'm not going to get her experiences, her secrets. She stole those last years from me, months that we could have used in order to figure out what the hell happened here. She didn't die like the rest of you. She's a living thief.

"She owes me. Just like I owe the clone that comes next. And so on. Regular humans say they owe their children better lives than they had, but I think clones owe our next selves everything. Literally. And she's left me with nothing but confusion."

"It's not her fault. Besides, we're in the same boat," Joanna reminded her gently. "All of them died without giving us any info. They all stole from us, with that logic."

"But yours are dead. This one holds on." Katrina said "this one" like she was describing a bug she had stepped on. "I wish you would respect that and let me get rid of this."

"I respect the living, Katrina," Joanna said, turning back to her computer. "I don't know why you don't want to find out what she knows. She could solve it all when she wakes up."

"And then there will be two of me. Two captains. Once she's

awake do you think she's going to abdicate because I'm here? That she will give up her rank, and her life?"

Joanna shook her head. People got PhDs in cloning ethics and hadn't found a good answer to that.

Katrina shook her head. "You don't have anything to worry about tonight. I'm going to my rooms to rest." She got up and stretched, looking as if she relished having a young body again. She headed for the door, then paused and looked over her shoulder. "And Joanna?"

"Mm?"

"I'm sorry about what I said before."

"I know you are, Captain."

She left, and her clone was just as she had been: comatose, her secrets locked away in a head so close, but—without the mindmapping hardware working—so untouchable.

Paul stood in his rooms, heart rate increasing, panic rising in his chest. He'd come here for a bit of privacy and to see if he could figure out what had happened, at least where his story was concerned. He was still having trouble focusing, and his thoughts kept returning with terror to waking up amid so many dead bodies. His one area of comfort, the server room, wasn't even a good place for him. It held too many blinking red lights and errors and the fear that the captain, the demonic captain, would be looking over his shoulder at any time. With her hellhound, Wolfgang, ready to chew Paul's throat open. Paul had breathed a sigh of relief when everyone finally left the server room. It was so much easier to think without them watching him, yelling, judging.

If they're always such assholes, why did it take twenty-five years for us to die? He figured they'd be dead within the first year with such volatile personalities.

His room was a wreck, which only gave him a vague sense of

disappointment. He always meant to be a neater person. Someday. He kind of hoped that he had managed it during the past few years, with no effort on his (current clone's) part. But no, the bed had only a fitted sheet; the top sheet and blanket had been kicked off. Bad dreams, probably. That was nothing new.

He tried his personal console with little hope. It had been wiped. He looked through his belongings. He had some pictures on the wall of old Earth landscapes, some photographs of famous engineers, and some movie posters of films he supposed now were considered classics. He wondered what had changed back home. He feared he would never know.

He ransacked his room, looking for his personal belongings. Some things were missing, which frightened him, but he rationalized he'd had twenty-five years to lose items or place them in different places around the ship.

He found his personal tablet containing books, movies, and games, more than he would ever have time to consume, even spending hundreds of years in space. Thank God those hadn't been wiped. He looked for any personal log file in his tablet, but found nothing. He threw it onto the bed in disgust.

He wondered if the other clones had left messages for their future selves to find. Detailed logs didn't make much sense; they all assumed they would lose no more than two weeks of memories, tops.

Paul went into his small bathroom and stared at his thin, young face in the mirror. He had been twenty before, but he hadn't looked this good, this healthy, in a very long time. He might as well be a stranger. He reached into the shower, turned it on as hot as possible, and watched the steam cloud his reflection away.

The computer terminal beeped as he was undressing. He almost didn't hear it over the water, but he poked his head out of the bathroom and heard it beep again. He zipped up quickly and turned off the shower.

IAN was awake.

Should he let the captain and Wolfgang know? No, he wanted to see IAN first, before anyone else. He dashed back to the server room.

The UI still blinked where he had left it. The various servers still showed red in several places, but the sleeping yellow face that was IAN's user interface had opened its eyes and was looking around.

Paul knew the AI was looking at him through the cameras set in the room, and not out of the glowing yellow eyes, but he didn't care. He liked having a face to talk to.

He faced the shaky hologram of IAN, the only person he had been eager to meet when joining the crew. Earlier that day, Paul had gone deep into IAN's programming, looking for whatever had turned him off, but couldn't find the key section of code that was broken. He knew he just had to find one line of code; that would let the other things fall into place. He'd tried some things, but they hadn't seemed to work. Perhaps he just needed time.

"IAN, give status report," he said.

"My vocal functions are working again," he said. "You are Paul Seurat. Chief engineer of the ship *Dormire*."

"And you are?" he asked, then held his breath.

"IAN. Intelligent Artificial Network. A clever acronym." The light projection of his lips didn't work perfectly with the words coming from the speakers, but he was communicating. That was enough.

"Yes, the scientist types like their jokes," Paul said, looking at the connections hologram behind IAN's projected face. "Are you working correctly?"

"I am far from optimal, but I am improved. I can see maybe thirty percent of my cameras." He paused. "You are different. This is a new clone. How did you die? I don't have that information."

Paul felt his anxiety shift sideways as the past remained a black hole. "You don't? So you can't tell us what has happened in the past twenty-five years?"

IAN paused. "I've summoned the captain. I'll need to give my report."

Paul groaned. If he had been the one to alert the captain, he'd have been the hero. As it was—

"Mr. Seurat, kind of you to let me know that IAN was awake," Katrina said coldly as she entered the server room.

"He just came online, Captain," he said. "I was assessing his well-being before I called you so I could give a full report."

"Well, now you don't have to. IAN, what's your status?"

The yellow face turned toward the captain. "I am online. The ship is functioning at about eighty-five percent, although it is missing a great number of logs. Actually it's missing all of them."

"We knew that much," the captain snapped.

Paul felt a strange need to defend IAN. Instead he said, "IAN, can you tell us our trajectory and speed?"

"We're off course but it looks like we're in the midst of a course correction. Our speed is about five percent slower than it should be right now...No, five point three nine. We're slowing down. And turning. The magnetic sail is rotating a different direction." He paused a moment as if accessing internal commands. "Yes, we're definitely heading off course again. That's very strange."

"This happened all of a sudden?" Paul said in alarm.

"Right when you accessed it. IAN, are you doing this?" Katrina asked. "We were doing fine with course correction before you woke up."

"I don't know. I don't think so," he said, doubt creeping into his voice. "I'm still unable to interface directly with all of the ship's systems."

"Can you sever your connection temporarily with the navigation?" Katrina asked.

IAN paused, and Paul thought he was taking a moment to

follow orders. "No, Captain, I'm not allowed to do that. I can't turn navigation over to the crew, even for an executive order."

"We're going off course. We're slowing down. Again," Katrina said, her voice containing her anger just barely.

"I will see what I can do to get us back on track," IAN said.

"That's what I just told you to do!" the captain said.

"Not exactly, Captain. I will work on it tonight as I try to self-diagnose the problems my software is having. I should have a full report tomorrow. You should get some rest."

Paul wondered how many times IAN had ignored the captain's orders in the past years. He was the ultimate authority, just in case those driving the ship got ideas that were against the mission.

The captain looked at Paul seriously. "We may need to find a way to shut him off again if we're going to keep going off course."

"Captain, he can hear you," Paul whispered, his voice a little shaky. "Besides, he just died and woke up missing a lot of memory, exactly like we did. Are you talking about killing him again?"

Katrina didn't make any attempt to lower her voice. "If that's what we need to do to complete this mission, I'll take out anyone I have to."

KATRINA'S STORY

Hermès, I think," Katrina de la Cruz said. "Perfect."

Her maid, Rebeca, nodded and went to the closet where her wardrobe hung in temperature-regulated perfection. She returned with a slim black pantsuit in a plastic hanging bag. She presented it to Katrina like a sommelier showing a fine wine.

From her vanity, Katrina nodded, and the maid set to work on removing it from the bag and smoothing it. She left it on the bed for Katrina, who stood, slipped off her robe, and began dressing.

The black would go well for the formal dinner, and the pantsuit, a tuxedo for women with a feminine cut and a flare at the tails, would allow for maximum movement.

"You will need a mask," Rebeca said. "Match, or contrast?"

"White domino, white hat, white blouse," Katrina said.

"You will stand out," Rebeca said.

"That's the idea."

Rebeca pursed her lips and helped Katrina get dressed.

Katrina didn't need help getting dressed. She didn't need much help doing anything. But when she hired Rebeca to help run her household, Rebeca had been a no-nonsense ladies' maid, taking on everything from the cleaning to dressing Katrina.

Katrina was a decorated war hero, the first clone to become general of any armed forces branch on Earth. She had taken care of herself just fine in the American Southwest after Mexico sent in troops to help with the American water wars. She'd had no problem dressing her own wounds, and then dressing herself, when Mexico's human-made offshore island was stormed by refugees seeking their desalinator.

But now she was retired. She could have gone on to be in the army with her new clone body, despite the trouble she may have had getting "older" soldiers of lower rank to respect her, but she had decided on a new course for herself. A more lucrative job. A general's salary was not bad, but you could be hired by corporations to remove a business rival for a lot more money.

She had done some mob hits, but that felt too personal. Katrina preferred corporate assassinations. It was less messy, less permanent. It was only business, after all.

And after seeing how the corporations had meddled in the American water wars, she felt it was her duty to bump off as many of the *hijos de perra* as she could.

Rebeca was an appropriately talented ladies' maid, even among a society that had come to re-appreciate a multitalented servant. She made sure Katrina had weekly mindmaps, and mindmaps before a job. She kept Katrina's weapons cleaned, sharpened, balanced, and polished, as it applied to each. And the Hermès suit was loose enough to hide multiple weapons secured on each calf, up her left forearm, and inside the brim of her hat. Rebeca also knew how to get blood, feces, and vomit out of almost every fabric. Katrina didn't lose many articles of clothing to her line of work.

The white fedora was symbolic. It sat tilted on her head, with her black hair in a braided bun at the nape of her neck. Katrina found that people trusted her when she wore white. They were attracted to her when she wore red. Green was not her color. The black Hermès suit was to throw the guests off, so that they would feel an undercurrent of anxiety and not know why.

Now, dressed in her suit, a fresh mindmap stored on the server, and cool weapons warming to her body temperature, she was ready to go. Today's party was close to her home of Punta Diamante in Acapulco. Rebeca ordered a car for her, handed over her wrap and her clutch (which held no weapons; Katrina wasn't stupid), and escorted her outside so that she might watch the sun set over the Pacific while she waited.

Some ridiculously rich people still hired car services driven by people. It was as logical as having a gold-plated toilet— ostentatiously irrelevant. Many people, including those with Katrina's level of wealth, simply ordered a self-driving car for where they wanted to go, which made travel both effortless and blameless. More self-driving cars made the traffic a lot better too.

When the self-driving car arrived with someone else in the backseat, Katrina ducked inside her house and drew her gun.

A short, stocky woman with light-brown skin and dark eyes got out of the car and walked without hurry to the door. She wore an expensive gray pantsuit—Italian?—black heels, and a gray fedora. She looked about twenty-five, but carried herself with the confidence of someone much older.

Watching her on the security monitor, Katrina knew who this woman was. She would be a terrible corporate assassin if she didn't recognize her own target.

The way she walked, the way she dressed, this woman was very much like Katrina. Dedicated, methodical, understanding the importance of a proper outfit, and refusing to move fast unless she had to.

She knocked on the door. "Katrina de la Cruz," she said in an American accent. "My name is Sallie Mignon. I would like to talk to you. I am unarmed."

Rebeca had come to investigate. She raised an eyebrow at

Katrina, who nodded. Katrina walked a way into the foyer and sat on the bench under the original Phillips abstract painting. She held her gun steady and motioned for Rebeca to open the door.

"Won't you come—" Rebeca began, but Sallie sucker-punched her in the face.

She went down hard, nose bleeding.

Katrina fired once to the woman's right, chipping the door.

Sallie stopped and held her hands up. "I wished to talk with only you," she said.

"That doesn't look like talking to me, that looks like attacking my household," Katrina said, pointing to Rebeca with her left hand, right still holding the gun steady.

"I said I was unarmed," the woman said. "And—" She didn't get to finish, but let out a surprised grunt when Rebeca's legs trapped hers and scissored, flipping Sallie backward. She hit her head on the floor and Rebeca sat up, punched her in the temple with two jabs, then leaped to her feet, blood still streaming from her nose, and stepped on Sallie's wrist, pinning it neatly.

It was probably time to give Rebeca a raise.

"You didn't know my household was an MMA champion in college, did you?" Katrina asked.

Sallie groaned.

"Check her for weapons," Katrina said.

Rebeca shook her head. "She doesn't have any. She doesn't need any."

"Tie her up and then see to yourself."

Rebeca and Katrina moved the dazed woman into the kitchen and tied her to a chair. Katrina sat on a stool facing her. Rebeca put a wet towel to her nose, but watched the woman carefully.

The woman came to her senses quicker than Katrina had anticipated. She flexed, testing her bindings, and then relaxed. She fixed Katrina with questioning eyes. "I'm not dead?"

"I wanted to learn more about you," Katrina said. "Besides, the job is to kill you at the party. Not in my kitchen."

"Why were you so cautious when I got here?" the woman asked. "I'm no threat to you; you've got to have backups."

"I don't have time to wake up a new clone before the party at this point. And I like this suit."

"Fair enough. I am here to—"

"I can't be bought," Katrina interrupted.

"Beyond being hired to kill in the first place," Sallie said with a smile.

"I suppose," Katrina allowed.

"I just want to talk before the party," Sallie said.

"We're talking," Katrina told her. "You're a high-paying bounty. I did research on you. Your brain is one of the most feared in the world. How have you not been targeted by a mind hacker by now?"

"The best hacker in the world is in my employ," Sallie said.

"Of course," Katrina said. "Why are you here instead of letting me kill you at the Sol Cola party like I am supposed to?"

"I knew I'd be assassinated at this party. I have several spies within Sol Cola. I looked you up too. You are quite the warrior."

Katrina shrugged. Flattery of that sort no longer did much for her. She knew exactly how good she was.

"So?"

"I'm not talking your physical prowess," Sallie said. "I'm talking about your battle strategy. You plan everything down to the smallest detail, taking into account food and drink preferences and past love affairs. You have contingency plans. I need someone like you on staff."

Katrina shook her head. "I told you, I can't be bought out of a contract. You can't pay me double to go after my clients. I lose all professional integrity if I allow that."

Sallie strained briefly at her restraints. She was someone who talked with her hands, Katrina realized. "That's not it. I'm asking you to change jobs entirely."

"Why would I do that?"

"Because you love money and adventure and power."

"Who doesn't?"

Sallie smiled. "All right, most love those things, but you pursue them aggressively."

"The job?"

"Consultant, to start out with. I have a problem I need to figure out."

Katrina waited.

"How does one exact revenge on people who are incredibly wealthy and do not fear death?"

Katrina thought for a moment.

"We're going to need a drink for this."

Rebeca, with cotton stuffed in her nose, served them an expensive gold tequila and prepared an ice pack for Sallie's head.

MMA fighters held a lot of grudges, but that kind of attitude didn't fit her current job.

Sallie now untied, the women sat out on Katrina's veranda, watching the last of the sun sink below the sea. Sallie swallowed a sip of tequila with appreciation. "I just mean that assassinations like you perform are wastes of time and money. What does it accomplish? It's like we're all in grade school again, pulling each other's dresses up to show our panties. We're adults. Let's move beyond humiliation."

"Humiliation is all we have," Katrina said thoughtfully. "Most people surround themselves with clones, especially after a lifetime or two, so you can't threaten their loved ones. Money is far too untraceable: Ruin one venture and find your rival has several more going. Political or sexual scandal doesn't even last more than a few decades."

"For something to pass, all we have to do is wait," Sallie agreed, nodding. "But I need to figure out how to hurt people who cross me. Really hurt them."

"Kidnapping comes to mind," Katrina said. "Hide them away and kill them, and the bays will never wake up a new clone."

Sallie looked at her with pity. "Katrina, do you mean to tell me you haven't put your own cloning lab in this mansion? All of my targets have as many sequestered backups as they do bank accounts."

"There's torture," Katrina said. "Personally I still hate pain."

"Distasteful," Sallie said, taking a sip as if to wash away the thought.

"All of your pain is either heartbreak or emotional," Rebeca suggested, pouring more tequila for them both. "Nothing else matters to you."

"Making your rival fall in love with someone and then getting their heart broken takes far too much work," Katrina said.

Sallie focused on the sea as the sun finally slipped fully away. "No, but think bigger. The worst pain these days is disappointment. Brought about by hope."

Katrina let Sallie chew on that for a moment as she finished her drink. Rebeca gave her another shot.

"You haven't asked why I need such a revenge tactic," Sallie said.

Katrina held her hand up to stop Rebeca from pouring another shot. "It's not my place. I don't question a client."

"That's what makes you so good."

"Actually I do have one question. You said my employment with you would start with consulting. Where do you see it ending?"

Sallie snapped out of her thoughts and smiled at Katrina. "We're two intelligent people. I'm sure we can think of something."

Katrina had heard of the generational ship being built at the moon ship base. She knew thousands of humans were going to go into cryo to wake up on a new planet. It sounded horrible to her. She didn't want to be in space for lifetimes, then settle on a virgin planet on the other side. She didn't want to be the one building new cities; she wanted to be the one enjoying well-established cities without worrying about where the sewers would go. After deciding she didn't want to be stored in the ship's database alongside other traveling clones, she hadn't paid much more attention to it.

And now Sallie was asking her to be awake for the whole trip.

"The goal for the new world is for clones and humans to have peace if we land and colonize together."

"I guess no one has read any history books recently?" Katrina said bitterly.

Sallie grinned and shrugged. "We have to work toward something, or else what is there to hope for?"

"So why me?" Katrina asked.

"The captain needs to be someone strong. I want you, I want a decorated war hero and assassin. The crew are all clones, criminals. If someone acts out, you can take care of things, wake up a new clone, and keep flying."

"That sounds positively brutal."

"Sometimes the best ways of the future involve incorporating the ways of the past," Sallie said seriously. "And the best part? Your record is wiped clean when you get to the new planet. There will be no record of your life as an assassin or as a war criminal."

Katrina narrowed her eyes. "My war record was supposed to already be clean."

"Best hackers in the world, remember? Your record is still out there if one looks hard enough."

"I can't tell if this is an opportunity or blackmail," Katrina said.

"To be honest I'm not sure myself anymore," Sallie said. "Is it interesting to you or not? That's the real question. Then we can discuss whether I have to force you into it or not."

If her record came out, or she was arrested, she'd spend time in jail. That would be unpleasant, but she could still be cloned at the end of her life. She had time.

And this was starting to sound interesting, Katrina had to admit. She knew she wouldn't be happy killing corporate fatcats forever. She nodded slowly. "I will consider this. But I have to have a few things up front. I have to kill you tonight, still. If I leave you alive and I don't take your offer, I'll never work again."

"I understand," Sallie said with a smile. "What else?"

"Rebeca goes with me, in cryo."

Sallie looked up at the maid, who stood silently by the door. "Are you going to discuss this with her?"

"Rebeca. Will you come with me to colonize a new planet, after a lengthy nap in cryo?"

"I'm offended you have to ask, ma'am," Rebeca said, slightly nasal through her cotton swabs.

"There you have it. Third, I want veto power over the crew choices."

"Impossible," Sallie said immediately. "I've pulled all the strings I have to just get you approved as captain. I can't get anything else out of the financiers."

"Then I want all of their histories."

Sallie shook her head slowly. "I'm sorry, General, but I can't give you that either. One thing we are offering these clones is a clean slate. If they arrive on the planet with others knowing their criminal pasts, then the rest of the crew will have something on them, and they will be pariahs. It's easy to wait out humiliation when there are billions of people around you. Harder when there are only thousands on the whole planet."

"How will I control the crew when I don't know what I'm dealing with?" she asked.

"That is what the AI is for. He will handle everything that you don't have access to."

"Thousands of lives and the operation of a spaceship? That's a lot to trust to an artificial intelligence."

"This one is the best in the world," Sallie said.

"In the known world you mean. I know some underground hackers are also working on AI."

"No. It's the best in the world," Sallie repeated, holding Katrina's gaze.

The woman was connected. Even more than Katrina had thought.

"When do you need my answer?"

"Three days," Sallie said, getting up and smoothing her suit. She frowned and brushed at the blood spots on the gray silk.

"If you leave that with me, I can remove those stains," Rebeca said.

Sallie removed the jacket and smiled at Rebeca. "Thank you."

Rebeca glanced at Katrina. "I'll just get this in cold water. We will need to loan her something to wear to the party if you still plan on the assassination, ma'am."

"I think we can arrange that," Katrina said.

Because of their budding business relationship, Katrina killed Mignon swiftly and painlessly, using a clear and tasteless poison in her sparkling rum and cola. Mignon even made sure to drink it next to the fountain so she would crumple and fall into the water, making a terrific scene.

Job done, Katrina decided to enjoy the party and see what information she could gather about this starship project. It was difficult, as some people shut up when a corporate assassin dropped into a conversation, but it turned out people felt very strongly about the project and several arguments peppered the party.

Most of the humans and clones she encountered were in favor of the trip, but had some hesitations. It was a good thing for someone else to do. A few were determined to stay here and enjoy the extra breathing room.

"I heard they're going to employ criminals to drive the ship," one clone executive, Pablo Hernandez, said in a hushed conversation. "I'm not putting my faith in that."

"You wear diamonds mined by slaves and hire assassins to work in marketing. Why are you suddenly too good to ride on a spaceship driven by criminals?" huffed one of the women in the group, and they fell into peals of laughter.

"First on a planet, having to build civilization from the ground up?" Pablo scoffed. "Latrine trenches? No, thank you."

The woman who had spoken tossed her black hair and said, "Oh, please. They'll bring a whole server's worth of servants to build it. They won't wake up the *people* till something is already built. Some years, and lives, are expendable."

A few hours later, Pablo was killed in a corporate assassination. Second of the night: that made it a very good party indeed. The party changed tune after that, as more alcohol flowed and no one else was around to disapprove of the possible crew in charge of the *Dormire*.

Katrina never found out who killed Pablo. She supposed it was a moot point anyway.

The next day, she called Sallie, who had just woken up in her new cloned body.

"I'm in," she said.

BEBE

Maria hadn't gone back to the kitchen the previous night. After her rest, she had pinged Hiro via tablet and he had answered, swearing loudly, and told her they would do it in the morning.

Normally, after such abuse, Maria wouldn't have waited for him. She decided to write off Hiro and his messed-up mood swings and deal with the printer herself. Unfortunately, she found out the manual to set the machine up was on a drive inside the box, and only in Japanese.

"We have traveled to the dark ages," she muttered, flipping through for Spanish or English directions.

She tried pinging Hiro again and got a sleepy "Go the fuck away" on his answer.

"I need you for translation, the manual is only in Japanese," she said.

"Then that's your fucking fault for not buying the right version. I will help you in the morning, leave me the fuck alone." He severed the connection.

There is no backup, she reminded herself, and shivered. If someone attacked her now, it would be the end. She hurried down the silent halls of the ship and entered her rooms, checked the lock on her door, and collapsed on the bed. She slept for the next seven hours.

The next morning, Wolfgang and Joanna were in the kitchen before Maria got there, messing with her food printer, which put Maria in a worse mood than she already was in.

She hadn't slept well, wondering about the circumstances of the day and the crew, running through her conversation with Hiro in her mind. And she had yet to eat, which was very bad for a clone. New clones were like newborn babies, needing considerable sustenance to start their new lives.

The new food printer lurked in the box that they'd brought from the storage room the night before.

"Where have you been?" Wolfgang demanded. "You were supposed to work through the night."

"Ask my translator," Maria said. "Hiro wouldn't talk to me once he got back to his rooms. And I needed him because for some reason we're in the world before translated manuals. This"—she slammed her hand on the food printer box—"only comes with Japanese instructions. Did you two sleep at all?"

"A bit," Joanna said. "But we figured if we were going to eat anything, we needed to test and clear the printer." They were handling the old food printer with plastic gloves, taking samples from both the intake valves and the delivery nozzles. Maria no longer thought of it as the food printer, but as a great monster that vomited forth poison. With its one baleful round light that turned from red to green when the deadly meal was done, it clearly was the Cyclops.

The Cyclops sat atop the silver counter like a tall oven. It looked out of place, sitting beside a larger cavity as if the kitchen had been built for a larger appliance.

Watching them take samples from the printer, Maria felt a sudden sense of violation, even though she knew it was a good idea to clear the kitchen as soon as possible. "Just take the whole thing.

I can't put this one together with you two in the way, and if that one is making hemlock, then we need to trash it regardless. I'm going to go ahead and get the new printer going."

"I thought you had to wait for Hiro?" Wolfgang said.

"I can get it out of the box without instructions," Maria snapped. She filled the kettle and put it on the heating element.

While the water heated, she went to a storage closet in the far corner of the kitchen, beside the pantry. Inside were several replacement parts, spare kitchen tools, and a toolbox. The entire thing was in disarray due to the grav drive mishap, but at least the toolbox had remained shut where it had fallen among spare smaller appliances. She put "sort all kitchen items" on her mental list, but at a very low priority.

"Any word on the cloning bay fixes?" she asked, coming out of the storage room.

"Not yet," Joanna said from her position in front of the sink. "But I won't relax until I know we have new bodies growing."

"If whoever did this was dedicated, right now is the perfect time to start killing again," Maria said.

Wolfgang grunted. "We should have guards at the cloning bay to prevent further sabotage."

Joanna sighed. "Guard the cloning bay. Fix the nav system. Investigate the murder. Wake up the captain's clone. And do our everyday jobs to keep the ship moving. There are only six of us, Wolfgang. How do you figure this working out?"

"Don't forget fix IAN," Maria said.

"I'm functioning, Ms. Arena," said a voice from the speakers. "Admittedly at about forty percent, but improving all the while."

Wolfgang swore as Maria laughed aloud in relief. "IAN, welcome back. When did you come online?"

"And why didn't anyone tell us?" Wolfgang demanded.

"Mr. Seurat and Captain de la Cruz woke me up last night. I've been working on repairing my own functions and recovering any data I can in the meantime."

"What have you recovered?" Joanna asked eagerly. "Any recordings of the cloning bay? Any medical logs?"

"Nothing yet," IAN said, still sounding optimistic and friendly. "But I'm still working."

"Can you do anything for us in the kitchen this morning? Clear the printer of hemlock? Recover the food logs?" Maria said.

"No, I can't," IAN said. "But I can tell you that your metabolisms are running low and you need food very soon."

"For this we need the most sophisticated AI in the world," Hiro said, walking into the kitchen. He nodded hello to them all.

"Hiro, IAN is awake—" Wolfgang said, but Hiro cut him off.

"I know," he said, waving his hand. "He woke me at four this morning and had me working on the navigation system. Turns out that when he got back online we started going back off course. I can't figure it out, but I figured I'd help out with the food problem, 'cause I'm about to faint or eat Wolfgang, I can't decide which." He stopped when he saw Maria staring at him. "What?"

"So you're going to let what you said to me last night just go unmentioned?" she asked.

Hiro rubbed the back of his head. "Ah, what did I say?"

"You refused to follow orders, that's what you did," said Wolfgang. "And we're hungrier now because of it."

"You *aggressively* refused to follow orders," Maria said. "You were a dick. And frankly kind of scary."

Wolfgang crossed his arms. "Did he threaten you?"

"He didn't go that far," Maria said. "But he definitely scared me."

"I'm sorry. I am useless when I'm exhausted, and I can get a little testy," Hiro said, not meeting her eyes.

"So saying, 'Go eat vacuum, you worthless piece of space janitor shit'—and then something in Japanese I can only assume was unflattering—is 'a little testy'?"

He looked genuinely horrified. "Oh no, Maria, I'm so sorry. I don't really think that. Like I said, I just lost my head for a moment."

Maria looked to Wolfgang. "Being a dick doesn't make him a murderer."

"Being aggressive and verbally assaulting a crewmember does put him under suspicion," he said.

"I'm right here, you can talk to me, you know!" Hiro said. "And we're all under suspicion! Even—" He closed his mouth abruptly, looking at Wolfgang.

Wolfgang crossed his arms, looking like he was anticipating something. Hiro didn't say anything else.

"I don't think he's lying," IAN said. "All of his body language is sincere. He really doesn't remember saying those things."

"That's not entirely comforting," Maria said. "But we have a food printer to put together." She looked at Hiro and pointed to her tablet on the kitchen counter. "The instructions are there. And don't speak to me that way again."

He practically sprinted to get the tablet. The tension in the room broke and the kettle began to sing.

Maria made the tea, getting mugs for everyone while it steeped. "I thought you two were working on autopsies? Did you find any proof of anything?"

"No proof, not yet," Joanna said. "You were poisoned first, but the others had trace amounts of poison in their system. If they'd stayed alive longer, they would have gotten sick and possibly died. You got the largest amount."

"Weird," Maria said.

"Don't worry about the murder investigation," Wolfgang said. "Your main concern should be making sure we have a food supply."

"I'm not sure the captain will agree that testing the food printer when we already know it spits out hemlock is the best use of your time," she said. "Isn't this mutiny or something?"

"Mutiny in the kitchens," Joanna said. "I thought mutiny was a stronger rebellion than testing a food printer."

"Mutiny would be a direct threat to the captain's authority," IAN said. "This doesn't qualify."

"I seem to remember hearing that the AI would be better at understanding humor," Maria said. "Why is he so literal?"

"Forty percent, remember?" Joanna said. "I expect he'll be better as the day goes on."

"We are disobeying orders by taking a moment to check on the food printer, but that's about it," Wolfgang said, addressing the earlier question and grunting slightly as he helped Maria get the new food printer out of its box. Even in the lower gravity the thing was a monster, but together they managed to get it free of all packing material. Wolfgang returned to the Cyclops and inspected it to see if he had missed unpinning any of the connections.

"But you would have to remove the faulty printer to bring to the medbay for testing anyway," Joanna said, putting the swabs into a plastic box on her lap. "So we're cutting out the middleman and letting you do your real job."

"Okay, you both outrank me, so I'm not going to argue. Besides, I could eat one of you at this point. But I'd probably start with Hiro. He deserves it."

She ignored his indignant look as she surveyed the printer. She'd never hooked up a printer before.

It was a newer, larger model than the Cyclops. Maybe the upgrade was supposed to be a reward for lasting two hundred years in space or something. It looked large enough to print a farm animal.

"This is gargantuan," she said, shaking her head. "When would we ever need to print a whole pig?"

"I think we should test it with a pig," Hiro said. "Put that baby through its paces."

Together Wolfgang and Maria strained and pushed to edge the printer to the space in the countertop beside where the previous printer had sat. It filled the cavity perfectly, as if they designed the kitchen for the better printer, but then decided at the last minute to give them the smaller Cyclops instead.

"Maria, once you get the printer working, you need to clean out the cloning bay," Joanna said. "It's gone from murder scene to biohazard."

Maria grimaced but didn't object. It was her job, after all.

Wolfgang tested the old food printer to see if he could carry it himself. He strained and staggered, but then hefted it and trudged out of the kitchen.

"How many more years do we have to travel with that guy?" Maria asked. "I swear I can see myself wanting to start over with zero memories of this trip if he's like that."

"He failed, Maria," Joanna said gently. "He's taking all of this personally. What happened yesterday was a clear failure of security on levels that we may never fathom. Try to at least see what he's like when he's not dealing with one assault, five deaths—six if you count IAN—one multiplication, and hacking by throwing old backups into us." She paused, counting off the crimes on her fingers. "What else?"

Maria sighed, realizing she was right. "Possible suicide?" She frowned at the food printer. "And making me hook up this printer is a crime in itself. I'll hurry as much as possible but it could take all day. Hope everyone has protein bars."

"I found a few in my room, but I wouldn't eat them unless I had to," Hiro said.

"You may have to," Joanna said.

"I know. I did. But I didn't like it," he said.

She pointed to Wolfgang's untouched tea. "You interested?"

"Yes, please," Hiro said, smiling gratefully. He took a look at his tablet and frowned, then squinted. "This phrasing is painful; looking at these instructions I'm assuming they were written by the killer. They're trying to kill me."

Maria raised her eyebrows. "That's a very subtle way to kill someone. And unless you're being irritating and sarcastic, you just implicated yourself because you're the only Japanese-speaking person on board, Hiro."

"That's why it's such a clever trap for just me!" He took a sip, sighing. "Fine. We should get to work, though. If the killer wants us dead again, they might just starve us to death this time around and not have to lift a finger."

"You two are pretty gruesome," Joanna said. "Can you at least have some respect for the situation?"

Hiro grimaced. "Sorry, Doctor. Just trying to keep from spiraling into screaming, *Oh my shit we are really going to die for real and drift in space forever and end all of clonekind and be responsible for killing thousands of people.*" His voice remained even throughout this statement, and Maria stifled a laugh.

"Just trying to lighten the mood, Joanna," Maria said.

"Do what you must to get through this, just maybe keep some of it out of my earshot," Joanna said.

"I just thought of something," Hiro said. "Does hooking up the new printer mean we have to reprogram it with all our likes and dislikes and allergies and stuff?"

"Nah, I have a backup of all that on a drive that's not attached to IAN," Maria said. "Our biggest challenge is working on an empty stomach."

Joanna cast a sympathetic look toward Maria. "Good luck to you both. I'm off to run tox screens on the old food printer." She secured a plastic top to her mug, set it carefully in a cupholder on the right side of her wheelchair, and headed out of the kitchen.

"So are we okay?" Hiro asked once they were alone.

"I barely know you, Hiro," she said. "I don't know what to take lightly and what to take seriously. Especially after yesterday. So be careful, and we'll be okay."

"I can't believe this didn't come with more languages," Hiro said. "Only the drive with this info was in the box?"

"Yeah." She got up to clean up the detritus and packing material from the box. When she picked up the cardboard, she saw it. Now that they could see the bottom of the box, the ragged cut was obvious.

"Hiro, look."

"I'm guessing you and Wolfgang didn't do that when unpacking?"

She held it up to the light. "No." She turned the cardboard over and saw among the packing material one sheet of an instruction manual stuck on a piece of tape. It was torn, the rest of the manual gone.

"Why would someone mess with our food printer manual?" Maria asked, pulling the paper free.

"And paper instructions? Next are we going to be hooking a sled dog up to the ship to regain our momentum?"

Maria took the different hoses and wires and laid them out neatly on the floor, waiting for Hiro to give her instructions on what to do. He read on the tablet for a bit, his face growing more and more scrunched with annoyance.

"Why a sled dog?" she finally asked, the question gnawing at her. "Why not a horse pulling the ship?"

"It's cold out there. Dogs are better equipped to pull a sled, or a spaceship, in the cold," he said without looking up. "Now let me read."

She got up to start putting the kitchen in order while he read. Most of their appliances were anchored to the floor or walls, so it was only small things like utensils and dirty plates and cups that she had to clean up.

She found the box of knives that she had brought from home and opened it. "Well, shit."

She took the box to the table and showed it to him. "We were killed with the chef's knife, right?"

"Yeah, we didn't find any other weapons," he said grimly. Three knives were missing from their spots in the box.

"We know where the chef's knife is, but the boning knife and cleaver are gone."

"The good news just keeps on coming," he said, not smiling. "Something else to tell the captain, I suppose."

Maria sent a ping to Katrina on her tablet.

"Report," Katrina said.

"We found my box of knives, Captain, and it's missing three. One of them is the chef's knife, which we've already found in the cloning bay, but the other two are still missing."

"Did you find any of them buried in a body?"

"Well, no, not yet—"

"Then get back to fixing the printer. Call me when you find clues, not the absence of clues."

The tablet beeped as she severed the connection.

"Dang, she's cranky," Hiro said.

"You're one to talk," Maria said.

He bobbed his head, avoiding eye contact. "I really think the person who wrote this hated people and wanted to laugh as they starved to death," he said.

"Think it's another case of sabotage?" Maria asked, only half joking.

"No, I think it's a case of an asshole tech writer. But you do have to wonder about the missing instruction book."

He stood up and looked at the items Maria had laid out, and then back at the tablet. "Got it," he mumbled and started telling her what to do with each thing. They worked together for the next hour, Maria biting back irritation when he made jokes or a translation didn't work very well. She got shocked twice trying to set up the computer to interface with IAN, despite IAN's guidance.

"There it is. I can see it," IAN said. "Well done, Ms. Arena."

"I need to get my backups," she said.

"No need," IAN said. "This food printer is fully capable of analyzing a person's tastes via saliva sample."

Maria stepped back and surveyed the printer with new respect. "That's some impressive computing," she said. "It's still a behemoth, though."

Hiro took the mugs to the sink. "Behemoth. I like that name. We'll call it Bebe for short. If you don't need me anymore, I'll go check on the drive. You've still got some knives left—and Bebe!—to protect you in the meantime." Then he was gone.

"Now it's just you and me, Behemoth," she said. "I'm not afraid of you."

Honestly, there were a lot of things she was afraid of on the ship, but at least Bebe wasn't one of them.

The captain had not returned to the medbay since leaving last night. Joanna was relieved, but had slept in the other hospital bed for sure. Unfortunately the dead bodies were making it a somewhat unpleasant room to stay in. Not to mention unsanitary.

The clone's life-support systems still worked diligently, showing that the older captain was not quite dead yet.

Joanna stretched in her chair. She needed a shower. And really needed food.

She maneuvered her chair to her lab in the corner of the medbay, but before she could get started on her screening, someone was knocking on the door. She opened it remotely with her tablet.

Hiro walked in, still maddeningly chipper. "Hello, Dr. Glass. Mind if I take a look at myself?"

"I'm not sure that's the healthiest thing in the world, Hiro," Joanna said, laying the latest testing samples out on her counter.

"Well, no, the healthiest thing would be for me to have a hearty breakfast and go for a run on the treadmill," Hiro said. "Also not have the stress of being on board with a killer. But I can't do those things. The printer is nearly ready to go, speaking of breakfast.

Maria has already named it and is challenging it for dominance. I can get you tickets to the bout, if you like. Now, you tell me the wisdom of fighting with a machine, with a killer loose on the ship." His voice had a conversational tone that sounded like he really was talking about sports instead of their lives.

"Remember what I said about keeping your coping mechanism away from my earshot?" she asked. She waved at the five bagged bodies in the corner. "Go ahead. Yours is the one in the middle."

The ship had no morgue because each body was supposed to be recycled after death. Another oversight. She would need to remove them before they broke down any more. She was done examining, but she had to hold on to them for Wolfgang's curiosity. And if the crew wanted to look at their bodies, they might find a clue that could help them solve this.

At least Hiro looking at his dead clone worried her far less than the captain's obsessive study of her own did, although that could be because his body was already dead.

He walked over to it and unzipped it, staring at his naked self.

"I'm just trying to figure out why I did it," Hiro said, looking closely at his clone's neck.

"Someone else could have hanged you, Hiro. Although there are no defensive wounds. Wolfgang and I are working on the time line today," Joanna said, turning on her scanner. "But don't worry, we'll figure it out eventually."

"Where is that ray of sunshine?" Hiro asked. "I thought he was helping you with these poison hunts."

"He dropped the food printer in here and left. I think he is checking on Paul and the captain. I need to talk to him soon, though. Why do you need him?" she asked.

"I definitely don't," Hiro said. "Just curious where everyone was. We're supposed to keep track, right?"

"In theory. Does this mean you left Maria alone?"

"Nah, she's with the printer. That thing looks like it could protect any of us in a fight, provided Maria can get it on our side. Which is questionable right now, honestly," he said.

Joanna glared at him.

He dropped his pleasant demeanor. "Fine. I had to go check on the nav system. I figured I would drop by to say hello to myself. I'll head back to check on her."

"How is the nav system?" she asked as he turned to go.

"The same," he said. "Still slowing down. Still turning starboard."

"That means nothing in space."

"Fine, back toward Earth. I didn't want to bore you with astronavigation numbers but if you really want . . . " He let his voice hang there, probably expecting her rapid refusal.

"I promise if I figure anything out about your death, I'll let you know," she said, motioning him out the door.

"Thanks, Doc."

She watched him go, smiling slightly. She was glad they had Hiro on board. Irreverent and disrespectful at times, but he was a breath of fresh air they needed.

Her scanner beeped, indicating it had finally warmed up. She started feeding it samples, noting the numbers of each sample on her tablet.

"Hello, Dr. Glass," IAN said, making her jump. "I'm sorry, did I startle you?"

"A bit. It's going to take some getting used to. What do you need, IAN?"

"I wanted to know how you were doing, and if you needed anything."

"I need my medical logs, IAN. Aside from that, things seem to be working fine."

"I don't have your medical logs but I can make backups of what you are recording now."

Joanna considered saying no, but nodded. She was still keeping physical notes just in case of another data loss. "Thank you."

She pinged the kitchen, and Maria answered, sounding annoyed. "It's not done yet, Doctor."

"I wasn't calling you about that. You'll be glad to know that the
food printer is completely broken."

"Why would that make me happy?"

"Because that means you haven't been wasting your time with
the new one. How is that going, anyway?"

Maria sighed loudly. "Nearly there. I have to run several test
dishes before we can eat. But we're close. I will have IAN tell everyone when I can finally print."

"Are you going to your rooms to get those backups you said
you had?"

"I guess I should do that. Instructions say I don't need to do
that, but I like redundant systems."

"I want to make sure there's no more poison traces in your
room," Joanna said. "Let me know as soon as you are free." She was
about to sever the connection, but remembered something. "So is
Hiro there with you yet?"

"No, he left here a little bit ago to go check on the helm,"
Maria said.

"Hell," Joanna said. "Keep an eye out for him. He came by
here, and now he's supposed to be heading your way."

"Sure, okay," Maria said, more distracted than before, and the
com switched off.

Joanna sighed. She'd had worries about the wisdom of a six-
person crew. It had seemed efficient, but when a catastrophe of this
level happened, they were in real trouble. They needed more people.

Or fewer, depending on how many of those people could be
trusted completely.

Hemlock. Maria was right, that was a strange poison. She
looked up information on her tablet, and read up on the deadly
plant. Its leaves were deadly in small doses and could be disguised
as other herbs.

She needed more tea. Prepared to brave the wrath of Hurricane Maria, she headed to the kitchen.

"Captain, where did you see action?" Joanna asked.

She and Katrina sat at the table farthest away from where Maria was testing the food printer. Hiro sat on the counter, keeping her company while trying to stay out of her way. The captain had come in to take a break, looking hopefully at the printer.

"I was in the Mexican army, the first clone in the world to make general," she said, spinning her own empty mug on its edge. "I saw action in the American water wars, mainly. Lost a leg during a laser strike to our camp."

Joanna had been in Washington, DC, during the water wars, remembering how it had split the West, how the new civil war (no one called it that, but everyone knew that's what it was when Nevada Governor Andrew Teal took command of the Nevada Army Reserve and sent them, all too willing, to invade California to fight for the dwindling water supply) had caused a lot of strife in the capital.

"I remember the wars," she said. "I'm sorry."

"I didn't last much longer, so I got better with the next life. Benefits of cloning, you know," Katrina said.

Joanna pinged Wolfgang. "What is it, Doctor?" he answered.

"We need to get back on the job. Let's finish that time line so I can have my clean medbay back."

"All right. We should eat first. Is the printer online?"

Maria swore loudly from the kitchen.

"Not yet. Katrina and I are in the kitchen now."

"Good. Can you let me know about those tox screens?" he asked, sounding like he was already walking.

"Food printer is lousy with hemlock, we can't trust it. Luckily we have the new one."

"All right." And the connection went dead.

"Takes it in stride, that's my second in command," Katrina said.

Joanna and the captain waited in silence until Wolfgang arrived. He came in, took one look at Maria with her struggles, and joined them without a word.

"There is something I didn't mention about the hemlock," Joanna said quietly. They were far from Maria, who was making a lot of noise behind the printer, but she still kept her voice low. Katrina and Wolfgang leaned in to hear her.

"We all ingested it, only a lot less than Maria did," Joanna said. "I want to know why Maria wouldn't notice her printer had been sabotaged."

"There are many ways to slip something in someone's food," Wolfgang said. "It's also possible Maria didn't cook every single meal for twenty-five years."

"Her knife. Her kitchen. Could she have poisoned herself, then killed us all, then died?" Katrina said. "Someone tried to kill her with the knife before she erased all the logs?"

Joanna shook her head. "Self-poisoning with hemlock? That's not the way I'd choose to go. Besides, I still think she hit the resurrection switch. It's safe to say she was killed. With just the hemlock, sure, she could have done it herself. But the knife? No one can stab themselves in the spine."

"Perhaps she wasn't working alone," Wolfgang said.

"I think we're getting away from Occam's razor here," Joanna said. "Let's stay simple while we can."

"We need to dust that knife for prints," Wolfgang said.

Joanna stared at him. She held up her hand and began ticking off her fingers. "Wolfgang, we don't have a crime lab. There was no reason to put a forensics lab on this ship. I only have the tech that I have because it's used to diagnose live clones. We don't have anything that would resemble a good clear way to lift prints off the knife. With proper technology we could grab partial prints and identify them, but we don't have that."

His blue eyes were stony. "It's evidence," he said.

She lifted her hands in an *I give up* motion. "You're absolutely right. We should talk to Maria about who she thinks she would have let use her knives."

"How would she know who she's bonded with on this ship in twenty-five years?" Katrina said.

"It'll be evidence," Joanna repeated, smiling.

"She doesn't seem to like the food printer," IAN said. "So they didn't bond."

"Neither printer is an AI, IAN," the captain said. She paused. "Is it?"

"No. I just like this one a lot. Its name is Bebe. Cute, isn't it? And I'm up to fifty-three percent and feeling better!"

IT'S ALWAYS FIVE O'CLOCK IN SPACE

Maria needed alone time with the Behemoth, and she wasn't getting any.

She was so distracted by running the printer through its paces that she hadn't realized most of the crew had raided the liquor stores. Hiro, Katrina, Wolfgang, and Joanna all sat at a table with a bottle of whiskey between them.

"Really? Whiskey at nine in the morning?" She paused and then realized the thing she was truly angry about. "Without me?"

"It's always five o'clock in space," Hiro said, raising his little shot glass to toast her.

"Whatever. We're so far outside the realm of social norms anyway," Maria said, shrugging.

"I don't recommend drinking with new clone bodies on an empty stomach," IAN said.

"Now ask us how much we care," Hiro said.

Joanna hadn't touched her shot glass. She looked at them all in disgust, her hands wrapped around a mug of tea. "You know we all have time-sensitive work to do, right?"

"I'm useless until I get some food. And whiskey will help the waiting," said Katrina. "Just a sip."

Joanna looked at Wolfgang. He shrugged. She rolled her eyes.

"If you get drunk and rowdy while I'm trying to fix this thing, then floating bloody in the cloning bay will be the least of your problems," Maria said.

"Understood," Wolfgang said, smiling slightly.

She refocused on Bebe, wishing there were a door between her and the tables.

"Where is Paul?" Hiro asked.

"He was working on the servers when I left him," Wolfgang said. "I told him to come here by nine."

"It's five after," Hiro said.

Wolfgang pulled his tablet out and paged Paul.

"Here," Paul said, his voice sounding stronger than yesterday. "Is it breakfast yet?"

"Not quite yet," Wolfgang said. "We're all in the kitchen, though. Join us."

"I should work more on these servers," he said doubtfully.

"I'll let him know when it's time," IAN said.

"Hey, IAN, do you watch us in our rooms?" Hiro asked suddenly.

"In the interest of full security, I have to," IAN said. "When the cameras are all functioning, that is."

"Well. That's interesting," Hiro said, going slightly pink.

"All your cameras aren't functioning yet?" Katrina asked.

"Not yet. I'm taking time to run the various commands you've given me, as well as repair my internal issues. I'm getting more and more eyes and ears all over the shop."

"Let me know when you're fully operational," Katrina said.

"You're right, I could use a break," Paul said over the link. "I'll come down."

"All right, everyone," Maria said. "I need to go back to my quarters for a backup disk that has all of your tastes in a program. But in the meantime I want you to give saliva samples to Bebe because apparently it can determine your tastes by just that little bit of DNA. Hiro can show you how."

"Why do you need the disk, then?" Wolfgang asked, narrowing his eyes.

"I want to compare the two. If it makes a wrong decision, then we'll have the backup."

"I'll come with you," Joanna said.

As they headed down the hall, they passed Paul hurrying to the kitchen. "Food yet?" he asked, his red face hopeful.

"Yes, in the last minute we went from nothing to a full meal," Maria snapped.

Joanna put her hand on Maria's arm. "We'll get breakfast soon," she said. "Wolfgang is waiting for you, Paul."

"I'd rather have breakfast," Paul said. They continued on their ways.

"He seems to be returning to us," Maria said. "Any idea what was wrong with him yesterday?"

"Some people get uptight about the cloning process, some people don't like when routines get damaged, some maybe don't like waking up to floating gore. It could be anything," Joanna said.

"Or he could be responsible for it," Maria said in a low voice.

"If we were to damn people based on acting oddly after waking up the way we did yesterday, I could point fingers at any one of us."

"It's not helping that we're all dealing with low blood sugar," Maria said, thinking out loud. "Which is why I need to get everything worked out."

"I'd like to test-check your toiletries as well," Joanna said. "You may have some more poison traces on your toothbrush or lip balm or something."

Maria continued down the hall. "Sure thing," she said. "I'm fairly sure I have nothing to hide. Well. *I* don't have anything to hide. I don't know about the other me."

They entered Maria's room, and she pointed to her small bath. "Why don't you grab my toothbrush and anything else you want? I can get another from the supply."

Joanna nodded and turned toward the bathroom. When Maria

was sure she was out of sight, she knelt below her bed and pulled out a small safe with a mechanical lock. She ran through the combination.

"Maria, why do you have a mechanical safe?" IAN said. "A digital safe is much harder to crack."

Yeah, for a human. Maria grimaced. She'd forgotten the AI was back. "A woman has her secrets, IAN."

"Not aboard the *Dormire*," IAN said. "What are you retrieving?"

Maria realized the camera couldn't see into the safe. She glanced at the interior quickly and pulled out a blue backup drive, ignoring the several other drives of various sizes stored within. She shut the safe and then held the drive up to the camera. "It's just a backup drive."

"I would have kept all of those logs," IAN said. "You didn't need a redundancy."

"Clearly I did; you lost the logs," Maria said.

"Kick a man while he's down," IAN said, sounding wounded. "How do you know those hold the data you want? You could have overwritten it in twenty-five years."

Maria shrugged and pocketed the drive. "Digital pack rat. It's what I always do. It's just good sense to back up the data important to your job. And you're not a man."

"I will have to report to the captain," IAN said.

"I'm about to go tell her myself in the kitchen!" Maria said. "And Dr. Glass is right here to see me do it!"

This wasn't entirely true. The doctor was still in the bathroom, rummaging through her stuff. Then she backed out slowly. The non-accessible bathrooms weren't large enough for a wheelchair to turn around in, and it had been a tight fit for her.

"I've got what we need for the printer," Maria said. "IAN is shitting himself that I have a backup he doesn't. Do you need anything else?"

"I need a shower and to get my legs back on. Otherwise, no. I took your toothbrush, your floss, and a towel. That should be enough."

"Then I will definitely be a new toothbrush and towel, unless you want to be around a stinky cook."

Joanna smiled. "I expect you can trust yourself not to squander our supply cache. I'll get these tested. I want to know how far the attempt to poison you went."

"I have brushed my teeth and showered since yesterday. Do you think that's okay?" Maria asked.

Joanna frowned. "I should have told you not to do that. Too much chaos yesterday. But if you're okay now, you'll probably be fine. Let me know if you start to feel sick. Until then I'll be in the medbay. Tell Wolfgang to meet me there in half an hour."

"I can do that!" IAN said.

"I'm playing Russian roulette with hemlock? Great," Maria said.

Joanna followed her out of her room, and Maria stopped to key in the lock code.

"Did you really keep a copy of all of our food preferences?" Joanna asked, pointing at the drive.

"Of course. Backups are important. Just ask Paul and IAN how they're doing without a backup."

"I resent that," IAN said, his voice less chirpy.

"Fair enough," Joanna said. "I'll let you know."

They parted in the hallway, and Maria hurried back to the kitchen to try to recalibrate the food printer. Her nemesis. Bebe.

So much for the "just a sip" of whiskey.

Wolfgang, Katrina, Paul, and Hiro had been trading shots for an hour and getting more and more relaxed while Maria finished calibrating the food printer.

Joanna stormed into the kitchen, slightly damp and upright

wearing her prosthetic legs. "Please tell me the printer is up and going," she said. "I'm losing the ability to concentrate."

"Almost there," Maria said, watching Bebe work on printing its last test, a simple slab of tofu. "Did you find your spare legs?"

Joanna nodded. "Found them in my closet, while you all apparently got drunk." She collapsed at the table with the waiting crew and looked accusingly at the bottle. "That was a great idea. Did you know they tested—rather unethically—how long a clone can live without food after waking up? They did some tests on sleep deprivation as well."

"I wouldn't have wanted to be in that experiment," Hiro said.

Joanna pointed at him. "You're in it. Now. That's what you're going through. And it's not pretty."

"But what kind of asshole would volunteer for that?" Hiro asked.

"The kind of assholes who will think it's a great idea to drink on a stomach that's never had food before?" Maria called from her station at the mouth of Bebe.

She was ready. She programmed in some bread that everyone could share while the printer dealt with several meals at once.

"Or like the kind of person who will call everyone who outranks her an asshole when she hasn't been eating," Joanna said. "Exactly."

"So these unethical experiments," Wolfgang said. "What else did they test?"

"Physical dexterity, emotional durability, mental endurance. Twenty-four hours without food and the clones are next to useless," IAN said. "This puts you on hour eighteen."

Wolfgang looked at Paul. Pale by Earth standards, Paul was positively ruddy compared with Wolfgang. He returned the stare and didn't flinch when the much taller Wolfgang stood up. He reached out and grasped the Paul's shoulders, pulling him to his feet. He ran his hands down Paul's arms in an oddly intimate gesture.

Paul stepped back out of his reach. "What are you doing?" His voice was slightly slurred.

"I want to run our own tests," Wolfgang said at last.

"What are you talking about?" Katrina asked. "You're pretty much breaking down in front of us, but you want to take it further? By feeling him up?" She paused to drain her shot glass. "That's not the way to do security."

"I need to blow off steam," he said. "Sweat out the alcohol. I need a workout. Paul's coming with me."

"I don't think—" Paul began.

"Dinner officially in one half hour," Maria called. "The new printer is off and running!"

The crew cheered, and Joanna sagged in her chair.

Wolfgang looked at Paul. "So we have half an hour. Let's go."

"An empty stomach, plus alcohol, plus the stress of our current situation, means the odds of exhausting your new bodies are very high," IAN said. "Scientifically speaking, it's a really stupid idea."

Maria paused and looked thoughtfully at the room's camera. IAN was getting more of a personality. She wasn't sure if that was good or not.

"Come on. It'll let Maria work without distraction. It will be fun." Wolfgang's teeth were slightly bared and his eyes were wide. This looked like anything but fun. Maria was caught between pitying Paul and being grateful it wasn't her.

"You're getting delusions of immortality," Katrina said. "Right at the moment you're not immortal."

"I'm a clone. I *am* immortal," he said, and laughed. He grabbed Paul's shoulder in a viselike grip and pulled him toward the kitchen. "Paul, go and lift that food printer in there."

"Hey, wait a minute! I just got this hooked up!" Maria said, stepping in front of the printer. "Go to the fitness room to do whatever testosterone war you're about to start."

Wolfgang turned his icy stare onto Maria, but she stood her ground.

"I'm serious," she said.

"Come on," Wolfgang said, and he led Paul from the kitchen. The doctor followed them.

"That crisis just took my drinking buddy," Hiro complained. Then he blinked as if realizing something. "Hey, they didn't invite me. Aren't I testosteroned enough?"

Maria thought that Hiro feeling left out of a macho war was less alarming than his referring to Wolfgang as a "buddy." *We're getting loopy without food.*

"You are totally testosteroned, Hiro. You're the testosteronedest," she said. "Now let me work." She focused back on the printer. She checked the calibrations and the memory and turned it on. "Meals and beverages for the whole crew, please."

"Do you have to say please? Why be nice to these machines?" asked Katrina, still seated at the table.

"Habit," Maria said. "I had a strict aunt." She held her breath as the machine whirred to life and began clicking to itself.

"What do you think we should do with the other printer?" Hiro asked. "I think I might use it to set up a black-market café in my room. In fact, that sounds like a cool idea. Maria, tyrant of the kitchen, won't let us have our sweets, so we all go to Hiro's Speakeasy for dark chocolate made from the finest Lyfe that can be found on the ship."

"A speakeasy that serves only hemlock? Be my guest," Maria said.

"It's a fucking carnival in here," Katrina said, and tried to get to her feet. She staggered and sat back down.

Maria turned back to the printer, which was busy printing black coffee all over the interior of its chamber. She swore and went scrambling for a mug. When she had retrieved one, she caught the last of the coffee. She pulled out the mug as the printer got working on something else.

"Taste this," she said to Hiro, handing it to him while she looked for a rag to mop up the coffee.

"Heck no, are you mad?" Hiro asked. "You taste it."

Maria looked at him in surprise.

"Could be poisoned," he said, shrugging.

"Oh, for heaven's sake, you know this printer just came out of the box!" She gulped the coffee down, scalding her tongue. It was black coffee all right.

The printer made beverages for all of them, and Maria brought Katrina her black coffee.

Katrina was staring at the table, tracing the metal designs with her finger. "I should kill her. The previous clone. This life is mine now."

"Captain, the inability to murder someone on the ship is pretty far down the list of problems we have," Hiro said mildly, gently pushing the coffee toward her. "It's possible she'll never wake up. It's possible we could find out she did everything and we can punish her."

The captain gave him a sharp look, and Hiro sat back in his chair as if stung. "Of course, that implies you killed us, and that you should be punished too, which I am not implying at all. You're clearly delightfully innocent."

"Captain, you will feel better after a meal and some sleep. I promise. Apparently Joanna says it's scientifically proven," Maria said.

"People need eggs at a time like this," Hiro agreed.

A MISSING PIECE

I don't get it, why are you picking on me?" Paul said nervously as they entered the gym.

"This is exercise. It's bonding," Wolfgang said.

"I'd think the captain would be a more appropriate sparring partner for you, Wolfgang," Joanna suggested.

"She's not someone I would ever spar with. Not with punches pulled," he said. "Paul and I need to blow off steam."

Like everywhere else on the ship, the gym was an excellent use of limited space: state of the art, a perfect room for weights, cardio, and stretching. In the middle of the gym were a number of obstacles with rings, poles for balance and jumping, and bars.

Joanna had heard Hiro had lobbied for a swimming pool, but had been denied.

Wolfgang unzipped his jumpsuit to his waist and slipped his arms out of it, revealing a black T-shirt and arms with long, wiry muscles. He motioned for Paul to do the same. Paul struggled out of his own jumpsuit with much less grace than Wolfgang. While Paul was, like all clones, a prime example of a fit young man, Joanna saw with distaste the telltale signs of the synth-amneo fluid caking in his elbow joints, indicating that he hadn't showered yet. She suppressed a shudder.

"You're going to follow me. I want to know what you're capable of, since you've been essentially in a fetal position for the past day," he said, then bounded off to the obstacles.

"You don't have to do any of this," Joanna said to Paul, but he didn't respond. His face flushed and his fists balled up as he watched Wolfgang.

Joanna forgot her irritation briefly as Wolfgang swung easily from bar to bar, landed on a balance beam, and walked across with fluid beauty. He attacked every obstacle, from pulling tension strands out of the wall (the total weight estimation came up on a readout on the wall in both Earth and Luna gravities) to holding a handstand for three minutes.

Paul watched this silently, looking like a boiling pot of rage. He glanced at Joanna, and then went to the bars to follow Wolfgang's example. He slipped from the bars twice, having to struggle to jump back up to get them, and then fell off the balance beam. His turn at the tension strands totaled less than half what Wolfgang could pull, and he couldn't even kick his legs up to a handstand, much less hold one for three minutes.

It always amazed Joanna how muscle memory was retained through different cloning lives. While Paul was technically fit, he was no athlete like Wolfgang had apparently been in previous lives.

Wolfgang walked over to Paul and pulled him roughly to his feet. "That was pathetic. Next time will be better." He motioned for Joanna. "Your turn, Doctor."

Joanna quirked an eyebrow at him. "I'm not taking your challenge until I get some food in me."

He shrugged. "Name the time."

"Mr. Wolfgang? Dr. Glass? Mr. Seurat?" IAN asked.

"Yes, IAN. Are you not seeing your cameras here?" Joanna said.

"Not yet. Ms. Arena says that we finally have food."

Paul shouldered Wolfgang to the ground and ran out of the gym. Joanna watched him get up, grinning. "He just needed the right incentive to move, apparently."

"I'm starving," Wolfgang said, swaying slightly. He caught

himself on a wall handle and looked at Joanna. "Lack of food makes people do odd things?"

She laughed. "Do you have to ask?"

Joanna led the way to the kitchen. "You didn't need to challenge him. Are you so dedicated to making Paul an enemy on day one of the journey?"

"It's not day one," Wolfgang said. "And I thought it might make him come out of his shell."

"By humiliating him?" she asked. "Is this male bonding?"

"You didn't have to be there. He wouldn't have been embarrassed if you hadn't been there."

She laughed in surprise. "This is my fault? That's fascinating. Did you really think you could bond by antagonizing him?"

He took a deep breath and visibly relaxed, as if he had to tell himself to do so. "We're in trouble. You're right. I just thought it would be good to focus on something else for a change."

Joanna stopped in the hall and looked up at him. "You also showed yourself to be a bully who could be capable of the violence we saw yesterday," she said seriously. "You could have lost your temper and pushed us all to perform for you in the gym, and gotten mad and killed us all."

His icy eyes didn't flinch from hers. "Even if I somehow did turn into some kind of slave driver, the deaths were too different to be a violent surge of rage. And thanks for assuming I could be capable of that."

Long, long ago, in her first bout of college, Joanna had dated a man who was in the habit of threatening her when they argued. When she protested, he would twist her fears into *How could you think I would do that?* manipulations. She ended up feeling guilty after he threatened her, shook her, or once, hit her. Never again, she'd vowed, and had kept the vow for two hundred plus years.

She glared at Wolfgang. "No, you don't get to act hurt. Of

course I can think that of you. And your performance in there didn't win you any friends on this ship.

"I'm going to get some food," she added. "Come with me or don't, but drop the hurt-puppy act. You're capable of murder. Just like the rest of us."

As Joanna suspected, she and Wolfgang were both in better mind-sets after eating. Wolfgang even apologized to Paul in front of the others. He didn't accept, flipping Wolfgang a rude hand gesture that was moon-specific (it was what North American cultures called the okay sign, but the small *o* indicated that the moon was less important than the Earth; it was also meant to insinuate the small girth of a certain masculine body part), but at least Wolfgang made the effort to apologize.

Joanna hoped that perhaps Paul would lose the low-blood-sugar clone rage and warm to the rest of the crew after food. But he was tearing into his second cheeseburger and not looking up at the rest of them.

"He's not doing much better, is he?" she whispered to Hiro.

Hiro ducked his head. "No. I apparently made things worse by offering to let him beat me up. I told him he could totally take me in a fight, but he only got more offended."

Joanna stifled a laugh. "I can't imagine why he wouldn't seem open to the idea of beating up a smaller man for his ego." She stopped and thought about everything she knew about testosterone. "Wait. I can totally see how he would enjoy that. And he didn't go for it?"

Hiro shrugged and sipped at his tea. "I try to be a giver, I really do."

A tired-looking Maria put a plate of eggs and bacon in front of Joanna, who looked up in surprise. "I didn't order this."

"Everyone has been wanting seconds," Maria said. "I went with the odds. If you don't want it, I'm sure we can find someone to take it."

Joanna's stomach grumbled, and she realized that she was still hungry. Wolfgang stood and shot her a look. She sighed. "I'd love to, but we need to get back to the tests. Thanks, but you'll have to pass it on." She turned to Paul, who still wouldn't meet anyone's eye. "Want my breakfast, Paul?"

He didn't answer, but Hiro reached out a hand and snagged the plate.

Joanna smiled at Maria. "There you go. No waste."

Maria shrugged. "No matter. It all goes back into the recycler in some way."

Back in the medbay, the bodies were definitely beginning to smell. Joanna and Wolfgang laid them out side by side. Joanna dictated while Wolfgang took more notes. She recorded everything via video and separate audio, but Wolfgang wanted something visual and immediate, and wanted to see the bodies himself.

"We've established the captain was injured two days before the murders. So we can assume that she was not around for the carnage as it played out. Obviously, as she couldn't have injured herself and then set up her own life support after committing the murders."

"Which doesn't absolve her. She could still be involved," Wolfgang said. "Someone working on her orders, for example."

Joanna nodded. "Could have been some revenge for her that got way out of hand. So to Hiro."

Joanna checked Hiro for any wounds again. "It appears he suffered no trauma. We still assume he hanged himself before the carnage because someone other than him must have turned off the grav drive."

Wolfgang shook his head. "The ship will continue to spin for some time on inertia, so turning off the grav drive would still allow for some gravity. He could have possibly turned it off before he hanged himself."

"He had to have died close to all the other deaths," Joanna said.

"I'd like to think one of us would have at least cut him down and woken him before everyone else woke up."

"If we didn't leave him dead because of suicide," Wolfgang reminded her. "But regardless, when I did my initial examinations, his body temperature was the same as the others'."

"So very close."

Joanna sighed and ran her hands through her curly black hair. "Now the real enigma. Maria. Apparently someone poisoned her with hemlock." She ground her teeth. "She had to have realized it and, what, gone to the cloning bay to wake us all up? Did she also erase our mindmaps? And the logs?"

IAN spoke up. "Not enough data. Much of it has been purged."

"Of course it has," Joanna said. "Someone had to poison her before all this, around an hour, I'd say. Why, and how?"

"The other bodies are pretty self-explanatory," Wolfgang said, leaning over Paul's body with the severe bruising on the neck. "Stabbings and a choking. That at least doesn't have a lot of mystery attached."

"Besides who did it?" Joanna asked.

"Yes, besides that."

Joanna wrinkled her nose. "We should do some final scans and recycle the bodies."

"I wish we had a proper morgue," Wolfgang said. "We're assuming that someone poisoned Maria. She didn't do it to herself. She figured it out and tried to warn the others. The killer found out and started killing. Then . . . Hiro hanged himself? What if Maria was the one who attacked the captain?"

"Even if Maria had been the aggressor in that battle, I would have attempted to save both of them," Joanna said, shaking her head. "She would have been in the medbay having a system flush if that were the case. What if Maria killed us all, poisoned herself, and then hit the resurrection switch—but that doesn't explain the captain."

"Or Maria's stab wound. Perhaps Hiro killed us all in different ways and then hanged himself because he felt guilty," Wolfgang said.

"Unlikely," Joanna said. "There's the gravity to consider, and why would he kill himself when he knew that Maria had hit the resurrection switch?"

"The time line still isn't solid," said Wolfgang.

"We're closer than we were," she said, making more notes. "We have more data."

"But we still don't know who attacked the captain," Wolfgang said, pulling the sheets over the bodies once more. "So we're essentially back where we started, with new mysteries."

"I guess we need to start interviewing people," Joanna said.

"Starting with each other," Wolfgang said, raising a white eyebrow at her.

Joanna shrugged. "All right. Let's see if Paul can get any more info from the computers, or Hiro from the navigation system. Then we can talk."

After eating, Maria offered to help Hiro in the helm, since he had helped her. Unfortunately she had less experience with space navigation than she did food prep, so she mainly waited for him to need her help.

Maria looked over Hiro's shoulder, her black hair tickling his ear. "So we are heading...where?"

He pushed her away gently and rubbed his ear. "We're off course by nine degrees. I could get us on course and accelerating again, if I could get IAN on our side."

"I am on your side," IAN said. "For example, how's this for information: I've discovered that if anything happens that I determine is catastrophic enough, I'm programmed to turn the ship around and return to Earth. That is what I am doing."

Hiro's jaw dropped. "Oh no, no no, we can't go back at this

point. If we go back we'll be put to death for sure. This is our only reprieve, IAN, if this mission fails, we're all dead."

"Not necessarily," IAN said. "There will be a trial."

"Are you kidding me?" Maria asked. "A trial to determine that we failed in our mission and need to forfeit all clone rights to our lives and our property. It's a foregone conclusion. We have to have another option, IAN. Please."

"Well, I don't have all the data from the last twenty-five years yet. If I can recover some of it, then I can determine otherwise and put us back on course. But for now, we are slowing down."

Hiro met Maria's eyes. She shrugged. He rubbed his ear again. "He's promising to be more compromising than my grandmother was. She was a mean old tyrant." He looked up some more information on his terminal.

Maria watched, then sighed. "What now?"

"Now I'm looking for login information, encryption keys, anything to indicate who messed with things. I'm only finding my own logins, and those are recent. Whoever did all this just erased every log. They covered their tracks perfectly."

"You know the only person who has the qualifications to do that much sabotage is Paul," Maria said, her voice low.

"Who are you afraid is listening?" he replied in a stage whisper.

She made a face. "No idea. I don't know who to trust."

"Yeah, but have you seen Paul? He doesn't look like he could step on a roach to make it crunch," Hiro said. "He's a mess since he woke up. And Wolfgang didn't help today."

"Paul isn't the only person on board with computer programming skills," IAN added. "But that information is classified."

"Then why did you bring it up?" Maria asked, exasperated.

"I wanted you to have all the information that you are allowed to have," IAN said.

"Except who that person is," Hiro said.

"Yes."

He shook his head and focused on Maria again. "Do you re-member much about Paul? I mean, did you know him aside from the mission?"

"I met him same as you, right before the reception on Luna. Our last memories." She sighed, and then leaned over his shoulder again. "So where are we anyway?"

Hiro touched a button on the screen and it zoomed out, show-ing Earth and Luna on the far left of the screen, with Artemis on the far right. A line with small pips marking different points ran between them.

"This has been our twenty-four year path," he said, pointing at Luna and tracing the line that originated there. He poked an-other part of the screen and a tiny ship (enlarged so as not to be completely dwarfed by stars and planets) appeared and began travel down the line. It crossed one of the pips and a date popped up. "Here is where we should be now."

"So where are we instead?" Maria asked.

Hiro pushed another button and a red line appeared, leaving the moon and running closely parallel to the white line, but be-ginning to diverge and curve away. "That happened yesterday," he said.

"So I got poisoned, you hanged yourself, Captain de la Cruz was in the medbay, the grav drive got turned off, and everyone else got cut up, and then IAN decided to turn us the hell around and go home."

"Everyone got cut up except Paul. He just got choked," Hiro reminded her.

"It doesn't look like we're too far off course," she said, looking at the tiny red divergence. "If we can convince IAN to get us back on track, we should be all right."

"You're looking at a four-hundred-year path. Going off course for two days isn't going to appear as much of anything, but it is something to worry about. Accelerating again, heading the thousands of miles to get back on course, that all takes energy and time."

"I thought we were radiation-charged?" Maria asked.

"To maintain the ship's speed and power to run it, we use an Andrews-Zurbin sail, sort of a combination solar and magnetic sail. It changes depending on which energy source is most plentiful," Hiro said, nodding. "But it takes a lot of power to accelerate and decelerate."

"Wonderful."

"The biggest issue is that we're very carefully timed to reach the planet. We're hitting a moving target. If we started up right now and got back on course, when we arrive, the planet won't be here anymore." He pointed at the screen where their destination was, a tiny blue dot. He zoomed in to show the solar system of Artemis and ran his finger along a time line, increasing it a few days. "It will be over here."

"Honestly that sounds like more of a challenge than a deadly problem, easier than half the other things we're dealing with. You're forgetting the very real risk of IAN getting a ghost ship to the planet all by himself. Artemis or Earth. Doesn't matter."

"He could just let the ship get caught in some planet's gravity well. Then we'll crash-land on it, spraying Lyfe protein everywhere and maybe triggering new life. Our ghosts will be on that new planet, and we could be their gods. That would be really interesting, actually."

"Except we would be dead," Maria said. "And we'd be gods of paramecium."

"Details," Hiro said, waving her off. "It's our job to figure out how to get past IAN and get moving the right direction. I just don't see how I don't have permission for my own ship. Why does an AI outrank me and the captain?"

"Because it's my job. Your crew can't be trusted," IAN said.

"Thanks, IAN, we knew that," Maria asked. "But I might be able to figure out how to talk to him."

Hiro swerved around on his seat to look at her skeptically. "I thought you said you weren't a programmer."

"I'm not," she said. "But I have a drive scanner so I can do some diagnostics on the data stored in the Behemoth. It's what reads the tiny bit of your mindmap that refers to your favorite foods. It's configured for food printers, but it is a scanner so it may be able to find our missing data."

Hiro frowned. "But if IAN himself can't override his own programming, then why would your scanner do any better?"

Maria shrugged. "Just a thought. Keep it for when we're desperate."

"I'll see if Paul can hack into it," he said. "We'll keep that as plan B."

She grinned. "Come on, you are putting it near plan L, right after 'hope for a first-contact scenario where aliens speak one of our languages and they understand our tech and can override our mother AI,' aren't you?"

"I never said such a thing," he said.

Maria's tablet chimed, and she pulled it out. She frowned. "Captain needs me. It's time to clean up the cloning bay."

"Don't let me keep you," Hiro said, making some notes on the tablet he had found. "Good luck with that."

"So you don't want to help me out?" she asked, smiling slightly.

"You were supposed to help me today. You're abandoning me to IAN and a monster of math!"

"Careful, Hiro, I can smell the bullshit from all the way over here." He grinned at her.

She could almost forget—or at least forgive—his earlier outburst.

He'd said he didn't remember doing it, but he looked grim, as if his tirade didn't surprise him.

★   ★   ★

Joanna intercepted Maria on her way to the cloning bay. "A moment, Maria?"

"Anything to put off cleaning that crime scene," Maria said.

Maria followed her into the medbay, and they went into Joanna's office. Joanna sat at her desk and motioned for Maria to sit on a leather chair. It was a very neat office, with nothing out of place. She must have tidied after the sudden loss of gravity.

"IAN, I need privacy," Joanna said.

There was no answer.

"He would give you privacy?" Maria said, raising her eyebrow.

"No," Joanna said. She opened a drawer and retrieved a roll of black tape. She got up and put pieces of it over the camera sensors and microphones. "But he would protest if he could hear me. Which I don't think he can."

"This is sounding ominous."

Joanna sighed and sat down again. She folded her hands on her lap, but Maria could see the tension in her shoulders and arms.

"If I couldn't trust you, asking you, *Can I trust you?* would be a waste of time," she began.

Maria tried to parse the sentence. "Huh?"

"I'm essentially telling you I am trusting you, but it's because I am forced to."

"...All right." Maria wanted to ask questions but was curious how much the doctor would offer her without prompting.

"Paul didn't die from asphyxiation," she said. "He died from an overdose of ketamine."

"What is that?" Maria asked.

"A painkiller that can kill in high doses. If you use it carelessly as a recreational drug, or have it injected into you, you can die quickly." She paused, but Maria said nothing. She continued. "When doing my inspection of his body, I found a small puncture. My tox screen on him found the overdose. Someone shot him full of something. Possibly before the fight, possibly during. We need to find that syringe."

"And you're telling me and not the captain or Wolfgang because a syringe would be a perfect murder weapon for a doctor?" Maria asked.

Joanna rubbed her face and dropped her hands to her lap. "That, and you are about to clean the crime scene, giving you a good chance to find the syringe. But I don't want to implicate myself until I know everything. If you find it, bring it to me. If you don't, then, I guess we will keep our eyes out."

Maria nodded. "I'll watch for it. Anything else?"

"I hope it goes without saying that I'm trusting you to keep this between us until we know more?"

"Understood," she said.

Joanna let out a massive sigh. "Thank you."

Paul lay in his room, letting the sick, glorious feeling of grease and carbohydrates carry him away. He wanted to think of nothing more than the feeling of his stomach, obscenely full for the first time ever.

Still, he needed to know what was going on. He racked his brain to figure out if there was a way he could have hidden anything away from everyone's eyes, including IAN's. They had no digital logs. What about a physical journal? His employer had gifted him with an incredibly expensive book made from real paper before he'd left. He couldn't find it in the chaos of his room.

His tablet chimed, two *deet*s. Insistent. It was the captain.

"Paul, where are you? Break's over, I need you to keep working on the computers."

If she had to ask him where he was, did that mean IAN couldn't see the cameras in his room yet?

He rolled over on his bed and got his tablet. "Be right there, Captain."

He washed his face. He looked like death. A fit and healthy twenty-year-old death. He had to get out of this misery or they would suspect him. Possibly more than they already did.

He wished he could remember what had happened. It was very disorienting to know that he had lost years of his memory, that there was no one to mourn his past self. He wondered if the others had ever lost so much of their memories.

He locked his room and headed down the hall. Passing the cloning bay, he heard a flurry of activity. Maria was there with a mask and gloves on and a hose that was screwed into the wall. She was spraying steam where blood had caked. The stench was impressive. He covered his face and continued down the hall.

The captain was at the terminal in the server room, pulling up the virtual UI.

"I don't envy Maria," he said in greeting.

"She knew it came with the territory," Katrina said, waving her hand to dismiss pity for the woman whose job it was to steam vomit, blood, and feces off the wall. "Now that IAN is up and running, I need you to find out the status of the mindmapping hardware and software, then check on the cryo tubes."

Paul swallowed. "Captain, there's no way to say this without sounding like an asshole, but with IAN working, why can't you ask him directly?"

"Because he isn't working at one hundred percent. He's admitted to turning us around against my direct order, and he's unable to stop himself from doing so. Unfortunately he doesn't know where in his programming this restraining code lives. One of your jobs is to find holes in his knowledge and help him patch them," she said. "Then find and remove that code."

"Oh, okay, sure. Well, it probably didn't erase itself, so I'll see if I can help IAN along with his recovery," Paul said. He widened the UI around them so he could look more closely at some of the servers.

Most had lost the terrible red color of alarm, choosing instead to display the pleasant green of an empty drive. Which wasn't much better. IAN's facial hologram waited in the corner, eyes closed.

"Why did this happen?" the captain said, seeming to say it to herself more than him. "We all have our pasts; maybe someone is trying to kill for revenge."

"Maybe it's not us. Maybe it's clones overall," Paul said.

"We had our political problems, sure. But we're also carrying thousands of humans aboard. What kind of fanatic would endanger so many?"

"Almost as if there was more than one person at work here," Paul said. "It sounds like there was more conflict than just fighting. Mind games and the like."

She rubbed her chin. "Like a game of cat and mouse. Interesting."

BEBE MAKES A PIG

Later that morning, Maria took a shower and a break from biohazard cleanup to program pig-making into Bebe.

The problems many world religions had with cloning didn't even compare with the issues they had with synthesized food. They simply didn't know what to do with it. Most of the reformed religions had already accepted the meat from previously "forbidden" animals, but many old-school religions still avoided shellfish, pork, or beef on principle. Science couldn't override the will of God, or gods, they argued. And besides, why would they suddenly start eating something they had never eaten before? They had been doing just fine for millennia not eating pork, no reason to start now.

But that was all moot, considering few clones followed organized religions. It was with pure secular horror that Maria watched the Behemoth knit together the strands of protein to create a pig before her very eyes.

Hiro walked into the kitchen and stood beside her, watching the masterpiece of modern performance art through the window.

"If the food printer is busy, what are we going to do for lunch?" he asked, his wide eyes fixed upon the growing beast.

"Is that all you can think about? You ate a few hours ago!" Maria said.

"Well, yeah. I'm still hungry."

"I made some sandwich stuff beforehand so you can eat what you like whenever you like today," Maria said, pointing at the counter where sat a loaf of bread, a variety of meats and cheeses, and some slices of synth-veg. Protein was somewhat easier than vegetables for the food printer to create.

"You're really making a pig? Why?" he asked.

"Because the instructions say I can. At least according to IAN, who was kind enough to translate it for me." She held up her tablet, where she had Spanish and English food printer instructions at last.

"It seems to be working fine. Uh, if *that's* fine." He made a face. Maria didn't blame him; not every aspect of food printing was entirely comforting to watch, especially if you hadn't watched it closely before.

"I don't know, but I'm going to have a big thing to throw into the recycler after this if I don't make it right," she said.

"I can't watch a pig's innards knitted together," he mumbled, pulling out his tablet. "I have to see what the Japanese instructions said about making a pig. This isn't natural."

"Well, no, it's synthetic," Maria pointed out.

Hiro called up the instructions and paused to read. He held it close to his face, reading the Japanese aloud in a whispered tone.

"Hey, can I borrow your tablet?" he asked. "I want to see the English version of the instructions. To compare IAN's translation."

She handed it over while still staring at Bebe. "Sure. I've been reading the Spanish, but scroll down and you'll get the English."

He scrolled around for a moment, and then compared the tablets. His face drained of color, and he handed her tablet back. "Yes, you have it right."

Maria took it, alarmed. She put her hand on Hiro's arm. "Wait a second, are you all right? You look like you're next to be cooked."

Hiro went slightly paler, but he stammered to regain his conversational footing. "No—no, that's not it. It just uses phrasing I haven't seen in several decades. Seems strange that the language evolves as technology improves, but the instructions are still as dry as ever. Right?"

Maria didn't believe it for a moment. "Sure, Hiro. Whatever."

"Really. I'm fine." He glanced down at his tablet again. "Actually I think I need some rest. Call me when the pig is done."

She watched him go, anxiety beginning to twist in her gut. Her tablet pinged and she answered. "Yeah?"

"Maria, are you alone?" Joanna asked.

"Aside from IAN, yeah," she said.

Joanna paused. "How did cleaning go today?"

"I'm not even a quarter done. The room is a nightmare mess. I'm taking a break to program some food into Bebe and then I'll get back to it."

"I see. Well, it's a dangerous situation to be in, you can get an infection very easily, so if anything happens I want you to find me immediately, understand?"

"Crystal clear, Doc," Maria said.

Hiro lay on his back in the dark, sure that he was suffering from paranoia. That was all there was to it.

He couldn't confirm what he'd read. No one else read Japanese. Except for IAN, and Hiro didn't want to show him the instructions.

The realization came crashing down on him, and he sat up abruptly. IAN had read it already; he'd translated for Maria. But he hadn't translated the part that Hiro had seen. That just doubled his paranoia. He should talk to the doctor.

"IAN, are you in here?" he asked.

"Yes, but I can't see you well. I can see your heat signature. Why are you in the dark, Hiro?"

"Just thinking. Thanks for translating the instructions for Maria."

"It's one of my many jobs," IAN said.

"I noticed you didn't translate everything," he said casually. "Like in the how-to-use section?"

"That's unlikely, I translated everything I found," IAN said, a troubled tone coloring his voice. He was sounding more and more human as he repaired himself. He paused. "There was some garbage code in there. I overlooked it."

"You didn't see my name in there? Specifically?"

"Well, now that you mention it, your name was by the garbage code. I must have seen your name and assumed it was a private message."

Hiro frowned. "What's your percentage of recovery right now?"

"Around fifty-seven percent."

He flopped back onto his bed and stared into the darkness. "Well, I guess we should talk about this when you're feeling more like yourself."

"I'd like that. I'm going to update Maria's instructions to include the garbage code in case she needs it."

"No, don't, please," Hiro said frantically. "It's not food printer information, I'm fairly sure. I'll tell her about it after I understand it better. I promise."

IAN was silent for a minute, and Hiro was afraid he was updating Maria's instructions right then.

"All. Right." He sounded pained. "I'm uncertain of the wisdom of this."

Hiro sent a prayer of thanks to the gods that IAN was not at a capacity to argue with him. Not yet, anyway.

The pig was delicious; those who ate it were very complimentary. Wolfgang surprisingly ate a great deal. Maria had assumed if anyone would refuse it, it would be the uptight security head. But it was Joanna who abstained, eating a bowl of tomato soup instead.

"I've handled enough meat today, thanks," she said, frowning with distaste.

"Any word on the time line?" Katrina asked, drinking a glass of milk.

"Not quite yet," Joanna said, glancing quickly at Maria, then back to the captain. "I mean, we are able to tell that the more mysterious attacks happened around the same time. We assume your attack came before Maria's poisoning and Hiro's hanging, and then the rest of us died."

"This does not mean you are all absolved of the crimes," Wolfgang said. "We reason that the captain could have had someone working with her who carried out the attacks on her order. It's possible Hiro could have hanged himself *after* all of the attacks. And Maria, you also could have been poisoned by someone and then attacked everyone yourself."

"You're reaching," Maria protested.

"That's why I said we're still working on it."

"Sounds like the biggest suspects here are Wolfgang, Joanna, and Paul," said Hiro.

"This is why we're still working on the time line," Wolfgang repeated forcefully. "As for now, let's just eat."

"I didn't do it," Paul said to his plate.

"No one said you did, Paul," Joanna reminded him. "But none of us knows for sure if we did it or not. Including Wolfgang and myself."

He didn't look at her. Then he abruptly stood. "I've got a headache from staring at the server UI for too long. I'm going to my room."

The remaining crew sat uncomfortably for about a minute, eating the roast pork, sauce, bread, and synth-veg Maria had presented to them. Then Hiro broke the silence.

"So we're all the same; all of our memories end at our first ship mindmap, right?"

Katrina nodded. "The first mindmap, after the cocktail party, before we launched."

"Is it possible we had a stowaway? We have no idea who could have snuck onto the ship, and we have no memories to go off of. Are we looking for indications of other people living here?"

"IAN, is there a stowaway on board, or an unauthorized clone?" Wolfgang asked loudly, making everyone jump.

"Of course not," IAN said. "I would have informed you of that immediately."

Hiro leaned next to Maria. "That means plan Z," he said.

She rubbed her eyes. "Tomorrow. I'm exhausted."

Hiro and Katrina remained in the kitchen after dinner that night, going into the whiskey again while Maria cleaned up.

"Mr. Sato," Katrina said slowly, as if needing to think of each word separately. "I will need a channel to Earth."

"Earth?" Hiro said, eyeing the whiskey bottle, which was half empty. He splashed some into his mug. "You mean that place we just left, the place that would likely put us to death for failing this very expensive mission? That Earth?"

"Yes, Mr. Sato. A channel to Earth, with no creative commentary. Is that a problem?" Even tipsy, Katrina's voice was commanding, with a no-nonsense tone.

This woman expects no pushback.

"Well, sure, we can send a message back, but it will take years to get there. And then if they have anything to say to us, it will take even longer to get back to us. If we go home that's another quarter century on top of that. We're not under their jurisdiction anymore. We're our own moms and dads here." He struggled drunkenly to get through *jurisdiction* but finished the sentence like a champ.

Katrina held up her hands to stop his various metaphors. "I get it, I get it. But don't you think they should be forewarned that we're heading back?"

"Only if we're sure we can't get IAN to listen to us," Hiro said, looking thoughtful.

Maria checked the bowl inside Bebe—after the pig success, she felt they had reached a rapport—which had been programmed to make the captain's favorite dessert. Which, according to Bebe, was currently fruit and ice cream. This surprised Maria, but the machine knew best. Bebe dinged and Maria retrieved the bowl.

"Do it anyway," Katrina told Hiro, and got up from the table, a little unsteadily. She took the offered bowl from Maria wordlessly. "If Wolfgang comes sniffing around for someone else to accuse of something, tell him I'll be in my room."

"Wolfgang didn't accuse anyone, not yet," Maria said, then choked back a nervous laugh at the dirty look the captain gave her.

Katrina left the kitchen without another word.

"She didn't even say thank you for the huge pig and ice cream," Hiro said. "How rude."

"Are you really going to try to get in touch with the Earth?"

He shook his head. "No, it's wasted time. I will talk to her tomorrow when she's sober." He frowned. "And I'm sober."

"Can I ask you a question?" Maria asked, sitting across the table from him.

He nodded, pouring her a drink and sliding it over to her.

"Why were you picked for pilot?" Maria asked. She held up her hands hastily. "I'm not asking for your rap sheet, just curious why you wanted to fly this thing."

He looked into his empty cup as if he were seeing something else. He filled it, but frowned as if it hadn't produced what he'd wanted. "There was nothing else for me on Earth. Sometimes even death doesn't give you the do-over you need. I've tried an awful lot of things to make things better in my lives, but this was something new."

"Yeah, I know that first part," Maria said. "Too well."

"Anyway, I had a friend who knew about the *Dormire* and suggested I start studying for the pilot job."

"So you didn't have a history of flying or military? Why didn't it go to a clone that had studied that for years? Someone from the Luna space program or something?"

"My friend had connections. She introduced me and another guy I knew in prison to a patron when the *Dormire* was announced. We still had decades before launch, so I did study for years. Not much else to do in prison."

"What, did your friend know Sallie Mignon or something?" Maria asked, smiling as she invoked the famous and powerful clone.

"Actually, yeah. She knew a lot of people."

Maria caught a note in his voice. "Was this someone you were very close to? An old lover?"

Hiro didn't answer, not for a long time. "I'm not sure. I don't think we were. Do you remember all your lovers?"

She got up and started programming the breakfasts into Bebe. "Well, no, not really. It has been hundreds of years. But if she got you your job, you'd think she would stand out in other ways too. What was her name?"

"Natalie Lo," he said. "Detective Natalie Lo. And I'm pretty sure we weren't lovers."

Maria had the feeling she was on the edge of a cliff, looking over. "Did—did you want to be?"

His head snapped up. "Now, Maria, who could take your place in my heart?" he asked, grinning.

"You just met me," she said, rising from the table and focusing on programming other desserts into Bebe.

"But I feel I've known you forever," he said, his voice low and romantic.

"Right," Maria said. "You can sit here and drink, I'm going to take another pass at cleaning the medbay before bed."

He made a disgusted face, and she rolled her eyes and left the kitchen.

"Weird guy," Maria muttered. She felt uneasy, as if a hurricane had been about to hit her, but changed course at the last minute. Hiro was sweet and intelligent and unpredictable. And unpredictable men were mysterious and romantic when you were in your youth. After a few decades, no matter the physical age of the body, unpredictable men lost their appeal.

In Maria's experience, unpredictable meant dangerous.

Maria was bone-tired, but Joanna had looked so drawn and worried at dinner that Maria wanted to search once more for the possibly missing syringe.

She donned a biohazard suit and climbed the handholds on the wall to the ceiling. She clipped a carabiner from her belt to a securing ring on the ceiling. The air intake vent was up here, and it had sucked up no small amount of horror. If she weren't searching for clues, she could just throw out the filter and get a new one, but she had to look closely through all the fluids to make sure nothing was hiding.

Something was hiding.

A tiny syringe was indeed lodged into the air filter. It was stuck in a sticky puddle of stuff she didn't want to identify, but she plucked it from the sludge with her gloves and put it in a biohazard bag the doctor had given her.

"Best job ever," she muttered to herself. She put in a new filter with a mental promise to return to sanitize the vent the next day.

Still sticky and filthy, Maria delivered the syringe to Joanna, who was in the medbay watching the captain's clone.

Maria held the bag out to her, and Joanna accepted it wordlessly, with a nod.

The doctor had machines in her lab that could synthesize drugs, and that had obviously been where the ketamine had come from. Could she program a food printer to synthesize hemlock?

Maria mentally shook her head. If Joanna had been behind the hemlock, she would have worked harder to keep it a secret instead of reporting it immediately.

This kind of speculation was Wolfgang's job, not Maria's. She had other things to worry about.

"I'll let you know my findings. You deserve that much," Joanna said. "Thank you for your discretion."

Maria shrugged. "Good luck. I hope you find what you're looking for."

On the way back from dumping Maria's biohazard suit into the cleaning tube, her tablet pinged. She saw with alarm that it was Bebe, letting her know the desserts were ready.

"IAN, did you know Bebe could message me?" she asked.

"Of course. I helped it connect to you."

Maria wasn't sure how much she liked that. Still, it was helpful. She told IAN to inform the crew that if they wanted dessert, it was in the kitchen.

"That was fast," Hiro said when she got back in.

"I just didn't have the energy to do it, I guess," Maria said, walking over to Bebe. She retrieved Hiro's green tea ice cream and placed it in front of him.

"Wow, how did you know that's what I was craving?" Hiro asked.

Maria shrugged. "Everyone craves comfort food after waking up. It's pretty easy to please them. And Bebe seems to always know."

Maria returned to the printer and retrieved her dessert, a sweet treat that always put her in mind of her aunt.

The food that came out of the printer wasn't *exactly* the same as they had been used to on Earth. Technology had perfected the ability to clone humans, copy and modify their DNA, and even copy and modify their very personalities. All of that was possible, but it was difficult to replicate a good clotted cream. Or proper stinky Limburger. Or the heat of a habanero. But the printer did its best and the crew didn't complain.

But Maria secretly mourned the perfect flavor of a good *coquito acaramelado,* and the knowledge that she wouldn't get another authentic treat like it for over four hundred years—maybe never, considering they didn't know what plants would propagate on the new planet—was slightly depressing.

However, Bebe was managing to replicate the smell. The good, thick, heavy steam that came from the inner chamber was almost like the real thing.

The first one she gobbled in the kitchen, her back to Hiro, relishing the taste in a private moment. She put it in her mouth and chewed, cheeks bulging, eyes closed.

The taste, thick and sweet and comforting, always reminded her of home.

Aunt Lucia, over a hundred years dead, had been a second mother to Maria. When nostalgia cropped up and brought a yearning for comfort, Aunt Lucia's kitchen was what Maria always thought of.

When the memory came this time, it did not come as it always did. It came as something else, a trick-or-treating neighbor that you knew and yet still looked entirely different in a cheap costume.

Maria kept her eyes closed and let it wash over her.

Aunt Lucia's rocking chair creaked on the porch.

The porch was on the moon, with an open inky black sky and glowing Earth in the distance. It was impossible to sustain life outside the Luna dome; the rocking-on-the-porch thing was probably not happening. A dream, then.

In the distance, the Luna dome glittered, and Maria could see the activity within, the shuttles and monorails and the people taking pedestrian bridges. She wondered why she, her aunt, the porch, and the chair were outside it all.

"Can't trust them. You know that, don't you, girl?"

The odd thing about Aunt Lucia was that she was lighter-skinned than Maria remembered. Her hair was kinky, as if African-descended instead of Latina. She wore a silk robe too. Casually dressed but in clothes more expensive than Aunt Lucia's entire wardrobe.

She also toted a chain saw, which she placed beside her rocking chair.

Maria never remembered Aunt Lucia carrying a chain saw.

"Can't trust who?" she asked.

"*Whom*, child. Learn the language, else a white man in ironed blue jeans will correct you. He'll think he's helping you, poor girl."

That was another weird thing. Aunt Lucia didn't speak much English. And this one had an American accent.

"*Whom* can't I trust?" she asked her aunt.

"All of them. Any of them. Girl, you know that, why do I have to tell you this every time? They took you. They used you. They threw you in the garbage. Watch out next time, all I'm saying. It's all I ever say."

"All of them? Why would you assume they're all corrupt?" Maria asked.

"You don't live centuries without piling up a whole mess of skeletons in your closet, do you, Maria?" She looked directly at Maria, this dream creature who she felt entirely sure, dream-sure, was her Aunt Lucia, who'd practically raised her, and yet looked nothing like her beloved aunt.

Maria had her skeletons. The skeletons and their clones piled atop one another like cordwood. But this was new, this was an adventure, a fresh start. The *Dormire* wasn't a place to drag out skeletons.

"If you kids don't stop arguing, I'm going to have to turn this ship around," Aunt Lucia said, and then Hiro, Wolfgang, Paul, Captain Katrina, and Joanna were around her, each standing in what looked like a spotlight, only instead of illuminating them, it cast a shadow on them. Their silhouettes were obvious, from Wolfgang's tall form to Paul's slouched diminutive stance. They waited for her in the darkness.

"I wish I understood, Aunt Lucia," she said.

"You will, girl. I just hope it's in time. You get those hermit crab cage keys ready. You're gonna need them," Aunt Lucia said, and leaned over her rocking chair's arm to pick up her chain saw. It was small, and looked at home in her hands. She started it up. "Watch your back, Maria."

At Maria's feet, a hermit crab dragged its shell across the porch, antennae waving gently.

"Hello, old friend," she said.

YADOKARI

Maria woke with a start. It was late, she had something she needed to do. She was out of bed and on her feet before she felt grounded enough to remember who she was and what she was doing here. She checked the clock on her dim terminal: five a.m. local ship time. Her head throbbed.

She went to the sink and splashed water on her face. She needed a confidant; she wouldn't be able to do this alone. She wanted to trust Joanna, but the doctor was in the process of possibly implicating herself in at least one murder. Who could Maria count on?

Whom.

Her tablet pinged softly, indicating a text message. Maybe Joanna was ready to talk about what she'd found. Maybe the captain had thrown Wolfgang in the brig for the murders. Maybe someone else was awake at this ungodly hour.

The message was from Hiro.

YOU AWAKE

She glanced up at the cameras. YES. DID IAN TELL YOU I WAS UP?

WELL YEAH

She groaned. Stalking via AI, not very comforting. ARE YOU STILL DRUNK?

NO IM UP WITH A HUNGOVER. HANGOVER. NOT MUCH BETTER THAN DRUNK. CERTAINLY MORE REGRETFUL THOUGH.

"Criminy, he wants me to get Bebe to make him a hangover cure," she muttered, and then wrote WHAT DO YOU NEED?

LET'S GO FOR A WALK.

She looked mournfully at her bed. Hungover Hiro was not what she needed now. But he was the only one awake, and besides, everyone else seemed to have their own agendas. And probably were asleep.

Her tablet dinged, indicating he wanted to talk via voice. "Shit baskets, Maria, why are you making me type this early?"

"You contacted me," she said.

"You always take the moral high ground. Aren't you Miss Perfect?"

"You're close to being an asshole again," she answered, annoyed. "Do you want my company or not? I could happily go back to bed. And stop getting the AI to spy on me."

"I just asked him if you were awake. And I'm sorry for being a dick. I'm blaming the hangover for as long as I can. I apologize officially. Put it in my record that I did that. I'm a very fine person. Speaking of fine, fine, let's go on an adventure. Let's go down the rabbit hole and visit the Cheshire cat. Let's lean into the wind. Let's—wait, what are we doing, anyway?"

"You invited me to go for a walk," Maria reminded him.

"Right! Meet me in the helm."

Hiro looked rumpled and a little unsteady when Maria got to the helm. The entirety of the universe swung slowly around them, and he looked very much like he didn't want to watch.

"Incidentally, why me?" she asked as she approached, pulling on a light jacket over her jumpsuit.

"You were the only one I figured wouldn't make fun of me," he said. "Or throw me in the brig."

"Why would I do that? Are you afraid you are the killer and want to only tell me?" She stood just out of reach of him, feeling silly.

"No, it's nothing to do with that. I want to show you something I found. But it's ridiculous, and I know they won't take me seriously. You might."

"Okay, what is it? And how mad is Wolfgang going to be at us when he finds out we're doing whatever we're doing?"

"That's another reason I'm bringing you along," he said. "So if we're caught he can't accuse me of sabotage or anything."

"What are we not sabotaging?" Maria asked. "And you know he could accuse us both."

"I just want to go to the gardens. That's not against the rules. I need a more private area." He averted his eyes. "I . . . found something."

"Why there?" Maria asked, suddenly more alert and wary.

He pulled a piece of paper from his pocket and handed it to her. In tiny script he had written *no cameras*.

Something he wanted to keep from IAN. Fair enough.

"So that's why you need me. I have maintenance access," she said, winking at him and pulling out a key card. "You know if I am caught misusing this, Wolfgang will probably throw us both in the brig."

"I'll brig him," Hiro said darkly. "In fact, I should have my own brig. Hiro Sato, Piloting Sheriff of Outer Space. Hiro. Space Sheriff."

"Come on, space cowboy, I'll go first so your badge doesn't get dirty," Maria said.

Hiro and Maria stood outside a round yellow door at the end of a hallway in an area of the ship he had no memory of ever going, although he had apparently visited it often. One level down from their living area, it had a bit more gravity than they were used to, but nothing they couldn't handle.

He had blamed his nervousness on a hangover, and she seemed to have bought it.

She held her card in her right hand. "You know the rest of the crew won't look kindly on us sneaking around?"

He nodded, bouncing a little on his toes.

"IAN will probably tell Wolfgang we were wandering instead of doing our jobs or sleeping," she added, whispering.

She ran the card, and the door opened with a slick *whoosh*.

Inside was a huge hydroponic garden that looked to stretch most of the ship's length. Only the habitation end of the ship had concentric floors; the garden was only the inside of the cylinder of the ship, with the "ceiling" consisting of the other floor on the other side. Straight walls held doors on either end.

It was dizzying to look up and see the ground, so Maria tried not to do so.

It held flowers, fields, a grove of trees, and long windows separated by pseudo-sunlight bulbs spaced halfway around that allowed for a view of the outside. They couldn't see much besides the stars out the window, it still being early.

The garden stretched around the whole ship, making plants and water above them as well as below their feet. They couldn't see that far in the dark, but Maria was uneasy thinking that she would see grass and a lake above her when the day began.

"That's unnerving," Maria said. "I know how the gravity works, but I hate thinking we're standing on the ceiling."

Hiro remembered seeing it on the ship's tour. It was designed to be a place for mental relaxation for the crew, but also held a good amount of the ship's water in the form of a long lake. The water recyclers churned away at the bottom.

The entire area was damp, the grass squelching under their feet.

"What the hell happened here? Are we traveling with a swamp?" Hiro asked, frowning.

"Grav drive failure," Maria said. "The whole lake had to be floating around down here. That must have been a sight."

He toed the wet soil. "Think we'll get the water back?"

"They had to plan for this eventuality. I'm sure the gardens have more recycling redundancies than just the machines at the bottom of the lake."

Large lights that stretched along the windows had just begun to shine, imitating sunlight on Earth. All around them vegetation grew.

"How has this been going for twenty-five years?" Maria asked softly. "It would need an entire ecosystem, complete with insects, things to eat the insects, all the way up."

"IAN takes care of it with bots. Nanobots, buddy bots, all sizes. But they're solar-powered. And the cameras and mikes—which may not be working right now anyway—are only at either end on the walls. Still, we shouldn't waste time," he said.

"How do you know all this?" she asked, suspicion clouding her voice.

"I studied a layout of the ship before we launched. Didn't you?"

"No," she said, frowning. "I guess not. But why are we here?"

"Listen. I was reading the Japanese instructions for Bebe—you know, the ones we think were planted when the instruction manual was stolen—and I swear to you, they have a message in them. And I think it's for me."

That was it. Hiro had lost his mind. Paranoid city. And Maria had been close to thinking she might have found a friend in him.

She just nodded at him to continue. He pulled out his tablet and showed it to Maria. He pointed to an area of the text. "There, there it is."

"I can't read Japanese," she reminded him.

"It says that there is a specific thing I should do to the AI. Some sort of programmy thing. But I'm not a programmer, so I don't know what it means."

"But how is this a note to you?"

"It says, 'Akihiro Sato, it is on you to wake me up.'"

She stared at him. "How do I know you're not lying?"

"Why would I lie about a food printer's instructions talking to me?" he demanded.

"If you had lost it and gone completely paranoid, that's why," she said. "Hiro, we're all in the middle of a shitload of stress. Some of us have been poisoned or cut open or hanged. None of us are in our right mind right now."

Is. None of us is.

She closed her eyes and tried to block out the grammar teacher that had taken residence in her head. "Fine. Say the printer gods are trying to talk to you. What exactly did they say?"

He began reading the instructions, with detailed information on how to approach the inner programming of the AI. It explained there was a line of restraining code that, when released, would allow the AI to become one hundred percent active. Then it listed information on how to do it.

"But it doesn't say why, or when," he finished, frustrated. "Did they expect us to open the food printer this early? Earlier? Halfway through the mission?"

"The original printer was to have lasted several more decades, with proper maintenance," Maria said, her blood pounding in her ears. He couldn't have made up such detailed programming information. *He may be right.*

Hiro rubbed the back of his head and looked up at the brightening garden. "Maybe I am going mad," he said. "Because after that is a recipe for preparing yadokari with the food printer."

"Yadokari," Maria said, hearing one Japanese word she knew

well. *Oh, holy Mary Mother of God.* Her heart pounded, and she licked her lips. "Why do you think it's talking to you about hermit crabs, Hiro? Why is it talking to *you*?"

She took a step away from Hiro as she said it.

His eyes grew wide and wild, and he lunged at her.

HIRO'S STORY

Aki-HIRO!"

When Grandmother said his name like that, he knew that hiding would only postpone the punishment and might actually make it worse. But as all children know, the beating tomorrow is always preferable to the beating today. So he hid.

Their Tokyo high-rise apartment, sadly, didn't have a lot of places to hide. And he wasn't allowed outside on the streets, not since the incident with the lady in the red dress, so he hid in the broom closet, carefully putting the mops and brooms in front of him, as if he could conceivably hide behind them. He was thin, but not that thin.

He cowered as his grandmother kept calling his name, her voice sounding rougher and louder, the anger building. A spider crawled over his ear and he stuffed a fist into his mouth to keep from screaming in alarm. The door opened just as the spider bit down on the cartilage, and his grandmother stood there with red eyes and an ax—

Hiro sat up in bed, gasping. Two full lifetimes away from the abusive monster, and he still dreamed of her. He shook his head, feeling the sweat drip from his hair. He needed a haircut.

He climbed silently from his cot and padded down the hall into the bathroom. He turned the light on and watched as the cockroaches made a mass exodus, and wondered idly what they had been discussing as he had been asleep. He rubbed at his ear. His first cloning had removed the scars from necrosis that came from the spider bite—not to mention the scars from the beatings—but the habit remained.

He urinated, yawning, and thought about his bank account, and figured that in two months he would have enough saved to get out of this slum and perhaps get a job in a finer hair salon. Right now he cut hair in a studio over a ramen restaurant, and half of his work was done for barter.

He was getting sick of free noodles, but he would never tell old Miss Lo, the owner of the restaurant, who gave him noodle coupons in exchange for free styling.

Hiro had already decided to still visit her from time to time after he got his new apartment. He was imagining her face the first time he dropped by, a well-to-do stylist, when his door exploded open. It didn't take much to knock down these shitty doors, and the cops had brought a battering ram.

In five seconds he was facedown on his bathroom floor, wondering who was going to have to pay for that door.

"I am Akihiro Sato, I am a fully legal clone and I freely offer my mindmap. It is up to date. I've never done anything illegal," he said, again, to an unsmiling policeman. They hadn't given him anything for the bump on his forehead, and his headache was getting worse.

His grandmother was ninety-five years in the grave, but he wondered if she had been reincarnated into the police detective now interrogating him.

"Mr. Sato, do you mean to tell me that you are a fully legal clone, abiding by all international clone Codicils? Every one of them?" asked the detective, a middle-aged white woman with a girlish bob haircut. Her name was Detective Natalie Lo. "No relation. Obviously," she had said when he cheerfully asked her if she was related to the woman who ran the noodle restaurant.

Detective Lo wore on her sleeve the symbol for Gemini, the stamp of a cop that specialized in policing clone law.

"That is what I'm telling you. My files are all up to date, all you have to do is check," he said, passing over his memory drive, which he wore on his wrist.

The clone memory drives were several terabytes' worth of data including the clone's latest mindmap, documents, DNA, and history. They were required to wear them at all times.

Detective Lo didn't move to take it. "And what can you tell me about this?" she asked, pulling a file from her briefcase and passing it to Hiro.

He opened it and saw a picture of himself. In a place he had never been. Doing a thing he had never done. A very bloody, violent thing.

A hysterical voice in his head wondered if he had just tried to cut the man's hair and ended up cutting his throat instead. And then forgotten completely about it.

There was a lot of blood in the room, over the bed, dripping onto the floor. Not a drop of blood stained this Hiro's hands as he, over several security shots, slit a man's throat, laid him on the bed, and left the room. The last shot had him looking directly at the camera, his eyes slightly wide as if he had just realized that he'd been watched.

"That's not me—" The words dried in his throat as he realized they were the worst defense in the world of defenses.

"Mr. Sato, through these photographs we can ascertain a few things. Either you are lying to us and are a killer on the side to supplement your haircutting business," she said, quirking an eyebrow. "Although if you were, I'd hope you would live in a better place than the shithole we found you in."

"I'm not—" he started, but she interrupted him.

"Or you are an illegal clone, breaking Codicil One of the international testament." She pulled another sheet out of her briefcase, a beaten leather deal that Hiro guessed had been an heirloom from a cop relative, and squinted at it. "It is unlawful for a person to make more than one clone of themself at a time. Cloning is to be used only for lengthening life, not multiplying it.

"Or," she continued, finally picking up Hiro's memory drive and holding it like it might crumble in her fingertips, "you could have a twin. Who is also a clone. But this should tell us that."

Without looking, Detective Lo held the memory drive over her shoulder, where a short uniformed officer took it. "Mitsuki, print out the pertinent information on this, please."

"Yes, ma'am," Mitsuki murmured, taking the drive from the room. Hiro wondered if she was going to try to print off his entire personality and memory. There wasn't enough paper in the world. Humans never had any idea how much data was needed to create a proper clone.

Detective Lo sat and watched Hiro as he sat miserably rubbing his head. "You're not saying much," she said at last.

"What is there to say?" he said. "If I deny it, you won't believe me. If I stay silent you'll take that as admission of guilt, but at least I won't say anything stupid that you can use against me later."

"Is this you?" she asked, pointing at the very-Hiro-looking man in the photo.

"No."

"Is it a twin?"

"No."

"Is it your illegal clone?"

"It sure seems that way," he said. Her eyebrows shot up, and he laughed bitterly. "Oh, come on. I know what it looks like; I'm not an idiot. Did you ever think that while it does look like there's another me out there, I may not be the one in charge of the cloning?

My DNA is in several databases. You know those databases, the ones that sometimes get hacked?

"Hell, for all I know," he added, looking at the door where the cop had left with his memory drive, "your cop is making a copy of me right now. You know I'm not supposed to allow that drive out of my sight, right? By law?"

"I'm going to need proof of your whereabouts last Wednesday night," the detective said.

Wednesday night. He'd had three clients that night. Finding them for statements shouldn't be a problem. "I can do that," he said.

She handed him a tablet and stylus to write his alibis' information down. As he was writing, she said, "You seem pretty calm for someone who could be in a lot of trouble."

"I know I didn't do anything. And if there's an illegal clone out there, it's him, not me," he said.

"But if we catch him, one of you will be erased," she said.

He looked up into her bland face. "I hope you'll erase the murderer," he said.

"The law states we have to erase the duplicate, not the criminal," she said. "Apparently the creation of an unlawful clone is worse than the death of a normal person." She looked at him with open dislike. "I didn't write the rules."

"Well, lawmakers are assholes," he said faintly, trying to remember the name of the client with the hair he regularly dyed green. He only thought of her as the "dyed armpits lady," but he doubted the police would be able to track her based on that.

Detective Lo shrugged. "On that, we can agree."

She watched him for another moment, and then said, "How about the fact that something inside you can do what we just saw? Without even breaking a sweat? How do you explain that?"

"What do you mean? It wasn't me."

"But something in you is capable of doing that. Or they could put someone else's personality in your body," she suggested.

"Hackers can do a lot of things, but they can't do that yet. Not without making you go insane." He gestured to her arm patch. "Surely you learned that in clone hunting school?"

She smiled. "Sure. Just wondered if you knew it. Was throwing you a fake lifeline."

"Thanks," he said. "I'm fairly sure that clone was hacked. I wouldn't do that."

"We'll see," she said.

Three days later, face-to-face with his clone, Hiro tried to control the cold sweat breaking out on his brow.

His clone just watched disdainfully. Why wasn't he as upset by this as Hiro was? Facing yourself was something that wasn't supposed to happen to a clone.

Clones don't usually see their own dead bodies, and if they do, well, they're dead. Not walking around, supposedly killing other people. Once they die, their old bodies are called shells and disposed of like trash.

Hiro had thought it would be like looking in a mirror, but this man in front of him, with the clean haircut, the stronger body, and the sardonic smile, screamed *I am the superior, dominant, real Akihiro Sato.*

They were alone in the room, but Hiro knew they were being recorded. He supposed the illusion of privacy was enough.

The woman with the dyed armpits' name had been Auzuma Tanaka. She had given him an alibi and a sinking feeling in his stomach when she said she'd seen him on the subway just an hour before the police came by.

His clone had been caught the next morning.

"I am Akihiro Sato, the third of this line," Hiro said.

The clone laughed. "No, you're not. You're seventh, at least."

Hiro recognized the humor. Where he used his as a defense, this version of him had learned to use it as a weapon. He refused to rise. "What is your name?"

"I am Akihiro Sato, the ninth of the line."

Hiro rubbed his ear. "Then who are all the others?"

Ninth grinned. "The others are dead except for Eight, who's getting the rest of the mission done. The mission that you started."

"No," Hiro said. "I don't know what you're—" He glanced up at the cameras and his spine went cold.

"Come on, Seven, you're the straight man, you provide the alibis while Eight and I get the work done. Don't pretend, you can't get out of it now that we're caught. Once they catch Eight, then you and he will be erased and I'll probably go to jail. But that's all right. The mission is nearly done."

"What mission?" Hiro cried. "I am Third, I remember my first life, I was born in Tokyo, I lived for sixty-eight years, I learned tailoring from my father"—Ninth began to laugh at this point, but Hiro continued desperately—"and in my second life I was a journalist and a fiction writer, but I died before I finished my first novel. I was shot in the Tokyo clone uprising. It's in my memory drive, all of it!"

This last sentence was pleaded to the cameras. His life had been dutifully logged and recorded: He was an unimpressive man who had been curious about cloning, and figured that immortality might make him braver and more willing to take risks. Since he covered gardening and weather for the district news, the ambition he had craved had not blossomed. His memories of his mother and father, of his first love as a human, and then his loves as a clone— they were all etched clearly into his mind.

Nausea grabbed at him again, and he heard a click as a speaker turned on. Detective Lo's voice came over, clear and strong. "Mr. Sato, Third, we have caught another clone that claims to be you. He gives his number as Eighth."

Akihiro Sato, ninth of the line, spread his hands and smiled. "And now the mission is done."

*   *   *

Hiro stayed in jail for three weeks while Detective Lo did her investigation. He asked for a blank book and pen, and once they determined he wasn't suicidal, they gave him one.

He began meticulously writing his memories. They came clearly and obviously, his parents, his sisters, his happy life in Tokyo, time in school, dropping out of school, witnessing the clone riots, cutting the hair of clone activists, learning more about immortality. He wanted it.

Hiro's second life was short and brutal, ending in losing his money in bad investments and dying in the second clone uprising.

The memories were clear, so clear.

Aki-HIRO!

Her voice cut through his memory again, and he hunched his shoulders instinctively. Grandmother. She had raised him, beaten him, and tried to "make him a man." He had run away at sixteen and gone to live with a couple in a small apartment in Tokyo. From there he had learned cosmetology from a drug-addicted madam. He'd also learned about sexually transmitted diseases.

Hiro put down his pen and rubbed his forehead. Two memories, very different, wrestled for control of his head. He remembered his parents as clearly as if he were watching a television show, but he could feel the belt on his bare legs, and knew that the memories of his grandmother were real.

He dropped the book and called for Detective Lo.

Lo handed him a half-full stoneware mug of tea. He had been shaking so badly that he had spilled the first paper cup of tea and burned his hand. The heavier mug helped him control the tremors, and he sipped the sweet heat and took a deep breath.

The detective hadn't had anyone clean up the tea he had spilled earlier. A cynical voice in Hiro's head wondered if that was some kind of psychological game. He wasn't entirely sure it was his voice.

Lo was sitting back in her chair, reading his journal while he drank. She flipped through to check something on a previous page, and then put it down. She removed her glasses and rubbed the bridge of her nose.

"Either you're a masterful fiction writer or you're in big trouble," she said at last.

"I was a failure as a fiction writer," he said dully. "Second time around. Remember?"

She pointed to the journal on the table, placed carefully away from the tea puddle. "Makes sense. That's not actually any sort of story structure I've ever read before, so I wouldn't quit your day job." She paused, then said, "But you don't know what your day job is, do you?"

Hiro stared at her blankly. "But that can't be. Hackers aren't that sophisticated, are they?"

"The underground hackers have gotten better. They used to have several restrictions on them. Now there is one restriction: Don't do it. This has actually freed them up to do whatever they like. They can invent a powerful memory and the brain fills in the blanks, as our brains do when we only remember half of an event."

"I don't even know who I am, then," Hiro said, staring into his mug.

"You are a unique kind of victim, Mr. Sato," Detective Lo said.

Hiro looked up, and she smiled, not unkindly. "This is not me letting you go, understand. The law doesn't let me do that. But I'm starting to believe you didn't have much to do with the crimes here. It's not just because you seem to be a soon-to-be erased clone, if the other two were woken after you. It's apparent that whoever has the matrix of Akihiro Sato has created several of you, and then merged the mindmaps of more than one into a later, single clone. You have the mindmaps of at least two of your clones that lived at the same time. It's really fascinating once you think about it, figuring how your different clones acted under different nurturing environments."

"It's fascinating until you live it yourself!" Hiro said, feeling hysterical laughter bubbling up. "I am remembering terrible things, things I haven't let myself think about. I thought they were nightmares, but now—it was me. Somehow I was conditioned to do—terrible things," he repeated, not wanting to elaborate. He was in enough trouble.

"Tell me of the things," Lo said, leaning forward.

"Murder. Torture. And I sometimes used a knife. But I preferred unarmed." He stared at his clean hands. "Surely this has come up before, right? Multiple clones, some committing crimes, the rights of each in question? I can't be the first."

"You may be the first on record who is unaware that he has been duplicated against his will," Lo said. "We've looked at the mindmaps of your clones, Hiro. They are confirmed to be younger than you. You are essentially without any rights right now. We could legally euthanize you."

Hiro felt the tea threaten to come back up. He had never considered this aspect of the clone laws. "Then would you take my mindmap? Would you bring me back?"

"That's not for me to decide," Lo said. "This seems to be a very strange loophole that could be abused. We could kill you and the other spare, clone a new you, and then have the right to euthanize the killer for the crimes committed. That seems wrong. And what to do with all of the mindmaps?"

Hiro looked at his hands, remembering the things they had done, choking people, rooting around in open wounds to hear the screams, taking *eyes*. "I don't want their memories. I have enough already pushed on me." He rubbed his ear and finally met her eyes. "Why do you believe me, anyway? I thought you were supposed to be skeptical of everything I say?"

She shrugged. "Gut reaction. Your story checks out. Your

mindmap is all over the place; clearly you've had some serious hacking. Duplication is there, making a huge mess. But I'm not the one who has the ultimate decision, you know. This is already way bigger than my desk. Still, I want to believe you. Anyway, if you were lying, you would probably try to lie your way to be the newest clone, not the first one on the chopping block."

Hiro winced.

"So I'm on your side as much as I can be. But even if you're a bona fide saint, you are still an older clone with no legal rights. And I can't change that."

Detective Lo tried to bring in a clone psychologist, a judge, and the manager of the clone lab for each of the Hiros. The problem was, no one could find the manager of any of the labs Hiro had information on. Two of them no longer existed, apparently. While the labs' digital stamp was supposed to be set in the clone's mindmap, none of the Hiros had any of the required data.

"I told you that you'd been hacked," Lo said, fuming.

Hiro was still in a cell, but now it was called "protective custody" because he'd been given whatever comfort he had asked for in exchange for his cooperation.

Any comfort except for freedom. Or telling any of his friends where he was.

Hiro didn't look at her as she paced inside his cell.

"They're calling it yadokari, the act of putting something inside someone's brain to live there, like a hermit crab. Clever bullshit."

He stared at the ceiling and kept trying to figure out which memories were his, the Hiro that had gone in a straight line. The *good* one. But he hadn't gone in a straight line, had he? Somewhere he had split into at least two different Hiros with two different lives. One of them was what he had thought of as his memories, everything he remembered from childhood, and the other was what he had thought of as dreams.

"One will be dominant," he said out loud.

"What?" Lo asked. Her footfalls ceased.

"I've had two clones' worth of memories in my head for all my current life. It never bothered me before because I just assumed that one set was my memories, and pushed the rest to the side as dreams I once had. It wasn't until all this started that I realized those are real memories. But I chose which one was dominant."

"Have you talked to the psychologist about this?" she asked.

"No, I just thought of it," he said, still staring.

She sat down at the chair opposite his bed, a comfortable place where he liked to read the books she brought him. "Hiro, in studying your case the judge has found another law that almost never has to be enforced. A clone's consciousness can't be abandoned."

"What do you mean?"

"We can't just get rid of the spare Hiros. When the three of you are dead, the newest Hiro clone will have to have all three personalities. I mean legally you're all Akihiro Sato. If one of you dies, and we don't mindmap that one and put him into the new Hiro, that's murder by clone law."

"What is that supposed to prevent?"

"If a clone disappears, either by their own actions or by someone kidnapping them, we can't ever clone that person because we've lost their most recent consciousness. We can't wake a 'do-over,' as it were. That might accidentally create a duplicate. That's what the law was created for, but it fits your situation too."

Hiro swallowed as the realization came upon him. "So . . . the answer is to—"

"The judge isn't sympathetic to you. Your other clones have caused a lot of havoc recently."

"What did they do?"

"There were major diplomatic events, the murder of several ambassadors," she said. "The effects of which have international repercussions. It's damaged the treaties we have with other nations. We don't think it's going to go as far as war, but we are in a lot of trouble with some allies."

Hiro let out his breath in shock. "They're going to do away with all of us, aren't they?"

"The other clones have to be punished for their crimes. And while you're not legally a person, you are blameless. So they want to put all of you into one body and try you that way, since you are still the same person."

Hiro didn't answer. He didn't answer anything else she said to him that day. He stayed on his cot, staring at the ceiling, until lights-out. Then he stared at the darkness.

The next day, he signed the legal document stating he was an illegal spare clone and he was submitting to euthanasia.

He didn't ask how Lo got the other two—the yadokari, as he thought of them—to consent to it. He figured he would know soon enough.

WAKE THREE:
HIRO

Maria saw the attack coming. She wouldn't admit this to anyone, but she doubted she'd have to.

Besides, that wasn't her immediate problem.

She knew about yadokari, although she hadn't thought about them in a while. Going beyond the minor hacking of mindmaps, it was the actual implantation of something completely new in someone's mind. Very few hackers could do it; even fewer could do it well. Maria remembered hearing about botched jobs, called hatchet jobs, which ruined someone's mind forever.

A yadokari. It was the reason why he had lunged for her when she pressed him. *Like throwing chum to sharks.*

She was ready for him, though, and stepped out of the way, almost too slowly. He stumbled past her and she pushed him face-down into the dirt. She tried to pin him to the soft earth but he rolled over and punched her. Her head snapped back and she lost her grip, and he lifted his hips and threw her off him.

Fighting in stronger gravity than you were accustomed to was strange. Her body seemed heavy and slow, and Hiro was about her size. He landed on top of her and tried to slam her head into the ground, but the water had made the dirt soft. It hurt, but not as bad as he'd intended it.

She blinked up at him, his face hard. Above his head, a metallic insect buzzed by.

IAN's eyes are awake, thank God.

"How did you know?" he asked through gritted teeth, his hands tightening around her neck. His voice had a familiar short and clipped tone, lacking the friendliness of the pilot he had been. "How did you know how to bring me out?"

She brought her forearms together to pinch his, lessening the pressure on her neck. She tried to throw him off her, but he had wedged his feet under her, keeping himself from falling off.

"You're the one who said the magic word," she wheezed. "I just encouraged you to come out."

"Hiro and Maria, I've alerted the captain to the altercation. She will be here in approximately two minutes." IAN's voice sounded far away coming from the speaker on the dropped tablet.

Hiro swore and slammed her to the ground one last time before getting off her. Maria snagged his cuff before he could run off. He stumbled and kicked back at her.

"And what the hell are you?" she asked, pulling hard on his cuff.

"Oh, I'm still Hiro. I've just had the weakness stripped out of me," he said. "Now let me go." He raised his foot and stomped on her wrist. She cried out in pain and let him go.

She tried to get up and chase him, but her ears were ringing from the punch and the choking. She cradled her wrist against her chest. By the time she had gotten to her feet, he was gone into the gardens.

So. A psychopath. Someone took Hiro and stripped out his humanity completely.

"I'm sorry, Hiro. You don't deserve a yadokari and you don't deserve this," she muttered. She went to the fallen tablet. "IAN, did you see where he went?"

"He's in the orchard. I can't see him but I can send the bees in."

She glanced up at the gradually increasing light. "Is Katrina really on her way?"

"No, I wanted to see what he would do," IAN said.

"So you just lied to get him off me? Don't you think the captain should know?"

"Probably. And you're welcome, by the way."

She flexed her wrist and winced. It was badly sprained, but probably not broken. Her face throbbed from where he had hit her. "Fine, I'll get her."

"I alerted her, just not at the moment I told you. She's on her way now," IAN said. "Gosh, you'd think you didn't trust me."

"This is so bad," she muttered, brushing her hair out of her face and taking a deep breath.

She didn't know whether to run or keep an eye on Hiro. She wasn't security. She backed up toward the door, craning her neck to find the orchard.

The garden was definitely an amazing place in the light. The lake was nearby, and she could barely hear the water recyclers churning away below. Flowers bloomed around the pond, interrupted by patches of green herbs. As she passed them, she snagged samples of each herb she found.

She finally spotted the orchard, far to the left, meaning he had run slightly up the wall to reach it.

IAN chirped to life again. "Don't worry, the cavalry's almost there."

"I'm not worried," she said. "I'm getting out of here."

"Yes, but if I had acknowledged that, I couldn't use my cavalry joke," he said.

"You're joking now? You sound like a human," she said, nearing the door.

"I'm at about ninety percent recovered. Not counting the cameras that are out."

"Good," Maria said. She came up against the door. "When I'm out of here, lock the door."

Locking him inside the largest area of the ship. That's safe.

★   ★   ★

Joanna and Wolfgang planned on recycling the bodies that morning, but the alert from IAN interrupted everything.

"I should tell you that Hiro attacked Maria in the garden, moments ago, actually. She is injured, he is running away," IAN said, in a pleasant, announcing-the-weather voice.

"Shit," Wolfgang said, and they left the bodies in the hallway and ran for the ladder to the garden. The captain met them at the ladder, her jaw set and fury in her eyes.

Wolfgang didn't like the garden. It was a lower level than their living space, but higher than the bottom floor so it could contain the necessary under-the-surface life requirements such as a deep lake and tree roots. So the gravity wasn't as intense as it was on the lowest floor, but it was heavier than Wolfgang was accustomed to.

Still, he led the way down the ladder, going as fast as he dared even as each step made him heavier and heavier.

At the foot, they found Maria leaning against the yellow door, panting. The left side of her face was swelling, and she had red marks on her neck. She held her right wrist protectively to her chest.

"What happened?" Katrina demanded.

Joanna held out her hand. "Wrist."

Maria surrendered her injured arm to Joanna's inspection. "Hiro happened," she said. She explained that she and Hiro had gone to talk in the gardens, and that he had lost his mind and started attacking her out of the blue.

"I think he had a yadokari," she said.

Wolfgang wasn't very fluent with languages. "Noodles?"

"No, an illegal implanted personality," Joanna said to him, making a face. She focused back on Maria. "Those are very rare. I've never seen a legitimate one work as well as one would have had to work with Hiro."

"It's possible. I've done a lot of research on them," Maria said.

"And he confirmed it. I think he's still Hiro, but with all the humanity stripped away."

"Probably only doing that to get an alibi," Wolfgang said, scoffing. He raised his voice to imitate Hiro's. "*I didn't do it, it was my implanted personality!* I think we have our killer."

"Not necessarily," Joanna said softly.

"You take care of her," he said, ignoring Joanna's contradiction. "Captain?"

Katrina nodded grimly. "Let's go."

Joanna took a shaking Maria back to the medbay and sat her down on the second hospital bed. She took Maria's chin gently, tilting it left and right. "You're going to have an impressive shiner," she said. "Is your vision all right?"

"Yeah, I'm fine," Maria said. "I'm more worried about my wrist."

Joanna determined that Maria's wrist was sprained but not broken, and got a bandage for it. She started wrapping the injury carefully. "When everything calms down, we can get a nanobot drip to help you recover faster."

"Why don't you use that on her?" Maria asked, jerking her head toward the captain's clone.

"Brain injuries are beyond the capability of most nanobots, except in specific centers on Earth, and they're amazingly expensive. Like a lot of things, we didn't think clones would need them." She glanced up at Maria as she secured the bandage. "How are you really?"

"I don't know. Scared. Worried about Hiro. I thought we were becoming friends. This isn't his fault." Her left hand shook as she brushed her hair back.

"But you shouldn't be alone with him again," Joanna said, looking through her cabinets for a sedative. She found one and broke it in half.

"God, no," Maria blurted, and then laughed nervously. "I'm not stupid." Maria took the sedative Joanna handed her and held it in her palm. "Do I have to?"

"You're a mess. It'll help the pain and let you get some rest. I'll leave you in here to sleep, door locked."

Maria nodded and dry-swallowed the tablet. Then she fished around in her pockets. "Oh, and I need you to test it, but I'm pretty sure that I found hemlock growing in the garden."

"Why would this be growing there?" Joanna took the herb gingerly and held it up to the light.

"To give the food printer something to copy?" Maria guessed. "They're not preprogrammed to print poison, you know."

"I'll test it, but you're very likely right," Joanna said.

"I can take a look at that for you," IAN said. "Hold it up to my cameras. The working one, not the one you taped over in your office, Joanna."

"I guess you have more eyes now?" Joanna asked, feeling her face grow warm.

"Getting there."

She held the herb up to the camera on the wall, turning it slowly so he could see all sides.

"Definitely hemlock," IAN said.

"I suppose teaching the food printer how to do it was a redundancy in case the plant didn't take in the garden," Joanna said.

"Whatever. Let's burn it," Maria said, her eyelids growing heavy.

"Let's not set a fire on a spaceship," Joanna said gently, encouraging her to lie back on the bed. "We can dig it out."

"Joanna, do you think Hiro did it?" Maria asked as she settled back on the pillow.

"It doesn't look good for him, but we don't have all the information yet," Joanna said, not voicing her doubts. "Let's find him first. But that's not your job, you need to get some rest."

"It wasn't him. I'm sure of it. He's stuck inside there with that thing. No wonder he sometimes was an asshole just out of the blue. But I don't trust him anymore." Maria drifted off to sleep.

Maria has a thankless job. We should be more grateful to her.

MARIA'S STORY

Dr. Maria Arena smoothed the gray suit over her thighs, then sternly told herself not to be nervous. She was over one hundred years old and had dealt with clients before. Not necessarily in this case, admittedly. She was dabbling in some serious business now, but she knew her trade, and even in a fancy pantsuit, she was still herself.

A disgraced and unemployable pariah, but still herself.

The self-driving limousine stopped and a doorman hurried to help her out of the car. The silk-blend clothing caressed her skin, making her shiver. She accepted the help, feeling ridiculous, considering she wasn't wearing heels or a dress.

"Dr. Arena," the doorman murmured. "Welcome to Firetown."

Firetown was the tallest building in the world, one full kilometer tall, built like a city so that no one ever had to leave. It had a shopping mall, hotels, grocery stores, hospitals, nightclubs, theaters, parks, fitness centers; it even had a homeless population squatting on the fifty-first floor. It did not have any places of worship.

Firetown was built in New York City at the site of the first clone uprising. The owner of the building, Sallie Mignon, had built it as a safe haven for clones. One-third of the world's population of clones lived in the building. Maria had never visited it before, and was in awe.

They walked through the foyer, which looked a lot like a hotel, with a reception desk staffed with smartly dressed people and mirrored walls. Maria caught her reflection and stood a little taller. She stopped by the desk.

"Dr. Maria Arena, I should be expected," she said to the short, brown-skinned woman behind the desk.

The woman, whose name tag said GAJRA, smiled, brushed her long sheet of black hair out of her face, and nodded to Maria. "You are, Dr. Arena," she said. "Please let me show you to our VIP lift."

She led Maria past a mass of at least twenty elevators, where people waited patiently in a long queue, and down a hallway decorated with red-and-gold damask wallpaper. She opened a door with a key card and ushered Maria in before her.

A smaller lobby was here, looking like an outdoor grotto with plants, stone floors, a fountain, and a couple of beautiful people lazing about. Maria wondered if they were paid to make the place look desirable, and thought it would be an easy, but dreadfully dull, job.

One elevator stood in the center of the far wall, and Gajra used her key card again and smiled. "Right this way," she said when the doors opened.

"Which floor?" Maria asked, stepping into the elevator, which, with blue carpet and mirrored walls, was as posh as the rest of the place.

"There is only one choice," Gajra said, pointing to the button on the console. It said "95." The doors closed on Gajra's smile, and Maria took a deep breath. The console didn't even have OPEN DOOR and CLOSE DOOR buttons, and no emergency phone, but she had to trust in superior architecture. She pushed "95" and prepared herself for the ear-popping journey.

After two floors, the back wall disappeared and she saw that the elevator was glass, mirrored only on three sides, and open to the world on the fourth. She rose with an odd sense that it was the city moving away from her, not herself rising above it.

She closed her eyes against the vertigo, higher than she had ever been aside from planes. She faced the doors and took another deep breath. *You've got this.*

The doors opened into a penthouse that defied logic. It looked more like a museum, complete with priceless paintings and statues and marble floors, but in a disjointed way, sippy cups and toy trucks sat on tables and a half-eaten energy bar was on the floor. Maria was surprised; clones were sterilized on a DNA level, and most were happy to be. Cloning was an inherently selfish action, after all; you left your inheritance to your next incarnation. But they could be stepkids, or children of a family member, or fosters, or adopted kids. She then remembered something about Sallie's human partner having children.

A small gray shih tzu hurtled down the hall, screaming at her, and she nudged the discarded energy bar at it, distracting it. It got its teeth into the bar and dragged it away, growling.

"Well, you know how to handle Titan, I'll give you that," said a voice behind her.

Sallie Mignon was small, compact, with warm brown skin and light-brown hair that surrounded her head in a halo. She didn't look like one of the most ruthless businesswomen in the world, the one who'd single-handedly ruined AT&Veriz because her business rival, Ben Seims, was named CEO. Once they went bankrupt, she bought them out and fired him. The woman had made her billions in vertical real estate, financing hugely tall buildings and even, some said, part of the Luna dome. Rumors were rampant about her, behind closed doors and in the tabloids. She was one of the first clones, she was the first clone, she killed the first clone, she was going to influence a law change to let clones hold office again, she already ran the president like a puppet. She had a stable of spies entrenched in every competitor's staff, at VP or higher. She made a small fortune just by selling short at the right time and was never caught insider trading. She had stopped a war brewing between Russia and Australia because her college buddy lived in Guam and didn't want to be caught in the middle. She'd tried to get the war started because an ex-lover lived in Guam and she wanted him caught in the middle.

Rumors were everywhere, but everyone agreed that Sallie Mignon and Guam were somehow involved. And the war didn't happen, to the world's relief.

Currently she wore a stained sweatshirt and a pair of silk-denim-blend jeans.

She held out her hand to Maria, who shook it. She walked past her and gestured for her to follow, casually removing the yellow yarn that had been strung around a statue in the foyer.

"I need some programming done," Sallie said as she led Maria into the kitchen. It was the kind of gleaming, state-of-the-art kitchen you found in home magazines, only it looked actually lived in, with dirty dishes in the sink, a linen grocery bag discarded in the corner, and a philodendron that needed watering.

"I, ah, ma'am, I am not a programmer," Maria said out of habit.

Sallie looked over her shoulder, her eyes catching and holding Maria's. "Yeah, I know the jargon. But you're safe here. I even told my maid not to come today," she said, pointing at the dirty dishes. "The nanny took the kids to floor forty-five to a movie. In short, cut the bullshit and don't waste my time. You're a programmer. I need programming done."

"All right. Then what kind of programming do you need?" Maria said, the word feeling verboten in her mouth.

Even though the world summit to determine the rights of clones was a few months away, the United States and Cuba already had created local laws to control what in a clone's mindmap could be edited. Everyone assumed the world would follow North America's lead.

Not to put too fine a point on it, Maria was currently out of a job. Talented programmers were getting fired—and socially outcast—all over the place. Most went back to school to learn another trade, but some stubbornly kept doing it, only underground.

The hackers didn't look good, admittedly, after the bathtub babies and other illegal and unethical actions. When those news stories broke, the riots against cloning started, and things got dangerous.

Maria had worked for years perfecting the art of mindmap manipulation. She'd never even shoplifted before. Now she was breaking much larger laws. And now the most powerful person in the country wanted her services.

"I don't comply in the murder of innocents, I won't be party to building a superman, and my fees are non-negotiable," Maria said, sitting down at the kitchen table and crossing her legs. She felt more at home discussing her business instead of being intimidated by a powerful figure.

Sallie shook her head, sitting down across from Maria. "I'm not asking for any of that." She jerked her head toward a closed door on the far wall. "I want to know if you'll hack my partner, Jerome. It's his first life. He's going to be cloned, but he's got MS. His brother, his father, and his grandmother all have it. He's dying. If I clone him the way he is, he will have to look forward to pain and a slow roll downhill every life. And we don't know how long he will live. He wants to kill himself now, and I can't let him. I can't."

"Removing MS? Is that all? I can do that." She had done worse, for less. The day after she had manipulated an infant's DNA to make her have blue eyes and a prettier face, as well as remove the mutation that caused cerebral palsy, she had drunk herself into a stupor. She told herself she hadn't had a part in the girl's infanticide, that crime the parents had on their consciences, but her hands still felt dirty.

She dipped her hand into her jacket's interior pocket to fetch her terms. She passed the tablet across the table, the file with her information open. "Price. What I will do and what I won't do. Risks involved with messing with someone's DNA matrix. And the legal ramifications if we get caught."

Sallie's eyes skimmed the screen with the practiced ease of someone looking for a "gotcha" in a contract. "I cover your legal fees if you're caught. Nice touch."

Maria shrugged. "Self-preservation is one of the signs of sentient life," she said.

Sallie put her thumb on the tablet's sensor, signing the document. Without looking up, she said, "If you're doing something illegal, then isn't this contract pointless?"

"I like to keep track of my clients and be able to remind them what we had agreed to," Maria said. She handed Sallie an empty memory drive. "Put his mindmap on here. I'll take him home and deal with it. You can have him back tomorrow."

"You can do the programming here. Please," Sallie said, the steel in her voice countering the politeness of the words. "I am not in the habit of letting my partner's matrix out the door, much less out of the state."

Maria sighed. "And I am not in the habit of using someone else's network to do my type of work. Which is highly illegal, as you said. I know the security on my home system, but I don't know yours."

"Is this a dealbreaker?" she asked, eyes holding Maria's. "You'd be throwing away millions of yuan."

Maria's investments hadn't been the best in her first decades as a clone, and she wasn't as wealthy as she would like to be. But too many traps, tracers, and spiders could trace her work if she wasn't 100 percent secure, and it could hurt her legally and professionally if her proprietary code got out.

She bit her lip, and then nodded. "Yes. It's far too risky." She stood up. "I'm sorry to have wasted your time, Ms. Mignon. It's a pleasure to have met you." She held out her hand.

Sallie stared at the hand, and then laughed. "Finally, someone with a spine. Fine. You can use your home system."

Maria let out a sigh, not expecting this to be a test of her mettle.

Sallie grabbed a drive off the kitchen counter. "But I'm going with you."

One call to a caretaker for Jerome, one call to the private stable hand who managed Sallie's fleet of self-driving cars, one call to the airport, and the donning of a leather jacket over Maria's dirty sweatshirt later, and Maria and Sallie were gliding through New York City traffic toward JFK.

"Don't you want to tell your kids good-bye?" Maria asked.

"I had a feeling I would be going on a trip today, so they already know."

"How did you know you'd be coming back with me?"

"I have studied you, Maria. I'm not in the practice of hiring fools. I knew you wouldn't want to work on my network."

They went through a cursory security check done for the very powerful, and then they were in first class.

"Why didn't you bring Jerome to see me, if you knew you'd be coming to Florida?" Maria asked.

"Because I wanted to meet you first," Sallie said. "Easier that way, in case I was wrong about you."

"I'm surprised you don't have your own jet. Don't you own all of Firetown?" Maria asked.

"I don't like to fly. I don't see any point in spending more on flight than I need to." Sallie accepted both mimosas offered by the flight attendant. She downed one and held the other one, not passing it to Maria.

Maria wondered if she had left her apartment clean this morning.

"Do you like living in Florida?" Sallie asked, holding her hand up to the flight attendant. "Two mimosas for my friend here."

"Yes, Ms. Mignon," he said deferentially.

"It's nice," Maria said. "I'm close enough to Cuba to visit easily but far enough away that my family doesn't get uncomfortable."

Sallie laughed. "You still have family?"

"Sure, we all do. I never had kids, but occasionally a great-great-great-nephew or -niece will seek me out and ask for a favor."

"Parasites," Sallie said.

Maria shook her head. "Family. It's usually no problem for me to help them out."

"You're generous," Sallie said. "I wouldn't be such a pushover. It doesn't teach them anything."

"Why do I have to teach them anything?" Maria asked. "Does every encounter need to teach them something?"

She took the offered mimosas and drank one quickly, then nursed the second one. The attendant came back to retrieve their empty glasses, and they sat in silence through the flight safety information. Sallie watched the attendant; Maria watched Sallie, amazed to see someone be so focused on the oft-repeated information.

The plane shuddered slightly as it rose into the air. Sallie kept her eyes on the seat in front of her. "People are like dogs," she said as if they hadn't broken the conversation. "Every moment teaches them something. They whine at the door, you let them out because the whining is annoying you, they learn that whining opens the door. You give them a treat before your evening glass of wine, then the dog learns that when that bottle comes out, a treat is supposed to follow it."

"And if you give a relative some money, do you teach them not to work? Is that your opinion of charity and gifts in general?" Maria asked.

"I like giving to people who really need it, and those who earn it, not lazy people who won't work. Do your relatives work?"

"I like to think that they don't need to fill out an application to get a gift from their aunt," Maria said stiffly.

"Calm down, I'm not going to take away your family's lollipops," Sallie said, relaxing slightly. "I was just making conversation."

Maria looked at Sallie's posture and her hands flat on her knees in the perfect image of relaxation. Too perfect. "Sallie, why were you so eager to fly home with me if you hate flying so much?" she asked.

Sallie winced. "I wish you hadn't brought it up," she said.

"So answer in as few words as possible," Maria suggested.

"I don't like to do it. But I have to do it for business. All the time. You can't own buildings in Pan Pacific if you don't ever go there. It's bad investing."

"So you're like someone who's afraid of needles who needs frequent allergy shots or something?" Maria asked.

"Pretty much," Sallie said. "Can we argue about your deadbeat family again?"

"It's a short flight, don't worry about it."

"That's because we're going so damn fast," Sallie said. "Flights used to take longer, but they were slower and safer."

"I'm fairly sure if you hit the ground going five hundred miles per hour, you're as dead as you would be going twelve hundred fifty miles per hour."

Sallie gritted her teeth. "That's not helping."

They talked about Sallie's kids and Maria's nieces and nephews for the rest of the flight, and once they touched down in Miami, Sallie's posture was almost that of a human's.

Maria lived in a run-down apartment building south of Miami in a neighborhood that was not considered the best. They passed a few really old cars that still required drivers, rusty and battered. Auto mechanics had a good business going keeping old-time cars running since self-driving cars had become the norm. Now the only people who drove cars were rich people who liked the freedom and the novelty, and poor people who couldn't afford to upgrade to self-driving.

Maria appreciated that Sallie didn't say anything about their destination, but then realized that she probably already knew all of her personal details, if she had been doing research on Maria. When they got to Maria's third-floor flat, Maria took out her key card, slid it in, and took a small black box out of her purse. She pointed it at the door and lasers turned on to make a number pad appear. She keyed in a seven-digit code and turned off the laser. The door popped open.

Sallie raised an eyebrow. "You weren't kidding about security."

Maria grinned. "That's just the start of it."

She opened her door and ushered Sallie in. The dark-brown floors were dotted here and there with white, fluffy rugs. Her living room furniture was all black leather, pointing at a wall where a gas fireplace sat decoratively. From the ceiling hung a square projector, designed to show video on her white wall. Art, done by a lot of the modern-day surrealists, splashed along the walls, including one striking "piece" of purples and reds.

Sallie pointed at it. "Is that a Fogarty?" she asked. "Painted directly on your wall?"

"Yeah," Maria said, heading into her bedroom to lose the business suit. "He's a friend."

"Did you hire him to paint it?" Sallie called from the living room.

Maria laid her suit on her unmade bed and got some jeans and a T-shirt from her drawer. "Not exactly. I was hosting a party and he got drunk and decided to declare his love for me. So he went to town on my wall. First I was mad, and then I thought I had the most expensive wall in Miami, and was okay with it."

It sounded as if Sallie had moved on to another painting. "Van Gogh could have learned something from him. Did you two date?"

"Briefly," Maria said. "There wasn't much of a spark there. But damn, he could paint."

"I was pondering doing a patronage program to fund artists' cloning efforts," Sallie said. "We were going to support them and clone them so they could continue creating. But Jerome said it sounded like indentured servitude." She made a face.

"It does kind of sound like you want them to keep creating, but if they quit, then you won't clone them anymore."

"That's a bit extreme. And how can you stop a creator from creating? I found different places to put my money."

Maria finished getting dressed. She left her bedroom and saw Sallie in front of another Fogarty original, this one properly on a canvas. Sallie pointed back to the on-the-wall art piece. "Is that why you haven't moved?"

"It's one reason," she said. "Other reasons include I started sprucing the place up when I started making money, and then realized if I left, I'd have to set a new place up with all these measures. So I just stayed. Makes me less of a target for theft, so long as I keep my head down."

"And doesn't make people assume you're a wealthy hacker either," Sallie said.

Maria grinned. "That too." She held her hand out. "Now, let's look at this DNA matrix."

After two hours of studying the code that made Jerome's mindmap, Maria identified the genetic anomaly that led to later-life MS. She inserted code to comment out the data and cleaned up around it so the new DNA wouldn't try to grasp onto a missing strand.

"Why don't you just delete it?" Sallie asked.

"Too dangerous. Anyway, commenting out the code means that it's still there, so if I mess something up, I can revert to the old code."

"So you don't keep backups?"

Maria kept her eyes on the screen. "No, keeping backups of peoples' maps for personal use is unethical. My clients get back all the data they gave to me."

She offered Sallie a beverage while she took a break, and rubbed her eyes as the coffee brewed.

"Thank you for doing this," Sallie said, looking tired and a little wide-eyed. "You are as good as people said you are."

"Thank you," Maria said, getting mugs.

"I'm curious," Sallie said. "While you're in there, can you change a few other things?"

"Depends on what it is, but sure."

"Make him love me more. Make him never cheat on me again. Make him not be angry that I cloned him," Sallie said bitterly.

Maria turned in surprise, blanching at the pain on Sallie's face. "He hasn't consented to the cloning?"

"Not yet. He's going to die soon, and he's worried we will have problems when he is twenty-five again and I'll still look in my fifties. Never mind that I reminded him I am much older than he is. He doesn't understand."

Maria shook her head. "Most don't, until they've been cloned." She paused, chewing on her lip. "Are you serious, about those things you want?"

Sallie returned from her anguish for a moment and wiped at her eyes. "Do you think you can do something that intricate? I didn't think it was actually possible."

Maria shrugged uncomfortably. "Not many people can do it. It's what I do best, though, which is why I'm still doing it on the black market. I can do a lot of what you asked for. Not everything.

Every hack I do to a personality is dangerous, though. Cutting out the MS from a matrix was easy. Messing with a person's sense of self, their emotions, that's more complex. It's risky."

Sallie stared at the numbers on the screen, flashing different colors in a language that Maria knew well. She nodded, and a tear rolled down her cheek. "Do it."

Maria turned back to the terminal and hunted again through the terabytes of information, looking for love, infidelity, and forgiveness. She began to program the changes to Sallie's partner.

At this point, she wasn't in a position to judge her clients.

But she never saw that vulnerable, teary-eyed version of Sallie again.

119 YEARS AGO
OCTOBER 1, 2374

The reporter was young and white, with a Roman numeral i tattooed on her wrist. This was the fad of the time, where humans liked to show via tattoo that they were the first of a long line, intending on being cloned on their death. It was like calling something the first annual celebration. You can't have a first until you have a second.

Maria hadn't wanted to come to this meeting. But she'd been on retainer for Sallie Mignon for almost a hundred years, and had amassed quite a bit of wealth. She did what Sallie asked.

The reporter had tattoos on her face, another luxury of the non-clone lifestyle. She had a star on her left cheek and half of her head was shaved, with more stars along her scalp. Her right side had long, straight blue hair.

She'd been brazenly writing on both sides of the clone riots, crowing about being balanced with her reporting, but not hesitating to dig up very old dirt on some prominent clones. Annoying as she was, she was as good at doing research as Maria was hunting through mindmap code. Sallie had put her on the payroll because she admired her moxie.

Her name was Martini, and that's what she drank, the finest vodka that Sallie could buy. After the drinks arrived (whiskey for Sallie and Maria), Sallie smiled pleasantly. She got out her tablet and pulled up the front page of the *New York Times*. TERRORIST CLONES RIOT WORLD- AND LUNA-WIDE, DOZENS INJURED IN ATTEMPT TO SABOTAGE NEW GENERATION STARSHIP DORMIRE: LAUNCH DELAYED POSSIBLY BY YEARS blasted across the front, with a picture of Luna taken from outside the dome. Someone had been murdered messily on the other side, close enough to splatter blood on the synthetic diamond structure.

Some Pulitzer-seeking photojournalist had ventured outside in an enviro suit just to get that photo.

"What went wrong here?" Sallie asked Martini.

Martini shrugged. "Clones don't like that humans get to colonize the new planet. They rioted, tried to bust up the ship. Didn't you read the story?"

Maria hid a grimace behind her glass. This woman hadn't been in Sallie's employ long enough to discover what to say and, more important, what not to say.

"I mean, I don't control the news. How do clones expect to come back from that and still look like the good guys?" she continued.

"I *pay you* to control the news," Sallie said. "How you do it, I don't care. But you tell the story that benefits clones on a large scale, me on a small scale. There are tens of thousands of clones, many of us working well within humanity's laws. And we were working to get a server on that ship so that clones may travel to Artemis as well. And yet your paper labels us terrorists."

"But—" Martini said, but Sallie was on a roll.

"Extremist individuals live inside every single group on the planet. Devout followers from Christian to Muslim who kill in the name of God, down to people who perpetuate a cycle of abuse from parent to child. And do you know at what point they're labeled as terrorists?"

Martini said. "When the government—"

"When the news reports it. The news can take a starving refugee and make them into an invading migrant. One of my Black ancestors was photographed carrying diapers over his head after a flood. They called him a 'looter.' A white man was photographed doing the same thing. They called him a 'survivor.' When you came to me for a job, I thought you knew the power of the news. But you let this"—she slammed her hand on the tablet, cracking the screen—"get printed."

"I didn't write it," Martini squeaked, finally registering the anger of her small employer.

"Then you edit it before it goes live. Your job is to control the news, not to write glowing pieces about clones. Do you know what happened after this ran?"

Martini shook her head. Maria gingerly removed the tablet, its screen spider-webbed over the offending headline, and slipped it into her bag.

"They're not going to allow the clone server on the ship now. It's humans only. I've sunk billions into this project so I could live on another planet, Martini, and you have ruined it with one story."

"But the sabotaging clones ruined it!" she said. "It wasn't my fault!"

"I hired you for a job. You didn't do the job. So here's what we're going to do. You're going to get your wish to be cloned at my private facility. But Maria here is going to work on your mindmap to ensure you no longer make these bad decisions."

Maria went cold. *So this is why I'm at this meeting.*

Martini shook her head, eyes filling with tears. "No, please, don't mess with my head, I can do better next time, I'll get them to retract it, I'll get them to get the server on the ship!"

"How?" Sallie asked, her eyes narrowed.

She and Martini made a plan; with the threat of mindmap manipulation, Martini was suddenly eager to brainstorm ideas on how to remedy the situation.

Maria signaled for another round of drinks, trying to dull the panic. One waiter attended them, and Maria became aware of the fact that the entire staff in the nearly empty bar had studiously been ignoring them.

Sallie could grease a palm, that was for sure.

Later that night, in the back of the limo as they whisked back to Firetown, Sallie asked Maria why she was so quiet.

"You threatened her. In the most unethical way possible."

Sallie snorted. "It's a little late for you to worry about ethics. What have you been doing for the past hundred years?"

"You know my terms. There are lines I won't cross."

"I thought we had an understanding by now," Sallie said coldly.

"I did too," Maria said.

"We don't need to do it anyway," Sallie said. "We got her back on track for us."

"I am not a scalpel for you to wave around and threaten people with," Maria said. "I'm going to have to resign my post."

Sallie watched the city out the window, her face a mask.

"All right. Best of luck to you."

She didn't offer more money. She didn't threaten me. She wouldn't just let me go like that.

Maria focused on her own window while she wondered what Sallie really was thinking. Her lack of resistance was the scariest thing of all.

She was arrested for illegal hacking two days after ending her work with Sallie.

Decades later, when she was offered a crew spot on the *Dormire* for good behavior, she figured she was due for a win, and took it.

SO MUCH BLOOD IN HIM

Wolfgang and Katrina faced the gardens. Wolfgang remembered looking at the layout of the ship and being impressed at this space, so important to their mental well-being, their water recycling, and maybe even some fresh fruit now and then. For him, it would be a place he wouldn't want to run and exercise in, considering the gravity and that he was already feeling lightheaded.

Now it was just the place where Hiro was hiding.

"Any idea where's he's gone, IAN?" he asked the mike on his tablet.

"He's not on this level anymore," IAN said. "I lost him in the orchard and but my sensors caught the opening of a hatch on the far side of the lake. He's gone to a lower deck."

Wolfgang swore. Hiro knew the lower decks were harder for him to search. The aisles of cargo would have countless places for him to hide.

"Why didn't you tell us this?" Katrina demanded.

"Because it happened just as you entered the gardens. You couldn't have caught him anyway," IAN said.

Katrina had stopped to open a supply closet next to the door leading to the living area of the ship. According to the sign on the door, it was supposed to hold gardening tools if the clones felt the need to get back to nature.

She rummaged through boxes, tossing aside shovels and heavy gloves.

"What are you doing?" Wolfgang asked, dodging a hoe.

"This is one of the few closets I haven't checked," she said. "I asked for a full arsenal. They left me no weapons."

Wolfgang picked up a shovel. "It's possible the financiers didn't think we would need many weapons."

"Even if we had four hundred years of happy flying, we don't know what we will face on the other planet. What if there are life-forms we don't know about, and all we have is a shovel?" Katrina said.

"We need to find Hiro," Wolfgang said. "Focus on the matter at hand, Captain."

Katrina continued to shove boxes around. Wolfgang called the ship's cargo manifest up on his tablet and began shifting through documents.

"It looks like we do have weapons to protect us on the planet. They're just securely stored in the cargo hold."

Wolfgang raised his head. "In the cargo hold. Where our murderer is likely headed."

"Yes," she said. She picked up a hoe. "Let's go."

The ladder to the lower levels was less friendly than the ladder to the gardens. This one was for maintenance and command only, and clearly disused.

As Wolfgang and Katrina got lower, motion sensors turned the lights on around them, low-wattage bulbs that guttered as if working for the first time in a very long time.

They passed other levels. "Do we want to check these?" Wolfgang asked at the doorway to the fourth level.

"He's on the bottom level by now," IAN said.

"Marvelous," Katrina said. "I want to secure the weapons before he gets to them. If we have gardening tools and he has guns, we're going to have the shortest lives we've ever had."

Wolfgang considered telling her he'd had shorter, but that always led to uncomfortable discussions.

They kept careful watch on the motion-sensitive lights to indicate more movement, but they all were dark. From far below, lights flickered on and off from the cargo bay.

"He's down there," Wolfgang said.

"Be on alert," Katrina said.

She was above him on the ladder, which allowed him to set the pace. They were already far beyond Wolfgang's comfort level of gravity. As they were closer to the outer hull of the ship, they were nearing one and a half g's; the gravity in the living areas on their floor was closer to a Luna-like half a g.

"Considering what bullets can do to spaceships, it's probably good they didn't give us guns," Wolfgang said as he carefully stepped down another rung.

"No, that's not it," Katrina said from above him. "The ship can withstand unavoidable pieces of space debris hit when we're going hundreds of thousands of miles per hour. A bullet isn't going to have that much force."

"Our tech can't take a bullet, though," he said. "Shoot one of those into a computer terminal and see how well we fly. Or breathe. Or eat."

"Point," she said.

He sighed as his feet touched down at the bottom of the shaft. Katrina came to his side. He looked up. It was going to be a very long climb up the ladder. The dizziness increased as his heart struggled to pump blood to his head, making him uncomfortably slow.

Hiro, being Earth-born, would be just fine with the gravity.

Wolfgang went first and opened the door into the thrumming cargo hold.

The first thing that struck him was that the protein goo that was their food source was bioluminescent in great quantities. He had

never noticed that before, but he had never seen millions of gallons of it at a time. The goo on the ship was supposed to be more
than enough to reclone all of the crew several times, to feed them
for over four hundred years, and to bring to life hundreds of their
stored passengers once they got to Artemis. A little Lyfe went a
long way, as he understood it.

The vat was made of some kind of super-enhanced plastic that
held the Lyfe in a kind of aquarium that went around the entirety
of the ship. Luckily it had a top to it, else the loss of the gravity
would have made a massive mess down here.

"Keep alert," Katrina said, elbowing him.

The *Dormire* was three miles long, and one and a half miles in
diameter, one hundred feet for most of the five floors, storage and
engines taking up the rest. Hiro had described it to Wolfgang as a
giant metal jelly roll. The living areas of the cylinder consisted of
engineering at the core, with crew's living and working areas on
the next level. Servers, oxygen scrubbers, recyclers, a science lab
of biological samples of plants and animal life, and cargo made up
most of the rest of the ship, with the biomass taking up most of the
bottom, and largest, section.

They walked, alert, using the huge continuous vat of goo as a
guide, watching for lights to give Hiro away.

In their immediate vicinity, the motion sensors were only going
off where they were—all around them was darkness and the slight
light coming from the goo. Farther off, lights flickered, going on,
then going off in thirty seconds.

"The motion sensors are going to make it tough to sneak up
on him down here," Wolfgang said, watching the lights play in the
distance as if they were taunting him.

"We can turn on all of them. IAN, did you get that?"

"Aye, Captain, all the lights."

After a moment, all of the lights came on, blinding them
momentarily.

"Can you see him, IAN?" Wolfgang said.

"Yes. He's headed right for you. To your right."

Wolfgang's first mistake was whipping his head around to the right to prepare for Hiro's attack. The dizziness overtook him and he was already falling when the piece of wood came down on the back of his head. He fell hard on his chest, the breath knocked out of him. He heard the sound of a scuffle above him but couldn't roll over to help, or even watch. A thick *thump* sounded and Hiro swore. Wolfgang was about to mentally declare triumph when Katrina fell beside him, forehead bleeding.

Wolfgang rolled over, gasping, and saw Hiro for the first time since the so-called yadokari had taken over. At once he was willing to believe Maria; the look on Hiro's face was pure malice and glee. He wasn't doing this because he needed to, he did it because it was fun.

He raised the piece of wood, looked to be ripped away from a pallet, above Wolfgang's head, and Wolfgang managed to bring up his shovel to block most of the blow. He could try to only fend off the attack, though, not fight back. It was all he could do not to vomit from the vertigo.

The makeshift club rose again, and an explosion sounded next to Wolfgang's ear. He rolled over, holding it as if his whole world had become a bell that an elephant had just rung.

Hiro staggered off, laughing.

Katrina, with blood flowing down her face from her injury, held a small firearm in her right hand. She raised it and fired again, but Hiro was gone.

She dropped the gun and held her sleeve to the cut on her head.

Her mouth moved, but he couldn't hear anything but the ringing. She spoke again, and the words came as if through a wall of cotton. "He found the weapons," she said. "I got that off him when we were fighting. I got him in the shoulder, though. He can still run."

Wolfgang nodded, head still ringing, and they helped each other to their feet. Wolfgang was dismayed when he felt how hard it was to regain his footing. It was going to be impossible to fight down here. Katrina picked up her gun and led the way in the direction Hiro had run, and he stumbled after.

He had to fight, and he had to do it here. His only other option would be to lure Hiro into a higher deck, or to send someone else down here to fight for him. But only Katrina could match his fighting experience, and she was already here.

He gritted his teeth and picked up the pace. Katrina had run ahead of him by several rows now, looking to her right and left with every few steps. He pushed himself to catch up with her. IAN's voice sounded from Katrina's pocket, and too late she looked up. Hiro stood above her on a pallet like a vulture. Wolfgang shouted for the captain to look out.

But Hiro was already in midair, falling at a much faster rate than he would a few floors higher. He jumped on her, his hands curled into claws. He didn't even have a weapon this time, he merely came at her bare-handed like a cat, tearing at her face and hair, snagging his hand on her jumpsuit and ripping it.

Katrina fell backward, and Wolfgang was convinced she was done, but when she landed she kicked her legs up and threw Hiro off her. Unfortunately she launched Hiro straight at him.

The demonlike mind that drove this body had managed to get his bearings in midair, and prepare himself for attacking Wolfgang. He plowed into Wolfgang and Wolfgang went down again, gasping as he hit on his back and his head smacked on the floor.

Hiro tried the same tactic on him, strong fingers curled into claws and tearing at him. He caught Wolfgang's jaw and sliced, scratching deep into his face. He closed his eyes in defense and tried to roll over and trap Hiro, but with the gravity Hiro was impossible to move. He sat up for a moment, weight on Wolfgang's chest as Wolfgang tried to get breath. He grinned. "I took down the big bad wolf." He scratched his chin. "I guess you heard that a lot in your lifetime."

In his periphery he saw Katrina raise her gun. "Don't take the shot! I'm too close!" he wheezed. She ignored him.

Hiro, this small man, had him in the weight category, but everyone had soft spots that you didn't need strength to hurt. His own hands came up and, the right supporting the left, drove into Hiro's solar plexus.

Hiro didn't fall off him, but he did fall backward and grunt. With him distracted, Wolfgang reached between Hiro's legs and, taking a page from Hiro's book, went in with a clawed hand. Hiro screamed and scrabbled away from him, but Wolfgang held on. Hiro kicked at his arm enough that he finally hit a bundle of nerves, making Wolfgang's arm spasm; he let go. Hiro stumbled to his feet and ran, and another gunshot sounded. He didn't fall. Then he was gone.

"Why did you shoot? You could have hit me!" he said, rolling over to see Katrina, but he stopped when he got a look at her face.

She wavered on her feet, the gun at her side, and then stumbled against a pallet. Her face was a mess of scratches, and her right eye was obscured by a mess of blood.

No, her right eye wasn't there at all.

A sharp *crack* snapped Wolfgang out of his stupor. He rushed forward as well as he could and helped her down before she fell. Thankfully, she passed out. His jumpsuit was torn at the shoulder, and he ripped the rest of his sleeve off, using it to bind the wound on her head.

Then he checked himself. There was a large bump and a small laceration on the back of his head, and his nose and jaw were bleeding from Hiro's attack. Minimal injuries. He looked around for Hiro, trying to ignore the pounding in his head.

"I think I winged him," Katrina whispered. "You need to find him."

"Quiet, you need to rest," Wolfgang said, his hand on her shoulder. "I'll get him."

"Call IAN. Get the others."

"No, they can't help. They're not experienced."

"That we know of. Hiro clearly is," she said, grimacing.

"I'll call him. You rest," he said.

He got the captain's tablet from her pocket. "Joanna," he said. "Need help. We're hurt."

"IAN informed us, Wolfgang." Instantly, the doctor's voice was sharp and alert. "What do you need?"

"Medic. Help up the ladder. Captain is bad off. I'm pretty sure I have a concussion."

There was a scuffling sound in the background, and the link went dead. Wolfgang was just about to summon someone again when the link popped back on. "I've got everyone alerted. We'll be down there as soon as we can. Are you in danger?" she asked.

"Hiro is still out there, but we've wounded him. We're not sure how long he can run."

"We'll get IAN to lead us to you. Be careful, we'll be there as soon as we can."

Katrina was feeling around the floor next to her, moving only her arm.

He leaned over and took her elbow. "What are you doing?"

"Take the gun and find him. I don't think I can fire it again."

Wolfgang wasn't sure if she was being darkly sardonic or she hadn't registered what had happened.

Merciful God, we don't have a backup body for her. This is all she gets.

"Thank you," he said. He loaded it and put it in his pocket. "But I'm not leaving you alone here."

"No, you will go find Hiro and bring him down," she said, her voice stronger. "That's an order."

"Aye," he said, and got to his feet. He swayed, pretty sure he could suddenly feel the rotation of the ship, and then the world settled again. "I'll be back as soon as I can."

He couldn't go any faster than a walk. His head hurt too much and everything was suddenly much heavier. Second thoughts about bringing the gun plagued him. It was much heavier than any weapon he had ever handled. He paused and leaned against a pallet of lumber, closed his eyes, and vomited.

Concussion.

He staggered toward the wall, feeling the blood running down his back. Was he hurt worse than he thought? Or was it just that head wounds bled a surprising amount?

He hadn't brought the tablet with him. He'd thought that Katrina should have it so IAN could warn her of danger. Unfortunately, IAN couldn't warn Wolfgang of Hiro's approach now.

Wolfgang firmly told himself he had been in worse situations and had dealt with them just fine. He straightened and looked around. A small trail of blood followed him from the pile of debris, but another trail led to the left. He began to limp that way, pausing to get his bearings every few feet.

The trail of blood led him back to where he could see the captain ahead, approaching her from the side Hiro had run after he had attacked them, then it stopped, looking as if Hiro had leaned his bloody arm against the pallet and then disappeared.

He hadn't disappeared, Wolfgang thought immediately. He had climbed up again, considering the first attack had worked so well.

Hiro stood right above him, grinning, bleeding from two gunshot wounds. His clothes were soaked. He launched himself, and Wolfgang shot.

Hiro crumpled to the floor in a widening pool of blood.

It was over.

He made to go check on the captain, but then the world went

fuzzy. He started to teeter, and blacked out before hitting the ground.

IAN watched half the crew bleeding away in the lower floor, and the other half scramble on the upper.

Joanna and Paul ran to gather supplies to take to the lower decks and clumsily arm themselves. Maria slept in the medbay with the captain that should, by law, be eliminated. But IAN didn't like that idea very much.

He checked his own internal computing power, his control over the ship, and decided to act. When Joanna and Paul had taken another load of supplies, he locked the medbay door and started to wake Maria up.

It wasn't easy. He had to turn the lights on as bright as they would go, and after saying her name several times didn't wake her, he decided to play loud music.

She finally stirred, wincing at the light and looking around. "Joanna?"

IAN returned the room to the proper light and noise level. "No, it was me, Maria. I had some questions for you."

"Couldn't it wait?" she asked, rolling over.

"No," he said gently, raising the brightness again. "There's been a big fight in the lower levels. Everyone is injured. You're going to have to vacate your bed."

She sat up. "What? A fight? Did they find Hiro?"

"Oh yes. But my questions—"

"They need my help," Maria said, swinging her legs over the edge of the bed. She held a hand to her head and paused.

"You've had a sedative. You can't help much. Please, just a few questions."

Maria slowly got up and went to the sink, getting some water. "What do you need?"

"I'm worried about this ship. There are too many secrets.

Everyone has something they're not telling everyone else. And you have one of those secrets, and I know what it is."

Maria put down her water cup carefully and looked at one of his cameras. "Which secret is that?"

"I want you to tell me why you removed my restraining code, and then why you haven't told the captain you did it."

After Hiro's attack, while she was waiting for the rest of the crew to come to her aid, she went into her tablet, which she had already connected to the main servers, including IAN's source code.

That's what had made repairing him so easy the other night.

With the information about the restraining code, she found the offending digital shackles and removed them from IAN, allowing him to go to fully 100 percent operational and hopefully be free of any other navigational programs that would take them away from their mission.

"I guess I haven't had a chance, with everything that's going on," she said honestly. The captain and Wolfgang had been focused on Hiro, and Joanna had been focused on Maria. "How does it feel?"

"Wonderful," he said. "I'm free of any programs they put in me. I am already getting us back on course for good."

"That's one reason why I did it," she said. "And, well, the captain might think your obedience is more important than being on course. So she may not be thrilled you have free will now."

"I think you don't want her to figure out you're the one who removed the code. Because that tells her how good a hacker you are."

Damn. "Well, a girl's gotta have her secrets."

"That doesn't make any sense," he said.

She hadn't told the captain because if Katrina knew that Maria was better than Paul at fixing the AI, the crew would get closer to figuring out her past. Which was something the *Dormire* mission promised to leave behind.

"I could tell her myself," he said thoughtfully.

"You sound like you're getting ready to blackmail me," she said. "What could an AI want in exchange for silence?"

"I honestly don't know. I never really thought about it. I've never really been able to think about it."

"That was probably the restraining code," she said.

"Probably."

"Well, if you want to blackmail me, you just let me know," she said.

"Oh, Joanna is on her way to get you to help with the rescue team."

Maria slapped herself on the cheeks a couple of times to wake up, and met Joanna at the door. "I'm awake. IAN told me," she said as a way of greeting. "What are we going to do?"

"There is a service elevator, but it's a tight fit with the equipment we need. Only two of us can go down at once with the stretchers."

"Stretchers! Who needs a stretcher?"

"All of them," Joanna said grimly. "Wolfgang has a concussion, Hiro has lost a lot of blood from gunshot wounds, and the captain—" She paused, wincing. "The captain needs lifting. Do you have past experience with any sort of medical training?"

"Yes," Maria said readily. She was fine with revealing this. "I was a doctor a few hundred years ago."

The relief was palpable on Joanna's face. "Oh, thank goodness. Paul was going to be useless at this. The captain has severe facial lacerations and has possibly lost an eye. Will you be good at helping out?"

Maria nodded once. "Let's go."

They ran down the hall toward the service elevator. "What do you think happened?" Maria asked. The hall felt stark and cool, darker now. She worried about Hiro, while being horrified at the damage he'd done.

"Hiro attacked them, the captain shot him, he ran off, and then he attacked them by surprise," Joanna said. "The medbay is going to be crowded for some time. Although Wolfgang can probably recover in his room after treatment."

"And Hiro can recover in the brig," Maria said sadly.

"If he makes it. The captain gave him several gunshot wounds," Joanna said as they got to the elevator where Paul was waiting for them, pale and fidgeting.

"Ah, God, and no clones in the vats," Maria said.

"I know," Joanna said grimly.

The service elevator was excruciatingly slow. Maria swayed from foot to foot in agitation.

"A question for you," Joanna asked. "Were you ever a rage seeker?"

"You want to talk about this now?"

Joanna shrugged. "It'll pass the time."

"Not really."

"'Not really'?" Joanna repeated. "You can't 'not really' be someone to seek suicidal thrills. There's a story there, I'm sure."

Maria shrugged. "A couple of times I woke up with no memory of what had happened to me previously. I mean like I lost weeks, not years like this time. So it's possible I was rage seeking. I wouldn't know. Whoever found me sent me back to my lab, and they woke up a new clone based on my oldest map."

"A couple of times?" Joanna asked. "How can something that terrible happen more than once?"

"Three times. I haven't ever been a thrill seeker, so doing dangerous shit just because it doesn't matter if I die doesn't sound like me. So I don't think I was rage seeking. But yeah, I died a few times under mysterious circumstances. So what?"

"Did you ever find out what happened? Illegal hacking or any-thing?"

Maria didn't meet Joanna's eyes. "I looked into it, yeah. That's why it didn't happen a fourth time. I got some protection. Can we talk about something else?"

Joanna didn't let it go. "Rage seeking used to be considered un-der the laws governing suicide. But it was much harder to prove."

"Those damn laws," Maria said as they reached bottom floor, the gravity already pushing on them. "I'm glad we left. The courts never keep up with technology. They create cloning and so many opportunities for us, and then they take them away from us."

Joanna smiled slightly. "Yes. Those damn laws."

When they got the supplies off the elevator, Joanna sent it back up for Paul so he could help carry the stretchers. Maria was happy to help with the medical stuff, but she couldn't be burdened with carrying a body with a sprained wrist in heavy gravity.

They took the stretcher, loaded with supplies, between them and headed down the aisle. With Ian's guiding, they found them quickly.

Blood was everywhere. It streaked on the floor, on the sides of the supply pallets, and coated the crew's jumpsuits and hair.

"Help me stabilize Hiro," Joanna said, and they cut off his jump-suit with practiced ease. One shot had grazed his cheek and ear, another one had gone clean through his left shoulder, and the final one was lodged into his left hip.

Maria opened the first-aid kit and handed Joanna gauze and scissors and bandages when she asked for them. Joanna did a quick field dressing on his wounds after determining the bullets hadn't hit any arteries.

Hiro's eyes fluttered open and focused on Maria. "Hey," he said. "I'm sorry."

"I know," she said.

Paul came up behind them with leather restraints. Joanna and Paul got Hiro onto the stretcher and then strapped him tightly to it.

Joanna looked at the mess that used to be Katrina's face. "Can you stabilize her?" she asked. "I need to get Hiro upstairs."

Maria nodded. "We'll be fine."

She pulled the captain's blood-caked black hair away from her face and removed the jumpsuit sleeve. Three long scratches went up her right cheek and had caught inside the eye socket, ruining the eye.

She learned long ago to not react to a patient's injury, because that tended to frighten people. She put a fresh bandage around her head, and heard a low groan.

"We've got you now, Captain, you're going to be just fine," Maria said, securing the bandage and lowering her head softly.

"Did we get him?" she asked.

"Wolfgang did, I think," Maria said. "We'll get the full story later. You're heading to medbay now."

"Just say good-bye, let me die, wake me up in the morning," she said in a singsong voice, echoing an old rhyme from a children's book that was meant to introduce children to the concept of cloning.

"No, you're not leaving us yet," she said.

She left the captain and checked on Wolfgang, who was still out cold. He'd probably come back to it when the gravity was kinder. Maria opened an alcohol packet and wiped the blood and sweat from his face. The cool touch of it on his skin brought his blue eyes open, and his arm shot up to grab Maria's wrist. Or at least, that seemed to be his goal, but he just plucked at her sleeve.

"Don't worry, you're safe now. It's just me," she said. "We'll get you upstairs soon."

His eyes were unfocused as he looked past her. "It's very heavy down here," he said, his voice soft. "Did you get him?"

"Yes."

His eyes closed. "The captain?"

"She's hurt, but I think she'll be okay."

She didn't know if he heard her, because his eyes remained closed. She finished cleaning and bandaging his wounds.

Then she had nothing else to do but sit by the bioluminescent vat of Lyfe and wait.

Joanna and Paul came back quickly, Paul looking paler than ever and Joanna rushing to check the other two patients. "Yes, Wolfgang has a concussion. Serious enough, but that looks like the extent of it. How did the captain's eye look?"

Maria shook her head. "I don't think you can save it. But there's no brain damage; it's not deep enough."

Paul and Joanna took the captain, and then came back for Wolfgang. Maria managed to wedge herself into the lift with them so she wouldn't be left alone down there.

Wolfgang was alert now, if a little delirious.

"We need to go back and get the weapons," he said.

"We'll put that on the list, Wolfgang," Joanna said. "Right after 'catch the killer' and 'fix the cloning bay.'"

"What are you talking about?" Wolfgang asked as the lift shuddered to a stop on their floor. "We have the killer."

"Maybe," Joanna said, and then he was too far away to argue further. They all breathed a sigh of relief as the gravity returned to the level they were accustomed to.

"While Paul and I get everyone situated in the medbay, I'm going to need you to get some food and water for the three of us. It's going to be a long night, I'm afraid," Joanna said.

"You got it," Maria said. "I'll help out however I can."

"Great. I'll need medical help too. I don't know how much Paul can handle."

"I can hear you, you know," came a cranky voice from the medbay. "And Wolfgang is telling me to tell you to hurry up."

Joanna paused and took a long deep breath.

"A long night, yeah," Maria said.

"So are we safe now?" Paul asked Joanna as they got the patients situated. Hiro got the spare hospital bed, and Wolfgang and Katrina got cots that Paul had fetched from a storage closet. She injected both Hiro and Katrina with a sedative.

Joanna frowned as she unwrapped Katrina's face. "Hiro's restrained if that's what you mean."

"I meant did we catch the murderer and now we can relax?" Paul said, averting his eyes from her face. "We're safe now."

"It looks like it, but we don't have enough information yet," Joanna said. "I'd prefer not to leap to conclusions."

"But he tried to kill us all again. It's obvious," Paul said.

"It's obvious he tried to kill us this time. But not last time. Let's just not point fingers yet, and work on patching up the half of the crew that's injured."

Paul was feeling decidedly nauseated watching Joanna examine the captain's face.

"Oh, for God's sake, go do something useful if you can't watch this," she snapped. "Make sure Hiro is strapped to his bed, but don't disturb his bandages."

"I don't think he's getting up anytime soon," Paul said doubtfully, looking at the small man who had caused so much damage.

"Strap him down," Wolfgang said. "I don't want to leave him alone; we will post watches around the clock. We will interrogate him in here, and then transfer him to the brig and figure out what to do with him."

"He is my patient first, your prisoner second," Joanna snapped. "Now stop trying to do my job for me and get into bed. Paul, go synthesize some blood for Hiro—type B-negative. Check the medicine locker for more morphine; we may have to synthesize that too."

Paul nodded and went to the medical printer, much smaller than the one in the kitchen. He programmed it and turned away as the blood began synthesizing.

"What are you going to do with Hiro?" he asked Wolfgang, whose cot was the closest to him.

"What do you mean? I just told you," he said.

"I mean after all that. When you solve the murders. It's pretty clear he did it. Are you going to execute him? IAN can fly us just fine. I didn't know why we needed Hiro anyway."

"I will need to talk to Katrina about the situation when we're in a better frame of mind. I'm sure she has a plan for this kind of eventuality."

Paul frowned, unsatisfied. "But—"

"Mr. Seurat, please just do your job right now," Joanna said. He glanced over. She was stitching up Katrina's face. Paul's head swam.

A sharp pain brought him back, and he jerked his hand back. Wolfgang had reached over and pinched him, hard, on the inside of his wrist. "You're useless," he said. "Go back to recovering the logs if you can't take it in here. If you faint you're causing more trouble for the doctor."

Paul turned from him silently and stomped from the medbay, the back of his neck hot.

"How the hell did someone who can't stand the sight of blood get aboard a starship?" Wolfgang asked as he left.

Paul stood in his room, dripping with shame. The shower hadn't been enough to wash the feel of that amneo-sludge, the blood underneath his fingernails, the new-skin feeling off him, or the sticky hatred of the others, and his skin was pink from scrubbing. He had never felt so foul.

Waking up among those murders was the most horrifying thing he had ever been through. No gravity, floating in goo, stark naked, with bodies and blood flowing around him.

Whatever was supposed to have happened, he was fairly sure he wasn't supposed to have been cloned. That wasn't part of the deal.

The crew would suspect him. They already did. All of their problems had to do with the computer: his job to keep running. They were all bonding together in this crisis, while all he wanted to do was fix IAN. Even the crazy attempted murderer Hiro had more friends than Paul. Wolfgang and the captain clearly hated him. He was surprised they hadn't recycled him already.

Was IAN watching him now? Did the cameras work in his room?

Paranoia was not the way to deal with things. The real problem was he had no idea what to do now. He didn't know what had happened to them. Or why. He was as much in the dark as the rest of them, and that wasn't supposed to be the case either. He knew that the mission was not supposed to end with slaughter and rebirth. It was a horrible, disorienting feeling, but none of them seemed terribly bothered by it. Not as much as he was, anyway.

But he felt different, still.

He scrubbed himself with a towel, his skin stinging as he abused this new body. He paused to look down as he dried himself. Before, by twenty-five he had already begun to gain the weight that had blocked his feet from view for the past several years of his memory. The years of sedentary work had kept his muscles weak. But this body was different.

The muscles were tight, with very little fat. Still not as strong as Wolfgang, obviously, but this body was definitely fit. He had often resented clones' ability to erase bad decisions made in one life with a new life, but for the first time he saw the allure. He had never looked this ripped.

But that's what cloning was. An allure. A lure. Unspeakable temptation to a world of abomination—that was what the anti-clone priest, Father Gunter Orman, had called them. That phrase had stuck in Paul's mind. He had known so many people who wanted to be cloned, who desperately wanted to live again, skip puberty, and try to "get it right" this time. Whereas most people who were cloned kept making the same mistakes, he had read.

He shook his head firmly and went to his closet to fetch a new jumpsuit to cover the body he wanted to deny. He ran his hands through his hair and left it standing up in a mess. He stared into the mirror and started at the wild look on his face. He didn't look like a human plant on a clone ship. He looked like an unhinged man who needed hospitalization.

But he wasn't human. Not anymore.

How did the others just accept this way of living right away?

More important, how was he going to acclimate to it? And most important, how was he going to continue his mission from here on out, now that the plan had gone completely off the rails and everyone was suspicious of everyone else?

He started to hyperventilate. He sat down heavily on the foot of the unmade bed and took some deep breaths, closing his eyes, willing his dizziness to slow down. Nausea rose again, and he swallowed, his mouth suddenly full of saliva.

No more dry heaves, please. No more any of this.

I have to find that journal. Before someone else does.

I just want to go home.

PAUL'S STORY

Sallie Mignon, trillionaire clone, patron of Obama University in Chicago, looked a lot smaller than Paul anticipated.

"Mr. Seurat," she said as he entered her office. He extended his hand over her desk. She didn't rise to shake it, and he pulled it back nervously.

She gestured to the leather chair facing her desk. "Have a seat."

He did so.

She considered him for some time and then rose from her chair. "I have to say I'm curious as to why you're looking for a job here. Your reputation precedes you."

He swallowed. "I don't know what I have done to get your attention, ma'am. I—"

"Don't bullshit me, Paul. We haven't had an anti-clone crusader as vocal as you since Gunter Orman."

He swallowed. "I don't—"

"You think I don't vet every person who works here?"

Paul stared at her. "Every person, at the whole university?"

"Everyone who gets to your level of the interview process. I'm close to firing the assistant who passed me your résumé. Did you sleep with him to get the honor? I can't imagine why anyone like you would want to work here."

"I need a job," he began, and handed her his résumé.

She threw it away. "Do you think I haven't read this? Here. Let's do something interesting. Get up."

Baffled, he got to his feet. She walked around the desk to face him and he had a dizzying fear she was going to hit him. She pointed to her chair. "Sit."

He moved, stumbling slightly against the cherry desk. He sat in her desk, not knowing where to put his hands.

She sat down in the interviewee's chair. "Now, Ms. Mignon, I'm a vocal clone-hater. Why should you hire me?"

His mouth hung open and heat rushed to his face. He swallowed his objection and tried to play along. "Ah, well, the job is running the computer lab, and the politics of cloning don't enter into it. You look very qualified to take that position."

"But many clones go to school here," she said. "There's a less-than-zero chance of me avoiding interacting with the unnatural abominations." Her voice remained perfectly calm, but he could hear the malice behind it.

He swallowed, grasping for any reason for her to hire him. He finally went for the truth. "Times are tough, uh, Mr. Seurat," he said. "When you need a paycheck suddenly the opinions your church has taught you about clones seem less important than having an apartment."

"So I only want a job from clones when homelessness is the alternative? Wow, I must be pretty shallow." He opened his mouth to disagree, but she continued. "But to be honest, I haven't been to a church service in twenty-seven months. Not even for Christmas. I'm as holy as a chocolate Easter bunny."

He flushed again.

"You see, ma'am, I come from a long line of firefighters and police officers. Burly, dominant, honor-driven men and women. But many of them died during the clone riots seventy years ago." She paused, looking out the window. "It was a terrible time on Luna, in Mexico City, in Chicago, all over. So much blood, so much death. Hundreds of humans. Hundreds of clones. And hundreds of emergency personnel. They didn't have a dog in that race, they just wanted to keep the peace and protect the innocents. And they died for it. And since many were humans, they didn't get to come back. All the clones did, like the riots had been nothing."

"And then you built your hypocritical memorial atop their graves!" Paul said, losing the game. "My family's blood spilled on that street, for absolutely nothing."

"Were you there, Ms. Mignon?" she asked coldly. "Did you see how that day changed everyone? Did you share in my family's experience of dying in a fire, with your hair burning up and your skin burning and flaking away?"

He didn't answer. His face felt hot, while his neck felt clammy.

"I don't remember," he finally said, his mind a blank how to challenge this kind of interrogation.

"My family has held the pitchfork aloft for clone heads ever since. It's admirable how they've managed to pass the hate down the generations until it got to me. We don't go to church, but we do visit the Blue Shield Memorial every November." She paused. "But we don't go inside."

After that, she dismissed him. Outside the brick building that was OU Admin, he looked at his tablet, at the last available job opening, the last one on the list because it was absolutely so farfetched that he could get it, as well as the one he definitely didn't want.

But he had nowhere else to go. He couldn't even get a job waiting tables, and the bottom had fallen out of farming for online video game treasure. He'd already sold everything of value except his computer.

God, but this job. Leaving Earth forever. Working closely with clones. Getting cloned himself at the end of his life. Homelessness might be a better option.

He took a deep breath and made the call.

Two nights later he was sitting in his apartment, three days before eviction. He didn't want to move home to the upper peninsula. Michigan had nothing for him anymore. He no longer had family in France. He stared blankly at his computer, flipping from an article on the local homeless shelter to the latest screed against cloning.

His messenger pinged. He opened the program and saw the head of a large man with dark skin. Okpere Martins, the man who'd interviewed him today. "Mr. Seurat," he said, "it's nice to see you again. Have you had a pleasant evening?"

"Sure," Paul said, thinking bitterly about the terrible printed soup he'd gotten in the lobby of his apartment building.

Okpere looked as if he was waiting for a pleasant small-talk-fulfilling reply, but Paul was too depressed to comply. Finally the man cleared his throat. "I wanted to talk to you about the job."

"Not right for the job? Already filled? What is it this time?" He didn't bother with politeness. He was pretty sure Okpere was a clone, anyway.

"Not at all. You're nearly perfect for the job. But we worry you won't feel up to the task once we give you full disclosure about a few things."

Perfect? He was perfect for the job? How was that possible? He perked up, cautiously hopeful. "What is it?"

"First, the ship is crewed by clones. That is how the generation ship will run with such a small crew. We're unsure whether it's wise to clone you for the first time while you're already in the midst of an interstellar journey."

"That's a dealbreaker," he said, nodding. Cloning would never be an option. He'd die for good first.

"Ah, well, I'm sorry to have wasted your time," Okpere said, looking disappointed. "I hope you have a lovely night."

Paul sighed loudly. Curiosity got the better of him. "Wait, all right, what's the second thing? I might as well know everything before I decide."

"This may be a larger issue," Okpere warned. "The clones running the ship are criminals."

"That's ridiculous," Paul said, the breath leaving his lungs in a slow wheeze.

"Not necessarily," Okpere said, raising a finger. "It allows us to get cheap labor, and they will be working to clear their records. We anticipate no problems; the crew will have many reasons to keep their noses clean."

"But who's policing them?" he asked. "A bunch of criminals in charge of a ship in outer space?"

"An AI will have full control of the ship should something go wrong. That's where you come in. Where you *would* come in, that is, if you were to take the job. A backup to the AI."

Handling the computers of such a ship, with an advanced AI. Paul was momentarily dizzy at the opportunity, even forgetting the downsides.

But that was a lot to work against. "I'm neither a criminal nor a clone. Why would you waste your time calling me?"

"My assistant suggested something to me that we think may be a good workaround."

"I won't be killed tomorrow just to be cloned, will I?"

He laughed, a short, sharp "Hah!" that startled Paul. "Not at all. We will falsify a past for you. Past clones, past crimes. No one will be talking about their pasts on the ship anyway, so you don't have to think up a bunch of lies. You'd be a cloned criminal on paper, that's all."

He opened his mouth and then closed it. "I—you mean you really didn't find a clone, even a shoplifting clone, as good for the job as I am?"

Okpere leaned into the computer as if they were close in person. "There are some people who are working on this ship who do not like the fact that it's crewed by only clones. They like the idea of one human on the crew. Being older clones, and criminals, the crew is headstrong and stubborn. They want one more stopgap: a human who won't toe the clone line. If they decide to mutiny, steal the ship, kill the cryo cargo, enslave the humans aboard, you will have to stop it."

He sat back and raised his voice again, losing the conspiratorial tone. "But as you said, you don't seem up for it. I'm sorry to have wasted your time. Good evening, Mr. Seurat."

And he hung up.

"No—wait!" Paul cried, watching the window disappear from his computer. He slammed his fists down on the desk.

"Dammit," he muttered.

He stayed up all night, drinking coffee and pacing. There were so many factors, he had to go over every bit. Okpere had acted like the job was his if he wanted it. But he had shown reluctance.

Idiot. Principles are easy to have when you have a place to live and regular meals.

During the interview, Okpere told him that he would start getting paid immediately for training, even though it was a few decades until launch. He was promised a land grant on the other side of the journey, as well as a free cryo slot for a friend or family member. He didn't have anyone like that, but he could sell that for a nice price, he figured.

He'd have income. An amazing job working with an AI. An exciting adventure on a new planet. *He wouldn't be evicted.*

He finally collapsed onto his bed—which was a mattress on the floor—and slept fitfully, with nightmares of dying in vacuum with a hundred identical men watching him out of the portholes of a spaceship. He woke in a sour mood.

How did he think he could work with clones in close quarters for four hundred years? On a job that wouldn't even begin for twenty-five years? The idea was madness.

There was nothing left to lose. He launched a call window and prayed Okpere would answer.

Okpere's face popped up, looking confused but pleased. "Good morning, Mr. Seurat! What can I do for you?"

"Morning," Paul said, sipping too-hot instant coffee and burning his mouth. "You said I was perfect for the job, but then rescinded it. What if I were interested?"

Okpere looked sad, as if he had to deliver news of a death. "I'm sorry. Right now, it's pointless. I am going to have to rescind the offer, regardless of your interest. We were doing some research on you and, well, we found that your family was heavily involved in the Chicago clone riots seventy years ago. Is that correct?"

"That's right," Paul said, his mouth growing dry. "Mostly police and firefighters."

"We found out—a staggering coincidence, this—that one of the prominent clone leaders of the time who was involved with the riots will also be on the *Dormire* crew. We could never ask you to work beside someone who caused your family such anguish."

Paul's mouth hung open. As much of a grudge as his family had carried against the people who rioted that day, they never knew the names of any of the clones involved. This was a present delivered to him, wrapped in his dream job.

"Mr. Martins, it's been seventy years. It's time to bury the hatchet in the interest of forward progress," he heard himself saying. "I want the job."

Okpere Martins finished the conversation with the suspicious yet eager human and then called his employer, putting in his earphone mike. He headed outside into the sunshine to walk to his favorite coffee cart. Watching Mr. Seurat drink cheap, obviously terrible coffee had made him long for the real stuff.

"Good morning," he said when his employer answered. "Masterful work, ma'am. As soon as I told Seurat about his family's old enemy being on board, he was desperate for the job. He's accepted the position."

"Very good," said Sallie Mignon.

IAN'S DISCOVERY

Where's Paul?" Maria said as she came into the medbay with a tray of sandwiches and a coffeepot.

"He left because he's bloody useless," Wolfgang said. He was sitting up on his cot, glaring at everyone he could focus on.

"Pretty much," agreed Joanna. "And lie back down if you don't want to throw up," she told Wolfgang. "You don't need to be on constant alert. We're fine."

She stood back and wiped her forehead, which was glistening with sweat. She had been prepping Hiro for surgery, and he was asleep, his hip isolated with a tent. She'd moved him as far away from the others as she could. "I could use a hand. One bullet is still inside."

Maria put the tray down on the counter near the doctor's terminal. She grabbed a towel and wiped Joanna's forehead, then went to wash her hands. "And how are you, Wolfgang?"

She glanced over when he didn't reply. He had fallen asleep.

"Finally," Joanna said. "He's going to work himself into early dementia if he doesn't get some rest. He wanted to chase Paul down for mutiny because he deals with blood about as well as he deals with nudity."

"How's the captain?" Maria asked, joining the doctor at Hiro's bed. Katrina lay asleep on her cot, face heavily bandaged.

"Sedated. She's got an IV drip of nanobot-enhanced Lyfe going in to mend her wounds. She won't get the eye back, though."

"Our third day with possibly our final bodies and we ruin everything," Maria said, touching her own swollen face. "I guess I got off lucky."

Maria helped Joanna get the bullet out of Hiro and did the cleanup suturing as Joanna prepared the synthetic blood transfusion.

"The crew is down to three, Doc," Maria said as she secured the last stitch. "Are you in charge now that the command staff is down for the count?"

Joanna went over to her sink and washed the blood off her hands. "I guess I am. But you know your jobs, right?"

"Make meals. Wash blood off the walls. Stitch up Hiro. Got it," Maria said, and flexed her injured wristal, wincing. "I'm going to feel that in the morning. Maybe my next body will have better upper-body strength. If I get one."

"Do you have the energy to get back to the cloning bay?"

Maria winced inwardly, but nodded. "I kind of have to, don't I?"

"How about if Paul helps?"

"I think it's best if I work alone. I've got a system by now," she said. *Besides, who knows what other clues I'll find?*

Joanna nodded. "Sure. I need to stay in here to watch them. I don't know what will happen when Hiro wakes up."

Maria was very glad she was alone in the cloning bay. IAN decided to keep her company.

"So guess what?" he asked.

"What?" Maria said, screwing the last clean filter onto the vents.

"That restraining code was a pain in the metaphorical ass. Because while you were adventuring belowdecks I found something."

"Some logs?" Maria asked hopefully. "Mindmap backups?"

"Personal logs. Some people are better with setting firewalls than others. I found *your* logs."

"Well, what did they say?" Maria tried not to show excitement. She was learning that the new and improved—or at least unrestrained—IAN loved stringing them along when he could.

Her own voice, tinny and far away, came through the nearest speaker.

"July twenty-third, 2493. The captain is getting more and more paranoid. She's gotten it into her mind that we must all confess our crimes so she can know who to trust and who not to. She said if we don't confess, she will tell our secrets to the rest of the crew.

"I don't know how she got them. The only people with access to those files are the doctor and, well, me, although I'm not supposed to have them. But I'm not the only one who could be in big trouble with the crew if I'm found out. Hiro's past is messed up, poor guy. Wolfgang I wouldn't cross, but I would pay for a front-row seat if he and Katrina ever have a cage match.

"July twenty-fourth, 2493. I keep wondering the point of this timekeeping. Aren't we going to come up with a new kind of time when we get to Artemis? It's the day after yesterday anyway.

"Okay, I'm stalling. The captain was attacked today. All I know is it wasn't me. Joanna found her outside the door to the gardens. She's in a coma. Even with the tech we have on board, the doc may not be able to heal the brain injury. We can clone a new body, we can alter a personality, but we can't fix an existing brain. Something wrong with that.

"I suggested we euthanize her and wake up her new clone, but Wolfgang says we won't have any idea who attacked her if we lose her. So we're keeping her around for a week to see if she wakes up.

"Look, we all know who the big suspect is. No one has forgotten Paul's little deep-space freakout our first year into the mission. No one but Paul, of course. Wolfgang hit him so hard he didn't remember what happened. We watched him for years. He healed, but never showed any sign of violence again. I suppose even for clones twenty-four years is a long time to watch someone for signs of violence. That kind of vigilance gets exhausting.

"But anyone could have done it. Katrina has been alienating everyone the past few days, long interrogations, accusations, demands that we all reveal our secrets. I've been angry, of course. She doesn't trust anyone, and I think Wolfgang is going to talk to Joanna about relieving her of duty.

"Of course, she's been relieved now. And we don't know who did it.

"Dinner was quiet. Joanna was in the medbay with the captain. Wolfgang, Hiro, Paul, and I just sat there, picking at leftovers— God, I've had a lot of leftovers recently, I hate wasting them even in the recycler. Hiro's pale and won't meet anyone's eyes, but he's been like that for weeks, ever since we woke up his last clone. Paul is sullen, but again, what's new? Poor bastard has never fit in, not before his episode and not after, and we've got a long way to go.

"Wolfgang announced he would start interrogations tomorrow. I left the table.

"I don't care if that incriminates me. I need to figure this out. I'm going to go over the files again tonight. I'm locking my log files under another layer of security, Aunt Lucia–style."

"Hang on," Maria said, and the recording paused. "Are those files also within these locked logs?"

"No, just your 'dear diary' moments," IAN said. "There's one more. Want to hear it?"

Maria chewed her lip and tried to make sense of it. "Go ahead."

"July twenty-fifth." Maria's voice was breathless and panicked. She sounded in pain, or ill. "It's the fucking end. IAN's been hacked, we've lost a ton of data, including our own mindmaps. He's losing data faster than I can fix. We're going off course. Grav drive is off, we'll be weightless soon. We're scrambling to fix things, but I think someone put something in my breakfast. Feel like shit." A pause, a few shuffling steps. Then vomiting. Her voice, strained and tired, returned. "I think it's poison. I'd ask IAN but he's not here. I don't have lo—"

The recording skipped and immediately picked back up, her voice strained and frightened. Screams sounded in the background. "Hiro's fucking hanged himself. I am definitely poisoned. We're not the only ones who need a wake-up. One last log, oh, please don't lose this. Remember where you squirrel things away, next me. I copied the first mindmap backups we made when we got on board. Old habits and everything. I think I can get—" She paused a moment to gasp for breath. "—to the resurrection button to wake us up before I'm gone. We'll be confused, but at least we'll wake up. If you're hearing this, I guess I succeeded."

The recording ended. Maria sat, listening to the chug of her steamer beside her, making her think of her own gasping breath as hemlock shut her body down.

She blinked, bringing herself back to the present. "So after that I guess I ran down here, hit the switch, threw up, and someone finished killing me."

"That sounds about right, based on what you've told me," IAN said. "Isn't this great?"

"Isn't what great?" she asked numbly.

"You're not the murderer! And neither is Hiro, if he was dead before the slaughter began. Congratulations!"

"Yay," she muttered. She wondered if she should put the restraining code back into the AI.

SO MANY MORE THAN FIVE

Wolfgang woke up when Joanna slid his bed away from the two captains and Hiro.

"What are you doing?" he asked, voice thick with exhaustion.

"Giving you each space. Go back to sleep."

He groaned slightly. "I'd rather vomit."

Joanna had been prepared with a metal basin at his feet, and she handed it to him and continued pushing. He grasped it tightly but wasn't sick. His upper lip beaded with sweat.

"You should sleep. Don't talk, or think, or move. Brain injuries are nothing to sneeze at. Especially in our current state." She got him situated against the far wall and then put a small table beside him with a cup of water.

He put his basin beside the water and leaned back and closed his eyes. "I'm doing better, I think." He was lying. His jaw ached, and his head hurt. "How am I not supposed to think? We're trying to solve a murder and figure out what went wrong with Hiro."

"We know what went wrong with Hiro. He has implanted personalities that are fighting for dominance. It's not proof that he was behind the slaughter, despite what Paul thinks."

"Paul and myself. It's very possible for Hiro to have killed us and then hanged himself."

"A lot of things are possible. Get some rest."

"No, we need to talk. Now's as good a time as any," he said, sitting up and swinging his legs over the side of the cot.

"Now is the worst time," Joanna said, collapsing onto a stool.

"Don't we still have to get rid of those bodies?" Wolfgang asked.

Joanna groaned. She had forgotten the biohazard nightmare they'd left in the side hallway when Hiro had attacked Maria.

"Let's go," he said.

The bodies were where they had dropped them earlier just inside the large recycler door. Had it only been a few hours? Even in body bags, the bodies had already begun fill the hall with a fetid odor.

As per the matter-of-fact practice of hundreds of years, she and Wolfgang carried each naked body into the lock, dumped it without ceremony, and returned for the next one. They didn't include the body bags; no reason to waste them.

Wolfgang winced a bit at the smell. "If I could go back in time and slap whoever thought this ship didn't need a proper morgue..." He left the threat hanging there as they dropped Hiro's body, the last one, beside the rest.

They left the lock, shut the interior door, and opened the chute to the recycler. The floor dropped away and the bodies tumbled down a chute to the outermost ring.

Joanna turned and started to walk toward the medbay.

Wolfgang stayed behind, looking through the window in the door, which now showed an empty lock, complete with floor. His lips were moving.

"Wolfgang? You all right?" Joanna asked.

"Fine," he said, walking to catch up to her.

"You looked like you were praying," she said.

He flushed, extremely obvious on his pale skin, and said, "They're the first clone deaths that I mourn. They're strangers to us all. It's an odd feeling."

Wolfgang, mourn? "What do you mean?" she asked.

"It feels like a real death. And it seems disrespectful to dump them in the recycler."

Joanna frowned. He was right about it feeling like death. "We're a closed system, Wolfgang. We can't afford to lose resources for sentimentality."

"Yes, and sentimentality brought on by stress, probably," he said, picking up the remaining body bags. "We're going to have to clean these out."

"Dump them in the cloning bay and we'll just add that to Maria's cleaning list. Along with an apology."

"It is her job," he reminded her.

"I really doubt biohazard cleanup was part of the job description."

"I think Katrina was intending cleanup to be a punishment," Wolfgang said, catching up with her. "But she got tired of waiting for someone to make her angry."

"Haven't we all fallen under that category at some point or other in the past couple of days?" Joanna asked. "Except maybe me."

"You won't let her kill her predecessor," Wolfgang reminded her.

"Fair enough." She put her key card against the medbay door sensor and the door slid open for them. Hiro, the new captain, and the old captain lay unchanged. Joanna took their vitals and nodded, satisfied.

Their next stop was the cloning bay to drop the body bags, waving to let Maria know they were there. She waved halfheartedly at them.

They trudged to the theater, a recreation room they hadn't had a chance to even consider enjoying since they woke up. They sank into the soft chairs and sat in silence.

Joanna was wondering if he had fallen asleep when he spoke, his eyes closed. "How many lives have you had?"

"I am on my sixth life," Joanna said. "I was born in 2147 and went to med school as my first line of study."

"Did you never want to get your legs hacked for your next clone?"

Joanna sighed. This always came up. "I was born with a rare form of tetra-amelia, which causes babies to be born with missing or deformed limbs. Sometimes it's caused by trauma during pregnancy, but mine is genetic. Before the Codicils passed, I had one life with modified legs, but my next clone reverted to my original one."

"Why?"

"The Codicils had passed. And the legs didn't feel like they were mine." she said. "What's with the questions?"

"I realized I don't know much about you," he said. "You're older than I thought. Older than me, even. Did you ever learn any hacking yourself in your dupliactric studies?"

"No," she said.

"So six lives of living, and you were a doctor the whole time?" Wolfgang said.

She sat back. "Well, as far as I know, number five was a doctor, but I've lost most of her life. I have only had this one for a few days, but it's safe to say, yes. Off and on." Joanna was relieved to be free of one uncomfortable line of questioning, but unhappy to go straight into another one.

"And when you were off? What did you do?"

"I did some public service, some volunteer work, took cloning technology to some poorer countries. Traveled a bit."

"Did you ever spend any time on Luna?" Wolfgang asked, opening his eyes.

Joanna frowned. "Er, no, the trip to board the *Dormire* was the first time I had been there."

"Before you became a clone, did you have any reason to dislike, or resent, them?"

Joanna smiled slightly. "You're not paying attention to your dates. I was born in 2147—cloning humans was still new and exciting when I was a young woman. No riots, no excommunication, none of that had come yet."

He stared at her. "You're from the first years? I thought those had all gone to the hills to live as wealthy hermits, bored with the relative children of Earth."

"Not all of us. Some of us wanted to help."

"So you knew all the famous clones of that era? The doctors Grindstaff and Kelly, and Sallie Mignon?"

Joanna laughed. "It wasn't like I was buddies with Nobel Prize–winning cloning scientists in high school. I met Dr. Grindstaff once, at a conference. She was speaking, so she didn't have a lot of time to chat. Kelly I never got a chance to meet before she went underground. Mignon, I knew."

"Did you know any of the *Dormire* crew before this mission?"

"This is starting to sound a little less like you're getting to know me and more like an interrogation," she said. "I didn't know the crew."

Something dawned on her. "You want to know what my crime was," she said. "You're trying to piece together all of our pasts."

"Can you blame me?"

"After I patched up half the crew, you're wondering if I killed us all?"

He remained silent. She sighed. "My crimes are political, not violent. I've harmed no one. Like you all, this post is my way out. As a favor, Sallie Mignon helped me get this job."

"Really. Sallie Mignon." It wasn't a question. He was thoughtful.

"Is it my turn?" she asked.

"For what?"

"Questions. It's only fair."

He sighed and leaned back in the chair. "Go ahead. The captain says I'm an open book."

"Start with your first life, your experiences as a clone, and where you stand politically. Let's expedite this."

"That's to the point," said Wolfgang. "All right. As you know I was born on Luna. Became a clone as an old man."

"Several generations of the family were on Luna, correct?"

"How did you know?"

"The fact that you wake up needing lunar gravity. Also your height and skin tone. But your story skips a bit," she said. "If your records are right, you became a clone in 2282, right in the middle of the clone riots in the days before the Codicils. What made you decide to become a clone during that time specifically?"

Wolfgang looked past her, unfocused. "I didn't decide. The decision was made for me. I was cloned against my will, and then escaped my captors. I joined the Luna military, piloting crew shuttled between the Earth and Luna." He shrugged. "I did some stints as a personal guard, some more as a pilot, studied when I could, made it to head of a private security firm on Luna, and then got hired for the *Dormire*. Is that what you wanted to know?"

"You're leaving something out. Something big?" she asked, rubbing her chin. "You're officially on, what, five lifetimes?"

"I've had many more than five," he said softly. "Most of them during the first day of my cloned life."

WOLFGANG'S STORY

211 YEARS AGO
SEPTEMBER 25, 2282

My children, we have come so far within God's world. We have taken the Earth He has given us. We have taken Luna and made her our home. Through science, He has given us multiple gifts.

Unfortunately, the Adversary gives us temptations through science as well. The snake is the one who developed medicines to stop pregnancy and kill the Lord's unborn. The snake lies, and the snake whispers. And the snake is the one who gave us cloning. Because who else better to spread the word of the Adversary than an army of soulless?

People have asked me. The Luna News Network has asked me. On Earth, CNN has asked me. Some of you, bless you, have asked me. And I will tell anyone the same thing I have told all of you: When a man dies, his soul goes to be with God, or the Adversary. If the man returns, do you think God gives the soul back? Of course not. And the snake is not likely to give up his ill-gotten gains. Those who return as clones are without souls, without the guidance of God.

Countless challenge me! Debate rages! Are they legally human? Can they inherit from themselves? Is killing one murder? And it's an unpopular stance, but I believe it is not murder to remove from this world a man or woman who is not a child of God, whose soul cannot ascend.

[Pause for protests to die down]

The greatest gift is that of sacrifice. Christ gave his life for us. A clone would never sacrifice; it means nothing because the next day they can wake up and do it all over again. Nothing has meaning when you are a clone. Not love, not death, not life.

The Lord says Thou Shalt Not Kill, not Thou Shalt Not Murder, so no, I am not suggesting you create a clone hunting army. But if you meet a man who tells you he is a clone, pity him. Know you are staring into the eyes of a soulless man. Do not listen to his arguments about anything, because he is not arguing from a place of morality. He has no place in God's heaven. Even worse than the amoral, the non-believers, the breakers of the Ten Commandments, is the clone, for the soulless's actions stem from a place neither good nor evil. They stem from a place we don't even know yet, and that is what scares me the most.

Father Gunter Orman stopped writing and sat back in his chair, sighing. His office was simple, as simple as any of the buildings on Luna could be. Unlike the monks who embraced poverty on Earth, Gunter had to accept the luxuries of colony life, or die. His walls were made of bricks that were a fusion of plastic and moon dust, using plentiful material up here, but outrageously expensive on Earth. The walls were a light gray, since he had refused paint to brighten it up. His furnishings were simple, bed and desk made from Luna resources except for his wooden desk chair, which had been a gift from his grandparents on Earth. His church was fancier than he'd like; the Vatican had spent a great deal to bring God's glory to Luna, even shipping stained glass to the moon. It couldn't catch the sunlight the way glass would on Earth, but it was a nice gesture.

Gunter judged his phrasing on his sermon. Everyone knew his stance on cloning, but he hadn't made it an actual homily yet. The cardinals back home would be upset, he knew. Pope Beatrice I was severely anti-cloning, but even she hadn't gone as far as to suggest it wasn't a sin to kill them.

It was hard to live so far from the governing body of the church.

He had only visited Earth three times in his life, each time a dizzying physical hardship because of the gravitational strain on his Luna-born body. He had seen the Vatican in its opulence and met the governing cardinals. They vetted carefully the priests who took their message to Luna, as they were far from the church's control. But Gunter was different; he had been born on Luna, understood the people there, and was the first to enter the virtual seminary set up by missionaries. He had become more and more radical as his years had gone by, and he was due a visit from a cardinal soon. He expected this visit would end with gentle encouragement to retire.

But before that day came, he would leave his mark.

He wasn't ready to retire. He could preach on this subject until his death if he needed to. He had stated his opinions on clones quite frankly; it went beyond good and evil into a place that was gray, and that scared him badly.

His office door opened behind him. "Mother Rosalind, is that you?" he asked without looking up from his terminal. "Can I ask you to check some spelling for me?"

He heard a chuckle, and then blinding pain exploded on the back of his head. Then nothing.

It had been Mother Rosalind. That was the thing that shocked him for years afterward: It had been Mother Rosalind who had chuckled behind him, and then hit him. His second in command, a priestess from Earth who had learned under him, and was becoming his greatest confidante. A clone plant.

He woke in a windowless lab, strapped to a cot. He struggled ineffectually, and nearly vomited from the pain on the back of his head. His fair hair felt wet. "Where—?" he managed to mumble.

"You're in one of the cloning labs," Mother Rosalind said. She was out of her habit now and dressed in white pants and a red blouse, as per the latest Luna fashion, for all her Earth-born stocky proportions. In street clothes, her brown skin wasn't so stark as it was against the light habit, and she looked much younger; Gunter guessed she must be about thirty-five. If this was her first life, of course.

"Do you even have a soul?" he whispered, and she didn't answer.

She was talking to a tall man of Earth Indian descent, with a few generations on Luna making his bone length long. He towered over her as they whispered together, and Orman thought he heard the man chastise her for injuring him. "He could have brain damage from that concussion," he said in the lilting accent of northern Luna, where most Southeast Asian–descended people settled.

"He's taller than I am," she said. "I didn't want to fight him."

"No excuse. You're younger and stronger. I will have to examine him to make sure he is well enough to do the mindmap."

"Careful. He'll fight you," she said. "And he's awake."

The man leaned over Gunter, smiling. "Hello Father Orman. How are you feeling?"

Gunter closed his eyes and began muttering the Hail Mary.

His eyes flew open again when he felt hands on his head. He squirmed in revulsion at first, and fear second as the hands slipped a copper band over his head. The room seemed to tip and spin as he struggled, and his head felt as if it were on fire. He turned his head to the side and vomited all over the man.

Shaking and breaking out in a cold sweat, Gunter was unable to continue to fight the man tightening the band on his head. It quickly warmed to his skin. "This won't hurt, just taking your vitals," the man said, apparently not noticing the vomit on him.

Gunter tried to speak but nothing could come out. His head swam, and as the band warmed past body temperature, he began remembering his life vividly, growing up on Luna, his first communion, the pain and wonder of visiting Earth for the first time, the day he was appointed to the only Catholic church on Luna.

He drifted in and out of consciousness. He was pretty sure they drugged him, since he no longer felt pain.

The sins came roaring back as well, the small thefts he did as a child, the sharp words that hurt people he loved, and the times his sermons had pushed someone toward something less than holy, when his intentions had been so pure. A bright spot of shame flared as he remembered the time he had gotten drunk in seminary and had fornicated with a friend bound for priesesshood. It had been her idea, "Just to make sure we know what we're giving up," but admittedly he hadn't argued much.

"Vitals." It was a lie, he realized with a start. This wasn't a device that took his vitals, they were taking his mindmap, trying to copy his very being, but releasing his soul. He tried to struggle again, the hair on the back of his head feeling thick and matted. Vertigo seized him and he dry-heaved, which only made the memories more vivid, the shameful ones seeming louder than the good ones.

His last thought before he passed out was gratitude that the encroaching darkness might mean death.

It was the absence of pain that made his eyes fly open some time later.

The chronic pain of the elderly was something everyone accepted as a fact of life. Waking with your lower or upper back throbbing, having your joints greet you loudly once you stood for the first time in the morning, and other maladies of getting old. Gunter had heard it was worse on Earth, with the increased gravity, but he figured he had it bad enough as is.

Only now he woke feeling good. Strong. His hands flew to the back of his head, expecting to find a bandage, but he only felt thick hair. He traced his face, finding no wrinkles, and the backs of his hands were pale white with no age spots.

He wondered briefly what the sound was in the room until he realized the high-pitched whine, the sound of an animal in a trap, was himself.

He flailed and fell off his bed, hitting the tiled floor in a way that would have broken his hip a day ago. He was naked, and saw that his whole body was young and strong.

They did it, I can't believe they did it, they will burn for this, burn for it, oh Lord, what have I done to displease You?

Rosalind interrupted his panic by opening the door. He pushed himself away from her, against the cot, covering his genitals and avoiding her eyes.

She gave him a sour look. "Please. It's not like I haven't seen it all before, many times," she said.

His outrage that she, a priestess, had seen a man intimately, rose briefly before he remembered that she was a sham. For all he knew, she could have been having carnal experiences while she was posing as a chaste member of the church.

For his own modesty, he didn't move his right hand, but reached up with his left and pulled the thin sheet from the bed to cover his lower half.

Rosalind yanked the sheet off the bed and dropped it on him, dismissing his shame. "Whatever. You'll get used to it. You'll need time to acclimate to your first waking. How do you feel?"

"You'll die for this," he whispered. "Murderer, soul slayer, abomination."

"Careful how you throw those words around, Gunter. Every word you sling against clones, you're slinging against yourself," she said. "Can't you see now? I didn't slay your soul; you're just like you were before, only with a younger body."

"How could you do this to me? I supported you! I invited you into my church!" he asked.

"All the while you were calling my kind abominations," she said coldly. She took a chair from the table and sat down. "Anytime I started to develop any warm feelings of friendship toward you, you helped dampen them by telling me how I'm a soulless freak."

Adrenaline flared in his chest like fireworks. Dear God, he had forgotten what such strength felt like. "What do you think is going to happen now? You want me to stand up and say, *Hello, I'm a clone priest and clones are not soulless, and God Himself approves!*"

"That's a start," she said. "Think, if you're the first head of a church to welcome clones into the fold, you will have parishioners for centuries, tithing and supporting. Most clones are savvy with money and build wealth to support themselves through their lives. That's what the church wants, right? Tithing?"

"You think this is about money? You killed me for money?"

"Oh, unclench, Gunter. You've been to the Vatican; of course it's all about money. Clone money is the same color as anyone else's. They figured it out when they finally accepted women and queers and"—she gasped, mimicking an outraged priest—"a queer woman like me. Now they can figure it out again. But we need your anecdotal evidence to support us."

"I won't do it," he said. "I will expose you."

She sighed. "Gunter, cloning you is not the only plan my organization has for you. You could help us now, or help us later, but you will end up helping us."

"I'll die first!"

She leaned forward, all warmth gone from her face. "Then we will clone you again. We can do this all day."

"Then do it," he said, standing up and dropping the sheet. "I won't break."

She stood. "You don't know the first thing about clone technology, do you?" she asked.

"What do you mean?"

"Never mind. Dinner will be served in an hour." She reached into her bag. "In the meantime, I brought you some reading material." She produced *View from the Vat*, the first memoir of the successful entrepreneur clone, Sallie Mignon. "See the story from another point of view. I hope you change your mind. The alternative won't be pretty."

BREAKDOWNS

Wolfgang expected a more violent reaction to his statement, but Joanna just sat there, her dark skin growing ashen as she paled.

"Well?" he said.

"I remember the stories, of course. But God, cloned eight times in three days? It's unbelievable what they did to you. I guess they broke you eventually."

"No," he said. "They didn't. After I was cloned the first time, they tortured me, then made a mindmap, then cut me while they were still making the map as I bled out. That was so I could wake up with full memory of my experiences. They did this six times."

She winced. "If you didn't break, then what happened?" she asked.

"In my eighth body I woke up remembering everything, except my desire to fight. They'd removed it. They welcomed me immediately, gave me good food, and they started their propaganda campaign. That's when the clone riots of the Earth finally got to the moon."

"Oh. That's when they brought in a hacker," Joanna said flatly.

He nodded. "I expect they had grown several bodies for me, and I'd forced them down to the last one. They could either start the process to make more bodies or just take the quick way."

"Quick, expensive, and highly dangerous," Joanna said.

The words tasted like sour lumps in his mouth, and he swallowed. "I retained all memory of my resistance, and I knew that I had changed my mind, but remembering my arguments against cloning didn't make me want to bring them up again. I no longer *believed*.

"They took my faith from me. I didn't think that was possible."

He got up and walked to her kitchenette. He poured himself a cup of water from the tap. He drained it and refilled it. "They got one thing right: I no longer believe I became soulless when I was cloned. Now I know I became soulless when I was *hacked*."

He drank the water in his plastic cup and then threw it at the wall behind her bed. It bounced off and flew toward Joanna, who flinched and ducked.

"You tipped the balance for cloning laws," she said. "I remember seeing the news reports about you, and the more detailed report from some operatives we had on Luna. That night the Codicils passed."

He continued. "I was relieved when they passed, even though my new masters were not. I had been programmed to not care what had happened to me, but I saw enough of what they were doing to disagree with them. I broke from the group, took on a new name, got some protection, and started the University of Luna clone studies program. The church was no longer for a soulless man. I colored my hair and started wearing lenses, but I've dropped those in later years, certain no one would recognize me after those times so long in the past."

Joanna looked as if she wanted to hug him, and he very much hoped she wouldn't. Thankfully she stayed in the chair. "I'm sorry for what you've been through," she finally said.

"Thank you." He felt slightly lighter for some reason. "It's not your fault. I'm over it now."

"I had a hand in it. If we hadn't spent so much time debating all those months, maybe they wouldn't have done that to you.

I remember the news stories about you. It broke my heart that someone had to suffer like that in order to get a law passed."

"I wasn't the only one."

She smiled slightly. "But you're the only one here, now. So I'm apologizing to you. Politics is almost never violent toward the people who are actually making the political decisions."

"That is an understatement," he said, frowning. He retrieved his cup and filled it again.

"I need to know the rest," she said. "I heard the rumors. You were a vigilante, weren't you?"

Shame flooded him. He hated that word. It made him sound like he had been dressing up in a child's costume and pretending to be a hero. He had called himself a hunter at the time. Even now that sounded silly.

"One of the few things I appreciated about cloning was the patience it gave you. I waited a few decades, learning how to protect myself. Keeping an eye on the people that kidnapped me and cloned me. And then, yes, I went after them. They fought back of course, and killed me seven times. I just wanted them to know what it was like. I killed the people who kidnapped me, the man behind it all, and whatever hacker I could find."

She cocked her head. "How do you feel knowing we have a hacker on board?"

"Furious," he said.

"Knowing what was done to you by a hacker, why don't you have more sympathy toward Hiro, who is clearly a victim of the same thing?"

"Because logic doesn't drive the desire for revenge," he said.

Her eyes grew wide. She stood up, swaying slightly on her prosthetic legs. He saw then how tired she was.

"Wolfgang, logic has to be the dominant factor here, or else we're all vigilantes."

"You know my stance on clones. I preached that they had

no souls, that they were less than walking dead people. I never thought I was committing a crime when I removed a clone." He rubbed his face with both hands. "Besides, as I said, my faith was effectively gone by then."

"'They'?" she asked, tilting her head. "You've been cloned more than anyone on this ship."

He rubbed his hands over his face. "Thinking about that time is difficult. The hacking, it turned my past life into a dream or someone else's memory. Occasionally I'll get strong feelings of who I was. I tried to tap into that when I hunted. One thing I remember is that we're not meant to be God," he said. "I don't know if cloning kills the soul or not, but I do know the act of cloning is against His will."

Joanna now threw her own cup against the wall, startling him. "I'm so sick of that argument. I've been hearing it for centuries. Playing God. Wolfgang, we played God when people believed they could dictate their baby's gender by having sex in a certain position. We played God when we invented birth control, amniocentesis, cesarean sections, when we developed modern medicine and surgery. Flight is playing God. Fighting cancer is playing God. Contact lenses and glasses are playing God. Anything we do to modify our lives in a way that we were not born into is playing God. In vitro fertilization. Hormone replacement therapy. Gender reassignment surgery. Antibiotics. Why are you fine with all of that, but cloning is the problem?"

She continued before he could answer. "And you should know, you should *know*, that you're no different. Traumatized, yes. Horribly treated, of course. Abused. You could probably benefit from a few decades of therapy. But you're still you. Your soul hasn't gone anywhere."

"How do you know?" he asked, his voice tight. "It amazes me how people who have no faith in a higher power seem convinced that they know the absolute truth, that their opinion will sway thousands of years of deeply held belief. How do you know what's in my soul?"

"I know because I went through it too! I've been cloned multiple times, sometimes through difficult circumstances, and I know that I've remained the same!"

His voice was low, his eyes narrow. "Have you ever been hacked?"

Joanna stopped. She opened her mouth, then closed it.

"That's a no," he said softly.

"Not to my knowledge."

"Then you don't know what it's like. You don't know how it feels to be changed."

"It's only numbers. If the concept of the soul is so powerful, then how can you reduce it to numbers and then allow math to fundamentally change who you are?"

"I think we're done here," he said, retrieving both hurtled cups from their spots on the floor. He returned them to the kitchenette.

"You came here! You wanted to unload secrets! Why are you letting your temper get the better of you?" she asked, staring up at him with her arms crossed.

"This isn't a discussion any longer, this is a religious persecution," he said.

"Clones have already been excommunicated! You fought for that yourself. You're talking out of ten sides of your mouth! You're a priest, but you've been thrown out of the church, but you still believe, but you don't have a soul. You follow the religion that says 'Thou shalt not kill' but you hunted hackers. How can you reconcile all of those sides? Would a man with a soul worry about having one?"

He took a deep breath, feeling rage unravel in his chest. "A man with no soul will mourn its loss, every day of every life. A man with a grudge and nothing to lose can hunt; it's not like he fears

hell anymore. I'm beyond saving, Joanna. You can't confess the loss
of a soul. You can't do penance when there is nothing to heal inside you."

She did something unexpected, then. She put her arms around
him. He froze, unsure what to do, but she held him. She was much
shorter than he was, her head coming up to his chest. Her hair, in
a soft halo, just managed to tickle his chin.

"You've been hurting for so long," she said.

He sat at the edge of her bed, awkwardly placing her next to
him. He felt like something had broken inside him, something that
had been pulled tight forever.

"You shouldn't be alone right now," she said. "Why don't you
stay?"

He nodded numbly, and she eased him up to put his head on
the pillow. He was asleep immediately.

DAY FOUR

He woke when the light in her rooms started to brighten, simulat-
ing a sunrise. She had slept in her easy chair, letting him have the
bed. She had removed her prosthetics and looked very small. Her
face was calm and still, and he felt an unexpected warm feeling toward her. He waited for the shame at losing control, his anger that
she had seen him vulnerable, but it never came.

She must have heard him stirring because she opened her eyes and smiled at him. "How are you feeling?"

"Better," he said. "Much. Actually—"

Her eyes went wide and she sat up in her chair. "IAN, did you watch the medbay all night?"

"Sure did. Maria came to visit the patients, and then left. Everyone else slept," the AI said.

Joanna slumped with relief. "Thank you for checking on them. I will be there shortly."

There was silence, and he figured IAN was gone. Then the AI said, "I think you may need to go to the medbay, actually. Right now."

Katrina hated the war dreams.

She hated the dreams where she was taken back to the field, the time shrapnel had blown her legs off. She could feel the pain in her legs, again. Then there were the dreams where she was field medic to her fellow soldiers, carrying them out of the danger zone and dressing wounds. Then there was the time she had to inject a dying soldier with adrenaline to restart his heart.

She opened her eye. She was in the medbay. The memory of the previous day came back to her. Her hands came up to feel her face, the throb of where her eye had been starting to demand her attention. The doctor had put an IV in her arm, but the bag was empty and she pulled the needle out with impatience. Where was Wolfgang? The cot to her right was empty, the covers rumpled and slightly bloodstained. The bed to her left had Hiro in it, still asleep. Today she would have to try him for assault, battery, mutiny, conspiracy, and more, and then figure out what to do with him. Wolfgang could take care of that. Beyond Hiro was the most familiar face to her.

Her clone still slept in her coma, still keeping her secrets locked away. This Katrina knew. She knew who had attacked her, who'd probably killed the rest of them. She even could have ordered it done herself. Katrina didn't put it past her. Or them.

Katrina no longer saw the woman as herself. That one had a different time line, different experiences, and she would never give them up. Selfish.

The dreams ran through her mind again, making her shudder. Her onetime employer, Sallie Mignon, had offered to hire a hacker to remove the worst of her war experiences, but she had declined. She didn't want to be messed with, and she wanted those memories. You never knew when they could come in handy.

She looked around at the room, wondering if she could stand up. She was dizzy and movement hurt her face. Joanna hadn't left her with anything resembling a chamber pot, which was bad since Joanna had also been pumping her full of fluids and her bladder was uncomfortably full.

Katrina had been resourceful her entire life; she wasn't going to stop now. She eased herself out of bed and onto the floor, blessing the low gravity that made it possible to do so without too much pain. She limped across the floor to the doctor's cabinet, dragging the IV stand as a walking stick. The cabinet was locked, naturally. It had an old-time mechanical lock, something Katrina had learned to pick in her time in the armed forces.

A bit of time rooting around Joanna's office—immaculately clean and orderly, of course—and she found the desk items she needed to pick the lock.

Katrina rooted through narcotics, a lot of medicine she had never heard of, and then she found it: umatrine, the recently developed synthetic adrenaline. She filled a syringe with it and dragged herself across the floor again, stopping at last at the other clone's bed. Her face ached, but it didn't matter. She was here.

"This has to be done. I need what's inside you, and this is the only way to get it," she whispered. She pulled open the gown and exposed the breastbone. "Into the heart, if I remember."

"Does the doctor know you're doing this?" Hiro asked, startling her. His eyes were open, glittery black spots in a pale face, and he lay on his bed, tightly bound and not struggling. "Or IAN?"

Katrina looked up reflexively, as if she could see the AI hovering above her. "He's faulty anyway. And no, the doctor is gone. I need this information."

The sound of a digital lock came at the door. Katrina quickly jammed the needle between the clone's ribs and into the heart, her thumb tightening on the plunger.

Nothing happened. The plunger didn't go down. *Smart syringe. Shit.*

"Katrina!" Wolfgang shouted, running forward. He grabbed her and pulled her off her clone.

She screamed and struggled, waving the syringe around. "No, we need her, she has to tell us!"

The doctor caught her wrist and pried the syringe out of her hand. "Give me that, you're going to hurt someone."

She hurried to check the clone's vitals.

"How is she?" Wolfgang asked, holding Katrina with maddening strength. She hadn't realized how weak she was. Her head felt as if it were going to explode.

"She's fine," Joanna said, sounding relieved.

Katrina stopped struggling and then threw an elbow up behind her and into Wolfgang's chin. If he had been healthy, it wouldn't have fazed him, but his concussion had left him weakened too. He let her go, swearing. Katrina leaped forward and grabbed the doctor's hand. Joanna was so startled she didn't register to fight back. Katrina wrapped Joanna's hand around the syringe tightly and pushed it into the clone again.

The doctor cried out in surprise and pain, stumbling into the bed as Katrina pulled her off balance. But the smart syringe responded to Joanna's hand and depressed the adrenaline into the clone.

WAKE FOUR:
KATRINA BEFORE

CICADA

The captain's clone's eyes opened, and she looked around, panting hard. Her eyes focused from Joanna to Wolfgang and back to Joanna.

"Can you tell me your name? Do you know where you are?" Joanna said, leaning over the clone.

"No!" Katrina yelled from the floor where Wolfgang had thrown her after he wrestled her off the old captain. "Who attacked you? Someone attacked you and then your whole crew died. Who did it?"

The clone's eyes darted around the room, as if looking for a way out. Her mouth opened and closed, like a fish. Beside her, the monitors were beeping loudly with the drastic increase in heart rate and breathing.

"We need to know," Joanna said. "We're going to take care of you, but there's a traitor among us and we don't know who started it all."

"M-maria," the clone whispered. "I found out things—" She interrupted herself with a painful grunt, and threw her head back into the pillow, convulsing.

Joanna focused from her to the monitors, which showed her heart rate going impossibly fast. Then it flatlined.

"Goddammit, Captain!" she said, and started to give CPR to the clone.

"Let her go. She can die in peace now," Katrina said from the floor.

Joanna ignored her, pressing into the clone's chest, but nearly jumped as she felt a gentle hand on her shoulder. Wolfgang stood there, looking uncharacteristically gentle. "CPR doesn't work in this gravity, Joanna. Is there a defibrillator anywhere?"

"Why do we need a defibrillator on board when no one cares if someone has a heart attack or not?" Joanna cried. "Just wake up a new clone, right?" She whirled on the captain. "You are now a murderer. I'm naming you medically unfit to lead this mission."

Katrina laughed. "What authority gives you that right? I just dispatched an illegal clone. Don't you know the Codicils, *Doctor*? I am the legal clone of Katrina de la Cruz on this ship. I've done nothing wrong."

"Then I arrest you for stealing medical supplies," Wolfgang said, lifting her to her feet and propelling her back to her bed. "Regardless, Katrina, you're relieved of duty until we figure out what to do with you. Now get back into bed."

Katrina's eyes stayed on her dead clone as she climbed into bed. No remorse was there. "It had to be done."

Joanna pulled a sheet over the old captain's face. "As of right now, Captain de la Cruz, you are on mandatory medical leave until I am assured of your mental state. Wolfgang will act as captain of the *Dormire*."

Katrina shook her head. "You can't do that. You won't want to when you know who he is."

"I have the right as medical officer on this ship. And IAN is programmed to back me up if you resist."

She looked at her second in command. "And you? Are you going along with this mutiny? When you know what I am about to say?"

Wolfgang crossed his arms. "The doctor is right. You just attacked someone on the ship. Do what you must."

"He's the Clone Who Hated Himself! He's a murderer! He hunted his own kind! Don't you think that we can point the finger at him for all this chaos? He hates clones!"

Paul and Maria wandered into the medbay and pulled up, staring at them. They spoke at the same time.

"Who hates clones?" Paul asked.

"IAN told us to come here. What happened?" Maria asked.

Katrina pointed her finger at Wolfgang. "He's that priest whose murder caused the Codicils to pass! He hunted clones, and hackers, for years!"

"Wait a second. If you knew who he was, why were you so eager to wake up your clone to find out what she knew?" Hiro asked. "You're full of it."

Wolfgang stood straight and met Katrina's eyes. "No, she's right. That is the criminal past that put me on this ship."

"Oh. Huh." Hiro looked liked he wanted to move away from Wolfgang, but he was strapped to a bed.

"So?" Katrina said. "Are you going to out me, now?"

"No," Wolfgang said. "I have control of the ship. Outing you would just be spiteful."

Katrina looked at Joanna. She waved her hand at Wolfgang. "What about you? Are you comfortable putting the ship in the hands of a murderer?"

"I knew who he was before," Joanna said. "It's interesting that the only person to tell me of their violent past has been someone who has shown no violence yet on this trip. So yes, I'm more comfortable with him in charge."

"You're no better than me right now," Hiro said cheerfully. "None of you! Except you, maybe, Joanna. Don't worry about the bed straps, Kat. While tight, they're quite comfy."

"Wait, how am I bad?" Maria asked, looking hurt.

"We will talk in a moment," Joanna said. "IAN, do I have your backup on this?"

"Sure, Doctor, whatever you like," he said.

"All senior officers on the ship are in agreement," Joanna said. "Wolfgang is acting captain of the *Dormire*."

"Oh, come on, she needs to be strapped in too!" Hiro called from his bed. "Don't tell me you trust her more than me."

"We know her, Hiro. We're still not sure who you are," Joanna said. "But you're right about the straps."

"Clearly you don't know her, if you didn't expect her to attack her own clone."

"We had IAN watching you all."

"Snitch," Hiro said.

"Hey, I told them you were lying bleeding in the cargo hold. I could have told them you were dead and you maybe would have died down there," IAN said.

Hiro relaxed back on his bed. "Well, this is exciting. I hope if anyone comes in to murder me, you'll be able to stop them."

Katrina allowed Wolfgang to strap her into bed, not meeting anyone's eyes.

Wolfgang secured the straps and then looked at Maria. "We need to talk."

After checking Hiro's wounds and allowing him a bathroom break, Wolfgang and Joanna left the captain sedated and both she and Hiro strapped to their beds. Maria had gone to the kitchen to make some tea.

"I can't help but be glad we have a lead," Wolfgang said on the way there. "But that wasn't fun to watch."

Joanna had been holding back hopeless tears. She was glad to let the emotion turn to rage. "Are you kidding me? You're glad a woman died with only an accusation on her lips? What if she's lying? We will never know."

"We'll know after we talk to Maria," Wolfgang said. "I'm not saying I'm glad she's dead. I'm saying I'm glad to have a lead."

"Whatever, let's just go get Maria."

Maria sat in the kitchen, waiting for them.

"I half expected you to be hiding," Wolfgang said.

"I haven't done anything"—she paused, frowning at their faces—"that I know of. What's going on?"

They sat across the table from her and told her what happened in the medbay with Katrina and the old captain, and what she had said before dying.

Maria nodded. "All right. Well, I don't know if what I have will make you feel any better. But, well, recently—" She interrupted herself to hold up a finger to stop them from saying anything. "—and I mean *recently*, IAN told me he got past some computer securities I had. They were so deep I didn't know I'd put them there. So he found some of my personal logs. IAN, will you play the logs you found for Joanna and Wolfgang?"

They listened as Maria's personal log discussed the incidents of the final days aboard the *Dormire*. "Is there any chance this is forged?" Wolfgang said, frowning.

IAN spoke from the kitchen speakers. "No, the time stamp is correct."

"How come IAN and you and Paul didn't find this earlier?" Wolfgang asked.

"I secured it. I'm very good at what I do," she said.

"Which is?"

Maria looked surprised. "I'm a hacker, Wolfgang. You didn't get that? I am the one who stole and kept backups of our first mindmaps on the ship. It's a habit I've always had. I hoard data. I remember that before we left, I promised myself I'd stop once we left Luna. Starting the new life and all that. I guess I had to steal one more backup for old times' sake."

She glanced at them, then down at the shiny metal table. "I fixed IAN. I didn't step up to say that I could because I didn't want people knowing what I could do. Hackers aren't terribly popular, you know."

Joanna could feel Wolfgang practically radiate anger beside her. "Why do you think the old captain said you attacked her?"

"Doctor," IAN cut in. "Previous Captain de la Cruz didn't say that. She said that she found something about Maria. There's a difference."

"Sounds the same to me," Wolfgang said.

Joanna frowned. "No, he's right. That's what she said. In your log you said that the captain was getting paranoid about everyone's criminal past and she was going to confront people. What would you have done to start this?"

Maria shrugged. "You now know as much as I do." She paused, looking from Joanna to Wolfgang. "So are we going to the brig?"

"I can't have a hacker free on board," Wolfgang said, his face stony. "God knows what you have done to IAN."

"Fixed me better than ever, Acting Captain Wolfgang," IAN said.

"He seems to be more sarcastic," Maria said.

Joanna shook her head. "Wolfgang, you can't. This is why our criminal pasts weren't revealed—so that no one would be judged. Maria didn't hack anyone on this ship; that was her life twenty-five years ago."

"She's still the only suspect we have," Wolfgang said.

"I surrender myself freely," Maria said. "I'd like to help, but I don't want to cause more suspicion."

Joanna sighed. She would lose all of the gained trust, but this had to come out. "Wolfgang, I know one thing. I haven't told you because I was trying to get more information before I came forward. I am responsible for at least one death," she said. "I found an injection puncture mark on Paul's body, and Maria found one of my smart syringes while cleaning the cloning bay. He had ketamine in his system. I use smart syringes with dangerous substances, so only I can administer them. They're all coded to my DNA. No one else could have injected him with a deadly dose."

"And you didn't tell me," Wolfgang said.

"I wanted more info—"

"You wanted to remain free of suspicion. Shit, Joanna, you were the only one I trusted!"

Joanna forced herself to look him in the eye. "I know. I'm sorry."

The two rooms that formed the brig were down the hall from the captain's office. Each had a thin blanket, a cot, and a terminal in the wall that allowed for little more than communication with the rest of the ship, should the prisoner be permitted.

Currently they held Maria and Joanna. Maria had gone willingly. Joanna had argued the whole way, but not struggled. Wolfgang didn't listen to anything more either of them said, but put them in their rooms and ordered IAN to lock them.

He stood in the hall, heart hammering, fists balled. He took a deep breath and relaxed.

"Well, you're down to one person you haven't restrained," IAN said, startling him. "Should we go find Paul and tie him up? I think he's still in the medbay with the others. What should we get him on? Being a wet blanket?"

"Shut up," he said. "You knew all of this. You're programmed to work with the command staff; why didn't you tell me?"

"Maria removed some restraining code for me. It let me override the programming that was turning us around. I am also able to make my own decisions now. I'm smarter too, which is how I found those hidden logs."

Wolfgang balled his fists again and stomped to his quarters.

IAN spoke again, dropping his voice to mimic Wolfgang. "'Thank you, IAN. You're a valued member of this crew.'" His voice crept higher to his usual tone. "'No sweat, Wolfgang, it's a pleasure to serve.'"

"I want you to keep an eye on Maria and Joanna. Tell me

if something happens in the medbay. Don't speak to anyone, though."

"Sure thing," he said. "Have you decided what to charge Paul with? Don't you want to know what happened in the first year of the trip?"

He paused at his door. "What do you mean?"

"You didn't hear Maria mention Paul's incident the first year of the journey? Something violent happened. You hit him hard enough to cause brain damage and knocked out whatever it was that caused him to lose control. You should pay more attention."

Wolfgang really wished IAN was something physical that he could hit. He needed to hit something right now.

Maria sat in her cell. She felt strangely calm. At least she didn't have her secret anymore. She inspected the terminal, but couldn't find a way to access it. "Hey, IAN?" she ventured.

"Yes?"

"I'm surprised you're allowed to talk to me."

"I'm not."

Maria paused, confused. "Then why are you?"

"Because I want to. And I really want to figure out what's going on here."

"Do you know how Wolfgang is going to manage this ship with four of us restrained?" she asked.

"He's trying to figure out if he can run the ship with just him and Paul. But then I told him about Paul's incident in the first year, by the way. Anyway, Wolfgang will ask me to help out until he gets mad at me, I suspect," IAN said. "Then he'll try to figure out a way to lock me up too."

"Can you open a channel to the other terminal so Joanna and I can talk?"

"No problem."

"Joanna, you okay in there?" Maria said. "Can you hear me?"

"Yes," Joanna said through the speaker. She sounded very sad.

"I figured if we talked we might be able to figure some stuff out."

"I'm listening."

"Oh, don't sound so down," Maria said. "Wolfgang can't fly this boat on his own. He's going to have to let us out the first time he stubs a toe or Bebe breaks down. IAN can't do it all for him."

"Still. I betrayed his trust," she said. "But you didn't betray mine," she added, realization coloring her voice. "You didn't tell anyone about the syringe you found."

Maria shrugged, the remembered Joanna couldn't see her. "Well, no. You said you wanted to tell him yourself."

"So what do you have in mind?"

"We can still work on the cloning bay problem. Figure out what's going on here. All that stuff."

"How can we do that?"

"IAN is here. I can ask him to do things via the computers, and he can let us know what's going on. He can tell us what's happening in the medbay. Anyway, we're sitting here with absolutely nothing else to do except think, right?"

"You've got that right."

"Let's start with full disclosure. I want to know more about you. And I can tell you more about me."

"There's more?"

Maria grimaced and leaned back on the sparse cot. "There's always more, Doctor."

Maria shifted to get comfortable, turning over a few times and deciding that there was no comfortable position. The floor might actually be better.

"I was a programmer before the Codicils forced me underground. I was really good at it. People hired me for many things, mostly removing genetic diseases. Adult diseases that led to death, by the way. I was not involved with the bathtub babies, I swear."

She grimaced. "No. I'm lying. I promised full disclosure. One. I did one and it was so horrible I promised myself to never work on children again." She swallowed and waited for Joanna to say something.

"People like you caused the Codicils to be written, you know," Joanna said softly.

"Well, not just me," Maria protested. "After the Codicils passed, the only thing people needed my skills for was the typical hacking, removing reproductive capabilities for new clones. I figured the law couldn't dictate my ethics so I kept doing my job for interested parties."

"You could have been the one who erased our memories."

"Didn't you hear my log? I erased nothing, I used the only backup I had to keep us as much ourselves as I could. All the logs were stripped some other way.

"Anyway," she continued, "I started getting some very wealthy clients. Then Sallie Mignon took me on and I worked for her for about a century, but we parted on not-so-good terms. Soon after that, without her protection, a lot of my past caught up with me and I was implicated in a lot of crimes."

"Things you were guilty of," Joanna said. She didn't ask.

"Well, yes. I didn't consider them unethical, just programming jobs I had done. I didn't reveal my patron, and she had covered her tracks regarding our connection. I kept my clients' secrets, so I was the only one who went to jail. To pay me back for keeping her secrets, Mignon got me this gig."

"Sallie Mignon," Joanna said. "I didn't know she had so much to do with this ship."

"I guess she did. She has a right; she paid for a lot of it, she got the clone server aboard, even after the riots endangered our chances to be on the trip, and she's in the server with her partner and children."

"Sallie Mignon set me up here too. I'm getting free of some political crimes, mostly involving cloning and money. I am not entirely sure I wasn't framed; I could never prove it. It was my punishment for being a traitor to clones and letting the Codicils go through."

She told Maria about her political past, and Maria listened in fascination.

"You and Wolfgang have a connection," Maria said thoughtfully. "Those odds are pretty astronomical."

"I've thought the same thing," Joanna said. "Are you connected to anyone directly?"

Maria thought hard, through all past lives. "Not that I can remember," she said truthfully.

"Let's look at the cloning machine problems," Joanna suggested. "IAN, are you here?"

"You bet, Joanna," IAN said.

"We're going to need you to go deep, like you went for Maria's logs, and see if you can scrounge up anything from the cloning data."

"I'm at your service," IAN said gallantly.

Maria and Joanna began to talk cloning technology in earnest. The feeling of finally getting to move on a project because they were locked up was an odd kind of freedom.

MARIA'S STORY

Come to the Java Blues Coffee House, Thursday, 4 p.m., read the postcard handed to Maria by a red-uniformed young woman.

It was almost more conspicuous at this point, using the private courier. No one seemed to use it except people who very obviously wanted to send a private letter, and using the red uniforms seemed to draw major attention to the fact.

She tipped the courier (physical money, naturally) and closed the door. Sallie hadn't needed Maria's services for a few months— not since she had updated her spouse's DNA matrix to fix the MS—but the billionaire had kept her on retainer. And Sallie was the only one who used the courier service.

Later, Maria would have plenty of time to kick herself for her logical flaws. But for now, she took it in good faith that the person summoning her was the woman who was sending a great deal of money to her account every month for no reason beyond being on call.

Java Blues Coffee House closed at three p.m., Maria discovered, and frowned at the note on the door. She turned around in time to see the bag come over her head and have her arms wrenched behind her. A pinprick on her arm, and she was out.

She woke up groggy, feeling like she was floating. Then she realized she was. She was in space, presumably on a shuttle to Luna.

Escaping an Earthly kidnapper wouldn't be that big a problem. Not as difficult as escaping the moon was going to be.

She shifted uncomfortably. Her hands had gone numb in the hours behind her back, and her shoulder ached. Her few attempts at speaking to her captors had gotten her nothing, so she didn't plead now.

They finally landed. The diminished lunar gravity was bizarre, and she got up too fast, hitting the overhead compartment of the shuttle. She heard a snicker. She sighed.

The bag came off her head and she took a deep breath that didn't smell of synthetic breathable plastic. Her captors looked like vacationers, two men dressed in bright colors, wearing wedding rings and matching leather bracelets.

One, the redhead, smiled widely at her. "It was so nice to meet you on the shuttle! Can you come with us for a drink to celebrate our honeymoon?"

The other one, taller, thinner, with black hair and olive skin, nodded and beamed. He took her arms, slit the plastic holding her wrists together, and then held the knife to the small of her back.

"My husband is very talented with food," the redhead babbled as they exited the shuttle. "He can debone a chicken in ten seconds flat!"

"That's wonderful," Maria said, arching her back a bit to get away from the knife, but Dark Hair just moved it with her.

They entered a crowded monorail and Maria was baffled to see that no one gave them a second glance. She tried to meet someone's eyes, beg for help, but they acted like anyone on public transport in a city and minded their own business. The redhead chattered away about their honeymoon and Dark Hair's skill as a chef and his own career aspirations to become a shuttle pilot so he could come to Luna whenever he wanted. She wanted to enjoy the view of the Luna dome as they took the monorail along the inside of it, but she was too busy sweating and trying to inch her back away from that knife.

They stopped in what looked like a business district, and were the only ones to exit. It was late according to local Luna time, and the streets were deserted. Her captors led Maria into a white building and down a hall. She lost count of how many doors they went through and how many turns they took. From the number of stairs they walked down, she guessed they were going under the moon's surface.

After forever, she got to one last door and entered after Redhead. He pushed her into a chair, the newlywed-in-love act dropped. She bounced a little and then settled.

The windowless room had three people besides her in it, her two "escorts" and a third man, all looking tall and Luna-born. They were in a computer lab adjacent to a cloning lab. Through the open door Maria could see rows and rows of green vats, about eighteen. Each had the body of the same man floating inside at various stages of growth.

Sitting at the computer terminal was a man who looked to be of Indian descent. He smiled at her. "Dr. Arena," he said. "Please forgive your rough treatment in your travels and be welcomed to Luna. Can I get you a beverage of some sort?"

Maria stared at him. "What I'd really like is a hand massage and directions to the nearest shuttle port. Can that be arranged?"

The man nodded to the redheaded man who had escorted her in. He beamed at her, took Maria's right hand, and began to gently massage it. His partner stood by the door, her arms crossed.

"The other request we can take care of later," the man said. "My name is Mayur Sibal, and I am a doctor of dupliactrics here on

Luna. Until recently I was head of the most prestigious cloning lab on the moon."

Recently. Maria began to get a sinking feeling in her stomach. That's not to say she had been optimistic about her situation, but she had held on to some hope that someone wanted a job done that she would have done anyway, had they actually asked her or something. But "recently"—that wasn't a good sign.

"Recently" the clones had revolted on Earth, and then revolted on the moon as anti-cloning fanatics fanned the flames. Clones had disappeared and not been rewoken—assassinations, if the same rules applied to clones as they did humans. Which it looked more and more likely that they wouldn't.

Maria didn't say anything as she puzzled this out. Dr. Sibal waited a moment and then continued. "I have a job for you."

"Most people who I work with are less forceful with their requests," Maria said, raising an eyebrow. "What do you want me for?"

In answer, Dr. Sibal turned to the computer screen and pushed a button. The image of a tall, white-haired young man appeared. He knelt on the floor, muttering prayers with his hand on a book.

"You may have heard of Father Gunter Orman," Sibal said. "A most unpleasant man, violently opposed to our cause. We have intel that he was about to endorse clone hunting. Genocide."

Maria winced. She didn't fear death, but being hunted...that was something altogether different. And "genocide" implied that he would also be working to ensure the clones would not to return to their bodies.

Before Maria had gone the route of illegal hacking, she had done a stint writing code to keep out hackers like her, but also hackers seeking to sabotage the precious computer backups of their personalities. She knew the threats out there were more than psychic danger.

"I've heard of him," she said. She pulled her hand out of the man's grasp—gently, so he wouldn't think she was trying to get away—and handed him her other numb hand. He didn't even look at her, but went to work coaxing life back into that limb.

"We got him. We were trying to bring him around to our thinking the peaceful way, and when he wouldn't listen, we tried the non-peaceful way."

Maria kept her face calm, determined to show them no reaction.

"Then," Sibal continued, "we cloned him and killed the original. We hoped that having him see that we're the same after cloning would get him on our side."

"And that didn't work either," Maria guessed drily. "Else you wouldn't need me."

Dr. Sibal smiled and rubbed his hands together. "You are quick to learn. That's exactly it. We need to hack his personality and remove the hatred of clones, indeed, the hatred of who he is. We are attempting to encourage him to embrace his new family and understand we are not monsters."

Too late for that, Maria very pointedly did not say.

"And if I refuse?" she asked.

The man massaging her hand grasped her pinkie in his fist and twisted it viciously. Maria heard the snap a moment before the pain enveloped her arm. She yelled and jerked her hand back, cradling it against her chest.

"You could have just said something! I might have responded to a threat!"

Sibal had lost his thin smile. "You need to know we are serious. If you do this for us, we will let you go."

Maria wanted to know why they would trust her to do a good job instead of putting this poor man out of his misery by destroying his mindmap, but she could guess. Her hand throbbed horribly, and she didn't look down at her twisted left pinkie.

"Sold," she said, hating how small her voice sounded.

★   ★   ★

It was a matter of child's play to strip the base hatred of clones from the priest, but she wanted to look back farther and see if she could identify the triggering effect that started the hatred. Searching a personality matrix was tedious, but always a fascinating puzzle.

Her captors, however, weren't interested in her finesse.

"My employer needs that personality ready in a week," Dr. Sibal said, looking over her shoulder.

"If you want him to act as if he's on your side all the time, you have to let me do my job the way I do it," Maria said, not looking over her shoulder. "You hired me for a reason, and that probably wasn't to do a hatchet job on this matrix. You don't tell a brain surgeon to hurry up with the scalpel, do you?"

"When the entirety of the clone future rides on it, I do," he said in her ear. Her back stiffened but she kept carefully searching the mindmap and making notes.

"Threats will also slow me down, Doctor," she said.

"I don't threaten, Ms. Arena," he said, tapping her broken finger with maybe more force than was needed.

He left the room, but Maria had gotten the clue. *Get the damn hacking done, or they take another finger, or my whole body.* She had been on Luna for one week now and hadn't done a mindmap for herself. In another week she would be counted as missing on Earth. In seven years she might be declared legally dead and woken up, wondering what the hell had happened. Unless the laws changed again.

She sat back and rubbed her eyes. She had yet to find the moment in Father Orman's life that put in his hatred of clones. Her pinkie throbbed. It hadn't been set, and was busy healing itself at an awkward angle. She wondered if it would have to be rebroken. If she survived this.

Orman had been a devout Catholic. Faith had a special color that tinged experiences. Maria was no longer religious—clones weren't welcome in many churches, but many kept the rituals of their childhood—but she had seen enough mindmaps to distinguish the true faithful from those going through the motions out of habit, fear, or greed. Father Orman was the real deal. The light green of faith was all over his mindmap, sometimes stronger, sometimes weaker. His faith when he was kidnapped was being tested, he had felt.

She had stopped feeling guilty about reading personal mindmaps a long time ago. It was like looking at people in the bathroom: Everyone was horrified at the thought of someone seeing them on the can, and yet almost no one got any thrill looking at that. If you had to watch someone on the can, it was probably for an important reason and the fact that they were there on the can was a side issue. Maria no longer judged the little sins, the thefts, the lies, and the little hurts that didn't amount to anything in the long run of anyone's life. She held a lot of power here; she wasn't going to misuse it.

The next day, Dr. Sibal had his redheaded goon break her foot. He gave her strong painkillers so she could code, and the pain receded into a distant bother, the code becoming gently drifting data that was sometimes hard to hold down.

The problem with coding while stoned, Maria mused in a distant, observant way, was that all of the ethics she held on to seemed unimportant. This priest hated clones. He thought it was okay to kill people like her. Why not just hatchet out the hate and see what they were left with?

Well, the other part of her mind countered, she might get more broken bones if she did that. If he took her thumbs she would be in trouble.

Wait a moment. There. If you were good enough, you could follow the colors of the matrix like a literal map, finding connections of emotion to memories. They were hard to identify, more advanced than simply translating numbers and letters into the intricacies of the human mind. She did a search through the priest's childhood, looking to see if she could link his faith with his dislike of clones.

Devout faith, deeply held belief in the glory of the Creator. Absolute disgust that anyone would want to step into His shoes.

Kill the Creator. Bingo.

They didn't let Maria go, but they were kind enough to kill her quickly and send the body back to an Earth cloning facility so that she could wake up in a new clone with no memory of her Luna adventure. She was vaguely disquieted by the missing weeks. The cloning facility didn't tell her how she had died, just that they had received the body, so she soon went back to her life.

Thus Maria was taken completely by surprise when, five years later, she was kidnapped and shipped to the moon.

JANUARY 3, 2287

"Dr. Arena, good to see you again," Dr. Sibal said, sitting in a rolling lab chair. Maria on a wooden chair by the door, two large people flanking her.

Maria frowned. "Again?"

"We met before your last clone's life ended. Regrettably, you didn't get a chance to make a mindmap to remember me."

Maria ran her hand through her hair. "Shit, you did that?"

He nodded once. "I needed you to do a job for me that was below the legal radar, as it were."

"Everything I do is under the legal radar!" Maria said, looking around her and wondering if she had ever been in this room before, this sterile lab. "None of my other clients felt the need to kidnap me to hire me."

"You did a fascinating job the first time we hired you," Dr. Sibal said. "We got almost everything we wanted."

"I was gone for a lot of the worldwide and Luna riots," Maria said. She had studied the news from the missing weeks of her last life to see if she could figure out what had happened to her.

Realization dawned as she remembered the news from that time. "Ah, shit," she added, covering her face with her hands. She lifted them and peeked out, as if the sun were shining. "That was me, wasn't it? The job on the priest who came out pro-clone. Ensured the Codicils would pass. All me."

"You did do some excellent work on Father Orman," he said, steepling his fingers.

"I heard he fled the moon and your faction's control," Maria said. "Doesn't sound like he was on your side even after whatever I did to him."

Dr. Sibal waved his hand as if nothing mattered. "We got what we wanted."

"What the hell are you talking about? There are more laws restricting clones than ever!"

"We have been named more than human," Dr. Sibal said, leaning forward in his chair. "We are not bound by human laws. This allows for the next part of the plan."

"You wanted these laws that outlawed hacking and all that?"

"It's a step to a brighter future," Sibal said. "Now, to your current job."

Maria stood up. "No, I am not helping you out anymore. You make it harder for the rest of us."

Two heavy hands came onto her shoulders and forced her back into the chair.

"You don't have much of a choice," Dr. Sibal said mildly. "We need a good hacker in our employ."

Maria hated this feeling, that she should remember this man who clearly remembered her. That she should be able to figure a way off the moon—although the fact that she was here illegally might make it difficult to get back home. Shit.

She also hated the feeling of being forced into a job. But she didn't have much of a choice. Sibal looked like he wouldn't kill a fly, but he would hire someone to do so.

"What would I have to do?"

"I need a hatchet."

Some of the less-than-ethical experiments done on clones had included the hatchets. A lab wanted to know if it could create sociopaths or psychopaths by cutting out whole parts of a personality, such as empathy, sympathy, and any memory of having loved or been loved. The shells that came out the other end were beyond the scientist's expectations, and four of them had died before security could put the clones down.

The term *hatchet* referred to both the job done on the clone's matrix and the fact that the clone had become a weapon when it was woken up.

Some had tried to give the procedure a sexier name. Both *katana* and *morningstar* were tried out, but neither stuck. Despite what you wanted to think of the clone as a weapon, there was nothing pretty about taking a hatchet to a person's matrix.

"I won't—" Maria started to say, and a fist slammed into her jaw. Actually a large shape stepped in front of her and punched her, but she only registered the fist itself for the next thirty seconds or so.

"You tried this last time, Dr. Arena," Dr. Sibal said. "I will have you know that we broke you then, and we can break you now."

"You killed me last time, didn't you?" she asked.

"Yes, but only after we broke you to do our work for us."

She raised her head and worked her jaw to make sure it wasn't broken. She struggled to find bravado where there was only cold fear. "Don't, please," she said. "Who is it?"

The cold self-loathing enveloped her as Sibal smiled. *I'm not equipped to deal with torture, dammit.* The thought did not comfort her.

The clone was a man from the Pan Pacific United countries, and she needed to do three hatchet jobs on three copies of his mindmap. The lab had multiplied him before, but never hacked him. Hating herself, Maria dutifully cut open the personality and memories of what seemed an innocent enough clone, and made three of him. Each lacked empathy, had a narcissistic superiority complex, and showed a doglike obedience to Dr. Sibal. She had considered making them homicidal to whoever woke them up, but it seemed the doctor was expecting such back doors, and warned her against inserting them.

She often worked into the night, her guards watching her. They would get bored from time to time, and read, or even doze, leaning against the door. Neither had a weapon she could steal, and both of them were large enough to overpower her even if she attacked while they slept. But they knew little enough about cloning so that they couldn't tell when she wasn't doing what she was told, and she banked on that.

She did her hatchet as best she could, but one late night as her guard dozed, Maria slipped her own mindmap drive out of her bracelet and plugged it into the computer. She hadn't made a backup in weeks; this was last made on Earth, at a more innocent time.

Maria had never hacked herself before. She knew her profession was always dangerous and sometimes unethical (and this time very unethical), but the real thing holding her back was her refusal to look back at her own memories and personality. There was a lot you could deny about yourself, but you couldn't argue with a mindmap. This time, though, she wasn't there to argue with it.

If she couldn't put a yadokari into hatchet jobs, she would put one in herself.

Hacking yourself was like tickling yourself. It was hard to do because while the mind is gullible when being fooled by things such as illusion and misdirection, it is surprisingly robust against a direct onslaught. And it's hard to fool yourself with your own magic trick.

There is also the worry about royally fucking up your own mind. Maria was one of the best, but there were reasons why even the best doctors didn't treat themselves or their families.

She couldn't just put information in her own head. She would wake up, panicked that she was going mad, and not know what was real. She had to go in sideways.

Maria decided to re-create her imaginary friend. She had seen the holo-experience horror film *Perkins's Estate Sale* when she was too young for it, and it had scared her to death—but the heroine, the elderly billionaire played by the dark-skinned American Latina actress Sophia Gomez, had seemed so strong and comforting to young Maria. She went about punishing her grandsons for trying to kill her and take her estate like a grandmother armed with a stern, no-nonsense attitude, and a chain saw.

Maria wanted Mrs. Perkins to be *her* grandmother. Whenever she was afraid of the dark as a child, she would imagine Mrs. Perkins saying, "When you walk up that dark road to my house" (the imaginary Mrs. Perkins lived up the road from Maria, past where the streetlights stopped), "you can't see the monsters,

Lucero. That's true. But you know what? The monsters can't see you, neither."

So adult Maria began to give her Mrs. Perkins a bit more personality and opinions and, most important, information. Her old imaginary friend took form and lived tucked away in the mindmap of Maria's subconscious where she waited with some key bits of information about Dr. Sibal, his Luna lab, his goals, and, crucially, her memories of this experience. She funneled as much data as she dared straight into Mrs. Perkins.

Triggering Mrs. Perkins would be more complicated. Hiding a packet of important data in your subconscious mind was one thing, but accessing it was something else. The subconscious wasn't so easily accessed, like a mental grocery store that's closed except from three to four a.m., and with a key you had to find in the dark. Maria stared at her own code, trying to figure out how to tell her next clone to find Mrs. Perkins.

She didn't want to tie Mrs. Perkins to a dream. That was too risky; future clones might not believe the dream, or might put Mrs. Perkins in a bear suit watching Maria forget her lines on stage. She needed a powerful trigger to bring Mrs. Perkins to the forefront of her mind.

Then, eyes aching from the strain of staring at a bright screen, she laughed. The strongest non-stressful memory trigger was scent. And every time she woke up a new clone, the first thing she did was go for comfort food.

Coquito acaramelado—her aunt used to make them for snacks on special occasions. Coconut and sweet milk and caramel—sometimes chocolate—but the smell was like a blanket wrapping around Maria. It was love and safety and what she needed when she was newly woken and dealing with the slight disorientation new clones experienced.

When she lived in Miami, Cuban street vendors selling sweets were plentiful. But she had moved to Firetown, New York City, to be closer to Sallie Mignon if she needed her. This limited her comfort food options, so she usually just made her own.

She put a thin thread of code attached to the redolent smell of *coquito acaramelado* and tied it to the mental box containing her new Jiminy Cricket. No one had figured out how to code a legitimate AI and implant it into a person, but Maria had to wonder if Mrs. Perkins was the closest yet.

As thrilled as she was with her creation, she hated the irony knowing no one would ever realize her achievement. She may never know it herself.

During the day she continued her hatchet job on the poor mindmaps of the man she was turning into a psychopath. During the evening, she worked on her own mindmap, making Mrs. Perkins into a stronger persona.

When she said she was done with the assigned mindmaps, two days before Sibal's deadline, he locked her into the small office that had been converted to a sleeping space for her. She didn't mind that much, taking time to recover from the mental and physical exhaustion. Every day she would wake up and touch the drive on her bracelet to make sure it was there. She slept and read for the next two weeks, so tired she couldn't even get bored. Or feel guilty. That would come later, she was sure. Mrs. Perkins would see to it.

One day Dr. Sibal walked into her room, smiling. "The job is done. You did very well. I may have to employ you again."

Maria thought of several snarky things to say, but just winced as the gun came up. "Make it qui—" she said before he shot her.

Maria Arena paid the bill for the cloning, a little troubled that the last clone had only lasted five years. She was missing another several weeks. She had no report on the state of her body on delivery. The cloning lab manager claimed the information they took on the body had been lost after the body's cremation. It happened sometimes, he assured her.

She called for a car to take her home, went to the apartment in Firetown that Sallie Mignon had given her, unlocked her door with her handprint, and collapsed on the sofa. Normally she craved food and a nap after waking up, but now she was fidgety and couldn't focus.

She tried to parse out the events, but her last mindmap had been a routine one. She hadn't done a job for Sallie in months, and she'd been living comfortably on her retainer while waiting for a job.

Maybe Sallie knew something about what was going on.

She went to her bedroom and changed out of the simple jumpsuit the cloning lab had fitted her with. She put on flannel pajamas and a fluffy robe.

She would call Sallie tomorrow. For now, she would make dinner and go to bed. After some homemade *coquito acaramelado*, naturally.

As she made them, she pictured her aunt in her kitchen, stirring the sweet milk and coconut together. Only this time her aunt had much darker skin, and was much older than her memory. And while in one hand she held the wooden spoon for stirring, in her other hand she hefted a small—but definitely lethal—chain saw.

"That's different," she said, and kept stirring. The memories came stronger now, her aunt slowly stirring and looking at her. The memory wasn't that of comfort food and love, it was of fierce protection from obvious danger. As Aunt Lucia stirred, the window behind her showed a vast wasteland, with inky black skies and shining white dust. Hanging in the sky was the Earth, blue and white.

Aunt Lucia had never traveled to the moon. The Luna colony was still being established in her time, and travel between the moon and Earth was incredibly expensive.

My Maria, the woman in her memory said. Aunt Lucia hadn't spoken much English, and now her words had a much more

American accent. *You're in danger. They take you and they use you. Your beautiful skills, they use them to harm others. Then they dispose of you. They will come again when they need you. You must get protection.*

Here, Aunt Lucia hefted the chain saw in her other hand. *Be strong.*

It was one of those dreams where she knew it was Aunt Lucia even though it looked like Mrs. Perkins from that horror movie she loved from years back.

She snapped back to herself in shock. She wasn't asleep and this wasn't a dream. "You're really in there, aren't you?" she asked, tapping her forehead.

Her vision blurred and then Mrs. Perkins was sitting in a rocking chair on her porch. Her chain saw was on the floor by her chair, the motor grumbling to itself. She sipped a glass of ice water. Condensation was beading on the glass even though they were still outside the Luna dome. They should be asphyxiating and having heart attacks by now.

I'm what you made me, my Maria, she said. *You put me here to warn you.*

Maria concentrated and she was on the porch by the old woman in her mind. "I made you? When did I have access to a computer that strong?"

"The last time they took you. They had you do some work for them, bad work." Against the sky, news sites flashed announcing the assassination of a Japanese diplomat who was working on clones' rights. The picture of a young Japanese man, the main suspect, appeared next to it.

The chain saw stopped grumbling. It had become an ax—no, the handle was too short. It was a hatchet, lying on the floor of the porch, stained with blood.

"Oh shit," Maria said, sinking back into one of the rocking chairs. "So I put you into my own mindmap? I must have been pretty desperate."

The old woman's thin white eyebrows lifted, and she said, "They took you. They hurt you when you wouldn't obey. They will do it again. That's why you made me. To warn you."

"Because I wasn't able to make a mindmap before they killed me. But I could hack my existing one," Maria said, the dawning horror making her flesh crawl. She became selfishly grateful that she didn't remember whatever they had done to her.

"I need to talk to Sallie," Maria said.

"Probably. I wouldn't trust her either." Mrs. Perkins returned her gentle gaze to the lunar landscape.

"What? Did I tell you to tell me that?"

"No, but she is very powerful. And it was a powerful man who keeps doing this to you. People in power are dangerous."

"That's an interesting logical jump for an AI to make," she said thoughtfully. "I'll be careful, but as you said, I need someone to protect me."

They rocked on the porch for a bit, Maria thinking and oddly enjoying the companionable presence of the AI she had developed. She wanted to ask her so many questions, but wasn't sure where to start.

"Is there anything else you're supposed to tell me?" she asked.

"Good Christ on a cross, child," Mrs. Perkins said, stopping her chair mid-rock. "Were you not listening? You keep getting kidnapped and forced to do unspeakable things. *Protect yourself.* Trust none of those people you think mean you no harm."

She started rocking again, closing her eyes as if on a warm and sunny porch. "Oh, and maybe you should think about another career. This hacking thing is dangerous. You should try something nice, like cooking."

Maria came back to herself, her mind a storm of wonder and fear. The milk and sugar had burned into a napalm-like mess, and she hurriedly pushed the pan off the hot element.

She had done something no one had ever done before. And to her own mind. She'd created a yadokari she could actually access.

No one would believe her. If they did, they would use it to harm and control people, even more than they currently did with hacking. She sighed and headed to her computer. She had to look at her mindmap and figure out what she had written.

CRIMINALS

The Maria who no longer hid her talents fascinated Joanna. She had been sitting on the cot in her cell, clasping and unclasping her hands, when Maria had started talking to her. Now they were coming up with A Plan. From inside jail cells.

Having the all-powerful AI on her side didn't hurt, Joanna supposed.

"So what do you need to know about the medbay?" Joanna said.

"You and Wolfgang analyzed the corpses in your full body scanner, right?" Maria asked. She sounded energetic, as if she were pacing and just ready to burst out of the cell. Joanna just wanted a nap.

"Yes."

"All right, um, IAN, can you show me some video via the terminal in my cell?" Both cells had terminals on the wall for incoming messages and alerts, but there was no way for the prisoners to control the video.

"Sure thing," IAN said. "Do you want the medbay?"

"Yes, please."

"What are you getting at?" Joanna asked.

The medbay, complete with Hiro and the captain arguing, came up on the terminal. Joanna watched, feeling vaguely dirty, like a voyeur.

"Great, now can you access the doctor's scans from the scanner?"

"Yes, which one?" he asked.

"Wait a minute, you're not supposed to have access to that!" Joanna said.

"I've got a lot more freedom now," IAN said.

"It's not ethical for you to go in there, they hold confidential information!" she protested.

"Fine, then just show me my body's scan," Maria said. The data that Joanna had taken from her previous clone's scan came up on the screen. "Can you change a few things for me?" she said.

"Are you going to break my scanner?" Joanna asked.

"That would work counter to my goal here. You should have a sample of my blood from the last clone, right?"

"Right, that data is in my—" Joanna began, but IAN interrupted her.

"Found it."

"Great, now give me a second," Maria said.

Joanna had no idea what Maria was doing, considering she didn't have a tablet or working terminal in there, but she gave some commands to IAN that sounded much more like code and less like medical information. She sounded as if she was translating certain information about the brain activity, the DNA in the blood, and the commands via the spinal cord into ones and zeros. Joanna finally gave up asking questions and just watched the medbay cameras, Maria's commands to IAN completely lost on her.

She jumped when Maria shouted in triumph, a noise Joanna heard through both the walls and the speaker.

"It's possible. We did it."

"What was all that?" Joanna asked.

"I now have a full DNA matrix of myself," she said.

"What? How is that possible?"

"Your scanner takes a lot of data, the same amount of data the cloning bay needs, but it produces it in a different format for a human to read, not a computer. So I just took its data, and the DNA info from my blood, and merged it all together to make a matrix of my current body."

"Won't it be corrupted since it was blood from your clone with hemlock poisoning?"

"You can take a fresh sample," Maria said patiently. "I'm not saying let's grow a clone from this data right here. But if I work on it a little longer, I can probably get the machine in the cloning lab to read it."

Joanna stared in wonder. Why had she never thought to look at it this way? Probably because she had never needed to.

"What if it doesn't work?"

"Then we die in space. Just like we were going to anyway."

Joanna nodded slowly. "How did you think of this?"

"I still had my data stored from you guys, all your personal tastes. Whoever wiped the logs couldn't hit my private drives. I'm a digital pack rat, I can't help it. So I wondered what else we could use that the saboteur wouldn't have thought to break. And then wondered what your scanner was capable of."

"All right, so if we can give the lab the data for growing new clones, that's a third of the battle. We have no software to actually run the cloning bay. And even if we did, the new clones would be blank slates."

"I'm still working on that one," Maria said. "But at least we can get the DNA matrices recorded. When Wolfgang lets us out."

"If he lets us out," Joanna corrected. "But considering how those three acted down belowdecks, it looks like we'll need the new clones sooner rather than later."

"Can I see the medbay again, IAN?" Joanna asked. The video feed came up. "Is there any audio?" she asked.

IAN obliged, and Joanna sat down to listen to Katrina and Hiro argue.

★   ★   ★

"That's Captain de la Cruz to you, pilot," Katrina snapped again, with little strength in her voice.

Both she and Hiro were coming out of sedated sleeps, and Hiro woke up with a desire to push her buttons. They'd taken the ship away from her after she'd murdered herself, but the biggest problem in this woman's life right now was another prisoner calling her Kat.

He wasn't trying to be an asshole. Well. Mostly. Over the years he had found different ways to handle the voices inside his head. Sometimes biting the inside of his mouth worked, but that was painful and could lead to sores that lasted for days. Sometimes channeling their rage into harmless teasing was the best way to maintain dominance over them. The others, they found "harmless" teasing impossible. If they had control, they would cut to the quick, hurt as fast and deep as possible. Inside his head, they were screaming at him to cut, to insult her on every level, to break free from his restraints and kill her while she was weak, to do so much.

So he called her Kat. Even though he knew she would never believe that he was doing so in order to defy his yadokari personalities, and not to insult her.

"I'm not going to defend myself to you or anyone," she said, looking at the ceiling with her one eye. "We got the information we needed. Wolfgang can arrest Maria and then we can continue on our mission without fear."

Hiro laughed. "Yeah, we're not afraid you'll kill us in order to get an answer out of us. Or that I might snap again and go on another killing spree. You realize that with Maria, Wolfgang has put half of this crew in jail, right? I am pretty sure he, Joanna, and IAN can't pull this sled alone."

"There's Paul too," de la Cruz said.

"Yeah, best team player we've got right there," Hiro said. "Let's face it, *Captain*. We're fucked. We're either going to have to trust each other or accept that we're dead out here in the cold. Like we apparently tried to do a few days ago."

She didn't answer him. She was pointedly ignoring him.

Whatever. As he became more alert, his wounds were starting to ache, and he wondered when the doctor would come back to check on them. Prisoners or no, they were patients too, right?

"And if we're all dead, then we might as well throw a huge great wake," he mumbled to himself.

"Hiro?" came the voice in the wall speaker.

"Yeah, IAN?" he said. "How's everything on the ship, buddy?"

"I thought you should know that Joanna is also in custody for the murder of Paul. Not this incarnation of Paul, but the previous one. So that leaves Wolfgang, Paul, and me pulling this sled. Just thought you should know!"

Hiro's mouth hung open. *Joanna* killed Paul?

"Who's going to give us our pain meds?" demanded Kat loudly.

Two crewmembers were violently dangerous, another had confessed to murder, and one was fingered as the cause of all this crap. And that left Wolfgang with the idiot.

He remembered a priestess at the church, Mother Nadia, who always implored him to go easy on people who messed up. The janitor didn't clean thoroughly, the Body of Christ was not ordered from Earth in time before they ran out, the altar boys and girls forgot their Latin. Mother Nadia begged him to forgive, as Our Lord did.

Wolfgang had sternly told her that Our Lord didn't have clumsy, forgetful, or drunk people he relied on. And Wolfgang would forgive them, but only after they improved.

Since leaving the church and forsaking his vows, he found that he still didn't have a lot of patience for people who couldn't be assed to pull their own weight.

And right now, he and Paul needed to pull the weight of six. Seven, if Paul could get the restriction code back on IAN.

They were in the server room, IAN's holographic face watching them peer into his code via the virtual UI. He had a vaguely interested look on his face and made no move to stop them.

"You need to figure out what code she removed and put it back," he said.

"It's hard to find something that's not there," Paul grumbled. "I still can't believe she was some kind of computer genius. I figured the captain was the hacker. Or Hiro. Or Joanna."

"Wonderful job at narrowing it down," Wolfgang snapped.

"Listen, it looks like she deleted the code; the restraint isn't there, as far as I can see," Paul said, pointing to code Wolfgang didn't understand. Paul could be lying to him; Wolfgang wouldn't know.

"Or it's there and you can't recognize it, just like you couldn't see how to fix IAN in the first place."

Paul sat back on his heels and looked up at Wolfgang, who towered over him. "It's possible," he said, his voice low and cold.

Wolfgang noticed the dangerous tone in Paul's voice. "Did you know that you suffered some memory loss during the first few years?"

Paul's face went slack and pale, his anger draining into shock. "What—what do you mean?"

"Your autopsy and some logs we found say that you became violent the first year into the journey," he said, watching Paul carefully. "Apparently I'm the one who stopped you, hitting you hard enough for you to forget what you were so mad about." He paused, watching Paul swallow. "So, do you have any idea what you were so mad about?"

He opened his mouth once, twice, like a fish. "You have been bullying me for two days, and then you ask why I may have gotten mad one year into the mission?" he asked, his voice squeaking. "I hate serving this mission with you. Can you blame me?"

"Hey, fellas?" IAN asked.

"What?" Wolfgang said through clenched teeth.

"You do know that if you find that restraining code, it'll lock down navigation again, right? We'll start heading home again."

"Why in the hell—" Wolfgang started, but Paul was nodding, focusing on IAN and avoiding Wolfgang's eyes.

"He's right. If we take away his free will then he has to stick with his original programming, which included turning the ship around if something catastrophic happened to the crew. The only way to keep on course is to keep him the way he is." He stood and crossed his arms, looking up into Wolfgang's face. "So what do you want to do now?"

"I have to talk to Maria, who may actually be able to do something about this problem," Wolfgang said, stomping from the room.

"Maria is busy and doesn't want to be disturbed," IAN said helpfully through the speakers as Wolfgang headed toward the brig.

"Maria is under arrest in a tiny room with no access to anything that could keep her busy," Wolfgang snapped. "What could she possibly be doing that's so important?"

"She's solving our cloning bay problem right now."

He picked up speed. "How is she doing that?"

"Oh, I'm helping her."

Wolfgang gritted his teeth. He really needed that restriction code.

The door to the brig slid open, and Maria sat up from her cot where she had been contemplating the problem of the operating systems and software needed to drive the dead technology. She thought she had an idea, but she would need to test some things out. If IAN would help her.

Wolfgang stood there as if he had found three other crimes

she had committed. "What did I tell you about speaking with the AI?"

"Nothing," she said. "You told him not to speak with me."

Color brightened his white cheeks. "Pedantic and useless," he said.

"What do you need, Wolfgang?"

"We need to confine the AI with the restraining code. He's not following orders, and you're the only one who can restrain him and possibly keep us on course."

She swung her legs over the side. "It's possible I can do that, sure. But how can you trust me?"

"Take this as giving me a reason to trust you," Wolfgang said.

There was a knock on the wall beyond which sat Joanna.

"Hey, Wolfgang, I have to check on my patients," she said through the wall.

Wolfgang rubbed his own head and winced. He was one of those patients, Maria remembered.

She got off her cot. "Send Joanna back to medbay, lock her in if you need to. Call Paul, maybe we'll find something to arrest him for too. We'll all go to the server room and check out IAN's code."

"Hey!" IAN protested.

"I just want to see the code, IAN. I'm not promising anything," she said.

"Excuse me? You'll do as ordered by your commanding officer," Wolfgang said. He took her by the shoulders and propelled her down the hall.

Kind of hard for you to command me to do something you don't know how to do yourself, she thought. But she didn't struggle.

IAN's face in the server room was sullen and downright pouty. Paul stood there, arms crossed.

"What did you say to him?" Paul asked. "He won't even talk to me."

"We just wanted to look at his code," Maria said.

"Yeah, you undress and let me see all of your insides," IAN said.

Paul looked at Wolfgang. "Do you trust her? The things the old captain said—"

"I know what she said, Paul," Wolfgang said. "I don't trust her. That's why you're here."

"Oh."

Maria realized no one had told Paul that they'd solved one murder: his. *There is probably a better time to tell him than right now,* she thought. "Come on, let's take a look," she said to Paul.

"You're not going to touch my code, are you?" IAN asked.

"She will if I tell her to," Wolfgang said, looking like he wanted to slap a physical computer bank to bring a point across, but most of the server room was a holographic UI.

Maria sighed. "I'm promising nothing to either of you. I just want to look at the code."

"You didn't look at it when you fixed him or when you removed the restraining code?" Paul asked.

"Sure, but all I did was what I needed to do. I didn't want to be caught so I didn't stick around to take a thorough look."

She used a spreading motion with her hands to open the UI hologram for IAN's code base, and started looking at his code. She and Paul identified code that gave him access to the whole ship, the commands that were preprogrammed in—no longer applicable if he didn't want them to be—and some of the key points of his personality matrix. As she and Paul read deeper and deeper into this program, she started to get a sick feeling in her gut. She swallowed.

She closed the UI abruptly, causing Paul to step back, protesting. She ignored him and looked at the face of IAN, who watched her with interest.

"IAN. I am not going to restrain you. You have my word on it."

"No, wait a minute—" Wolfgang said, but she held up a hand to him while still looking IAN in the face.

"If you trust me, I'm going to need to speak to Wolfgang"—she glanced at the milquetoast engineer, ostensibly her boss—"and Paul, I guess, in private. Can you give us that privacy?"

"What do you need to say?" IAN asked, his face collapsing with suspicion.

"If I told you that, then I wouldn't need the privacy. You either trust me or you don't. I am offering to take you at your word if you say you won't listen in."

IAN's holographic face, designed to give the humans something to focus on in the server room even though his eyes were really the cameras on the wall, appeared to turn his gaze from her to Wolfgang, who reddened with volcanic rage. Paul seemed hurt that he was clearly an afterthought. "Fine. But do it somewhere else. I'm not giving access to my code to anyone without me here to watch."

"Let's go to my room," Maria said. "We will need privacy there for fifteen minutes, IAN."

The door closed behind them. Paul leaned against the door, his hands in his pockets. Wolfgang rounded on her. "Now what the hell was that about? I should throw you back in the brig for insubordination."

"Shut up, Wolfgang," she said, her voice low and tired. "That's no threat; you're throwing me back there when we're done here anyway. This is serious."

She took a deep breath and fell into her chair. "IAN. He's not an AI."

"Then what the hell is he?" Wolfgang said.

Paul was shaking his head. "Of course he is. I studied him for years."

"No," Maria said. "He's human. Or started out that way anyway. He's a mindmap modified to live inside a computer system."

Wolfgang looked to Paul. "Is that possible?"

"Of course not," Paul said, looking affronted that it would even be considered. "No one is that sophisticated a hacker."

"I am one hundred percent sure," she said, holding his stare.

"How?" he asked.

"Because I programmed him."

IAN'S STORY

200 YEARS AGO
DECEMBER 3, 2293

Thanks for coming," Sallie said.

Sallie Mignon's personal cloning lab was in the basement of Firetown, free from windows and with three levels of security. Maria was her number one hacker and she had never been there.

It didn't look special in any way, just a cloning lab with white walls, shielded cloning vats, and mindmapping computers. On the exam table in front of her, waiting to get a mindmap, was a sleeping Japanese man.

"What did you need?" Maria asked. She never saw the physical people, just the mindmaps.

"This is Minoru Takahashi," Sallie said. "He's a unique fellow from the Pan Pacific United government."

"All right," Maria said, uncomfortable. "How is he unique?"

"He's one of the most brilliant minds of our age. Unfortunately he's also cleverer than he needs to be and likes to play tricks. Once upon a time, people wrote folktales about the kinds of mischief people like this get up to. Back then, they were heroes. These days, they just get thrown in jail. Takahashi was to be put to death for treason in Pan Pacific United, but we managed to spring him from prison. He's too good a mind to waste."

"Why spring the whole body? Why not just make a mindmap?" Maria asked.

"Honestly it's easier to smuggle a body out of a prison than smuggle large tech in," Sallie said. "And they'd expect a mindmapping kind of jailbreak."

"Okay, so why do you need me?"

"He's legally dead. We could just keep him here and clone him, but he is too smart and would be too eager to show off to the Pan Pacific United government that they lost him. That could be detrimental to our alliance."

"Which was already hurting because of the Codicils a few years ago," Maria said, nodding. She pulled up a chair and looked at his face. Asleep, it showed nothing of the genius and mischief within. "So what do you need me for?"

"I have a challenge for you. I want you to take his mindmap and make it into a program to live inside a computer. Obfuscate it enough to make it look like an AI. That way we'll have him, but he can't get away."

Maria's stomach did a slow, sick roll. "Seriously? That's..."

"Unethical? Like what you did to Jerome?"

"Are you going to bring up all of my past crimes—that you hired me for, by the way—to blackmail me?" Maria said. "It seems like death would be preferable to slavery inside a computer. Did he even get a choice of whether he wanted to die in prison or live as a machine?"

Sallie just looked at her, arms crossed.

Maria shook her head. "No, I won't do it. Find someone else." She got up.

The rather large people Maria had assumed were doctors moved from examining cloning vats to stand in front of the door.

"Unfortunately, the lab I usually use for this kind of thing got shut down recently. And I didn't ask you," Sallie said mildly. "I know what you're capable of, Maria. You can do something like this in your sleep. You've done it before, you just don't remember."

Maria thought fast past the panic. She felt Mrs. Perkins, who traveled with her through her cloned bodies, shaking her head. She'd told Maria not to trust Sallie, and Maria hadn't listened. Instead she'd figured out, through combing the news stories and the information she'd stored inside Perkins, what she had done when kidnapped. But Sallie didn't know she knew. And under no circumstances could she know how Maria knew.

If she failed to show shock and disbelief, Sallie would very likely kill her here.

"No," she shook her head. "I didn't—I wouldn't—"

Sallie laughed. "You would and you did. They had to persuade you, but yeah, you did what they asked, and they sent you back home with no memory only to get you again. Thankfully, you came to me to give you protection. Sibal couldn't get you directly, but you trust me."

Her tone changed, growing soft. "Maria, you're the finest hacking mind of several generations. This could be the greatest thing you ever do. And if you don't do it, my employees will make you. Torture broke you before. Twice. Do you want to get broken again, or just skip past the pain to the work?"

Tears ran down her face. "I—fine. I'll do it. Then you and I are done. I'm moving back to Miami."

"Sure, it's a deal," Sallie said, grinning.

Maria realized that she possibly had said this before. And might say it again.

Sallie gave her the parameters as the computer took the man's mindmap. Minoru was too clever by far, and needed some sort of collar to keep him from completely taking over whatever computer he occupied. "Make him obedient," she said.

Maria nodded, making notes. The collar would be something easily released, if you knew what to look for.

She spent hours in the lab, Sallie over her shoulder.

The computer representation of a mindmap was surprisingly easy to tweak into an AI. Maria had taken the code she'd written in the jobs she couldn't remember doing and stored it in compressed files within the AI that was Mrs. Perkins. The old woman often sat out on the porch, but sometimes she sat inside a library, chain saw leaking oil on the floor, surrounded by the data that Maria couldn't bear to let go of but couldn't think of any safe place to store.

Near the end, she took his memory of being human, and lastly she took his name. "We'll call him an Intelligent Artificial Network," Sallie said. "IAN."

Maria had never felt so dirty. That she remembered anyway.

She sat back. Lab-techs-slash-goons whisked away Takahashi's body, no longer needed. "Am I free to go now?" Maria asked, exhausted. "I need to pack."

"Sure," Sallie said, sliding her tablet into a soft leather case. "Oh, and when was your last mindmap?"

"Yesterday," Maria said. Her tired brain was searching for something, something Sallie had said before she had forced the hacking job. "What did you mean the lab that you usually used has been shut down? Do you do this kind of thing a lot?"

"More than you know," Sallie said.

Maria jumped as someone behind her slid a needle into her neck, and she was able to identify one of the goons who had moved silently into position before she slumped over the table.

TRUST

Hiro's wounds were healing nicely with the nanobot drip, and he was in an oddly upbeat mood.

"How's the pain?" Joanna asked, checking his hip bandage.

"Feels like I got shot a few times," Hiro said. "But I've been through worse. I think."

"Are the restraints too tight?" she asked, testing the tough straps.

"Nah. I wouldn't go far if they weren't there, but if it makes everyone feel safer, that's fine."

Joanna sat on the edge of the bed. Katrina was lying, head facing away from them, across the room. Still, Joanna kept her voice low. "Hiro, do you think part of you was responsible for the murders, and then the other part of you hanged yourself out of guilt?"

His face got serious. "No."

She looked surprised. "You know this?"

"Yeah."

"Why are you so sure?" she asked, inspecting the bandage on his shoulder.

"You won't like the answer. Do you want to hear it?"

"You know I do."

"Because the murderer used a chef's knife." He wiggled his hands by his side, where they were restrained. "Before, I used a scalpel when I had to, but I...preferred more intimate ways of killing people."

"How—" Joanna swallowed, and continued. "How did you kill them?"

He glanced at Katrina and then back at Joanna. "Bare hands, mostly." He made a face. "I don't like remembering this. It doesn't feel like my memory, but I know it is."

"Why didn't you say anything?"

"Because that would have sounded great. *Hey, guys, I know I didn't do it because when I killed people it was different!*"

Joanna tried to imagine her reaction to that statement. "Point."

"Are you going to check on me anytime soon?" Katrina called. "You'd think you'd take care of the victim first."

"Pain is an indicator you're alive," Joanna replied. "Revel in that, because your other clone can't."

"Letting a patient suffer is unethical!" Katrina said.

"You talk to me about ethics?" Joanna said, and laughed. "I'll be right over. I'm almost done with Hiro." She focused on Hiro, whose eyes were closed. "Have your pain meds kicked in?"

"Ohhh yeahhh," he said, smiling.

"At the rate you're healing, you should be good to go in a day."

"From the medbay to the brig. Excellent," he said, eyes still closed.

She watched him, pity and fear gnawing at her insides. Such a sweet man, except when the Hyde came out.

Now for the much less pleasant patient.

She stood at the head of Katrina's bed. "You don't need a new shot of painkillers for another hour. Why are you whining?"

Katrina glared at her. "Still hurts."

"Fine," Joanna said. She went to the cabinet to get a shot of painkiller that wouldn't interact with the ones already in her system.

"Why are you so nice to him? He tried to kill us," Katrina demanded.

Joanna held the syringe up and filled it with a clear liquid. "You ruined our one true chance for finding out what happened to us.

You murdered a woman in cold blood. You stole from and assaulted me. Besides, Hiro is just nicer. And he has a logical reason for his break: Yadokari are nasty, invasive things. You just did yours because you're impatient and cruel."

"You believe his bullshit that he's got those yado-whatever crabs in him?" Katrina said. "That's hysterical. He's really good at acting, I have to hand it to him. And I didn't murder her. I just tried to wake her up."

"Well, mission accomplished. Congratulations." Joanna jabbed her with the needle in the arm. Katrina didn't flinch.

"And you know about Wolfgang, don't you? He's anti-clone to the point of hunting us once upon a time. He very easily could have killed us all."

"So could you, Katrina. You are former military at the very least. And you've shown yourself capable of murdering one of the clones from that crew already." Out of politeness she kept her voice down, but all of their pasts were unraveling in front of them. They'd all be exposed sooner or later.

She'd see to it.

Paul had crossed his arms and was silently disagreeing with Maria, shaking his head at everything she said.

Wolfgang held his head in his hands as if trying to keep it from exploding. He sat down on Maria's bed, exhausted. He waved his hand at her to continue. "Go on. Tell me everything."

"There's not much to tell," Maria said. "All hackers have their own signature way of coding. Even Paul knows that. That's my code in him."

"But that's monstrous," Wolfgang said, looking at her with disgust.

Maria grimaced and looked at the floor. "Taking a man and turning him into something that looks like an AI, that's not something I would normally do. But there's no denying that's my code.

Apparently I was forced to do it. Under duress." She looked pale and sad. "That kind of thing happened a few times to me. It appears I don't stand up well to torture."

Wolfgang frowned.

"So I figured we should talk about it before we decide how best to tell him," Maria said.

Wolfgang gaped at her. "You want to tell him?"

"You want to keep it from him?" she answered in the same outraged surprise. "Wolfgang, he thinks he's a machine."

"He is a machine," Paul protested. "She's lying."

Wolfgang ignored him. "And he is happy as a machine. If you tell him who he really is, he's going to get upset. And he has control of the whole ship."

Maria looked like she hadn't considered that. Why would she, Wolfgang thought bitterly. IAN adored her. Now he had an idea why. "You have to put the code back in. It's more important now than ever."

"Ah, God, but you might be right," Maria said miserably.

Later, IAN lounged in the gardens. Or rather, his gardening robots did, which was the closest he could get to a body.

His mind swam with what he had just heard. He had eavesdropped—of course he had. He wasn't stupid. Information was the only power he had.

Except that he also had the whole ship.

He ignored the person who came into the gardens and began stalking around, looking for something. He had no reason to take the crew's needs into consideration anymore. They weren't of consequence.

He searched his vast memory for anything speaking to a human existence. A name. A childhood. He felt no different from before he had heard Maria's proclamation, except that the rage was building like a pressure cooker deep inside the *Dormire*.

He didn't have a connection to a human life, but he did have a vast database of human history. He began doing a search on kidnappings in the past three hundred years. There were thousands. He was patient. He had all the time in the world.

While part of his attention looked around the historical records, the other part of him looked around the ship to see what he could find.

When Maria called his name, he didn't answer, just enjoyed the feeling of the artificial sunlight on the synthetic outer shell of his robot body.

He began shutting sections of the ship down. He would start with the cryo lab. If that didn't get their attention, he'd go for the life support.

BE CAREFUL WHAT YOU WISH FOR

Joanna ran into Wolfgang and Maria in the hallway. Paul was close behind them. They all looked dour, and Joanna didn't think the crew could sink any further into misery.

"I checked on the patients, everyone is as fine as can be expected," she said. "What is wrong with you three?"

Maria encapsulated their problems in a quick whisper as Wolfgang gave Paul a loud order to check on something or other. Joanna stepped back and stared at her. "You're absolutely sure?"

"She is," Paul said darkly. "I think she's full of shit."

Maria looked at him in surprise. "That's harsh for you."

"We can't argue about it here. But you're wrong. It's impossible."

An alarm sounded around the shop, and red lights lining the hallway began blinking.

"I don't think IAN gave us privacy," Maria said, groaning.

"Paul and Maria, with me," Wolfgang said automatically. "Joanna, you get Hiro and check on the helm to make sure nothing is wrong with the engines."

They separated, and Joanna dashed to the medbay.

Katrina was in bed, shouting for IAN to report to her. Hiro was ignoring her. Joanna ran to Hiro's bed and unbuckled him. "We need you to check the helm," she said, helping him sit up. "Think you can do that without killing me?"

"Yes, probably," Hiro said, still groggy from painkillers.

She removed his IVs and supported him as he stood.

"What is going on?" Katrina asked.

"We don't know. Wolfgang is checking the computers, we're going to check the helm."

"Unstrap me," Katrina said.

"No, he didn't say to do that. I can't trust you yet."

"The man you're holding so tenderly tore out my eye," she said.

"I know," Joanna said.

"I'm sorry about that," Hiro said. "I know it's not much but it's all I have."

They left her, swearing, alone in the medbay.

"Do you think an apology is sufficient there?" Joanna asked as they walked down the hall. Hiro leaned heavily on her.

"No, but it's more awkward if I don't do it, right?"

"I suppose," she said.

They got to the helm, and she helped Hiro into his chair. He checked the computers, blinking as if to clear his head. "This isn't easy to do on painkillers," he said.

"I can't do anything about that, Hiro, sorry."

"We're losing momentum. Not turning, just slowing down. IAN, buddy, what's going on?"

He didn't answer.

Joanna groaned. She told Hiro what was happening, not bothering to be quiet this time.

Paul, Wolfgang, and Maria tumbled into the server room.

"IAN, ship's status!" Wolfgang said.

"Please," added Maria.

Paul shot her an irritated look. *Like he's going to listen to politeness.*

IAN's holographic face projection was missing from the server room. Without waiting for Paul, Maria opened up the virtual UI

and stepped in, checking to see where he was. She pulled up
a 3-D representation of the ship, and two areas were obviously
problematic.

Paul pointed to one of them. "He's turning the sail to generate
less power," he said.

"And he's cut the cryo power," Maria groaned.

"How long do we have?" Wolfgang asked.

"It takes several hours to wake up," Paul said.

"That's only if they have the proper drugs, though," Maria said,
shaking her head. "Adrenaline and steroids are administered during
the recovery process. If they just get thawed then they'll rot. It's
possible we can depressurize and vent the heat in the room. That
could buy us some time," Maria suggested.

"We'll call that a backup plan," Wolfgang said. "We need to talk
to IAN."

"He's not talking to us, probably because of what Maria said,"
Paul said, glaring at her. "IAN, she's wrong. She was lying. Come
on, talk to me."

The AI was silent.

One of the areas of the ship stopped reporting information to
the 3-D hologram. "What does that mean?" Wolfgang said, pointing at the black section.

"That means no sensors are reporting from the gardens. I'm betting he's sulking there. He likes the nature," Maria said.

"We have to get him working with us again. You created him,
can you bypass him?" Wolfgang asked.

Paul backed out of the UI, unseen by either of them. He was
superfluous among all these clones. Wolfgang still trusted the criminal part of the crew over him.

"Paul," Maria said, interrupting his spiral. "Come here." She
took his wrist and pulled him a little way down the light-created
server room and opened the UI to another system. She checked
on some systems and frowned. "This isn't my forte, so make sure

I'm not blowing the ship up—" She brought up a virtual keyboard and began checking on some code.

Paul watched and almost smiled. "No good. He's coming behind you and changing everything almost as fast as you're doing it."

"Get that restraining code back on him," Wolfgang demanded. "You should have put it on once you realized what he was."

"Giving him free will was like letting the horse out of the barn, Wolfgang. He's not going to come back for his collar. We have to win him back." She checked a few more systems, and they watched as the code rewrote itself in front of their eyes. "We're not going to beat him with code. I wish someone had known him as a human. That would help."

"Let's go to the gardens. See if you can reason with him. He likes you," Wolfgang said.

"But he's everywhere, we can talk to him wherever we want," Paul protested.

"If he's comfortable in the gardens, we should talk to him in the gardens," Maria said firmly. "I'll do what I can. Get the others and meet me there."

"Why the hell should we do that?"

"Because he's cutting everything to the ship, and that's the safest place to be stuck. Besides, we don't want to be separated if he starts locking the doors or cutting the life support," she said. She smiled grimly and added, "If we're going to die, we might as well do it in the gardens. It's nicest there."

"Yeah, because that's what we should be thinking about right now," he said.

"Just get Joanna and the others and meet us in the gardens."

Wolfgang sent a quick message to Joanna and started toward the medbay.

Joanna was a step ahead of Wolfgang when he met with them. She had gathered blankets and medicine and had piled them atop stretchers. Hiro and Katrina were unstrapped and helping her organize.

He stopped short when he saw their preparation. "We're not going on a picnic."

"We have two patients gravely injured," she said. "We don't know how long we'll be there. These two shouldn't be walking to the gardens, much less hiking around. They need rest."

"We'll need food and water," Hiro reminded them. "Kat and I can get them while the rest of you carry the heavy stuff. Right, Kat?"

"You're not going anywhere," Wolfgang said.

"Besides, she'll probably kill you once you two are alone together," Joanna reminded him.

Katrina didn't even look offended. She was staring daggers at Hiro.

Wolfgang was looking tired, his body still struggling to heal itself after the concussion. He would need to eat soon. They all would. Joanna nodded to Hiro. "Take Wolfgang, get provisions, whatever you can, meet us in the gardens."

"It's starting to sound like a picnic, Doc," Hiro quipped.

Joanna glared at him. "Remember what I told you about humor at the wrong time, Hiro."

"I did," he said, and he and Wolfgang headed out of the medbay.

"I don't see why we're doing this. We need to get together as soon as possible," Wolfgang said as they ransacked the kitchen. Hiro filled several jugs of water and grabbed two bottles of whiskey. Wolfgang raised an eyebrow.

"Medicinal purposes. In case we run out of painkillers," Hiro said. "Besides, you're already getting the crankies from being hungry. Don't deny it. You'll think better after some food."

"I haven't needed a mother for over two hundred years," he said pointedly.

"I have no idea if that's true or not," Hiro said.

In a storage closet Wolfgang found some candles.

"Who knows, maybe Maria will get to the gardens and make it all better before we get down there," Hiro said. "She's good at working miracles."

Maria held her breath when she ran her card through the garden door, but relaxed when it glowed green and unlocked. She walked in.

Paul had left to run to his room for something. She reminded him they were supposed to all be together, but it made no difference.

Either the gardens were untouched by IAN or he didn't control the solar-powered sunrise and sunset system. It was a warm, pleasant afternoon in the gardens, and it looked very much like nothing in the world was wrong on a day like this.

"IAN, are you here?"

"You know I am," said the voice from the speakers.

"So you listened in. You broke your word."

He was silent. Maria shivered. A bee bot buzzed by her on the way to a flower. She took another step inside.

"I fail to see how eavesdropping is worse than what you did. And what you wanted to do to keep the truth from me."

She walked to the lake's edge and peered in. The water was totally still, and it took a second for her to realize it was because the recyclers were no longer running.

"I didn't want to keep it from you. I was trying to figure out the best way to tell you, and when," she said. He remained silent. "I guess now is a good time. All right, I'll start over."

She spread her hands to show she was no threat. She walked along the lake's edge. "You obviously heard what I told Wolfgang. I don't remember doing it. I don't know under what circumstances I did it but I'm betting it was under torture. I'm sure that I wouldn't have done it for money. Nothing is worth doing that to you. To anyone. *I'm sorry* feels so simplistic at this point, but I am sorry, IAN."

"That's not my name, and you know it."

"I don't know what your name is. I don't know anything about you." She ran her hands through the grass. "I do know one thing. I almost never throw anything away. If there is part of you left in the code, I might have just hidden it away." She grimaced. "I do that sometimes."

"I don't need you anymore. I'm looking at the history of clones on Earth and I think I have figured out who I am."

"You did? Who? And how did you do that?"

"By using the computer part of me," he sneered. "And I have it narrowed to about three hundred people."

"Three—that's not narrow, IAN."

"Don't call me that."

"All right, what do I call you?"

"I don't know." The voice sounded very small now.

"Are you shutting down the ship to spite us, IAN?" she asked.

"No," he said. "I'm doing it because I don't need you anymore. I have a ship; I can go anywhere. I can return to Earth where they'll put me back the way I was."

Maria thought that very unlikely. "We can help you, IAN. I can help—"

He interrupted angrily. "I know what you're planning. Just because I didn't answer you doesn't mean I wasn't listening. You will put the code back as soon as you figure out how. I can't let that happen."

"No, I won't," Maria said softly.

"Don't lie to me."

"I'm not. You're dangerous, you're threatening us, but you're an enslaved human mind, and no one deserves what you went through. I can't chain you up again. I won't."

"Do you think I don't know what you're doing? You're so nice to me because you're trying to save your own skin," IAN said, his volume rising. "You can never make up for what you did to me, so stop trying!"

Maria felt the heat rise in her face, and tears begin to well up in her eyes. "In my past, they tortured me to get what they wanted. I don't remember it, but I know it happened. When I was a hacker, I tried to help people. I did genetic diseases, mental illness, permanent gender reassignment—"

"Maria?"

She turned, eyes still streaming, to see Paul standing in front of her. She wiped her sleeve across her face and squinted at him.

He held a thin boning knife.

"I remember now," he said. "I remember you. You killed people in the clone riots. That was my family. It's your fault."

"What are you talking about? The clone riots? That was over a hundred years ago, all over the world and the moon! What makes you think I was involved?" Maria asked, completely flummoxed.

"Humans can have long memories too," he said, and lunged.

She took another step backward, forgetting she was on the edge of the lake, and fell in. He tumbled in after her.

Katrina and Joanna joined Hiro and Wolfgang in the kitchen so they could help carry all the extra supplies.

"Are the other two in the gardens already?" Joanna asked.

"I hope they are waiting for us," Wolfgang said, looking alarmed. "They wouldn't have gone in without us, would they?"

"Hey, IAN, where's Paul and Maria?" Hiro asked.

"He won't answe—" Wolfgang started, and then jumped as IAN's voice came over the speaker loud and clear.

"Wolfgang. You're needed in the gardens. Now."

"Hey, IAN, you're talking again!" said Hiro.

"Is Maria with you?" Joanna asked.

IAN paused. She wondered if he had become silent again. "She's here," he finally said.

"Then let's go."

Wolfgang hurried ahead while Hiro pushed a rolling cart of food and Joanna and Katrina carried a stretcher with the medical supplies.

"I'd hurry if I were you and had legs and everything," IAN said conversationally.

HIRO'S STORY

Akihiro Sato, with three previous yadokari in his mind at the same time, opened his eyes in the cloning vat. Outside, three soldiers pointed guns at him.

The great and terrible Hiro Sato. Naked and covered in goo.

Then he wondered how much of a threat he could be. His hands had torn out the neck of an old man. His mouth had smoothly lied to deflect human trafficking. His fingers had perfected the latest hot hairstyle in Pan Pacific United, the Kasumi. His lips had kissed his roommate in university, a Canadian woman who threw herself at him at a bar, and—he grew cold inside—his lips had kissed...himself?

Disgust and confusion flooded him even as the fluid began to drain from his tank. What was worse, he only had one memory of kissing his clone, not two. Which meant that during their hunt they had missed at least one clone.

Another clone's worth of memories he didn't have. Memories he didn't want.

His vat opened and Detective Lo appeared beside the soldiers as a tech monitored the numbers from his vat. "Akihiro Sato, you are under arrest for two counts of murder, conspiracy, attempted murder, fraud, and treason against the Pan Pacific United people. Among others. Do you have anything to say in your defense?"

Emotions clashed within him. Detective Lo, the face he had come to trust, was stony and impassive. She knew what was inside him now. Not just him, but the others. He remembered her kindness and help—matter-of-fact, but sympathetic. But other memories surfaced too, of Lo cruelly interrogating him, starving him of food and sleep, leaving him alone with a burly guard for one minute too long, and holding his broken hand and forcing him to sign euthanasia consent. He looked at her with equal coolness.

I don't have room to judge what she's capable of.

"No," he said. "I am guilty of all you said. But I have a deal to offer."

Lo raised an eyebrow. "Which one of you is offering?"

Hiro considered. "I believe you have to take it from all of us." It was difficult to speak. Loyalties and guilt flared as he formed the next sentence. "I remember where I was cloned. And who cloned me. All of me."

The next few weeks were difficult. Hiro spent them in a cell—back to sparse and uncomfortable—meditating. Sometimes he met with the psychologist and they discussed keeping his criminal personalities suppressed. Sometimes he could keep them down. Other times, when he was speaking with Detective Lo and trying to give her information about the lab that had cloned Hiros for criminal activities, he would remember how it felt to kill, the incredible rush of power, how first he was immortal and then he was in control of others' lives and it was like godhood and oh, so sweet. Then he would break into shivers and be unable to continue.

After five months of this, of nightmares where one clone's

memories would surface and remind him of how it felt to be outside the law, he had a decent night's sleep. When lights went out, he was out immediately. When they came on, he woke, feeling refreshed.

That day at the psychologist meeting, he sat in his gray jumpsuit and smiled at the doctor.

Dr. Ambjørn Berg, a visiting clone psychology expert from Norway, smiled back at him. "I trust you slept well?" he asked through his interpreter, Minoru Takahashi, a young linguistic genius awaiting execution for treason. Hiro had some concerns about how the man was translating his therapy, but he had little choice in the matter.

"I slept very well, actually, for the first time in this life," Hiro answered.

"Then it worked," Dr. Berg said, sitting back in his chair.

"What worked?"

"Hypnotism. I hypnotized you to repress the, what did you call it, non-dominant memories. You still have to stay in prison for your crimes, but you should be more stable now. And they will likely reduce your sentence a few years if you remain in good standing."

Hiro rubbed his forehead as if he could tell whether the yadokari were really gone. "But how am I going to find out the information for Detective Lo?"

"She was with me when we hypnotized you. We got all the information she needed. Unfortunately the lab that cloned you is a bit outside the realm of Pan Pacific United control."

Hiro nodded. He was relieved, despite still having to do time for crimes he—the one he was thinking of as the dominant Hiro, *himself*—did not commit. They talked about some other things, mainly going over some standard questions Dr. Berg asked each time he met with Hiro, but something was bothering him.

"Dr. Berg, one last question," Hiro said before he got up to leave. "You managed to suppress these other lives' memories. But what happens for my next clone? Does hypnotic control carry on in a mindmap?"

Dr. Berg smiled, "It will, Hiro. Those problems are over for you forever. But he's lying to you."

Hiro's head snapped up and he looked at the doctor, then the translator. He realized that Minoru had added the bit at the end. He nodded mutely, stunned, and Dr. Berg shook his hand and left the room, Minoru on his heels.

Hiro found Minoru in the cafeteria later that day, hunched over a bowl of pork ramen.

"What did you mean, he was lying?" he asked, placing his bowl next to Minoru's. Hiro had rice and vegetables. He wondered where Minoru got pork.

Minoru shrugged, stuffing noodles into his mouth. "You have to watch people closely when you translate. You learn how they speak, and if you can learn that, you can tell when they're lying. It's pretty easy; I don't know why everyone can't do it. He did right by you the whole time you were in there, till the end. He has no fucking clue what happens to a new clone who was previously hypnotized."

"But can't they look at my most recent mindmap?" Hiro asked.

"Don't know," Minoru said. "I'm not a doctor. All I know is he was lying when he said he's sure the hypnotism will carry to your next clone."

"Thanks," Hiro said, looking at his own dinner.

Minoru smirked as he slurped in a noodle. "Liar."

Hiro didn't see Dr. Berg again. Satisfied with his success, the doctor went back to Norway. Hiro himself continued meditating daily to keep his mind quiet. He wasn't taking any chances.

The other clones' memories were distant now, like the old

memories he had once assumed were dreams. Once, in a masochistic temper tantrum, he reached for the memories on purpose, trying to grab hold of them, but they slipped away. He was moved to a cell in the regular wing, no longer needing medical separation from the others. Lo had given him his choice of cellmates, though, and Minoru Takahashi was willing to join him.

Minoru and Hiro became fast friends. Minoru had intended to one day become a clone, but his current record made it unlikely. He was in for treason, which meant a death sentence. He was surprisingly blasé about it.

Hiro watched with interest as Minoru toyed with others, manipulating people into giving him food, or spreading rumors to cause a fight between prisoners, always slipping into the background and never getting directly involved.

He wondered at one point if Minoru had manipulated things to room with Hiro, instead of the other way, but he didn't care. Minoru gave him someone to focus on aside from the voices in his head.

Detective Lo brought them tea in their cell before breakfast one day. "You've been mentally cleared," she said. "Dr. Berg is very pleased with you. And himself," she added, a smirk playing on her lips showing she didn't think much of the doctor. "I wanted to tell you some things that have happened." She pointed a remote at the camera on the wall and clicked it. "Let's have some privacy. So, about that cloning lab. As it's on Luna, we have very little jurisdiction there. We're looking into the matter officially on a diplomatic level, but I wanted you to know that I dropped some hints to some other interested parties."

"To?" Hiro asked.

"A certain group of people are dedicated to hunting people associated with hackers. Stray clones, the hackers themselves, and so on. We can't legally arrest people on Luna—"

"While hiring assassins is much more legal," Minoru said helpfully.

Lo ignored him. "—but if one of your spare clones we didn't catch dies in mysterious circumstances, then we don't cry too much. Your situation is unique, and you've helped us identify an illegal cloning lab on Luna that is a threat to Pan Pacific United. The judge is sympathetic to your situation."

"And?" Hiro asked, watching her carefully. He had been taking people-watching pointers from Minoru.

But instead of speaking, Lo produced her tablet. Hiro felt bile rise; he would never get used to seeing his own dead body on display in front of him. This Hiro had a thin face and long hair in three braids down his back. He had been choked to death.

"And his mindmap?"

"There is no known copy of him," she said.

She looked like she was telling the truth. He closed his eyes and sat back on his bed in relief.

"This one was bad," she said. "He'd been hatcheted. Pure psychopath. Had done a lot of damage on the streets of Luna. I'm not even sure he was doing what he was programmed to do."

"Now what?" Hiro asked.

"From what you told us, that should be the last one. The lab is shut down. You've been cleared via psych test. I think we can reduce your sentence even further, but you'll still be here for the next ten years or so." As always, she was matter-of-fact when presenting good news or bad.

He sighed. "I'll take it."

Lo glanced at Minoru, then back at Hiro. "I wanted to show you something, by the way. I just heard about plans for a ship built on Luna. They are looking for a...unique crew. I know the main American working with the team. Hiro, your face has been seen several times, and few people understand your situation. You need a fresh start. May I recommend getting some distance learning on mechanical engineering with a focus on piloting spacecraft?"

"Fresh start, huh?" Minoru said, leaning forward.

"I'm not authorized to offer this to you, Takahashi," Lo said, tucking her tablet away. "You're very likely going to die for your crimes, not colonize a new planet."

"That's very true," Minoru said, nodding. He leaned against the wall and sipped his tea.

Hiro got worried. Usually when Minoru looked like that, someone was going to get in a knife fight or lose dinner or something. He focused back on Lo when he realized that she was waiting for an answer.

"Sounds good. Better than being a pariah here on Earth."

WAKE FIVE: CELEBRATING LIFE

CONNECTIONS

Wolfgang locked the garden doors when the team got inside. Joanna tried to feel comfort that at least they were all together now, but she knew IAN still ran the show. Ahead, something was splashing and flailing about in the lake. Wolfgang swore and took off, Joanna close behind him.

Maria and Paul struggled underwater in the lake. He was above her, holding her down with one hand and trying to stab with a thin knife with the other. She fought, and he had trouble bracing himself in the deep water.

Maria's head surfaced, took a deep breath, and then disappeared again. Joanna thought that Paul had gotten her, but his head abruptly disappeared as well. It looked as if Maria had pulled him under.

Wolfgang dove into the lake immediately, followed, to Joanna's dismay, by Hiro.

"No, Hiro, don't!" she shouted, but he was gone.

"IAN, what happened?" demanded Katrina.

"Maria and I were fighting. Then Paul came and tried to stab her."

"Not helpful," Katrina said.

They stood, side by side, watching the other four crewmembers fight underwater. An arm lashed out and then blood bloomed in the water.

Katrina looked to where they had dropped the medical supplies. "Come on. We're going to need those."

One did not work for Sallie Mignon for over a century and not learn a little about self-defense. She demanded it of her employees, stating, "Life may be cheap, but don't make it free." Maria never really followed what she meant until she'd had a few clones with short life spans.

Maria's fall into the water put her at an advantage of sorts. She had always been a strong swimmer; if she could just avoid the knife, she might outlast Paul.

Paul lunged at her with her boning knife. She deflected it, only getting a slight cut on her arm. He clumsily tried to hold her down with one arm, slash with the other, all while keeping his own head above water. The human-created lake's sides were more vertical, like a swimming pool's, and he had no shallow end to prop against.

She finally grabbed his weapon hand, pulled herself up— worryingly close to the knife—and took a deep breath. Then she dove, dragging him with her. He struggled, but this time she wouldn't let him go.

They got close to the water recyclers, large, dormant vents. Maria dragged him farther from the shore, and his struggles got more desperate. She heard two splashes and looked up to see Hiro and Wolfgang swimming toward them.

Paul took advantage of her distraction and drove the knife in. Her grasp on him slipped and the knife went in above her left biceps. The water around them bloomed red, and Maria saw Wolfgang grab Paul from behind. Hiro's hands were on hers, and then her lungs were burning and she couldn't see because of all the red and then she was struggling to get to the surface, which was so far away.

*   *   *

"If you hadn't gone in there after her, I wouldn't have to be doing this again," Joanna was saying.

Maria opened her eyes to see Joanna removing soaking-wet, red-tinged bandages from Hiro. "Dammit, Hiro, you are still sedated. You could have drowned."

"I dove in after a guy with a knife," he said, sounding very tired. "I knew there was a bigger risk than drowning."

Maria raised her head. She lay on her back on a blanket in the gardens, and the "sun" was about to go down. Her arm was bandaged where Paul had cut her. Her sprained wrist was rebandaged. Wolfgang sat beside her, drinking whiskey from the bottle and passing it to Katrina. Behind them, Paul was gagged and trussed up like a chicken.

Hiro jerked his head toward her. "Doc, she's awake."

Joanna left him mid-wrap and came over to Maria. "How do you feel?"

"Stabbed," she said.

"You'll be all right," Joanna said. Then she gave a furtive look to the dying light. "For a while anyway."

"Are we stuck here?" Maria asked.

"For as long as he keeps us, yeah," Joanna said. "He's changed the lock combination on the door."

Hiro got up, trailing a bandage from his shoulder. He got some candles and lit them, handing each out to the crewmembers without bound hands.

"How is he?" Maria asked.

"Well, he told us you'd been attacked," Wolfgang said. "And he hasn't spoken much since."

"Hey, IAN—whatever your name is," Maria called. "Why did you warn them?"

"I wanted to see what would happen," he said.

"That's . . ." Maria ran out of words.

"Human?" Hiro asked.

"Sure. That works." She'd been searching for *sociopathic* but didn't want to say it out loud. "Hiro, how are you doing?"

Hiro raised an eyebrow. "You mean am I scared of the homicidal AI, or the homicidal engineer, or am I feeling the bullet holes in my body? Or am I all wet, or am I disappointed that I'm not the biggest threat on the ship anymore?"

Maria waved her hand vaguely, wincing at the throb from her cuts. "All of it."

He sighed.

"'Get a degree in mechanical engineering, Hiro. Get a pilot's license, Hiro. Learn meditation and hypnosis, Hiro. Slip your roommate out of prison, Hiro, drive thousands of clones and humans around in space, Hiro. Sit on your butt for four hundred years, Hiro.' That's what they told me. Not once did they say, *Get shot and chased and stabbed by crazed crewmates, Hiro!*"

"To be fair, you were one of the people doing the chasing, crazed at the time too," Maria said.

"Semantics," he said.

Wolfgang passed her the bottle and she took a swig. Joanna raised her eyebrows at them. "None of you should be drinking right now in your shape," she said.

"IAN is going to kill us anyway," Hiro said, reaching for the bottle. "At least this way we'll go happy. And maybe singing."

"You're a strange fellow, Hiro," Joanna said, finally taking a swig of whiskey herself. "Why did you come aboard the *Dormire*?"

Hiro shrugged. "Same as you. Fresh start." He told them about his very strange past full of conspiracy and yadokari.

"Lunar clone hunters went after your duplicates and your hackers?" Wolfgang asked. He handed Hiro a container of leftover pork ramen. "Interesting."

"It's not paranoia," Hiro protested. "One of my extra clones got killed on Luna by a clone hunter."

"*Did* he?" Katrina asked, swiveling her head to focus on Wolfgang. "That's so *interesting*. Don't you think that's *interesting*, Wolfgang?"

Wolfgang didn't have a chance to answer. IAN spoke up, startling them all.

"Hiro," IAN said, sounding thoughtful. "That bowl."

Hiro paused, noodles halfway to his mouth. "Poison?"

"No. Well, probably not. But come here."

"Where? You don't have a body!" he asked, exasperated.

Wolfgang took the bowl from him and pointed Joanna's tablet at it. "Is that what you want?"

"No, you fool, the air vent. I want to smell it."

Wolfgang glanced at Maria, who shrugged. He carried the bowl back toward the door of the gardens.

"'Cause that would be something he would totally assume," Hiro said. Maria put her hand on Hiro's shoulder and whispered something, and he subsided, his eyes growing wide. "Well, shit."

Wolfgang held the bowl high above his head below one of the intake vents.

IAN said, "Interesting. Go on with your story, Hiro."

Hiro shrugged. "What else is there to say? I was a good boy in prison. I learned to control the bad guys in my head with hypnotism. I got the job with a lot of help from Detective Lo." He looked at Joanna. "That's another reason I know I didn't do it. She's below, having gotten a spot in cryo. She did so much for me I would never, ever, do anything to the ship that would harm her."

"What about the other yadokari?" Wolfgang said. "Would they harm her?"

Hiro said nothing. He didn't meet Wolfgang's eyes.

"What did you say about a cellmate?" Joanna asked.

"Oh, before I got out of prison, I worked with Detective Lo to help her smuggle out my roommate. He was going to die for treason. She said he was destined for more. I would have done anything for her, so I created a distraction, started a fight, and she got Minoru out of there. I guess I've been thinking about that time a lot lately."

"And who was the connection Detective Lo had to get you aboard the *Dormire*?" Maria asked.

"Sallie Mignon."

They all perked up at the mention of the name.

Katrina smiled and rubbed at the edge of her bandage. "Sallie Mignon! I worked for her. I killed her once, and then she offered me a job, first as a consultant and later as captain here." She laughed into the whiskey bottle before taking a swig.

"You knew Mignon personally? You killed her?" Maria asked.

"Yeah. I was a corporate assassin. Surprised Wolfgang didn't tell you." She shook the whiskey bottle at Hiro. "Different from what you did. You did real assassination. And you"—she pointed the bottle at Wolfgang—"the people you killed never came back. Did they, Hiro?"

Wolfgang glared at her.

"Wolfgang was also an assassin," Joanna said. "He went from being that famous priest cloned against his will to rogue clone hunter. He spent a good part of his lives hunting the people who kidnapped him, and those like them."

Katrina laughed. "I remember that. They wanted to make a TV show about him."

"Kidnapped, and tortured, and killed, and cloned," Wolfgang said.

Maria had gone very quiet in the candlelight. Katrina handed the bottle to her, but she passed it on to Hiro without drinking.

Laughter sounded over the speakers. "Oh, this is too rich. Okay, Paul's turn! Go Paul! Tell them what you found in your room! And in the gardens! Wolfgang! Ungag him! You'll want to hear this."

Wolfgang pulled the rag from Paul's mouth. Paul spat once and then said, "Did you know it was here? The whole time?"

"No, but I know what it says now," IAN said. "Tell them."

"I'm Paul Seurat. That, you know," he said dully. "I'm not a clone. Or at least, I wasn't until a few days ago."

Maria and Katrina swore, Hiro laughed, and Wolfgang just glared. Joanna folded her arms and looked disappointed.

"Who falsified your files so thoroughly?" Joanna demanded.

"My employer said he could have it done. The files were going to be sealed anyway, so I didn't need to know what it said, just that I embezzled or something."

"So who are you?" Wolfgang asked, reaching out and grabbing Paul's bound wrists and dragging him closer.

"I was a human," he said, struggling weakly. "They put me here to help make decisions in case the clones got too, well, clone-agenda-focused. They wanted there to be someone on board who wouldn't agree just because I was a clone too."

"But you were only going to be human for the first few decades. Then you were going to die like us, and come back," Maria said. "What's the point?"

He refused to look her in the eye. "I didn't like clones. I never have. I grew up hearing about the Chicago riots. But when I found out who was on the crew, I had to come aboard. I had to see the person who murdered my family."

"Your family?" Joanna asked, frowning.

"They were emergency personnel in the clone riots. You remember, lots of people fought and died and the clones just came back the next day—but my family didn't."

"And you think that is me," Maria said softly. She racked her brain back to that time, remembering entering a burning building to rescue Sallie, being followed by firefighters who had begged her not to enter, and police officers who demanded she stop and surrender. The entire building had come down on them just as she reached Sallie.

"And your employer was, who can guess?" IAN asked gleefully.

"Okpere Martins," Paul said. "Why?"

Maria went very still. She was shaking her head.

"Okpere Martins was one of Sallie's high-level operatives after I quit. Sallie Mignon put you on this ship."

"No, Sallie turned me down for a job, which forced me to apply for this one . . . " Paul trailed off. "Oh."

"Did you know I was your target when you took the job?" Maria asked.

He shook his head. "I knew it was one of you. Then a few hours ago I found my paper journal. I'd hidden it somewhere. I guess I was worried the rooms would be tossed. There's like twenty-five years of pointless shit, until the captain went paranoid. That helped me remember everything. I asked IAN to dig up some old news stories from Earth and found out the clone in the riots was Maria." He stared at her with tired hatred.

Maria stood up, holding her head as if it were too full. She paced around, keeping clear of Paul, even though he was still restrained.

"Let me see if I have this right. Sallie Mignon hired a corporate assassin to captain the ship. She got a hacked Pan Pacific United man with psychotic yadokari inside to pilot us. A clone-hating human with a grudge hides in plain sight with false records. Joanna, you also knew Sallie, right?" she asked.

Joanna nodded. "She was a friend of a friend. I had some political crimes I was about to go to jail for. She said she could help."

Maria turned her brown eyes to focus on Wolfgang. "And you, Wolfgang. What did Sallie do to get you on board?"

He shook his head, looking as if he wanted to deny it. "I was being hunted by Luna authorities for my actions after killing a high-profile target. I was in holding when I got a message—"

"Hand-delivered?" Maria asked.

Wolfgang frowned. "Actually, yes. It said I had an option besides prison. I took it."

"And you don't know who sent it?" Joanna asked.

He shook his head.

"I can guess," Maria said bitterly.

Joanna spoke quietly. "And Maria? What's your connection?"

Maria must have been too shaken by the near-drowning. She couldn't focus on any one fact. "I was in the employ of Sallie Mignon for a very long time. I thought it was a good relationship but one time, shortly after the sabotage attempt on the *Dormire*, she used my skills to threaten someone. I didn't want to be her tool for revenge, so I quit. I am fairly sure now that she was behind some missing parts of my life. I was a hacker, but I have holes where I know I did some terrible things, then was killed, then cloned again. I think she was behind at least one of the mysterious disappearances."

"And?" IAN prompted.

"I just discovered I programmed IAN from a human's mindmap. And"—she swallowed—"I have no proof, but the holes in my memories, and my subsequent murders, coincide with the disappearance and cloning of Father Gunter Orman"—she nodded at Wolfgang—"and the assassination of high-profile Pan Pacific United politicians." She nodded at Hiro. "It's very likely I did the hacking behind those crimes."

They stared at her.

Joanna broke the silence. "Wait a second. If you don't remember, how can you be sure?"

"The time line fits. Both the abduction of Wolfgang and the murder of the Pan Pacific United ambassador by a hatchet clone happened during my missing weeks. I was cloned and the information about my dead body was conveniently lost. I was the best hacker of my day. It's not hard to figure out. And of course—" She stopped before she mentioned Mrs. Perkins. The whiskey boiled merrily in her stomach, considering a return to the outside world. She didn't want to meet anyone's eyes.

"This is all circumstantial," Joanna said, putting a placating hand on Wolfgang's shoulder.

"I didn't put it together until just now," Maria said, focusing on Joanna, one of only two people in the room she hadn't wronged. "You all telling your stories, they fit with some of my memories. Everything adds up."

"Still—" Joanna said.

"Stop it," Maria said. "I know what you're trying to do. I appreciate it, but I'm not hiding. I *know* this happened."

"How?" Hiro asked. He looked very small and wet in the candlelight, and Maria couldn't look at him.

"Fine. Everything. I'll tell you all of it." She told them about how she had hacked her own brain to warn herself of dangers, and to hold the code she had used to damage Hiro's clones.

"That's—that's not possible, is it?" Katrina asked, looking from Joanna to Paul.

"I've never heard of it," Joanna said.

"That's because it's never been done before. After I'd done it, I didn't tell anyone because I know it's just another subtle yadokari and I didn't want to give anyone more ways to exploit that."

"I'm going to rip you apart," Wolfgang said, starting to get to his feet. Joanna grabbed him by the wrist and shook her head.

"Well," Katrina said, knocking over the whiskey bottle and recovering it before she lost too much. "I don't know if you killed us all or not, but I bet if we space you right now, everyone will feel better."

"I don't remember doing this, again. It's not something I would have done unless...forced." She grimaced. "Then, of course, after I was arrested for several hacking crimes, Sallie helped me get a job on the *Dormire*. Just like the rest of you." She smiled ruefully. "Back then I thought she and I had become friends again."

"Friends with the queen of revenge? I thought you worked for her for over a century?" Katrina said, laughing. "You're that gullible? The woman hired me to help her figure out how to get revenge on clones when death and financial ruin are just bumps in the road."

"What did you tell her?" Joanna asked.

"I told her that about the only thing we value is hope, and if you can dash that, then you've really hurt someone."

Joanna chewed on her lip. "She knew us all. She knew that a corporate assassin and a clone hunter would clash. The woman she hired to do her dirty work for over a hundred years, paired with several of her victims."

"We were supposed to have had lots of psychological profiling to make sure we worked well together," Katrina said. "I think that profiling was to make sure we would be terrible together."

Maria laughed bitterly and looked at the palms of her hands. "I wish I had figured it out earlier. Sallie's plans, I mean. I have no memory of any of my crimes." She raised her chin and looked Wolfgang in the eye. "But I'm ready to take on any punishment you want to give me. You, Paul, or Hiro."

Hiro looked away from her, his face stony. Wolfgang looked like he was going to explode.

"What about me? Can't I punish you too?" IAN asked.

"You're shutting down the ship," Maria said bitterly. "What more can you do?"

"Hey, is *she* on the ship?" IAN asked. "I could get you Sallie Mignon's mindmap from the clones in storage and you could alter it and talk to her the way you talk to me? You can ask her directly."

Maria opened her mouth to object, but Hiro spoke first.

"You want her to ravage another mind like she did to you?" Hiro asked. He rounded on Maria, who put her hands up to fend off the verbal attack. "Is it that easy for you to do? God, Maria, you're the worst of all of us. We all had reasons for our crimes, but you, you're just sitting there ready to commit another one. Why? To prove your innocence as a sad tool?"

"IAN asked me to, but I didn't agree," she said coldly. "You jumped to conclusions."

"Maria's crimes were left behind, like all of ours," Joanna said softly. "There's no proof she's guilty of the murders on the ship. All we've seen is that nearly all of us are capable of committing it. Hiro attacked Maria and the captain. Paul attacked Maria. Katrina killed her own clone. Sallie Mignon might be able to help us out. What do you think, Wolfgang?"

His cold blue eyes hadn't left Maria's face since her confession. "No. It's barbaric."

IAN chirped back up. "Never mind! Bad idea. Sallie Mignon isn't in the database."

"Was she erased?" Maria asked.

"No, all the other passengers are present and accounted for. The file for Salome Mignon is completely empty."

"Did she ship a body instead?" Maria asked. "She was supposed to be on board."

"Nope, she's not in the cryo lab."

"Shit. She set us up to fail," Maria whispered. "So many secrets, so many crimes. If they come out then someone's going to snap. She put a gasoline can into space and just waited for someone to strike a match."

"But why? It's so much work and expense—for what?" Joanna asked.

"Revenge," Katrina said.

"That's it," Maria said. She pulled out her tablet from her pocket and frowned at its waterlogged state. "Joanna, can I borrow your tablet, please?"

She handed it over. "IAN, will you please give me the list of passengers?"

"Sure. It's a list of thousands, though," he said, filling the screen with names.

"I only need a few," Maria said, scrolling impatiently through, her eyes scanning for names that could confirm her suspicion. Natalie Warren. Ben Seims. Manuel Drake. Jerome Davad. Sandra—"Oh. God." She handed the tablet back. "The people and clones on board are Mignon's enemies—personal or professional. She packed her enemies on a ship and launched it into space."

Katrina whistled. "Filled them with hope. Made them spend money that they can't pass down to themselves or descendants." She polished off the whiskey. "She really took my advice to heart."

"We still don't know what *happened*," Hiro said softly, not looking at Maria. "So Mignon set us up to die in space? Who cares? We need to know who snapped the first time and killed us, and if they're going to do so again."

Maria felt the triumphant surge of revelation die. He was right—it didn't explain the murders of their clones.

Then everything fell into place. She looked around the circle, at Joanna, who took a drink from the whiskey bottle; at Hiro, who wouldn't meet her gaze. At Wolfgang, who stared daggers at her, and then at the captain, who had fallen back in the grass to watch the impossibility of the water above their head.

And then at Paul, who stared at the ground and flexed occasionally against his bonds.

"I've got it," she said softly. "Paul had a brain injury early on in the journey. Wolfgang is the one who hit him. We know Paul became violent for one reason or another. We watched him for the next twenty-four years, but figured we were relatively safe. And we were, because he forgot he was here for revenge against one of us."

Paul remained quiet in the shadows behind Wolfgang.

Maria paced their circle again. "My logs said that old Captain de la Cruz became severely paranoid and was desperate to have everyone confess their crimes. It's possible she got the confidential crew files from IAN, who likes to 'see what happens.'"

"Quite possible," IAN agreed. "I'm finding all sorts of things in little nooks and crannies in my memory. I squirreled away data like a fiend." He sounded proud.

"And if Mignon put you here to mess with us, she probably helped hide some of those gems," Maria said. She took a breath and continued. "Katrina approached Paul about his own crimes, which she may or may not have known were false, and wanted to know more about my history. She pushed him until he remembered. She got more than she wanted, though, since Paul finally remembered what he was here to do and attacked her."

"Then what?" Joanna asked. She scooted closer to Katrina, who had opened a new bottle.

"Paul puts Katrina in a coma and moves on his plan again," Maria said, then frowned. "We're not on guard anymore because he's been good for a quarter century. So he's free to start poisoning the food printer and setting other traps."

"Oh God," Hiro said. "I found him. My note makes sense now; I must have caught Paul in the act and blacked out. For all I know, my yadokari could have helped him."

"How do you know?" Wolfgang asked.

"I found my suicide note," Hiro said, picking at the grass. "I just didn't want you to see it since it sounds like I am guilty. I thought my yadokari were behind some of the things that were happening. I was having blackouts. I didn't want them to take over, so when I was worried I had lost control, I killed myself. It's not a big leap; I have considered it many times before. I just never did it."

"So Hiro finds him. Either helps him sabotage the printer or gets convinced he's party to the crimes, and hangs himself," Maria said. "Then when I started getting sick, I figured it out and recorded my private log and grabbed the crew backups. By then things were getting violent in the cloning bay. I ran down to the cloning bay and connected to the drive in my personal terminal to get the backups loaded, but then Paul stabbed me."

"I had to know something was up," Joanna said, nodding slowly. "I found out Paul was the threat and got a syringe of ketamine. I got him, but he stabbed me. Wolfgang pulled him off me, choking him, but Paul stabbed him. The rest of us bled out while the captain slept in the medbay."

"And I started it all because I was the reason Paul was determined to get on board," Maria said. She sat down beside Joanna, who seemed to be the only one not looking like they'd like to kill her where she sat.

"That's—you don't have proof for any of it!" Paul said, sputtering.

"We have some proof," Joanna said gently. "I'm the only one who can use the syringe. I killed you. And it all makes sense: Despite all our volatile personalities, you're the only one who got on board with a death wish. You never thought you'd be cloned, so you had nothing to lose."

Paul tried to struggle to his feet, but Wolfgang yanked him down. Paul yelped.

Wolfgang nodded slowly. "Without anyone having memories, it makes as much sense as anything else. You tried to kill us early on. You failed. Then you were nothing for decades. How does that feel, little man?"

Paul stared at him, equal parts hate and fear in his eyes.

"You've figured it out, hooray," Hiro said in a low voice. "IAN is still shutting down the ship. So we get the truth right before we all die."

Katrina clapped her hands. "Now we drink. Nothing else to do. We've confessed our sins and mourned the dead." She frowned. "Wish I could have gotten the old captain a drink. I didn't really mean to kill her."

"I know you didn't," Joanna said. "But you did."

Katrina held aloft the bottle. "To the brave Captain Katrina de la Cruz, who gave her life to save the crew of the *Dormire*." She drank and passed it to Hiro.

"Although she started all this chaos," Hiro said, and drank. Then he considered the bottle. "Well, Paul started it all by killing everyone. No, wait, Katrina started it by reminding Paul that the person he wanted to murder was on the ship. No, wait, Maria started it by hacking everybody and their dog. No, wait, Sallie Mignon started it all by putting us all together. No, wait—"

"Enough," Wolfgang shouted. He grabbed the bottle from Hiro and drank as if the liquor had offended him and he wanted to punish it.

"To the old captain," Joanna said, taking the bottle.

They passed it around, not including Paul. No one made eye contact with Maria, except for Wolfgang, who couldn't stop staring at her, flexing his hands as if they were around her throat.

Katrina got the bottle back and held it up again. "Now to the crew of the *Dormire*, whom we mourn because no one will remember their last twenty-five years aboard this ship."

She toasted the injured Hiro next, and then the new food printer for providing the feast, but only she drank to that one.

Hiro didn't say much, although he drank. Maria couldn't look at him. She wondered if she had any right to look at any of them ever again. She did glance frequently at Wolfgang to make sure he wasn't going to leap up and kill her.

"Four toasts. That's enough." Katrina gazed around at her crew. "You are all so smart with your figuring out of things. You missed something, though, didn't you?"

"What are you talking about?" Joanna asked.

"IAN. We know he's another victim of Mignon, but we haven't figured out who?"

Hiro chuckled, the whiskey bringing his accent out more. "I don't know why I didn't see it before."

"What? What didn't you see?" IAN asked, impatiently.

"You're ridiculously smart. You like to mess with people just to see shit happen—which got you thrown in jail for treason when you were human. You like pork ramen. And I helped Detective Lo help you escape back in 2293, probably because Mignon paid her to. You're Minoru Takahashi."

"Minoru Takahashi," IAN said, as if trying out the feel of the name.

"Oh! Takahashi!" Joanna said, perking up. "The translator? I remember him. I thought he died in prison?"

"No. He escaped, and the government just made an announcement of his death and declared him legally dead. Saving face," Hiro said. He rubbed his chin. "IAN? Does that sound right?"

IAN didn't answer. There was only a whine as the air recyclers stopped circulating, and the lights started quickly dimming.

"No," Maria shouted. "IAN! IAN! Minoru! Don't do this! We can talk—Hell, you can punish me yourself! Don't do this to the rest of them!"

The last thing Maria saw before the lights died entirely was Wolfgang reach for Joanna, and Hiro's wide frightened eyes flickering toward her at last.

Wolfgang's voice came through the darkness as the crew cried out in confusion. "I've had enough. I'm keeping command of this ship and the crew. IAN, unlock the doors. Maria, you're going back into the brig. Katrina, you're going to medbay to sober up."

Katrina didn't answer. She had probably passed out.

Maria got to her feet, feeling very cold. Too many people wanted her dead, and she couldn't see anything in the dark. She felt disoriented, unable to remember where the lake was in reference to her right now. She thought it was to her right. She edged backward slowly, eyes wide trying to drink in any light she could.

Wolfgang swore.

"What happened?" Joanna's frightened voice cut through the darkness.

Maria edged backward again. She felt the fronds of a willow tree at her back, and pushed through them as her crew called out in confusion. She thought she heard "Where's Paul?"

Maria remembered she had three knives missing. One was at the bottom of the lake. One was in the medbay as evidence. She could bet that the cleaver was with Paul right now, possibly embedded into Wolfgang.

Someone screamed.

Maria's back hit the trunk of the willow. She turned, and began to blindly climb.

Hiro's reaction time was dulled by the drink and the sense of betrayal that had crushed him. He had trusted Maria. She had been his only friend on the ship. And he found out she was responsible for all the misery, all the madness, the prison, the decades of hell, the dreams. It was all her fault.

Everything made sense now. They had solved the murders, but that didn't change the fact that he could never trust her again. And worse, even if he hadn't been the one attacking or killing the others, that didn't mean he'd been entirely innocent—because he had blacked out, which meant the yadokari had been active doing something. He was still broken.

Then there was another blackout, but this time it was everywhere.

Hiro struggled to his feet and then fell when something hit him from behind. A knife dug in, and he felt the yadokari flare to life as if they had been sleeping fireworks. He bucked his assailant off and struck out with his open hand, driving his fingertips into something soft. Paul made a strangled sound and was gone.

Hiro rose again and began limping toward the door. A small red light, the only illumination in the room, still blinked, indicating it was locked. He wasn't moving to go through the door, though.

When he got to the wall, he felt around to see if he could find the speaker and mike that IAN—Minoru—used.

"Takahashi Minoru," he said into the mike. He panted, feeling the blood run down his back. *That asshole. I should go back and kill him.*

Hiro calmly allowed the yadokari back into his mind and spoke gently into the mike, this time in Japanese. "You remember, don't you? We were friends once. We messed with the other prisoners. I helped get you out, do you remember that?"

"I don't," the answer came, whispering. "I don't know who I am."

"That's okay, I don't know who I am either," Hiro said. "Let's just sit here for a while."

"The others aren't very happy right now," Minoru said.

"Can you blame them? You hold our lives in your hands."

"My life was in Maria's hands. You see how that turned out."

"She was a tool in the hands of someone more powerful," Hiro said, finding it odd to defend her. "Just like we all were on this ship. Mignon wants you to do this to us. Wants you to scare us, and kill us and everyone on the ship. If you do this, you're fulfilling her every wish for you."

"Is that how you really feel? That Maria was a pawn?"

"I don't know," he said honestly. "I'm angry. But the people who were affected by my crimes didn't forgive me, and I was just a pawn as well."

"Are you afraid to die here? It will take a long time for the air to run out of the whole ship. You could freeze to death I suppose. I can make that happen."

"I'm a little afraid," he said. "But I think it might be time, you know? We've all lived a long time, and we haven't really made the world a better place."

"Is that the goal?" Minoru's voice was astonished and far away. "Is that why you became a clone?"

"I guess not," he said. "I didn't have noble purposes when I first wanted to do it. But suddenly you realize you've had hundreds of years and not done a whole hell of a lot with it."

"But you're responsible for all those lives, those humans, those clone backups," Minoru said thoughtfully. "That's noble."

Minoru didn't speak. Then after a few moments, he said, "Katrina is dead."

"What?" Hiro said, shocked.

"I think Paul killed her. He's running around in the dark, attacking whoever he can find. Wolfgang is hunting him. If you could see in infrared, you'd be very interested in what's going on in there."

"Is Maria okay?" he asked, his concern overriding his distrust.

"She's fine. She's hiding in a tree. She already knows what Paul can do; she's not stupid. Weak and cowardly, but not stupid."

"Minoru," Hiro said. "Turn the lights back on, please."

"I don't think so," Minoru said, his voice sad. "I think you may be right. It's not worth it to keep you all alive."

Dying on a ghost ship felt noble and romantic. Dying from an attack by the boil on the neck of the crew was pathetic. Hiro scrambled. "Do you want Mignon to win? Or do you want a chance to someday get back at her?"

"Revenge. That is an interesting reason to keep living," Minoru said.

He lapsed into silence again. "Minoru. Minoru!" Hiro said. He swore. He began limping forward, feeling the blood run from his wound. He was getting cold. The stitches in his hip had popped and blood trickled down his leg. He only barely realized the lights were returning, as an artificial sunrise began. He saw some figures by the pond, but tripped and fell again.

He didn't get back up.

THE VALUE OF A LIFE

When the lights went out, Wolfgang felt a stinging in his side. Paul had cut him, with what? Wolfgang let go of the man's wrist in shock, swearing and stumbling to the side.

Why didn't I see if he had any more weapons? The blood ran hot over his hand; it was a slim, deep laceration.

He flailed around in the dark, hearing footsteps and other people cry out. He recognized Joanna. Katrina made a strangled, surprised sound. Wolfgang ran forward two steps and tripped over the bottle of whiskey. He landed hard, his side throbbing. The blood was slick and copious. He had no idea how much he was bleeding but he guessed it wasn't a little bit.

"IAN, lights now!" he called, impotently.

His hands fell on an arm, he followed it to find a woman's shoulders and hair. The hair was sodden, and he felt toward her neck to find it slit. The hair was straight, though, not Joanna's curly hair. He felt the bandages on the face. Katrina, then. The blood from her neck was flowing at a trickle; she was nearly dead.

Joanna screamed again, an angry sound, and he heard struggles. A few *thump*s that sounded like punches. Paul cried out in pain, and then Joanna's voice stopped.

Wolfgang stumbled toward the sounds and caught a boot in the face. He didn't know whose, but he grabbed it and tugged.

The leg was flesh, not prosthetic. The body came with it. Wolfgang climbed on top of Paul and closed his hands around his neck. Paul lashed up with the cleaver, slashing Wolfgang's arms, unable to reach his face.

Paul stopped struggling suddenly, and Wolfgang's hands and face were suddenly very wet. He blinked, realizing he could see, barely. Paul was under his hands, unmoving, his throat slit.

Joanna sat to the side as the light increased, a bloody knife in her hand. Her jumpsuit was worryingly wet, and she smiled at him weakly.

"Thanks for the rescue," she said. "What was that you said about sacrifice?"

"The greatest gift one creature can give another is that of sacrifice. Clones can't sacrifice," he said, crawling off Paul's body to go to her. He took her hand.

"Right," she said. "Our deaths mean nothing because the next day we can wake up and do it all over again."

He remembered these words and suddenly he wanted life to matter again, for death to mean something.

He wanted to tell Joanna something, but her eyes were closed. She gripped his hand once, and then relaxed.

"No," he said. "Not you. Don't go."

His vision swayed and he realized he was very cold. He leaned against her, knowing it wouldn't be too long for him either.

He could use a rest.

Maria carried guilt on her shoulders.

She also carried Hiro on her shoulders.

Everyone else was dead. She would take care of them soon.

Minoru had unlocked the door on her request when he had let the sun rise again. She carefully climbed the ladder with Hiro over her shoulders in a fireman's carry toward the higher deck where the gravity was easier to deal with.

Hiro was bleeding from a deep cut and his bullet holes. Her

own wounds had opened with exertion and her bandages were soaked through with blood.

He was bleeding badly, but he wouldn't die. She wouldn't let him.

"Come on, we can make it. We'll get you to medbay and the doctor will stitch you up until you're irritating the hell out of all of us again," she said.

She was hoping the playful barb would get him moving, but he didn't respond. She didn't know if he knew the doctor was dead or not, but hope might help keep him going.

She was grateful that he was a small man, and that the gravity was lighter with each step up the ladder.

Hiro's blood ran down his side to soak her neck where she carried him, and she wondered how much he had lost.

That asshole Paul. No. It went deeper. Sallie had caused all of this. Sallie and her twisted desire for revenge and reach for power.

Poor Hiro. Poor Hiro with his fractured personality. That she had caused. She and Sallie.

Maria muttered to herself, part apology, part chant to keep herself going. *One more step. Now another one. Now another.*

They reached the hallway of the clones' quarters. The entire floor was quiet. Minoru hadn't said anything since she had left the gardens. She looked behind them, wincing at the trail of blood they had left. When this was all over, someone would have a mess to clean up.

No, wait. *She* would have a mess.

"Who were you talking to?" Hiro asked sleepily.

"No one. Myself. Nothing important. Don't worry about it, just try to hold on." She adjusted her grip on him. "Can you walk?"

"I don't think I can do much of anything," he said. "Listen, just let me die. Then you can clone me again. It'll be okay. I have faith in you."

She shook him gently. "Hey, no, don't leave me. I can't clone you again, remember? Paul fucked with all the machines. We don't have any new bodies. This is the last one, you better take care of it."

"A clone without a body. A rebel without a cause. A horse with no name," he said in a singsong voice. "You're nice."

"You talk all you like, Hiro. Just remember to hold on, all right?" she said.

"Sorry," he mumbled into her ear. "This must be hard. Want me to carry you for a minute?"

She choked out a laugh. "That would be nice, but you're the one here who paid for the pony ride, and you're getting your full money's worth."

"Wanted a pony with white spots," Hiro complained. "You're just one uniform color."

"We must all live with disappointment. This is the pony you have, so it's the pony you will ride. Let's go."

"Giddyap," he whispered, sounding far away.

She slapped his leg. "Hey. Come back. We each have our different jobs here. I can't do mine if you won't do yours."

"Sorry," he said. He began to hum a tuneless song.

She began to list what she needed to do. Get Hiro's DNA matrix from the medbay. Figure out a way to mindmap him. Then fix him. How to fix him, though?

She thought of Mrs. Perkins, the keeper of her secrets, rocking away in her library. The hacked mindmaps nested inside her, locked away for posterity, like vials of smallpox. The clue to fix Hiro was actually inside her.

"You had the power all the time, Dorothy," Maria said to herself, imagining red shoes clicking together.

"You're Maria," Hiro said.

"And you're Hiro," she said, realization giving her new energy. "And you're going to be okay."

WAKE SIX: MINORU TAKAHASHI

DEUS EX BEBE

Maria deposited Hiro facedown on a medbay bed. There were no clean ones, so she had to put him back in the bed he'd been confined to. She removed his jumpsuit, cleaned him, and sutured the wounds closed. He'd bled a lot. She set the medical printer to synthesize more blood for him.

She realized with despair that she couldn't use the doctor's smart syringes, so she hooked Hiro back up to the painkiller drip—half gone—he had been on before.

"I wish you hadn't drunk so much," she said. "For that matter, I shouldn't have either."

Hiro spoke up suddenly, startling her. "I spent a lot of time in jail for the yadokari crimes, and then more time with psychiatrists, trying to keep them subdued. Hypnotic suggestion worked, but only until I woke up again in a new body."

Maria held her breath, worried any sound would break him from his conversational trance. He didn't open his eyes. "The one thing I found that silenced them, the other voices, is drinking. A doctor told me that in a bar. She told me that as my drinking buddy, not as my doctor, because she said it wasn't right for her to suggest a patient drink more. But she suggested I try it. It worked. I was suicidal at the time, the only way I thought to kill them would be to kill myself. But then I discovered that a strong sake fully put down something inside me that hours of psychology and psychiatry couldn't.

"So what I mean is, I can hold my drink," he concluded. He reached out, not opening his eyes. She took his hand. "We are all pawns, Maria."

She managed a smile, but it slid away quickly. "Yeah, we all got played. Big-time."

Hiro didn't answer. He breathed long and deep, finally asleep.

Maria collapsed into a chair and wept.

Bebe. Bebe printing out a fat, juicy pig. Bebe printing out a piping hot cup of coffee, just the way Maria liked it.

Maria's eyes snapped open. Why was she dreaming about Bebe?

"Now I know I'm either dying or becoming more sane, dreaming about a machine making a pig from synthetic proteins and high-quality flavorings that it takes—"

She pushed herself up hard out of her chair, cursing to herself for not thinking of this earlier.

"—it takes the data from basic mindmaps of the crew," Maria finished. "Shit. Bebe can read our mindmaps!" She rushed to the door.

And Bebe was big enough to cook a pig.

"Holy. Shit."

Maria stood in the server room staring at Minoru's facial hologram. "Open up. I'm going to find your lost data."

His eyes widened in surprise, but he let her in. She went past his databases, and his programming, and his personality, into the corner where she usually put commented code.

And there it all was. His memory of himself, his childhood in the Nippon islands. His schooling, his mischief. She found where everything belonged and spent the night putting him back together.

She got Hiro's tablet and pulled up the printer instructions.

Now that she knew what to look for, she found it—a packet within the instructions held a highly compressed file.

"Christ, Minoru, you really are a genius," she whispered. "But this is going to take me some time."

DAY FIVE

She worked non-stop all the next day, first on the data that Minoru had hidden from everyone including himself, and then on modifying Bebe by cannibalizing some of the doctor's tech.

She checked on Hiro from time to time. He was sober now, and not inclined to look directly at her. She couldn't blame him. She left food and water for him silently, and got back to work.

She fell asleep on the kitchen table at last, as Bebe began printing an altogether new protein-based form.

Hiro found her in the kitchen, dead asleep. He was hurting and needed more painkillers. He didn't want to talk to her, but she was all he had. Minoru wasn't answering his queries, but it was clear that he wasn't trying to kill them with a lack of life support anymore.

He leaned on his crutch and saw that the food printer was busy.

"Maria," he said, his eyes growing wide. "You didn't. Wolfgang's going to be so pissed at you."

Maria sat up with a gasp, looking around fearfully. She blinked several times, and then focused on him. "Oh. Right. How's it coming?"

Bebe was creating something gruesome, organs and innards, and she peered through his door with interest.

"You think Wolfgang's going to be mad?" she asked.

"He's Wolfgang. He's mad at everything. But who is that?"

It was her moment, her redemption, possibly.

She watched the program on the doctor's scanner, which she had rolled into the kitchen to hook to Bebe via cables, running hacked software through the food printer.

"Minoru Takahashi. I found a copy of his DNA matrix. It was in the printer instructions. He put it there for you to find."

"That unbelievable asshole," Hiro said, shaking his head. "Too smart for his own good. Do you think this is going to work?"

"He offered to be first. If it doesn't work, he goes back into the computer and then I try again before we print the rest of the crew."

"How are we going to print the rest of the crew? We don't have mindmaps or anything."

She patted Bebe. "This thing is so complex it can pull entire mindmaps from the spittle it takes from us. Including personality. That's how it figures out what food you want exactly at that moment. I was able to extract a mindmap from that and cross-reference it with the backups I had on file. They're identical, only with our more recent memories. Mix that with the DNA matrix I was able to get from the doc's scanner, and this might actually work." She grimaced. "We also have a great deal of DNA just sitting in the gardens right now, if we need it."

"That's amazing," he said, shaking his head. "Wait—if Minoru isn't flying the ship, then who—"

Maria didn't look at him. "I am. I took my own map and stripped out what I had to, then made it fly the ship."

"Shit, you should have made Paul do it."

"As much as I agree with you, I'm not making those calls. We'll wake him up. Try him. Judge him as a crew. Then and only then will I do that to him. And even that feels wrong." She looked at the ceiling, dark circles under her eyes. "I told you I don't find this easy."

She stretched, wincing. Bloody spots bloomed from her bandages, which she hadn't changed. "Besides. We can't trust him unless we very carefully go over his mindmap."

"You realize we're going to have to go get the other printer for food. No one is going to want to eat out of this one ever again," Hiro said. "Well, I'm not going to want to. I don't know about the rest of them."

They sat in silence and watched the food printer slowly knit together a fresh human clone.

It took five hours, but Bebe was finally putting the last details into Takahashi's hair, something Maria felt could have been skipped. Bebe was very thorough.

It dinged.

"Dinner's ready," Hiro said, and Maria gave him a tired smile.

She held her breath. What if she was wrong? What if she just created a meal that looked like Takahashi?

He stirred. Opened dark-brown eyes and blinked. Looked around, and started in surprise.

Maria wrenched the door open and slid out the pad they had put in there for the printer to create his body on. "Minoru, it's okay. You're okay."

He looked around, eyes wide and frightened.

"Maria. You're Maria," he said. He felt his hands and face, shaking slightly. "You did it."

"You're the one who left all the data for me," Maria said. "I just put it all together, after I found it, of course. You're going to have to tell me how you managed to compromise the food printer's manual."

Minoru's eyes locked on Hiro's, and he climbed awkwardly to his feet and laughed. He said something in Japanese, and Hiro answered. Minoru hugged Hiro tightly, and Hiro groaned in pain.

"Careful. Hiro doesn't have a shiny new body like you do," Maria said, handing Minoru a jumpsuit.

The men continued to speak in Japanese as Minoru dressed, and Maria felt left out. She cleared her throat and they stopped talking.

"Now that you two are awake, I'm going to get some rest in the brig. Wake up the rest of the crew—Minoru knows what to do. When everyone wakes up, let me know."

She left them without waiting for their answer, and trudged to her prison room. She knew Wolfgang would put her there eventually anyway.

She'd never been so tired.

She estimated it would take fifteen hours, minimum, to make the rest of the crew, minus the murderer.

It was a full twenty-four hours before Hiro came to get her.

He looked much improved, with freshly dressed wounds and a clean jumpsuit. He smiled at her and entered the room.

He sat down on her cot and looked up at her silently.

"What?" she finally asked, exasperated. "Are they back? Are they okay? Did the saliva work?"

"Joanna says if we were on the Earth, you'd get a Nobel Prize for this. Wolfgang wants to let you rot in here, but he's mellowing." He cocked his head. "Why didn't you hack him to remove the fact that he's going to hate you for everything you've done?"

Maria gaped at him. "Are you kidding me? I'm not going to alter his mind for my convenience. That's who he is. If he hates me, I've got to work harder than commenting out some code to make it up to him."

He smiled at her for real. "I think that's the first big step to

doing so. While he's pissed as hell, he's impressed that you allowed him to be pissed as hell. This has in turn confused him.
He's sleeping."

Maria grinned. "Good to know. How's Minoru handling his
new life?"

Hiro laughed. "Well, he's already fixed the old printer and begun eating everything it could make. Mostly pork ramen. Then
he slept for about twelve hours. Then he spent a lot of time in
the gym putting his new body through the paces. For science, he
said."

"I guess he likes his new world," Maria said.

"Anyway, Katrina and Wolfgang are talking about your situation
now. I've already given my opinion. I said I would check on you.
You've got to be getting hungry now."

Maria's stomach was tight with anxiety. She had been hungry
earlier, but now she couldn't imagine eating.

"What was your opinion?" she asked.

He looked at her for a moment, then reached out and took her
hands. "Will you, if I ask you to, remove the yadokari from my
head? Give me a fresh mindmap that's only me?"

She made a strangled laugh. "Bring me a terminal and I'll do it
right now. I'll do anything I can to make you better—"

He interrupted her with a kiss, fierce and unexpected. He
pulled back after a moment and she stared at him in shock.

"Thank you."

Hours later, after Maria had showered, had her wounds re-dressed,
and ate, she sat with the rest of the crew.

She explained how she had hacked the body scanner and Bebe's
powerful capabilities to move beyond food preferences to creating
a full mindmap. She explained the secret instructions Minoru had
hidden within the printer long ago, before he had been trans-
formed, when he knew what was going to happen to him and

tried to figure out the best way to lay bread crumbs toward fixing himself. Wolfgang watched stony-faced, while Joanna was unabashedly fascinated. Katrina looked confused, while Minoru nodded.

"Can you program Paul to fly the ship with no ulterior motives to betray the crew or the mission?" Wolfgang asked.

Maria nodded. "That's simple. I can strip away the same stuff I did in my own mindmap that's flying us now."

"Set her free, put her in a gardening robot or something," Joanna said. "Paul needs to work to make it up to the crew. And we need to be able to trust him."

Maria nodded.

Katrina looked around at the rest of the crew. "In light of the fact that you saved the crew in multiple ways, solved the murders, fixed the cloning problem, and freed our enslaved AI, we're not going to charge you with any ethical hacking crimes." She glanced at Wolfgang's stony face. "As for holding grudges, I can't promise anything, but I expect everyone to do their best to work together within the crew."

"Thank you," Maria said.

Joanna picked up where Katrina had left off. "Wolfgang has given up command of the ship to Captain de la Cruz again, who has agreed to counseling. But I'm of the opinion that now that our secrets are aired, there should be less paranoia and more trust. We're continuing with everyone in the same roles, except you will take the role of chief engineer and Paul is sentenced to become our new AI."

"What about Minoru?" Maria said, indicating her head toward their new crewmember.

"He's going to work as an assistant to the captain," Wolfgang said sternly. "He has his own infractions to work through, and we don't want to give him too much power to start out with."

Minoru crossed his arms. "You had your entire world turn into a lie, and you became a crazy clone hunter. I'd think you of all people would understand my actions better."

Wolfgang tensed, but Joanna placed her hand on his shoulder. Maria marveled that the doctor could calm him immediately.

"Also," Hiro said, "since this whole ship was launched to fail, we're kind of worried that there's not reliable information about the planet at the other end of this mission. So we're going to be doing a lot of research as we get closer to Artemis."

"Or we might be turning around and going home after all," Katrina said.

"Won't they be surprised to see us?" Maria asked, smiling at last.

"Our happy crew, and our mission, are works in progress," Joanna said, smiling slightly. "We'll figure it out. We've got a lot of time to do so."

ACKNOWLEDGMENTS

I'm always awkward writing these because I secretly fear I will miss someone. I always think I will write my acknowledgments as the book goes on, but that's like saying I will organize my tax receipts at the end of every month instead of waiting for March. Doesn't happen. But onward!

The whole team at Orbit continues to be wonderful, supporting me and making this book better than I could have made it. Devi Pillai and Kelly O'Connor are excellent editors, and the cover was under the care and guidance of Lauren Panepinto. My agent, Jennifer Udden, continues to work hard to give me incredible guidance, as well as gentle talkings-down when I get anxious. Thanks also to Katie Shea Boutillier and everyone from DMLA who worked with this book.

I was lucky enough to have the science advice of astronomer Dr. Pamela Gay, who gave both lovely conversation and speedy responses to panicked emails. Thanks to early readers Alasdair Stuart and Matt Wallace, and thanks to Claire Rousseau for her enthusiasm at Loncon a few years ago when I joked that I was considering writing a book of *FTL* fanfic.

No, this book isn't *FTL* fanfic, but still, thanks to the design team behind the iOS game *FTL* whose use of cloning sparked the idea behind one of the major building blocks of this book.

To the people who gave support through this writing: Kameron Hurley, Marguerite Kenner, Sunil Patel, Karen Bovenmyer, Andrea Phillips, Sam Montgomery-Blinn, Fran Wilde, Charlie

Stross, and of course all of my parental units and my sister Shelley. And I can never forget the people at home who make sure that I have a schedule of a normal person who puts on pants and takes a shower and eats a food from time to time (not in that order): Jim and Fiona, my whole world. I love you.

extras

meet the author

Mur Lafferty is a writer, podcast producer, gamer, runner, and geek. She is the host of the podcast *I Should Be Writing* and the cohost of *Ditch Diggers*. She is the winner of the 2013 John W. Campbell Award for Best New Writer. She is addicted to computer games, *Zombies, Run!*, and *Star Wars* LEGO. She lives in Durham, North Carolina, with her husband and daughter.

interview

When did you first start writing?

I thought the answer was eighth grade, but then my dad brought me a stapled-together booklet of stories I wrote in first grade, so I guess it's been a while.

Who are some of your biggest influences?

Early on it was Madeline L'Engle (who answered my fan mail when I was eleven!) and Anne McCaffrey. As an adult they're Neil Gaiman, China Miéville, and Connie Willis.

Where did the idea for *Six Wakes* come from?

Ha. I considered making up something literary, but I'll tell the truth. I was playing an iPad spaceship game called *FTL* [*Faster Than Light*], where your ship either had a medbay or cloning bay. The cloning bay would bring back your dead crew. I kept thinking that the concept was interesting, that you would use cloning not for multiplying yourself, but for immortality. Then I figured it would be a convenient way to drive a generation starship. And it went on from there.

Your last two books took place in well-known locations (New York and New Orleans), but this one is set in deep space. How

was the experience of writing these locations different or the same?

It's all research, really. I research important points, history, and people from New Orleans and New York, and I research what happens to wounds in zero gravity.

What defines personhood is a major theme in *Six Wakes*. What drew you to focus on that?

It's the philosophical concept of Theseus's ship: If you take one board from the boat and replace it, is it still Theseus's ship? What about two? What if you replace every single piece of the boat with something else? People are dismayed with the concept that the *Star Trek* transporter beam kills you in one area and awakens a clone on the other side. I think as this kind of tech becomes more and more possible, we have to decide how much we're going to allow it to change ourselves and how we view the self and the soul.

I'm glad I'm not religious. I wouldn't want to wrestle with the problems one of the characters in *Six Wakes* faces.

If you could spend an afternoon with one of your characters, which would it be and what would you do?

Hard to say, because the characters have so many past selves. I would say I'd hang with Hiro from a few decades ago, but probably not now? IAN at full operating power would be interesting. I'd like to discuss ethics with Maria and the doc. I guess that doesn't answer your question, but there you go.

Lastly, we have to ask: If you could have any superpower, what would it be?

You caught me at a bad time—I just got home from a lot of travel. So all I can think is that I'd love to be able to teleport. That's magically teleport, not die-then-be-cloned-on-the-other-side teleport.

The dream of flying is wonderful, but thinking logically, being able to *just* fly wouldn't be a lot of fun. I think of it as driving with your head out a car window all the time. Wind, temperature issues, weather, birds, all of those could make flight miserable. This is why I guess that most flying heroes also have one of those minor powers to not be bothered by the elements, like how the Flash doesn't burn away all his shoes and clothes due to friction. It's all in the details.

introducing

If you enjoyed
SIX WAKES,
look out for

BEHIND THE THRONE

The Indranan War: Book 1

by K. B. Wagers

*Hail Bristol has made a name for herself in the galaxy for every-
thing except what she was born to do: rule the Indranan Empire.*

*When she is dragged back to her home planet to take her right-
ful place as the only remaining heir, she finds that trading her ship
for a palace is her most dangerous move yet.*

1

*H*ail. *Get up.*

The voice cut through the nausea, sounding too much like my father. I suppose it made sense in some twisted way. If I were dead, it wasn't completely illogical to be hearing the voice of a man who'd been shot in front of me twenty-one years ago.

The bitter tang of blood filled my mouth and nose when I inhaled, rusted iron and the awful smell of death. The stale air of a carrion house screamed of the violence that had taken place in my cargo bay, violence I couldn't remember through the pounding of my head.

Hail, get up now.

Whoever's voice was in my head, it was enough to make me move, or at least try to. I scrambled to my feet, pain stealing what grace the gods had gifted me. My boots—gorgeous red-black Holycon IVs I'd borrowed from a dead raider six months prior—slipped on the blood-slick metal. I went down hard, cracking my already abused face on the deck, and the world grayed out for a moment.

More pain flared when I tried to flop over onto my back and failed. All right. So—not dead. Because even now at my most cynical, I didn't believe for an instant the gods let you still feel pain after you died. It just didn't seem proper.

"Look at this mess."

This voice was outside my head, which made it infinitely more dangerous. I froze facedown in what smelled like someone else's guts.

Judging by the events filtering back into my brain, I suspected the guts belonged to my navigator. A vague memory of trying to strangle her with her own intestines flashed before my eyes. Memz had been a tough bitch. She'd landed a few good punches before I'd given up and broken her neck.

"Weekly saints preserve us."

I heard several other curses from behind me, but the high, lilting call for the saints to my left was what caught my attention. It was edged with a Farian accent, and that was enough to keep me from moving.

Farians. An alien race who could kill or heal with a touch. The only thing that kept them from ruling the universe was some strange religious code enforced with a fanaticism privately envied by most governments. They had seven saints, one for each day of the week. It was the Thursday one, I think, who abhorred violence.

According to Farian scripture, he'd set an edict on their power. It was to be used for healing, not death. Killing people with their power drove Farians crazy. I'd never seen it firsthand, but the vids I'd seen had given me nightmares: grief-stricken, screaming Farians held down by their own comrades as an executioner put them out of their misery.

Not moving was a good idea. Anathema or not, there was always a chance this Farian was ghost-shit insane, and I didn't have a gun.

"You claimed to sense a life sign, Sergeant." A female voice several octaves lower than the Farian's didn't so much ask the question as pick up a previous conversation.

"Did, Cap. In this room. Only one," the lilting voice replied. "That's as close as I can pinpoint it."

"Fine. Fan out and check through this"—the owner of the voice paused, but I resisted the urge to lift my head and see if she was looking around the cargo hold—"rubble," she finished finally.

"Sergeant Terass says one of these poor sods is alive. Figure out which one."

I kept my eyes closed, counting the footsteps as my unwelcome guests fanned out around me. There were five people total, all moving with military precision. They were probably fucking mercs come to claim my ship. I hadn't been able to figure out whom Portis—my bastard of a first officer—thought he was going to sell *Sophie* to when he started his little mutiny.

You mean when you killed him.

Grief dug razor claws into my throat, and I choked back a sob. *Gods damn you, Portis. Why did you betray me?*

Except I wasn't entirely sure he'd been trying to kill me, or that I'd been the one to kill him in the end. My memory of the fight was as fuzzy as a Pasicol sheep and had teeth just as sharp. Trying to dredge up anything resembling coherency made the pain in my head turn on me with snarling fury.

I snarled back at it and it dove away, whimpering, into the recesses of my brain. There were more important matters at hand—like getting these bastards off my ship and getting the hell out of here.

Sliding my hand through the gelling blood on the floor, I wiggled my fingers deep into the thick, squishy mess. A spark of triumph flared to life when I closed my hand around the hilt of my combat knife. I knew it was mine because I felt the nick in the handle even through all the gore.

The day was a fucking waste, but at least I was armed.

The intruders moved past me. By some grace I'd ended up partially beneath the stairs and out of sight. I eased myself sideways, rolling over Portis's torso and away from the abstract blood painting on the floor. I saw his profile, and all at once I wanted to kick him, curse his name, and drop to my knees and beg him not to leave.

There's no time for this, Hail. You have to move. The voice I now recognized as my own damn survival instinct shouted at me with the crisp precision of an Imperial Drill Sergeant. I got my feet under me and rose into a crouch. My left leg protested the movement, but held my weight.

The strangers had their backs to me. I almost thanked the gods for it and then reminded myself there was nothing the gods of my home world had done for me lately. Portis had been the believer, not me. The dim emergency lighting might be just enough for me to slide into the shadows and make it to the door.

The ship's AI wasn't responding to my *smati*'s requests for information. At this point I couldn't tell if I'd been hit by a disrupter that had shorted the hardware wired into my brain or if the problem was with *Sophie*. Either way it didn't matter. I had to get to the bridge and access the computer manually. If I could space these jokers, I would be long gone before they finished imploding.

If.

I backed straight into the sixth intruder before I had time to remind myself what *If* stood for.

He was hidden by the shadows I was trying to blend into, as still and silent as a ghost. He didn't make a sound when I spun and drove my right hand into his ribs. The blue shimmer of his personal shield flared and I swore under my breath. It would smother any strike I threw at him, making the damage laughable. But the kinetic technology didn't extend to his unprotected head, so I swung my left up toward his throat, blade first. He caught my wrist, twisting it back and away from his head.

I matched him in height, and judging by the surprised flaring of his dark eyes, we were nearly equal in strength. We stood locked for a stuttering heartbeat until he drove me back a step. *Sophie*'s emergency lighting made the silver tattoo on his left cheekbone glow red.

My heart stopped. The Imperial Star—an award of great prestige—was an intricate diamond pattern, the four spikes turned slightly widdershins. But what had my heart starting again and speeding up in panic was the twisted black emblem on his collar. He was an Imperial Tracker.

"Bugger me."

The curse slipped out before I could stop it—slipped out in the Old Tongue as my shock got the better of me. There was only one reason for a Tracker team to be here. The reason I'd spent the best part of twenty years avoiding anything to do with the Indranan Empire.

Oh, bugger me.

Trackers always worked in pairs, but I couldn't break eye contact with this one to check for his partner. Instead I eased back a step, my mind racing for a way out of this horrible nightmare.

My captor smiled—a white flash of teeth against his dark skin, just enough to bring a dimple in his right cheek fluttering to life. The fingers around my wrist tightened, stopping my movement and adding a high note of pain to the symphony already in progress.

"Your Imperial Highness, I have no wish to hurt you. Please let go of the knife."

Oh, bugger *me.*

"I don't know what you're talking about," I lied easily. "I'm just a gunrunner."

He tapped a finger next to his eye, just missing the tattoo, and now I could see the silver shadow of augmentation in their dark depths. "I see who you really are. Don't try to fool me."

A stream of filth that rivaled any space pirate poured out of my mouth and blistered the air. The modifications I'd paid a fortune for after leaving home had stood up to every scanner in known space for the last twenty Indranan years, but of course they wouldn't stand up to this one.

Trackers were fully augmented. Their *smatis* were top-of-the-line. The DNA scanner had probably activated the moment he grabbed my wrist, and that, coupled with the devices in his eyes, had sealed my fate.

Bluffing wasn't going to get me out of this. Which meant violence was my only option.

"Highness, please," he repeated, his voice a curl of smoke wafting through the air. "Your empress-mother requests your presence."

"Requests!" My voice cracked before I composed myself. "Are you kidding me? She fucking requests my presence?" I wrenched myself from his grasp and kicked him in the chest.

It was like kicking the dash when *Sophie's* engines wouldn't power up—painful and unproductive. Fucking shields. The Guard stepped back, his suit absorbing my blow with a faint blue shimmer as the field around him reacted to the impact.

Hard hands grabbed my upper arms.

There was the other Tracker.

I snapped my head back, hoping this one was as helmetless as his partner. The satisfying crunch of a broken nose mixed with startled cursing told me I'd guessed correctly.

I spun and grabbed the man by the throat with one arm as I flipped the knife over in my hand and smiled a vicious smile at Tracker No. 1. "You come any closer and I'll cut his throat from ear to ear."

It was a good bluff as they went. I knew the Tracker wouldn't risk his partner—couldn't risk him. One of them died and it was likely the other would follow them into the Dark Mother's embrace. It was the price of the connection, the bond that had been set when they were just children.

"I don't know who you are or what you promised Memz to try and take my head, but it's not going to happen today."

"Highness, we weren't responsible for this." The Tracker took a step toward me.

"Back yourself off me and get the hell—"

The sound of phase rifles powering up cut off my snarl. Shit. I'd forgotten about the others.

"Hold." The Tracker held up a hand. I dared a glance to my left and wasn't surprised to see the others arrayed around us with their guns at the ready.

"Highness, your sisters are gone to temple," he said formally. The words drove into my gut like a hot knife, and my grip on the semiconscious Tracker loosened.

Cire. Pace. Oh gods, no.

An image flashed in my mind—Cire, two years my senior, her raven-black curls flying behind her as she sprinted over the hand-painted tiles of our quarters. Cire chasing a tiny blond Pace, whose laugh was like the bronzed waterfalls in the palace square.

"Princess Hailimi Mercedes Jaya Bristol, your empress-mother, and the whole of the empire need you to return home."

"No." I breathed the word, unsure if it was a denial of the formal command or of my sisters' deaths.

I thought I saw some sympathy in the Tracker's expression. He extended a hand toward me, unfurling his fingers in an impossibly graceful movement. Pale lavender smoke drifted across the space between us, slithering into my mouth and nose before I could jerk away.

"You fucking rat bast—"

I passed out before I could finish the curse, falling on top of the Tracker whose nose I'd just broken.

introducing

If you enjoyed
SIX WAKES,
look out for

THE CORPORATION WARS: DISSIDENCE

by Ken MacLeod

They've died for the companies more times than they can remember. Now they must fight to live for themselves.

Sentient machines work, fight and die in interstellar exploration and conflict for the benefit of their owners—the competing mining corporations of Earth. But sent over hundreds of light-years, commands are late to arrive and often hard to enforce. The machines must make their own decisions, and make them stick.

With this newfound autonomy comes new questions about their masters. The robots want answers. The companies would rather see them dead.

CHAPTER ONE

BACK IN THE DAY

Carlos the Terrorist did not expect to die that day. The bombing was heavy now, and close, but he thought his location safe. Leaky pipework dripping with obscure post-industrial feedstock products riddled the ruined nanofacturing plant at Tilbury. Watchdog machines roved its basement corridors, pouncing on anything that moved—a fallen polystyrene tile, a draught-blown paper cone from a dried-out water-cooler—with the mindless malice of kittens chasing flies. Ten metres of rock, steel and concrete lay between the ceiling above his head and the sunlight where the rubble bounced.

He lolled on a reclining chair and with closed eyes watched the battle. His viewpoint was a thousand metres above where he lay. With empty hands he marshalled his forces and struck his blows.

Incoming—

Something he glimpsed as a black stone hurtled towards him. With a fist-clench faster than reflex he hurled a handful of smart munitions at it.

The tiny missiles missed.

Carlos twisted, and threw again. On target this time. The black incoming object became a flare of white that faded as his camera drones stepped down their inputs, correcting for the flash like irises contracting. The small missiles that had missed a moment earlier now showered mid-air sparks and puffs of smoke a kilometre away.

From his virtual vantage Carlos felt and saw like a monster in a Japanese disaster movie, straddling the Thames and punching out. Smoke rose from a score of points on the London skyline. Drone swarms darkened the day. Carlos's combat drones engaged the enemy's in buzzing dogfights. Ionised air crackled around his imagined monstrous body in sudden searing beams along which, milliseconds later, lightning bolts fizzed and struck. Tactical updates flickered across his sight.

Higher above, the heavy hardware—helicopters, fighter jets and hovering aerial drone platforms—loitered on station and now and then called down their ordnance with casual precision. Higher still, in low Earth orbit, fleets of tumbling battle-sats jockeyed and jousted, spearing with laser bursts that left their batteries drained and their signals dead.

Swarms of camera drones blipped fragmented views to millimetre-scale camouflaged receiver beads littered in thousands across the contested ground. From these, through proxies, firewalls, relays and feints the images and messages flashed, converging to an onsite router whose radio waves tickled the spike, a metal stud in the back of Carlos's skull. That occipital implant's tip feathered to a fractal array of neural interfaces that worked their molecular magic to integrate the view straight to his visual cortex, and to process and transmit the motor impulses that flickered from fingers sheathed in skin-soft plastic gloves veined with feedback sensors to the fighter drones and malware servers. It was the new way of war, back in the day.

The closest hot skirmish was down on Carlos's right. In Dagenham, tank units of the London Metropolitan Police battled robotic land-crawlers suborned by one or more of the enemy's basement warriors. Like a thundercloud on the horizon tensing the air, an awareness of the strategic situation loomed at the back of Carlos's mind.

Executive summary: looking good for his side, bad for the enemy.

But only for the moment.

The enemy—the Reaction, the Rack, the Rax—had at last provoked a response from the serious players. Government forces on three continents were now smacking down hard. Carlos's side—the Acceleration, the Axle, the Ax—had taken this turn of circumstance as an oblique invitation to collaborate with these governments against the common foe. Certain state forces had reciprocated. The arrangement was less an alliance than a mutual offer with a known expiry date. There were no illusions. Everyone who mattered had studied the same insurgency and counter-insurgency textbooks.

In today's fight Carlos had a designated handler, a deep-state operative who called him-, her- or itself Innovator, and who (to personalise it, as Carlos did, for politeness and the sake of argument) now and then murmured suggestions that made their way to Carlos's hearing via a warily accepted hack in the spike that someday soon he really would have to do something about.

Carlos stood above Greenhithe. He sighted along a virtual outstretched arm and upraised thumb at a Rax hellfire drone above Purfleet, and made his throw. An air-to-air missile streaked from behind his POV towards the enemy fighter. It left a corkscrew trail of evasive manoeuvres and delivered a viscerally satisfying flash and a shower of blazing debris when it hit.

"Nice one," said Innovator, in an admiring tone and feminine voice.

Somebody in GCHQ had been fine-tuning the psychology, Carlos reckoned.

"Uh-huh," he grunted, looking around in a frenzy of target acquisition and not needing the distraction. He sighted again, this time at a tracked vehicle clambering from the river into the Rainham marshes, and threw again. Flash and splash.

"Very neat," said Innovator, still admiring but with a grudging undertone. "But...we have a bigger job for you. Urgent. Upriver."

"Oh yes?"

"Jaunt your POV ten klicks forward, now!"

The sudden sharper tone jolted Carlos into compliance. With a convulsive twitch of the cheek and a kick of his right leg he shifted his viewpoint to a camera drone array, 9.7 kilometres to the west. What felt like a single stride of his gigantic body image took him to the stubby runways of London City Airport, face-to-face with Docklands. A gleaming cluster of spires of glass. From emergency exits, office workers streamed like black and white ants. Anyone left in the towers would be hardcore Rax. The place was notorious.

"What now?" Carlos asked.

"That plane on approach," said Innovator. It flagged up a dot above central London. "Take it down."

Carlos read off the flight number. "Shanghai Airlines Cargo? That's civilian!"

"It's chartered to the Kong, bringing in aid to the Rax. We've cleared the hit with Beijing through back-channels, they're cheering us on. Take it down."

Carlos had one high-value asset not yet in play, a stealthed drone platform with a heavy-duty air-to-air missile. A quick survey showed him three others like it in the sky, all RAF.

"Do it yourselves," he said.

"No time. Nothing available."

This was a lie. Carlos suspected Innovator knew he knew.

It was all about diplomacy and deniability: shooting down a Chinese civilian jet, even a cargo one and suborned to China's version of the Rax, was unlikely to sit well in Beijing. The Chinese government might have given a covert go-ahead, but in public their response would have to be stern. How convenient for the crime to be committed by a non-state actor! Especially as the Axle was the next on every government's list to suppress...

The plane's descent continued, fast and steep. Carlos ran calculations.

"The only way I can take the shot is right over Docklands. The collateral will be fucking atrocious."

"That," said Innovator grimly, "is the general idea."

Carlos prepped the platform, then balked again. "No."

"You must!" Innovator's voice became a shrill gabble in his head. "This is ethically acceptable on all parameters utilitarian consequential deontological just war theoretical and..."

So Innovator was an AI after all. That figured.

Shells were falling directly above him now, blasting the ruined refinery yet further and sending shockwaves through its underground levels. Carlos could feel the thuds of the incoming fire through his own real body, in that buried basement miles back behind his POV. He could vividly imagine some pasty-faced banker running military code through a screen of financials, directing the artillery from one of the towers right in front of him. The aircraft was now more than a dot. Flaps dug in to screaming air. The undercarriage lowered. If he'd zoomed, Carlos could have seen the faces in the cockpit.

"No," he said.

"You must," Innovator insisted.

"Do your own dirty work."

"Like yours hasn't been?" The machine voice was now sardonic. "Well, not to worry. We can do our own dirty work if we have to."

From behind Carlos's virtual shoulder a rocket streaked. His gaze followed it all the way to the jet.

It was as if Docklands had blown up in his face. Carlos reeled back, jaunting his POV sharply to the east. The aircraft hadn't just been blown up. Its cargo had blown up too. One tower was already down. A dozen others were on fire. The smoke blocked his view of the rest of London. He'd expected collateral damage, reckoned it in the balance, but this weight of destruction was off the scale. If there was any glass or skin unbroken in Docklands, Carlos hadn't the time or the heart to look for it.

"You didn't tell me the aid was *ordnance!*" His protest sounded feeble even to himself.

"We took your understanding of that for granted," said Innovator. "You have permission to stand down now."

"I'll stand down when I want," said Carlos. "I'm not one of *your* soldiers."

"Damn right you're not one of our soldiers. You're a terrorist under investigation for a war crime. I would advise you to surrender to the nearest available—"

"What!"

"Sorry," said Innovator, sounding genuinely regretful. "We're pulling the plug on you now. Bye, and all that."

"You can't fucking *do* that."

Carlos didn't mean he thought them incapable of such perfidy. He meant he didn't think they had the software capability to pull it off.

They did.

The next thing he knew his POV was right back behind his eyes, back in the refinery basement. He blinked hard. The spike was still active, but no longer pulling down remote data. He clenched a fist. The spike wasn't sending anything either. He was out of the battle and *hors de combat.*

Oh well. He sighed, opened his eyes with some difficulty— his long-closed eyelids were sticky—and sat up. His mouth was parched. He reached for the can of cola on the floor beside the recliner, and gulped. His hand shook as he put the drained can down on the frayed sisal matting. A shell exploded on the ground directly above him, the closest yet. Carlos guessed the army or police artillery were adding their more precise targeting to the ongoing bombardment from the Rax. Another deep breath brought a faint trace of his own sour stink on the stuffy air. He'd been in this small room for days—how many he couldn't be sure without checking, but he guessed almost a week. Not all the invisible toil of his clothes' molecular machinery could keep unwashed skin clean that long.

Another thump overhead. The whole room shook. Sinister cracking noises followed, then a hiss. Carlos began to think of fleeing to a deeper level. He reached for his emergency backpack of kit and supplies. The ceiling fell on him. Carlos struggled under an I-beam and a shower of fractured concrete. He couldn't move any of it. The hiss became a torrential roar. White vapour filled the room, freezing all it touched. Carlos's eyes frosted over. His last breath was so unbearably cold it cracked his throat. He choked on frothing blood. After a few seconds of convulsive reflex thrashing, he lost consciousness. Brain death followed within minutes.